PERSONAL WAR,
WILLIAM'S TRIUMPH

by
Dave Aquino

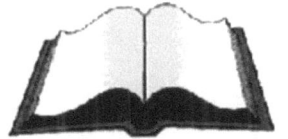

CCB Publishing
British Columbia, Canada

f

Personal War, William's Triumph

Library and Archives Canada Cataloguing in Publication
Title: Personal war, William's triumph / by Dave Aquino.
Names: Aquino, Dave, 1981- author.
Identifiers: Canadiana (print) 20190072865 | Canadiana (ebook) 2019007289X |
ISBN 9781771433846 (softcover) | ISBN 9781771433853 (PDF)
Classification: LCC PS3601.Q557 P47 2019 | DDC 813/.6—dc23

Cover artwork credit: Love hurt © vectorism | Canstockphoto.com
Candle on black © TDPanian | Canstockphoto.com

Publisher: CCB Publishing
             British Columbia, Canada
             www.ccbpublishing.com

Contents

Chapter 1: William Finally Gets the Big One 1

Chapter 2: A Gathering of Gentlemen 18

Chapter 3: William's New Buddy 40

Chapter 4: Celebrations and Sorrows 54

Chapter 5: Man in His Power 70

Chapter 6: Steak and Lobster 89

Chapter 7: Into the Flood Again 111

Chapter 8: You Opened Fire and Your Mark Was True 125

Chapter 9: A Small Regret You Won't Forget 145

Chapter 10: It's Just a Fantasy 159

Chapter 11: In the Jealous Games People Play 177

Chapter 12: The Winner by a Knockout 195

Chapter 13: Cherry Bomb 207

Chapter 14: Runaway Train 225

Chapter 15: The Fool 241

Chapter 1

William Finally Gets the Big One

A text message for Cherry came in from William Defreno at 4AM……

"Cherry, I am on my fucking hands and knees, with tears in my eyes am I am begging you for forgiveness for what I have done. Please God Cherry forgive me and don't do anything more to me. Please DON'T …… don't do it!! I'm coming to you admitting I made a mistake and begging you to forgive me. I'm so sorry Cherry, I'm so sorry Cherry, I'M SO SORRY!!!!"

………… Four Months Earlier…………

William Defreno stood behind the bar of his restaurant, Moe's Diner, stocking liquor for the evening rush. At a nearby table, his general manager and longtime best friend, Riley, muttered to himself as he did that week's books.

"Did you buy thirty-eight cases of dog biscuits?" he asked William looking like he really didn't want to know the answer.

"Maybe." William opened a can of Coors from the fridge under the bar and took a long sip.

"William!"

"I sent them to the lady who complained about the dog crap in the parking lot, ok?"

Riley put his black wire rimmed glasses on the table and rubbed his eyes. "That's not a business expense."

"Sure it is. Public relations!"

Riley kept his eyes closed as he leaned back in his chair. He tilted his head up towards the ceiling and sighed. In the late afternoon light William saw that a few gray hairs stood out among the black ones at Riley's temples.

William turned to check his appearance in the bar mirror. Not bad, he thought, checking his own blond hair for any gray. He didn't see any. There were maybe a few lines around his eyes, but he still looked young and felt younger. In fact, sometimes William still felt like a kid wearing a grown up body. He adjusted the collar on his crisp white dress shirt and went back to setting up the bar. They opened for dinner soon and were sure to be busy as usual.

"Mail here yet?" William asked. He'd slept through most of the day while Riley had run the diner for lunch.

"Haven't seen it."

"Keep an eye out, would you? Give it to Cherry when it comes."

"Expecting anything important?"

"Might be." William took another sip of beer. "Cherry's helping me with some loan papers. She thinks it's time I quit living in a shack behind the diner and bought a house."

Riley looked stunned. "Careful there, pal. You own a diner in the hotspot of town and you haven't been arrested in years. Now you wanna buy a house? You're getting dangerously close to being a respectable adult."

"Never gonna happen." William grinned. He set his beer down on the bar and picked up a rag to finish wiping down the counter.

The front door opened. William looked up, ready to tell whoever had come in that they were still closed, only to see another longtime friend Mitch walking towards the bar. It looked like Mitch had had another rough day at the hospital. He had dark circles under his red rimmed eyes and at least a day's worth of stubble on his chin. His sandy brown hair was getting long and shaggy again.

William noticed that his old friend was getting chubby. Mitch's scrub top stretched tight against his ever expanding beer gut. William figured his old friend had just come by to let off steam by talking trash and mooching up as much free beer as he could get away with.

"Evening gentlemen," Mitch said as he climbed up onto the bar stool. "What's good?"

"William's buying a house," Riley said as he gathered up his paperwork to put away.

"No way," said Mitch.

"It was Cherry's idea," William said. "And it's not for sure yet, we have to wait to see what the appraiser has to say."

"You know," said Mitch. "I don't understand why you don't use Christina's real name. She's not a club worker anymore."

"She prefers Cherry. She says the way I say is cute." William smirked.

Mitch just rolled his eyes. "Cute or not, you should have more respect. I wouldn't want people thinking *my* girlfriend was still a stripper."

"First of all," William said as he pointed his finger at Mitch. "You don't have a girlfriend. Second of all she was *not* a stripper. She was a massage therapist. She only worked at The Love House for three months."

"Yeah, stripper, hooker massage therapist, all the same thing," Mitch replied.

"It's not the same!" William protested. "It's hard to get work when *The Man* slapped her with a permanent felony for standing up for herself."

"Ok, fine, you win. Just saying that stigma sticks with someone forever."

"Cherry is a very respectable person. She gets plenty of respect in her new job as a self-defense instructor. She was a Staff Sergeant in the Marines and fought intermediate MMA. Nobody with half a brain disrespects that woman."

"And she can do loan documents?" Mitch asked skeptically.

"Yep. She's even better with business stuff than I am. She's good at details. I mean really good." William's face flushed as he suddenly recalled just what effect Cherry's attention to detail had on his nervous system...

"She's a good lady," said Riley. "Smart, talented and decent looking."

"Yeah. How did such a great gal end up stuck with some loser like William?" Mitch said as picked up William's can of beer. "You gonna finish this, Wilhelmina?"

William was staggered that Mitch would want to finish an open can of beer. The good news was this was his chance to make a wisecrack back.

"Sure, Mitch," William said. "You can have the rest of it, good buddy. I was kissing Cherry last night, so drinking out of a can I drank out of is as close as you'll get to kissing her."

William turned to pull himself a fresh beer from the tap. The alarm on his wristwatch beeped. William pulled his bottle of Wellbutrin out of his pocket, popped one into his mouth and washed it down with a sip of his beer.

"Should you be mixing those with alcohol?" Riley asked looking concerned.

William glanced at the Glaxo Smith Kline bottle for a moment. "It's just beer." he replied.

"Better be careful, William," Mitch taunted. "If Cherry catches you doing that she'll probably cane you."

William laughed, trying not to picture Cherry standing over him with a wicked looking rod in her hand.

"Does it bother you how tall she is? I mean she's almost 6 feet, just like you are?" Mitch asked.

William shook his head; he was right about Mitch just wanting to come to the diner to drink free booze and verbally abuse whoever he could.

"Only when she wears heels," William protested. "In heels she's gotta be like 6'1" or something. Why would that matter? So, she's kinda big 'n strong. Anything else wrong with her? She's a few years older than me too!"

"Bet she's got a killer roundhouse kick with legs that long." Mitch grinned wickedly.

"What are you getting at Mitch?"

Mitch shrugged. "Just wondered if it worried you that your girlfriend could possibly put you in the hospital if she wanted."

"Never thought about it." William shook his head. "I don't spend my time sizing myself up against my girlfriend."

"Are you sure you're not in denial, William? With all the donations your diner gave to the Battered Women's Shelter, they would probably give you a premier room," Mitch heckled as some beer spilled on his shirt.

"Yeah, just keep dancing on the landmine field, Mitch." William answered. "Is there a particular reason you're putting my balls through a salad shooter tonight?"

"Well," Riley interrupted in hopes of saving William from Mitch's verbal abuse. "I think he's just jealous that it didn't work out as well with the girl he met."

"Oh?" William said with an evil sneer in his voice, "Spill!"

"Oh, come on, man, that could happen to any guy," Mitch replied and looked away.

"Spill!" William repeated with a chuckle.

"Maybe Riley should just tell, he seems to be a better story teller than me and loves to laugh at my disgrace," Mitch said and he finished the last of the beer and crumpled up the can.

"Want another beer before Riley spills your story?" William asked. He filled a glass from the tap without waiting for the answer, knowing it would be yes.

"I don't think you really need to know every last detail," said Mitch. "Honestly, it's hardly worth telling. Maybe we should get back to talking about William's domestic problems."

"Tell the story, Riley, before the *paying* customers show up," William said, glad to shift the mockery back to Mitch.

"Well," Riley started. "Prince Charming here took his whole paycheck to The Love House--"

"Ok," Mitch interrupted. "I had just gone to the bank to cash my check; there was no need to stop at home first to put the money away."

"Anyway," Riley continued. "He meets the hood rat of his dreams at our city's premier gentleman's club and spends enough that she decides to go with him after work and party at his place."

"Go on!" William said.

"Well, they were drinking and playing video games and then ran out of smokes. She so kindly offers to take his car go get some more from the store."

"How sweet," William said.

"Yes, well, maybe twenty minutes goes by, an hour, two hours. Mitch's Audi and the bitch are not coming back."

"My sweet Lord," William laughed.

"Ya know," Mitch defended. "How was I to know? I mean she was a little rough around the edges, but I didn't think she would do that."

"What video games were you playing, Grand Theft Auto?" William sneered.

"Freaking cops didn't come for three days and just said 'we'll look for it' I mean, wow," Mitch said.

"Well," Riley said. "At least Cherry has enough brains to share with William so he doesn't do shit like that."

"Hey," William said. "She may have the brains, looks and class, but I can make a killer Long Island Iced Tea. Took me years to perfect which tequila goes best with which rum and vodka. Last week two guys from *Life Behind Bars* magazine came in. They said they'll do a story on the diner if I spill my secret recipe."

"Yeah, no kidding!" Riley added. "Since this town got gentrified we sell like thirty Long Island's to every one beer. The hipsters love it here and they tip well."

William beamed with joy that Riley was making excellent money working for him and never once seemed to regret that he never became the engineer he'd dreamed of being. As the three of them talked trash and snickered, the bar crowd started trickling in. Riley and William hurried the last of their prep work as the hostess and wait-staff took up their positions for the evening.

"Showtime boys," said William, knocking back the last of his beer.

Just then, Cherry came through the door. Her long blond hair hung loose around her shoulders, every strand neatly brushed and shining. She wore a tight fitting kelly green knit top that showed off her large chest and light colored stonewashed jeans that wrapped around her muscular legs like a second skin. Her favorite black motorcycle boots gleamed with fresh polish. Excitement sparkled in her wide blue eyes.

Her intense presence as she came through the door made the three of them, as well as other customers, jolt for a second.

"Uh oh, William! Better hope she didn't see you drinking while you work!" Mitch said as Cherry headed straight for them.

William watched Cherry strut towards him with a mixture of dread and excitement. He panicked a little when he saw something in her hands but relaxed when he realized it was a large manila envelope that was torn open at the seal. He guessed she must have grabbed the mail on her way in.

When Cherry smiled William's brain stopped working completely. Elation swept over him. He didn't know if it was the pill kicking in or just the effect Cherry's presence always had on him. Though William had tried many times he couldn't quite describe the feeling in words. The closest he could come was to think of it as himself being a big wound and her being a big band aid. He never would forget the night he purged his plan of self-destruction to her and how much she cared.

Cherry came around behind the bar. The smile on her thin lips grew even wider when she looked him in the eye. Before William could speak, she pulled him close and kissed him long and deep.

A round of whistles and cat calls went up from the customers at the bar. William did his best to pretend he didn't hear them.

"Uh, hi," he said stupidly when she pulled away.

"Hi yourself," Cherry answered in her delicate feminine voice.

"Drink?" William asked.

"Maybe later I'll have one. Unlike you, I don't drink while I work and you promised you wouldn't either." Everyone could tell Cherry's voice had shifted, taking on that steely authoritarian tone William found both intimidating and exciting.

"It's just a beer; it's not like I drink whiskey while I work," William replied.

"Yeah, you save that for nighttime."

"What do you mean?" William pondered.

Cherry got out here phone and showed William the *drunk text* he had sent her at 3:45 AM.

"Incense peppermints the color of thyme..... Dead kings many things I can't define.......who cares what game we choose......Little to win, but nothing to lose....."

"I'm sorry, an older boy made me do it," William laughed.

"What older boy?"

"His name is Johnny Walker. He's two hundred years old," William said trying his best to hold in his laughter.

"Maybe it's time we not allow you to play with Johnny anymore," Cherry replied.

"Well, you know I---"

"William," Cherry interrupted. "May I speak to you in the office, please?"

"Uh-oh! William's gonna get it!" Mitch shouted.

"Sure," William said, suddenly nervous again. He set down his empty beer glass and followed Cherry.

"Think she'll use the wooden paddle or a leather strap?" Mitch asked Riley. Mitch laughed and Riley chuckled and shook his head. William, who could hear better than average, told himself to not even acknowledge Mitch's comment.

Once inside the small office next to the diner's kitchen William shut the door. He remained standing while Cherry made herself comfortable in the padded leather desk chair. For several long moments she just sat there, looking at William the way William imagined a hungry wolf would look at a nice plump rabbit.

William shifted his weight from foot to foot, trying to quash the nervous anticipation building in his gut. "So, uh, did the appraisal come?" He asked in a shaky voice. "Is it good news? How's my debt to asset ratio looking?"

Cherry was silent a moment longer.

"Take your pants down," She ordered in a calm, commanding voice.

"Oh! Why?" he asked, suddenly afraid Mitch had been right.

Cherry got up and came over to him. Standing close, she rested her arms on his shoulders and cupped the back of his neck in her hands. "Because I want to cross an item off my bucket list."

"Okay," said William. Cherry's right hand moved down his chest. Her fingers lightly skimming the fabric of his shirt, until she reached the waistband of his pants. *Oh boy,* thought William. He hoped the noise of the kitchen would be enough to cover whatever Cherry was about to do.

"What...um... ah...I... uh... Did you have something specific in mind?" William wondered.

"Mm-Hmm," Cherry said, fingers still busy at his waistband. William felt his knees go weak.

"Um, what's this bucket list item you want to do?" said William.

"I've always wanted to sexually pleasure a millionaire," she replied.

Confused, William tried to figure out where this was going. Did she want to date someone else?

"Gee, honey, the only millionaire I ever knew was Randy Casner, and he's still in prison."

"Not anymore."

William's eyes bulged. They'd let Casner out? William wondered if he'd paid his life insurance premium recently. Even if they'd released him, though, William didn't think old Randy would get his fortune back.

"I'm sorry, I don't know any millionaires," said William.

"What on earth are you talking about?" Cherry asked. She looked completely baffled.

"Randy Casner is the only one I knew of."

Cherry laughed. "I don't want Randy Casner, dummy. I want you to do my bucket list."

"Sorry to tell you, tocts, but I'm not a millionaire!"

"Oh, but you are."

William shook his head. "How?"

"Well," Cherry began. She walked back to the desk and pulled out the papers. "They say our little city is the next boomtown, like Vail or Aspen, and your diner is on a prime downtown lot. The appraiser said it's probably one of the most valuable pieces of real estate in the whole city. And that's just the building. The business itself is worth just as much. You have almost no debts and you've invested well. It all adds up."

William came up to look over her shoulder. There it was in black and white. The appraisal with seven digits on it, but he still couldn't believe it. He grinned. "Looks like I finally got *the big one*."

"Shall I have Riley bring us some champagne?" Cherry wondered.

William shook his head. "I want to wait 'til we close to break the news. This town is full of people who hate me. I'd like to keep this quiet for awhile."

"Oh, it's too late for that. People know what you're worth. You're getting noticed."

"Great." William said flatly. "Just what I need. Another target on my back."

"Getting some attention isn't necessarily a bad thing, William. Look what else came today." Cherry handed him a smallish white envelope addressed to him by hand. William opened it slowly. Inside he found a professionally printed card inviting him to a special meeting for local business owners the following evening.

"Oh geez," he said. "They must have the wrong William Defreno."

"Can't be, hon. You're one of a kind."

"You don't really want me to go to this thing, do you?"

"Of course you should go. Why don't you want to?"

William sighed. "These are Casner's type of people. Most of them were his good buddies once upon a time. I don't think they'll be too glad to see me there."

"They will if they're smart. Casner is history. You're the future."

"I don't know." William began pacing the room. "I'd have to take a night off from the diner, get my suit cleaned, iron a shirt.... I don't have time to do all that by tomorrow."

"I'll help," said Cherry. "I'm off tomorrow. I can take your suit to the cleaners and iron your shirt. All you have to do is get dressed and go."

"What about the diner?"

"I'm sure Riley and your staff can handle it and if anything happens they'll call you."

"Gee, honey, I still don't know. These are *normal people* who are just gonna think I'm weird and persecute me. I'm gonna to have to make small talk and pretend to like people who would probably love to ride me out of this town on a rail."

"No one wants to ride you out on a rail, William. They invited you. They want you to be there."

"What if someone remembers me from the paper? What do I say if someone brings up my past?"

"Own it. Talk about how hard you worked to turn yourself around. Remind them of who you are now."

William still hesitated. He felt like a Roman being asked to walk into the Coliseum and face the lions.

"I suppose you want me to use barbecue sauce as aftershave, too," he said.

"Um, no," Cherry said looking amused. "Just maybe try not to smoke too much. We don't want you smelling like an ashtray."

"Cherry..." William whined.

"And be sober for once."

"What if I don't?"

"Oh geez, no!"

"Well then," Cherry replied. She crossed her arms and gave him a stern look. "Maybe I'll take your buddy Mitch's advice and invest in a wooden paddle."

"Oh, you heard that, huh?"

"You bet I did. I'm blonde, not deaf."

He put his arms around Cherry's waist and pulled her close.

"Burn, baby, burn," said Cherry. She rubbed her hips against him. "Compliments aren't going to get you out of this. But if you go, I'll make you a nice dinner afterward."

"Dinner is good." William's stomach grumbled. He hadn't eaten anything yet that day and Cherry was an amazing cook.

"And maybe we'll take care of that other little item."

"Other item?"

"Bucket list," said Cherry. She playfully scraped her teeth on the side of his neck.

"Well, I'd hate to make you wait to fulfill your fantasy," said William.

"You need to go eat something," said Cherry. "And I have a self-defense class to teach and a paddle to shop for."

"Oh." William's stomach dropped. Cherry laughed at the worried expression on his face. William felt like strangling Mitch for giving her such ideas.

"Good old Mitch," she said, "putting Starla's unwanted kids through rehab."

William groaned at the thought of Mitch losing his entire check and car to the girl from The Love House. He knew his friend couldn't afford that kind of setback and would have to work a lot of overtime to make it up. On the upside, he wouldn't be in as much if he was picking up extra shifts at the hospital. And maybe he wouldn't go giving Cherry any more ideas. Cherry's mind was devious enough without the help.

"I guess I'll go," said William. "Say something nice in my eulogy."

Cherry looked stern. "I want you to keep a positive attitude about this. You could do a lot of good at that meeting."

"Yes, I'll try to stay positive, toots."

"William, can we pretend we're not in middle school. How about we learn some class and respect before tomorrow. How about saying *yes Ma'am?*"

"Yes ma'am," William said, unsure of whether she was trying to teach him to be polite, being sexy and playful or making it clear that she wasn't going accept less than his utmost respect when she was working this hard to help him.

"That's better. Now go get something to eat." She gave him a kiss on his cheek. "And don't forget to zip up your fly."

William blushed. "Yes Ma'am," he said half sarcastic.

The next day, William woke to the sound of his alarm clock blaring. He shut it off and sat up, pleased with himself for not hitting snooze, even if it was two in the afternoon. One of these days he was going to have to start getting up during the day like a *normal person*, but for today he'd figured the best way to keep his promises to Cherry was to sleep until as close to the meeting time as he could get away with.

He saw he had a text message from Cherry.

"I'm gonna throw the book at you if you don't get some decent sleep for tomorrow."

"What?" William said. Finally he realized he had sent her a drunk text at 3:30 in the morning.

"Oh no Mr. Bill the jury has decided to throw the book at you...... THUNK!! OHHHHHHH"

He laughed out loud as he reached for his lighter and pack of cigarettes. They weren't there. He looked around the room. There they were on his dresser, locked inside a small clear plastic cage with a luggage sized brass combination lock. Next to them was a bottle of water, a banana and an energy bar with a post it note stuck to it. His clean shirt and freshly pressed suit hung on a wall hook nearby. William shook his head in amazement. What had Cherry done while he'd slept all day?

He got out of bed and went over to the dresser. "Drink me." had been written on the bottle of water in black marker. William twisted the cap of the bottle and began to drink. As he held the bottle up he noticed more black letters at the bottom. He put the cap back on and turned the bottle over, but from the outside the letters were backwards. He could only read them by tilting the bottle back while he drank from it. He chugged the water, watching the message slowly appear. "Eat bar," they said.

William picked up the energy bar and read the note. "I know better than to try to make you eat a full meal when you're nervous, but figured you could choke these down. XOX, Cherry."

That woman... William tore open the package and bit into the gooey slab inside. He chewed mechanically, trying not to think about the taste or texture. As he went to throw the wrapper away he noticed another note on the trash can. "Shower," it said.

William went into the bathroom. Another note on the mirror said "meds." He obediently swallowed his pills.

After a brief shower, he paused again to look at himself in the mirror. He lingered a moment, debating with himself. He couldn't remember when he last shaved. His face had uneven patches of scraggly hair that refused to lie in one uniform direction. He looked like a hobo. If he shaved, though, he'd look about twelve instead of thirty-five. Cherry had unhelpfully not made this decision for him. Sighing, he reached for the shaving cream. Better to be mistaken for a teenager than a bum, he thought. Besides, at least being freshly shaved came with a few perks.

He came back out to the bedroom. He about jumped out of his skin when he realized letters had appeared on the banana peel.

"Get dressed," they commanded. William stuffed himself into the stiff dress shirt and suit. As he put his car keys into is pants pocket he found another note.

"06-23-16," it read. "Have a smoke then come see me in the office."

William grinned that he didn't have to try every combination in the world to open the box.

A few minutes later he presented himself to Cherry in the diner's office. She looked up from the spiral notebook she was writing in and smiled at him. Her eyes narrowed when she spotted his tie.

"You don't know how to tie a tie?" she asked.

"No, I only ever wore a suit to court." William paused, thinking for a moment. "Actually, I'm not even sure I wore one then. I was usually in an orange jumpsuit and chains."

"You wore a suit on our first date." Cherry smiled at the memory. "You had your tie tied correctly then."

"Riley did it for me."

"Not surprised, we need to nick name him *Smithers*." She reached out and retied his tie. "You look very nice in a suit, dear."

"Thanks. Better than an orange jumpsuit?"

"Yes, much better. I hate orange jumpsuits, but I do like seeing you in chains," Cherry said with wickedness in her voice and eyes.

"Oh my," William said hoping the line cooks outside the office didn't hear that. Then she looked down at his feet.

"William, you can't wear white socks with black loafers."

"I don't have any black ones," said William, suddenly feeling self-conscious.

"Take mine. They should be in the drawer of your nightstand."

"Ok."

"Did you eat your banana?"

William sighed. "Do I have to?"

She gave him *that* look, the one that warned him that he was in mortal danger, but that it was going to be a very fun way to die.

"I could give it to you as a suppository instead," she replied.

"Fine, I'll eat the God damn banana!"

"Good." Cherry kissed his cheek. "Hurry back. We have work to do."

William dashed through the kitchen, out the back door and across the narrow alley to his tiny bungalow. He could feel the eyes of the kitchen staff following him as he hurried past. Thankfully, none of them said anything.

He ducked inside. As quickly as he could he changed his socks, ate his banana and washed his hands. He gave himself a final check in the mirror before hurrying back to present himself to Cherry again.

"Very nice," she said, almost purring.

"Thanks."

"Now down to business." Cherry tapped the notebook in front of her. "You're going to meet a lot of important people tonight. I have a little background on each of them to help you break the ice." She fanned out a handful of index cards. "And a few cheat sheets so you can remember it all."

William hesitated. "Will that help?"

"Researching people is always a good idea. They know all about you. You'll be at a disadvantage if you don't know them."

"Do I care?"

"You should," Cherry said sternly. "None of these men hold any office or position with the city government, but every one of them has influence over those who do. The city council may vote, but these are the men that tell them what to vote for."

"More dirty deals." William shook his head. "I thought this town was finally past that."

"Sweetheart, no human government ever has or will move past that. Those with ambition will always take advantage of those who don't."

Once again the image of walking into the lion's den popped into William's head.

"I don't think I'm the ambitious type. I just want to serve drinks and get some sleep once in awhile."

"You have plenty of ambition, passion and drive," said Cherry. "That's why I love you. You just use yours for higher purposes than they do. That's why I'm proud of you."

"Wow," said William. He didn't know what else to say.

15

"These men, William, they are scavengers. They are the second rate opportunists who moved in on the wreckage after you took Casner down and took advantage of the sudden power vacuum his absence created. They think they have money and power, but the truth is they only have as much power as people let them have and none of them have even one clear asset. They look rich, but most of them are so heavily leveraged they couldn't scrape up enough cash to order a pizza. You could buy all of them tomorrow and still have change left over."

"Think I'd rather buy a pinball machine."

Cherry laughed. "So would I. But these men are exploiting this town and everyone in it, and somebody has to change that."

"And I'm that somebody?"

"You're the only one who can. You aren't like them, but you're one of them now."

William looked down at his simply cut off-the-rack gray suit. "Maybe I should wear a cape."

"You don't need a cape. You just need to make them feel like you're their friend. Find common ground. Be interested in what they have to say. Talk about things that are important to them."

"Should we hold hands under the table?"

"William!" Cherry gave an exasperated sigh. "You aren't selling yourself to these jerks. You're just making a few friends."

"Ok, ok, I'll smile and make small talk and pretend I like these clowns." William twisted his face into an exaggerated grin that was more horrifying than it was friendly. Cherry did not look amused. William figured he'd better quit while he was behind.

"I'll try, ok?" he said.

"That's all I'm asking." Cherry kissed him lightly. "Now let's go over my notes."

An hour later, William stood up from his chair. His head spun from all information he'd just absorbed. He hadn't crammed this hard since high school. William hoped Cherry was right about the data being useful. He now knew the detailed background of all the current issues affecting city politics and the local business community as well as the name, age, business and family ties of everyone who would be at the meeting.

16

William had marveled at who had been connected to whom. He never would have guessed half of those bonds existed. Their little city was held together by one big tight knit web of backroom deals and secret friendships. And The Love House, of all places, was right in the center.

"Your old boss is a real piece of work, isn't he?" William said to Cherry.

"You have no idea," Cherry replied, rolling her eyes. "Sometimes I'm sorry I let him keep his kneecaps."

"Mean lady. Wish me luck tonight."

"Good luck. Too bad you slept so late. We could have had some fun after you finished your homework."

"Had to get my beauty rest." William said. He lit another cigarette with his Zippo Lucky Strike lighter he had since high school.

"It's ok, I'm into delayed gratification." Cherry smiled wickedly. "But you're gonna pay for making me wait."

"Looking forward to it."

William went out the back door of the diner. He climbed into his old reliable Chevy Impala and sat behind the wheel for a moment, taking a few deep breaths to steady his nerves. Finally, he turned the key and drove off into his shiny new future.

Chapter 2

A Gathering of Gentlemen

The meeting took place in a private room on the second floor of a *Gentlemen's Club* located about two blocks away from The Love House. Conveniently enough, both places had the same owner. Girls from The Love House doubled as wait-staff at the Gentlemen's Club, saving the owner money while also acting as walking advertisements for the services available at their sister establishment.

As William entered the room he was approached by a young waitress.

"Something to drink?" she said. William thought the twenty-something year old waitress looked cute in her outfit even though she was way too skinny and short compared to what he was used to in a girl. Having been a waiter himself he could see right through her empty smile and fake flirty behavior.

"Iced tea," William replied.

"Lemon?"

"Why not."

As she walked by the other men they were not so direct and polite.

"Come here little cutie," One of the guys who was old enough to be her grandfather said. "Hey, come here I said, I wanna tell you something."

"Yes, Mr. Nichols," she replied with a smile.

"Me and the guys are having a social meet-up this Sunday at lunchtime. I would like you to come. Take my card," Mr. Nichols said as he handed her a business card.

"Thank you, sir. I'd love to."

"Now, now, I mean it, don't just take this card and throw it away later. Text me now so I have your number and you don't drop so far off the map that I can't even reach you by carrier pigeon. I want you to reserve your spot right away. Space is limited and I only invite the best."

"Sorry, Mr. Nichols. I don't carry my phone while I'm working, but I'll text you as soon as my shift is over."

"Just be sure that you do. It's a good time you won't want to miss. Hey, even my good friend, Harold, here, who's in the Rotary club, wants you to come, don't you Harold?"

"For sure, she'll have a great time," Harold replied with a dirty smile.

"Hey, hey, Harold I saw her first," Mr. Nichols replied after a laugh.

"I'll come. What may I get you guys to drink?"

"Me and Harold will have a dry Tanqueray No. 10 martini. Now listen hun, when you make it do not leave the vermouth in. Just swish it around the ice and then remove it. I cannot stand too much vermouth in my martini."

"Will do," She said with her phony smile. "Your martini will be perfect, and I'll make sure I text you about Sunday."

Just to take his mind off of the obvious fact he didn't fit in, William watched her make their martinis. He noticed she didn't even put any vermouth in the drinks. She came back and served them to Harold and Mr. Nichols.

"Very good darlin' you'll go far," Harold said. "There's still just a little too much vermouth, but as long as we see you Sunday we won't get too mad about it."

"Yes, sir, I'll be there!" she replied. William thought the girl's teeth were going to crack from the effort of maintaining her fake smile.

William could only laugh that they just had to complain just for the hell of it. Was it a way of being flirty or showing off their authority or just being a general classic prick? If these were the men who made the rules there was no doubt how the city had so many corrupt cops and a huge meth operation going on in the past.

The girl passed him again. "Oh!" she said. A moment later she finally brought him his iced tea. She gave him a genuine smile. "Sorry about that."

"No problem," said William. He figured he'd get distracted too if he had idiots like that harassing him while he was working. Hoping to make up for the crappy way she was being treated, he decided to take a little time to be extra nice. "Great job on the tea. It's brewed just right."

"Thank you, Sir," she said, fluttering her eyelashes at him. She stood so close that William could feel her body heat. "May I offer you anything else? It would be my pleasure to serve you."

William took a long sip of his iced tea. "Thank you, but I think I'm good for now."

"Yes, sir, but do keep me in mind." She gave him a flirty wink before sauntering off.

The dozen men sipped their cocktails and chatted among themselves while waiting for the meeting to start. William stayed off to the side by himself, trying not to look like he could hear them.

"Hey, who's the kid over there?" A guy with a cowboy hat and a mustache asked the man next to him. William pretended to not know it was him they were talking about.

"Not sure, Tom," his friend said. "I think his dad owns that new car dealership on the interstate."

"Nah, I know him. He ain't got kids."

"I think I've seen that kid with his mom down at The Grotto," someone else chimed in. "Yeah, that Cherry girl who worked for Hank. I didn't know she even had a son. Didn't the lady who owns that place also work for you, Hank?" He continued.

Hank shook his head. "No, she wasn't one of mine. Wish she had been."

"Didn't the guy who bought Moe's Diner steal Cherry out from under you awhile back?"

"He didn't steal her. I cut her loose. That gal was pure psycho."

"Hot, though," said Tom. "The crazy ones always are."

"Ain't that the truth," another added.

The men laughed. One of them looked over at William again. "If he's Cherry's son, he must be the step-kid of the William Defreno who owns Moe's Diner."

"Probably, that's nice of Daddy to bring him along. It's good for the boy to get an education. Too many dads just hand their business over to their kids without even teaching them anything."

"He'll learn fast if Angel gets a hold of him. She likes 'em young." Hank said.

"Is he legal?" Tom asked.

"I'm sure he is. Just ask Mr. Franklin."

"Yeah, I'm sure old Ben'll vouch for him with the ladies." said Hank. "Just keep him away from the liquor. Damn liability laws."

The fact that the guys were degrading Cherry and the fact he looked too young for his age made him slip deeper in isolation Finally, they talked about something else. Tom's cowboy hat swung back and forth as he shook his head.

"I don't understand how this country got so turned against honest businessmen. Used to be we could make a good twenty-five to thirty percent return on an investment. These days we're lucky to get fifteen."

"Tom, nothing's been the same since the 80s," said Mr. Nichols.

"It could be, now that the communist bastard is out of Washington."

"All in good time, gentlemen, all in good time." Mr. Nichols said as looked at his watch. "Hell, it's getting late. Let's get started. I want to be home in time to catch the basketball scores."

The men took their seats at the thirty foot long mahogany table. Again, William found himself separated from the others by a short distance. Now that he could see everyone clearly, he noticed that he was by far the youngest, thinnest and had the most hair out of everyone.

"Is this Defreno guy coming or not?" Thomas asked someone. Everyone looked down the table at William.

"Hi guys!" William waved. "Name's William Defreno. Thanks for the invite. Nice club you got here." A wave of surprised expressions went around the table. It suddenly got very quiet. Once again, William tried to ignore the open stares.

"Oh," Thomas said. "You're dad's the lucky som' bitch who owns the most prime piece of property in town?"

"My dad doesn't own the diner!" William replied.

"Sorry, I meant your step-dad? We invited him; I hope he didn't get lost at The Love House,"

"My dad was killed in the Civil War," William joked. "I'm William Defreno; I own the diner."

"You're William Defreno?"

"Yeah, that's me," William replied. "You are?"

"Thomas Moore, I own the lumber yard here in town."

"Oh, ok, everyone likes lumber," William said feeling stupid already.

"Mr. Defreno." The chairman nodded in his direction. "Glad you could join us."

The chairman had to be somewhere in his 70s. He wore a black suit with a red power tie and had his thinning gray hair slicked back. His beady green eyes darted around the room taking in the group at the table. Finally, he reached out and began tapping the glass of water in front of him with a long metal spoon.

"Order, order, this meeting will now begin. First off, I hope our wait-staff has taken good care of you gentlemen."

"Wait-staff needs bigger tits," Mr. Nichols whispered to Thomas Moore.

"Perhaps we should start by letting our guest introduce himself," said the chairman.

William stood up. No one made eye contact. He noticed most of the members actively whispering among themselves.

"Um. Hi. Good evening." The whispers didn't stop. Nobody turned to pay attention to him. He continued on anyway. "My name's William Defreno. I own Moe's Diner. As most of you know I started at the very bottom and worked my way up, so if anyone understands the struggles of small businesses it's me. I'm looking forward to working with you all to make our city a better place."

He sat back down. Only the chairman smiled at him.

"First item on the agenda," said the chairman. "The proposed fee on disposable bags council woman Martha Stout submitted to the council last month. They vote on it Tuesday."

"Good old kill-a-business Martha," Mr. Nichols blurted out.

"Can we get it voted down?" Thomas asked a sandy haired man in a dark navy suit whose name tag read Scott Smith, City Council

22

District 3.

Scott shook his head. "We're gridlocked. The city only has four districts and old man Honest Abe in District 2 will do whatever Martha says 'cause he wants to relive his youth through her. That leaves just me and Ted to oppose and half the time Ted sides with her too. When he doesn't, the Mayor breaks the tie and he almost always sides with her since most of his big money donors come from her district."

"Why is that woman still plaguing this town?" Tom asked. "I thought old Dumbo ears gave her a job in D.C. last year?"

"He did," Hank chimed in. "Then one of those internet bozos found a picture of her throwing a bucket of pig manure at a cop during a civil rights rally back in '62 and the boys in Congress didn't confirm her appointment."

"Damn. I thought she was finally gone," Thomas said.

"Well, at least they didn't replace *Hail to the Chief* with the *Wicked Witch*," Scott said.

"But what are we going to do about Martha?" Mr. Nichols protested. "If we could get rid of her, we could get some tax relief, get some projects going, get some industry and get some law and order back!"

"She's up for re-election again this year. We just gotta find someone who can beat her this time." Hank said.

"You got somebody in mind, Hank?"

"We're still evaluating our options," Hank replied. "I'll let you know something soon."

"Moving on," said the chairman. "That concludes our old business. Does anyone have any new business?"

William figured this was his chance. He shot his hand into the air.

"Yes, Mr. Defreno?"

"Well, you know, speaking of tax relief, can anything be done about the association fees? As a business owner, I am forced to pay these fees that are supposed to pay for snow removal and street sweeping. However, I don't feel that I am getting what I am paying for. They don't plow my street for days after a storm and the gutters are always full of litter. It makes a bad impression on customers and drives away business. I would suggest making association fees optional instead mandatory. Only require payment if the services are actually delivered. That way our struggling businesses don't end up paying twice for the same service."

"We'll take that under advisement," said the chairman. "Does anyone else have a proposal to put forward?"

"I have a grievance against one of our members," said Mr. Nichols.

"Proceed, Mr. Nichols," said the chairman.

"According to city ordinance, goods are to be taxed, but services are not. Yet every time I go to The Love House, old Hank there charges me sales tax to see the girls. I think that's only further proof that women really are goods if they can be taxed like goods."

The whole crowd including the chairman laughed and even hooted a little. William might have thought it was funny himself if he hadn't been so disappointed. He had expected a group of concerned business owners who cared about the city they lived in, not a bunch of old men acting like drunken frat boys in a dorm.

"Now, now," said Harold. "We all know our friend Hank doesn't sell women. He just rents them out by the hour and there's gonna be tax on that pussy." There were more guffaws of laughter. "Scott, does the city code dictate whether or not taxes are charged on rentals?"

"I, uh, don't believe rented items are taxed," Scott answered.

"Alright, boys, alright. I'll repeal the Pussy Tax," said Hank. "But that means the girls will make a little less, so tip 'em extra nice, ok?"

"Well now, that depends on how nice they are to me," said Mr. Nichols.

"Oh, they'll be nice," said Hank. "I make sure of that."

Disgust churned William's stomach. These were the men Cherry had had to appease to make a living? He knew she'd had it hard after her conviction. He was proud of her for standing up for herself in the fight that got her arrested, but he hated that she had had to demean herself so much. He was thankful her current boss had taken a chance on her and she didn't have to work the clubs anymore.

The waitress came by again. "More tea?"

"Can I get a whiskey sour?" William asked. He was not going to make it through the rest of this meeting without a drink. The waitress looked at Hank. He shook his head.

"Sorry, hon, I don't think I can do that."

"Just the tea, then."

What she brought back was a very pretty looking half iced tea, half lemonade in a tall frosty glass. William looked confused. The waitress winked at him again. William sniffed the drink. Then he took a sip. Bless that girl. She'd spiked it. William savored the sweet taste of the Southern Comfort as it gently soothed his jangled nerves.

"Thank you," he mouthed across the room. She simply nodded. Then he noticed the writing on his napkin. "Sherry," it read, followed by her phone number. William tucked it in his pocket.

"Is there any other business?" asked the chairman.

"Not unless we can get Hank to consider repealing his Cup Fees as well," said Mr. Nichols.

"Sorry boys, those stay. The bigger the boobs the more you pay."

"Aw, come on, give us guys a break," said Harold.

"Those fees encourage growth in the city, the kinda growth I like," Hank chuckled.

"And it boosts the economy! Boob jobs create jobs!" Mr. Nichols chanted.

William's spirits sank. Again, he had hoped these powerful men would understand the struggles that people Cherry and he went through. He'd hoped they could be convinced to accommodate those who were felons, uneducated, unsocialized or just generally down on their luck. Apparently, though, all they cared about was making more money and stroking their egos by degrading those they saw as being beneath them. William now knew that if he suggested they try to make real changes to help others he would get laughed out of the room.

"We will now draw this meeting to a close," said the chairman. "See everyone next week."

William slinked towards the door.

"Hey, hey! Willie!" Thomas called. William turned to look at him. "Tell Cherry 'hi' for me. I spent a lot of Cup Fees on that lady."

"Tom!" Mr. Nichols blurted. "Don't say that about his mother, geez!"

William's face flushed as more laughter erupted. He tried to back away, but could still hear them trash talking.

"Man, she was a pistol!" said Mr. Nichols. "What are her testosterone levels?"

"Probably, higher than yours," Harold chimed in. They had drunk so much they were getting sloppy. They leaned against each other to stay upright and their laughter shook their old heavy bellies.

William turned to go, shame still burning on his face.

In the parking lot, William picked his way through the rows of Mercedes, over accessorized dully pickup trucks and SUV's, until he finally came to his humble old Impala. He sat in the driver's seat in the dark silently watching the other men swagger across the lot to their vehicles as they talked and laughed. None of them stopped to talk to him.

A text message beeped on William's phone. He read it, thankful for the excuse to avoid eye contact with the men walking past without waving or saying good bye. The text was from Cherry.

"Dinner's about ready. How did the meeting go?"

William groaned. He dreaded the thought of telling her about how humiliated he'd been. He would tell her eventually, but he couldn't face doing so just yet.

"Be there soon," he texted back. "Tell u when I get there."

He put down the phone and started the car. Yes, he would be there soon, but first he needed a drink.

The part of town near the club was not familiar to William, but he didn't want to deal with the noise and stress of the diner. So he just drove around for a few minutes in search of a bar. He passed chic boutique restaurants and dance clubs that sprinkled among upscale shops and art galleries. William shook his head in amazement. Two years ago this area had been nothing but vacant lots and empty warehouses. Now expensive lofts looked out over downtown and the old rail spur had become an urban walking trail.

Around another corner he finally found a quiet, dark looking bar set up in the basement of an old stone building. The gold letters on the green awing over the steps read "Ale Haus." Inside, the place was clean, but worn. Cheaply framed production stills and posters from vintage movies broke up the dark paneled walls. Bare bulbs in black wire cages hung down from the ceiling, casting warm yellow light that made the hardwood floor seem to glow. Groups of people clustered around a handful of the light colored wooden tables. A few more sat in dimly lit booths towards the back.

William took a seat at the bar, glad to have it to himself. A tall, thin young blond guy with sleepy green eyes framed by Elvis Costello style glasses came over to take his order.

"Coors Light in a can," said William.

"Sorry, man." The bartender shook his head. "We don't have beer in cans. And we don't sell Coors."

"Really?" William said with genuine surprise. "I thought that was illegal in this state."

The bartender just gave him a blank stare.

William sighed. "Ok, what do you have?"

"We have Heineken or Fat Tire in bottles and about two dozen local microbrews on tap."

"How about whiskey? You got that?"

"We have Bushmills."

Somehow William was not surprised. He told the bartender "two fingers, neat."

"Yeah, I need to see your I.D. first, man."

Annoyed, William flipped open his wallet and laid his driver's license on the counter.

The bartender poured William's drink and then wandered off. William put his license and wallet away. He picked up his glass and then immediately put it back down. He picked it up again, only to set it down again without taking a sip. He wasn't sure what was wrong, but he couldn't seem to let go of the uneasy feeling in the pit of his stomach.

William scanned the room in the mirror behind the bar, watching each person closely. Something about the dark haired guy in the maroon dress shirt at the table in the far corner seemed familiar. William shook it off. Then the man's eyes met his in the mirror and the feeling of recognition grew stronger. He tried to go back to his drink, but the prickly feeling on the back of his neck made him realize the dark haired man was still watching him.

Finally, William turned around on his stool. The dark haired man grinned as he got up and approached William.

Along with his maroon Ralph Lauren shirt the man wore well-tailored dark gray slacks paired with Gucci loafers, a Cartier Roadster watch on his wrist and a gold and diamond ring sparkled on the pinky of his right hand. It matched the gold and diamond chain the man wore around his neck. A saint's medal hung from the chain, but William couldn't tell which one. The guy looked to be around 5'10" and had a tight, lean shape to his body with a fresh looking tan.

Looking at the man again, William realized that he had been at the meeting, though he had been a silent observer rather than an active participant. Still, William wanted nothing to do with him and his frayed nerves left him in no mood to be polite about it.

"What? You gonna make fun of me too?" said William.

"No, no, seems that job is taken," The man replied.

"Yep!"

"Hey William, my name's Buddy. I wanna help."

"Help me how?"

"I'm a life coach, I make money off people like you."

"Oh really?'

"Yep, I know your whole story; I always research my clients before I consult them."

For some reason the voice and that phase 'I always research my clients before I consult them' rang a bell. William's jumped for a bit at the fact he may have met this man many years ago.

"Buddy, did you used to drive and old blue Cadillac with handcuffs hanging of the trailer hitch?"

"Well, certainly that's a possibility; anyway, enough about me, let's talk about you. You, William, let's talk about you."

"What about me? I was the God damn object of ridicule in there."

"I know. I was there. Here, take my card."

William glanced at the slick blue business card. It read in bold lettering *Better Beginnings* the slogan underneath said *Success takes the man out of the gutter, we take the gutter out of the man.* Then *Buddy Richfield* and his cell phone number.

"Tell me Buddy, what you know about me? William asked.

"I know you pulled yourself up from the street, took down a drug lord, beat the criminal justice system, bought a local business, turned it around and now you are worth over a million bucks. Yet you still can't seem to get the respect of your peers."

"Who says I want it?" William swallowed his drink and slammed the glass down on the bar.

"William, my man, everybody wants respect, but very few know how to get it. That's where I come in."

"Yeah? And just how are you gonna get it for me?"

"Come on over to my table. I'll tell you about it."

"Thanks for the offer, Buddy, but I have to be somewhere."

"Dinner with the lovely Miss Cherry, right?" Buddy winked at him.

William was both surprised and angry. "How do you know about Cherry?"

"I told you, William, I know everything."

"Um, yeah." William was starting to feel a little uncomfortable about this stranger's seeming obsession with him. "Listen, do you do this for everybody or is this just my lucky day?"

"I try to help as many people as I can. I coached half these guys. Mr. Nichols was once like you. He made a fortune off Bitcoin. But he spent his whole life being everyone's bitch slave that he had no idea what to do once he was in charge. But he took my program and now he's a man in his power. You can be too, if you work with me."

"Well, that sounds fascinating, Buddy, and I'd love to hear more about it, but right now I'm late."

"So be late," said Buddy. "Men in their power are always late. Only people pleasers and yes-men show up on time."

"Are you serious?"

"Of course I'm serious. Think of this: when you're in court and it supposed to start at 9AM. You know darn well the judge doesn't come out of his chamber till at least 9:30."

"Yeah, I did always notice that, Buddy," William said remembering the wreckage of his past.

"That's intentional, William. The judge does that to let everyone in the courtroom know he's the boss. All those people have busy lives and places to go and things to do. Yet he lets them know that him finishing his coffee and doughnut is much more important than all their important shit put together. That way, when he comes out, the people are already intimidated by him before even hearing his voice. He's letting everyone in the room know he doesn't seek even a morsel of their approval of him.

"When you're in charge, William, you need to do everything to let the people around you know that. Yes, William be a little late and hardly apologize for it."

"Wow, I didn't know that's why the judge did that. I thought it was just to give me time to commit suicide in the courtroom."

"It works dammit! And don't apologize for it. Hell, never apologize for anything. This damn apologizing thing I see so many dumb-asses do. Let's say you spill something like water on your new date. Just simply laugh and maybe say 'oh spilled some water on you' or something. These stupid guys that apologize profusely every time they make a mistake will always be 'workers' not 'bosses' and will always have women that treat them like the yes-man they are."

"Never apologize?" William asked.

"Yes, I know, sounds terrible right? But apologizing is weakness. A *Leader* has no weakness. A *Leader* realizes he is allowed to make a mistake and doesn't need to apologize for his errors."

"Cherry really doesn't like it when I'm late."

"Cherry. Cherry, Cherry, Cherrrr-rry, cherry, bay-bee." Buddy mockingly sang to the tune of the old Four Seasons song. "Is Cherry your girlfriend or your nanny?"

"Excuse me?"

"Forgive me for being blunt, but I always feel it's best to be honest. It is part of my job to tear people down so that I can rebuild them. I'm just saying, it seems like she has you on a pretty short leash. Who's got the balls in your relationship, her or you?"

"She just wants what's best for me."

"By bossing you around like a kid?"

"She doesn't, ok? She just... helps me."

"By putting you in situations where you look ridiculous and feel miserable."

"She doesn't do that."

"Oh yeah? Whose idea was it for you to come to the meeting

tonight? Yours or hers?"

"Hers," William admitted weakly.

"And I bet she made you wear the suit too, didn't she?"

"Well..." William suddenly thought it might be better to keep silent.

"I thought so." Buddy shook his head. "Man, William, you need help bad. No one is ever going to respect a man whose girlfriend has his nuts in her purse and then makes him carry the purse."

"I don't know, Buddy," William said. "My friends seem to like me ok. It's just the assholes like the ones tonight I can't get anywhere with."

"William, those assholes run the city," Buddy said quietly. "You want your street swept? Your sidewalks shoveled? You want your taxes reduced? Those are the men that can make it happen, but you gotta make them respect you first."

"And your program will make them respect me?"

"Guaranteed."

"Ok," said William. "I'll give it a shot. When do we start?"

"Fantastic! Meet me back here tomorrow night at seven. And lose the monkey suit. Dress how you feel comfortable."

"I'll be here."

"Great. Oh and don't tell anybody!"

"What? Why?"

"William, my man, I hate to break it to you, but a lot of your so called friends only hang around because they like seeing you down. If they know you're trying to improve yourself they may fight you on it or try to talk you out of doing the program."

"You really think they'd do that?"

"It's possible. I've seen it happen."

William suddenly felt depressed. Would his friends really try to keep him down if they knew?

"Ok, Buddy, I'll keep quiet for now. See you tomorrow."

William stood up to leave. As he pulled his keys out of his pocket his pill bottle fell out and hit the floor. Buddy picked it up. Before William could stop him, Buddy had read the label.

"Oh man," Buddy said as he clicked his mouth a few times. "Brainwash pills?"

Buddy shook the bottle at William. "Let me guess, these were Cherry's idea, too?"

"No," said William. "My therapist suggested them."

"And who suggested the therapist?"

"Cherry thought therapy might help me."

"Cherry thought therapy might help me," Buddy repeated in a mincing whiny voice.

"Well, it has," said William.

"Yeah, I bet," Buddy said back in his normal voice. "Helped you learn to be her obedient little patsy. Wow, William, you are going to be my most challenging case yet."

"Glad I can make it worth your while," said William. He grabbed the pills out of Buddy's hand. "See ya later, Buddy."

William left the bar without looking back.

Cherry lived in an older subdivision on the east side of town called "Paradise Cottages." The neighborhood had first been built in the mid-80s for mid-level professionals and young couples starting families. The cottage style houses had been designed simply with few embellishments to give them any character. These homes were meant to be temporary, lived in for a decade or so before the occupants traded up to something better, as such, they were made fast and cheap.

The low quality materials had not held up well over time. The vast majority of the houses had patched roofs and decaying window frames. Shadows of darker paint on exterior walls showed where shutters had once been. Cracks ran along the mortar of the chimneys. Pot holes and fissures ate away at the streets and the constant battle against snow and ice in the winters had left the sidewalks pockmarked and buckled. Overgrown cottonwood trees hung over the streets, dropping piles of decaying leaves in the gutters. Weeds grew in the seams in the concrete.

Still preoccupied by his conversation with Buddy, William drove through the maze of streets in the subdivision automatically making the turns that led to Cherry's street without really thinking about them. Traffic was always heavy at first because the subdivision only had one main road in and one out.

It wasn't until he saw her house in the distance that the warm glow Cherry always gave him pulled him out of his trance like state.

Buddy's voice in his head faded away, growing quieter and quieter the closer he got to Cherry. By the time William had parked in front of the house, Buddy's voice was gone completely.

William walked along the steep driveway to the opening in the unfinished split rail fence, slivered and warped by age, that surrounded Cherry's dry, but neatly kept, front lawn. The nice parts of this house were the corner lot, two car garage and huge park across the street. He followed the pathway of cracked cement up to the small, quaint brick and frame cottage.

Like the others, Cherry's house also showed its age. The roof of her covered porch sagged a bit and much of the paint had peeled away from the two elegant pillars that held it up. Cherry did her best, but it was hard for her to keep up with the constant stream of expensive repairs that the thirty-five year old house required.

Of all the amazing things about Cherry, that was the quality that awed William most. No matter what came at her, she got up and kept fighting. The same spirit that had brought her success in the ring had carried her through life, keeping her going when she had all reason to give up. Unfortunately, the felony assault conviction had ended her fighting career, but it hadn't held her down for long.

Though she had been banned from fighting, the judge had agreed that mitigating circumstances had been present and had given her a suspended sentence. As long as she got therapy and committed no further crimes she would be spared prison. Though the conviction had cost her many opportunities, she still worked hard to carve out the best life she could within her limited means.

Though the metal screen door was closed, the front door stood open, spilling warm light onto the porch. William's eyes swept over the comfortably furnished living room to the left of the front door and the dining room and U shaped kitchen straight ahead. He peeked in but didn't see Cherry anywhere.

He opened the screen door cautiously and stuck his head through. "Cherry?" he called. She didn't answer, but a heavy thump followed by chains jingling indicated she was in down in the basement. He followed the sound down the hall and paused at the top of the stairs before calling her name again.

"Hi honey, come on down," she answered. There was another

thump and the chains jingled again.

When William reached the bottom of the stairs he could see the heavy bag still swinging around. Cherry stood in front of it, wearing black yoga pants and a tight royal blue V-neck t-shirt. She wore her hair back in a high pony tail and a folded purple bandanna wrapped at her hairline to catch sweat. Baby pink polish coated the nails of her bare feet. As William watched, Cherry's long leg swung up again, delivering a roundhouse kick to the bag that sent it flying. Cherry then dropped into a crouch, spun around, jumped back to her feet and kicked the bag with her other leg, sending it the other direction.

"Wow," said William.

Cherry just smiled. She did a quick series of stretches while she waited for the bag to come to a stop. William enjoyed watching her move. The tight clothes she wore hugged her body in a way that left no doubt of her gender. He looked around the room to distract himself before he completely lost all blood flow to his brain.

A professional quality mahogany pool table covered in traditional green felt stood in the far left corner, lit from above by a hanging light. Gleaming wooden cues hung neatly in the rack on the wall behind it. Cherry rarely, if ever, used the table, but she kept it "for sentimental reasons," she'd told him.

The only other items in the cottage's nine hundred and sixty square foot basement were the heavy bag and a weight set with a bench covered in tan vinyl that had worn away in spots from constant use. The amount of weight currently loaded on the barbell made him wonder if she had another man in her life that came over to use the bench press. One glance at the sleeves of her shirt made it clear that she was indeed the one using it.

The only decoration on the unfinished walls was the state flag Cherry had painted on wooden lathes held together with brass screws.

William noticed a pile of red fabric pooled on the floor. He looked closer. His stomach dropped when he realized what it was. He hadn't known she'd planned to wear *that* dress for him tonight. He got the sudden feeling he'd missed out big by letting Buddy talk him into staying at the bar.

Cherry noticed where he was looking. Smiling sinfully, she bent down to gather up the dress and shoes, making sure William got a good view of her cleavage as she did so.

"Meeting ran a little long, huh?" she asked as she straightened up.

"Yeah," William said lamely.

"How'd it go?"

"Okay, I guess."

Cherry frowned as she studied him. "Hmm. Your pretty blue eyes don't look that ok to me. Did you get anything to eat?"

"Not really."

Cherry came over to inspect him closer.

"But plenty to drink though," she said, laughing a bit. "Come on, let's see if dinner is still salvageable."

William followed her upstairs into the kitchen with blue walls, lace curtains and white cupboards with silver toned trim. He sat down in one of the turquoise chairs at her table in the dining room.

Cherry placed a salad in front of him. As usual, William picked out the tomatoes and olives to eat and set the rest aside.

"Finish your salad, please, William," Cherry said sternly. "We don't waste food in this house."

"Yes, Cherry," he said with a grin on his face. He pulled the plate back to him and dutifully finished the rest of the pile of vegetables. Usually, he enjoyed playing this little game with her, but tonight his earlier conversation with Buddy spoiled the fun. With each bite of salad Buddy's comments came back to him. "Is she your girlfriend or your nanny?" "She keeps you on a pretty short leash."

Hoping to silence Buddy's voice in his head he studied Cherry's living room. He liked her full-size L shaped sofa and big screen TV with surround sound speakers. Being gloomy, he just stared like a zombie at her full service cable box and large high end DVD player. The only thing he didn't like about the house was that there was no access to the garage directly from the house.

He glanced down the hall and could see her queen size mahogany bed covered in silk sheets. He knew from experience that she hadn't chosen the bed frame with round solid wood antique posts by chance. The smell in the house indicated she had just had the sofa and carpets professionally cleaned. Even with her scrawny gray cat living there the place smelled like fresh laundry.

He noticed on her bookshelf the copy of a book of short stories that had his short story "One More Year" in it. He smiled as he remembered giving it to her and confessing why he wrote it. He was glad the bad feeling he had then was gone but always feared it would come back. Cherry had saved him once, but he felt like he could still backslide down into that same dark place.

He wondered why he didn't feel more successful. He was a millionaire, yet he still lived in a 500 sq foot shack behind the diner that didn't even have a full kitchen. Then he remembered the house he'd rented back when he was a teenager had also been a 100 year old one room hovel no bigger than an average garden shed. It depressed him to realize the nicest place he'd ever lived had been the bland condo he and Annie had shared in Reseda with its beige walls and balcony overlooking the freeway. No wonder nobody took him seriously. Would Buddy's program really be able to change all that?

Cherry brought their dinner to the table. William looked down at the meatball sub smothered in homemade marinara sauce with gooey layers of melted cheese and the giant pile of crispy golden steak fries on his plate. It looked delicious. Cherry sat down to eat her own dinner. William suddenly had the feeling that the sandwiches on their plates weren't the only meatball subs at the table.

"So tell me about the meeting," Cherry said in a tone that made it sound more like a command than a request. Like a little devil on his shoulder, Buddy's voice piped up again, "who has the balls in your relationship, you or her?"

Then her sparkling blue eyes looked into his and Buddy disappeared again. William sighed and leaned back in his chair.

"I don't know, Cherry. I don't think those kinds of meetings are for me. They were all rude and no one even paid any attention to me. They kept talking over me and nobody listened to anything I had to say. I felt like a bug under their shoes."

"I'm sorry you got treated that way," Cherry said sympathetically. "But don't take it personally. They treat everybody that way because they think making other people feel small makes them look bigger, but really it just makes them assholes."

"I guess," William said glumly. Then he remembered the men had been nicer to the waitress serving them than they had been to him. Even though she'd been belittled, too, at least they'd considered her useful. "I just want to feel important," he said sulkily.

"You are important. Businesses like yours are the lifeblood of this city. Guys like that just sit on their butts all day sucking other people dry, but you work hard every day. That's what keeps things moving. You actively contribute to the economy, they just take from it. Not a single one of them would have a penny if it weren't for the people like you who actually generate income."

"Well, what if I don't want to have to keep scraping for everything I get? What if for once I want to sit back and let other people do the work for me?"

"You aren't like that though, William. You are the type that has to work, otherwise you'll go crazy."

"Yeah, maybe. But why does it have to be so hard? Why do I still feel like a loser? I'd just like a little respect for once in my life, is that too much to ask?"

"It doesn't. There's no reason you can't take time to enjoy your life. And you are not a loser. You are a young, healthy man who worked hard to get where he is."

"So what's next? More work? Do I keep living in my little shack and come home at the end of the night reeking of kitchen grease?"

"You use what you've been given to help make the world a better place."

"And how am I going to do that if no one will even pay attention to me? Hell, the chairman of that meeting tonight didn't even know who I was. He thought I was your son."

"Was that Lawrence?"

"I don't know, I wasn't paying attention," said William. He took a vicious bite out of his sandwich and chewed loudly.

"Well, he's an idiot. They're all idiots."

"Yeah, but they're the idiots who have all the power in this town."

"Not all of it."

"Enough to get to make the rules. You should have heard them tonight, Cherry. Talking about who they wanted in office and whether or not it's fair to charge tax on the girls at The Love House. It's like politics is just a big game to them."

"It's not a game, William. The decisions that get made in

37

meetings like those have a direct impact on people's lives. That's why I wanted you to go, so you could speak up for those people."

"*Her perfect little patsy,*" Buddy's voice whispered in William's head.

"Well, I tried, but they didn't listen, so I guess we're out of luck."

"So, make them. You have just as much right to be there and have your ideas heard as they do."

William shook his head. Cherry just didn't understand. Buddy understood, though. He was starting to think Buddy had been right about everything.

"Look," said Cherry, "I know it's hard. It was very brave of you to go to that meeting and speak up. I'm proud of you. And, I got you a present to reward you for it."

"Oh?" William perked up a bit.

Cherry smiled and placed a package wrapped in brightly colored gift paper on the table. William took it. With deliberate care, he slowly began to open the gift.

The paper revealed a bottle of Evan William's Cherry Reserve Kentucky Whiskey. The bottle had a large logo of two cherries on it.

"Look," Cherry said. "It's got 'William' and 'Cherry' on it. We're like two cherries William. I got it for you. Save it for a special occasion."

"What kinda occasion?" William said as he looked at the slogan on the bottle that said 'The smoothness of Evan William's with a sweet Cherry taste."

"Well, I hate that you drink so damn much, but I do know whiskey can help celebrate victory or drown out sorrows. Don't drink it unless you have victory or sorrow."

"Thank you, Cherry," William said feeling misty eyed.

"You're welcome." Cherry leaned over and kissed him. "You matter, ok? You matter more than all those jerks put together. Don't let them bully you. They have no right to shut you out."

"I don't know how," said William. "How do I get big and powerful like them?"

"You don't have to be big and powerful like them. Just be yourself," said Cherry. "You are perfect just as you are. Find your own door to the promised land. Believe in yourself a little more and they'll start believing too."

"Maybe," said William, but he felt skeptical. Did Cherry really believe that or was Buddy right; that she just wanted to keep him down so she could keep him under control?

He believed she really cared about him. Maybe she really did just have his best interests at heart. Then again, maybe she didn't. Did she respect him? Or would she only start to if he stood up to her?

"I have an early class to teach," Cherry said as she gathered the dishes.

William stood up. "Guess I better go home then." He headed towards the front door. Just before he reached the threshold she called his name. He turned around to meet her, only to see her holding out his pill bottle.

"You forgot these," she said. He took the pills and put them in his pocket.

"Gee, thanks," he said sarcastically.

Cherry's eyes narrowed as she studied him carefully. "Did you take those today?"

"Of course I did. Why?"

"Just making sure. I know how out of control you get when you don't take them."

"Oh." Well, now he knew.

William unintentionally slammed her front door behind himself as he left.

As he walked down the steep driveway to his car he pulled the pill bottle out of his pocket and shook it. He studied the little pills jumping around inside.

"Be myself, huh? I've been myself my whole stupid life. All it ever got me was beat up, arrested, dumped, rejected, persecuted and spit on."

He shook the pills some more.

"Ahh, fuck!" He said as he threw the bottle into the street and listened to the plastic bottle break and pills scatter everywhere.

Chapter 3

William's New Buddy

The next day, just before 7PM, William parked down the street from the Ale Haus. He walked up the street at a slow pace watching the happy productive office people rush around him, yapping away on their phones as they power-walked down the sidewalk. Groups of people stood in the doorways of the restaurants and other bars, chatting and laughing. Here and there someone smoked.

William wondered why he felt completely alone despite being in the middle of the evening rush. This feeling often overtook him. He could sense the gap between himself and the people on the street. It was as if he saw them all through a window instead of being part of the same world they lived in.

William entered the bar. The same bartender stood behind the counter. Plenty of stools were open but this time he opted for a table. He chose one towards the back where he could watch the door. He sat there for what felt like a long time waiting for Buddy. For the first time in his life he wished he had a phone that did more than make calls. At least that way he could do something to pass the time instead of sitting there looking like an idiot.

Finally, Buddy came in. After a quick look around he spotted William and waved. William waved back but didn't move. Buddy paused in the doorway for several long moments before approaching William's table.

"Good man," Buddy said in a loud, approving voice. "That's one lesson down already. Don't ever come to people. Make them come to you."

William shrugged. "I guess," he said.

Buddy didn't sit down. "Hey, listen, I got really busy today and never got to eat. Let's go around the corner and hit up Marylou's. I'm starving."

William's stomach rumbled. He realized he hadn't eaten all day, either.

"Sounds good to me." He followed Buddy out the door. He thought the bartender gave them a hostile look as they left but he couldn't be sure.

Marylou's turned out to be a diner two blocks away that looked like it had seen better days. Silver duct tape patched tears in the clichéd red vinyl booth seats. Most of the ones near the windows had faded, turning a pinkish yellow with patches of gray where years of friction had rubbed the setbacks thin. Cracks and scratches ran across a black and white checkerboard linoleum floor and foot traffic had completely worn the color off of in places.

Buddy slid into a booth in the back corner near an alcove that led to the bathrooms. William sat on the opposite side of the table. Menus were already on the table. William picked his up and tried to ignore the sticky spots on the laminated wood table top and the thick dust on the windowsill. He wondered when the health department had last come through.

The waitress, an older blonde woman with wide hips and no chest, stomped her way towards them in her sea green uniform dress and white apron.

"What'll it be?" she asked with a sour expression.

Buddy ordered a double bacon burger, fries and a side of chili. William, knowing better in a place like this, stuck to a slice of key lime pie and a coke with a straw. He was very thankful the straw came in a paper wrapper.

While they waited for their food, William gave Buddy some more background about his past. Buddy, however, seemed to have heard it all already.

"If you already know everything about me why do you keep asking?" William finally said, getting annoyed.

"It's like when you see the doctor," said Buddy, pausing to chew a bite of his burger before he continued. "He doesn't just start poking and ordering tests, he asks about your symptoms and medical history first, right? This is the same way. I know the facts, but I don't know how you feel about them. I need to see what happened to you from your point of view before I can know how to help you."

"I got screwed," said William. "Some big jerk decided to make life hell for a teenager whose only crime was to be a better athlete. Even though I won in the end, it's like I suddenly became everyone's punching bag. People have been taking shots at me ever since. It's like the fight with Casner broke me or something and everyone knows it. I'm weaker than they are and they all take advantage."

Buddy nodded sympathetically. "Been there, my friend; been there many times. I was always the dog that got beat, until I figured out how to play by their rules and beat them at a game I never wanted to play."

"But why?" William protested. "Why does everything have to be big games and power plays? Why can't it all just be straight?"

"Because resources are limited and competition is how our species keeps evolving. The winners get the choicest bits and everyone else fights over the scraps. That's why we fight wars, why dating is such hell, why businessmen are so ruthless and politics gets so ugly. Everyone wants to be top dog, but very few people know how to turn the fight in their favor."

"You figured it out though?" William asked half sarcastic.

"I did, but then I started feeling guilty, you know, because I saw everyone around me still suffering. Guys like you who have everything going for them, but are being held for ransom by bad friends, poor self-esteem and disrespectful women without even realizing it. So I had to do something. I felt like, you know, one of those Buddhist saints who reaches Nirvana but comes back to earth to guide others. I couldn't keep my new gift all to myself."

"I guess that makes sense," said William. "So what have you got for me?"

"Well, my friend, first of all, you need to understand that I don't offer my program to just anybody. The stuff I teach is forbidden fruit and for good reason. Not everyone can be a *Leader*, and not everyone deserves to be. Somebody's gotta be the grunt. It's not up to me to change that. It's just up to me to help the people who belong on that tier claim their rightful place. Someone has to have real talent and potential to be worth my time, but I've studied you for years, and I know you're ready."

William's eyes widened as he realized Buddy *was* the guy in the Cadillac who had been obsessed with him back when he was a teenager.

"So why me?" William wondered.

"Because your story is incredible! You've earned the right to be number one. Someone just has to show you how to set yourself free."

"I have to admit I'm tired of fighting and struggling all the time. I'd like some smooth sailing and respect for once."

"Money, power, women, respect, it's all yours for the taking." Buddy proclaimed. "All you have to do is follow the program."

"So where do I start?"

"You start right here," Buddy said. He tapped the side of his head. "Change the way you think and change your life."

"That sounds too easy."

"No, it's not easy. Breaking a lifetime of ingrained habits is hard, but it is simple. It's just like replacing fuses. Replace a bad thought with a good one."

"Just like that."

"Just like that," Buddy repeated. "But not everyone can do it. Too many people give up because they can't make the commitment to themselves to do better."

"So I don't have to like move to the side of a mountain and live in a cave for a year or something?"

Buddy laughed. "No, but you do have to make the commitment to change. You have to make the time to put yourself first."

"How much time?"

"We can cover the basics in about a week if you can commit to meeting every evening."

"Could we break it up into like weekly meetings or something? I don't know if I can take that much time away from the diner all at once."

"William, do you own that business, or does it own you?" Buddy asked.

William sputtered.

"Don't answer that." Buddy held up a finger. "I already know.

Look, William, it is your business and it is great that you are so hands on in running it. However, that doesn't mean you have to be chained to it all the time. Do you see Thomas Moore out there hauling lumber? Does Hank hang around The Love House and polish the furniture?"

"No," William said. "I had never seen any of those guys before tonight and I use their businesses all the time."

"That's because they trust things to run themselves. They hire people to do the work and sit back and enjoy the rewards. You've earned that right, too. You just can't let go because you still think like a grunt."

"Not entirely. I didn't plan on working this much but hiring people is hard. It was just easier to do it myself."

"Hiring people isn't hard." Buddy proclaimed. "You only make it hard if you don't know how to be the boss."

"Riley mostly handles that. I just mix drinks and wait tables."

"So everyone still sees you as the servant you used to be instead of the successful man you are now."

"Oh," said William. Things were starting to make sense.

"Not to mention, doing all the work yourself is really selfish. You keep talking about wanting to help the downtrodden but here you are monopolizing jobs that could help someone turn their life around."

"Never thought of it that way," said William.

"That's exactly my point. Riley is a good manager. Hire some people, back off and let him do his job. Take some time for yourself."

"Well, it has been awhile since I had a break," William agreed. "I'll ask Riley if he'd be ok with me taking a week off."

"Wrong," said Buddy. "Riley is your employee. You will *tell* him that you are taking some time off, not ask him if you can."

"But--"

"No buts! You are taking charge as of now. You are the boss. Act like it."

William paused. He had never in his life had a time when someone wasn't telling him what to do. He didn't know if he knew how to be in charge of himself.

"What if he asks why? What do I tell him?" William wondered.

"Tell him you do not need to justify your decisions to your

employees."

"Wow."

"Yeah, I know, it sounds harsh, but if you want respect you have to insist on getting it. Put him in his place."

"I don't know if I can do that."

"Yes, you can."

An awkward silence fell. William rocked the glass ketchup bottle back and forth across the table while Buddy chomped away on his fries. He finally swallowed and looked up at William.

"I know," said Buddy, "You think I'm an asshole. All my clients do at first. All I'm doing is untangling the web of bullshit you've been conditioned to believe all your life. All through school we're taught 'play nice', 'work hard', 'do as you're told', 'get good grades', but nobody ever tells us why. We never once are taught what the grades mean."

William thought about that for a moment and realized that a lot of what he learned in school didn't help him much.

"Why is getting an A in 7th grade science class worthy of reward?" Buddy continued. "How will this help someone? No, we're taught to do what were told and always be the good guy and always make everyone happy and that this pot of gold will be waiting for you. But it doesn't work that way. All being the good guy gets you is stomped on while the people who make their own rules climb over you on their way to the top."

"Yeah," William added. "I did try breaking the rules, and all it got me was jail time."

"Really? Because I seem to recall that it was only when you broke the law and took matters into your own hands that you finally cleared your name and brought down the people attacking you."

William found himself shocked again. He couldn't believe how right Buddy was. Even though he was innocent, fighting in court had gotten him nowhere. If he hadn't gone rogue he would be sitting in a prison cell instead of a rundown diner booth.

"Listen to me carefully, William," said Buddy. "This is the most important thing you will learn from me. In this world there are *Yesmen* and leaders. *Yesmen* play by the rules and get kicked around all their lives. Leaders make their own rules and don't care what anyone thinks about it. You've gotta decide which one you want to be."

"Thought I'd already decided, Buddy, that's why I'm here."

"Good. Now start acting like a *Leader*."

"But what does that even mean? The only 'leaders' I've ever seen are bullies that like to boss people around."

"Ever seen any of those old gangster movies? The guy in charge never yells, never moves, never dirties his hands. He just sits there at his back table speaking so quietly it's almost a whisper. Always calm, always still, but his word is God's own law. People live or die by a wave of his finger. That is being a *Leader*. A *Leader* is in control and he knows it, and he makes sure other people know it, too."

While Buddy went on, William zoned out and had a quick daydream of himself in one of Marlon Brando's old roles. He was seated in a dark room while a group of silent, hostile men in dark suits waited to do his bidding. Riley stood next to his desk in a pinned stripped suit and fedora. He pictured Mitch seated in front of him waiting to be lectured.

"Time and again I have invited you into my diner." William started to say to a scared Mitch. "I have fed you like family, and yet you disrespect me. You mock my success when you have none of your own."

"Please accept my deepest apology, Don William," Mitch begged.

"Excuse me, Don William," A waitress said, "Table 4 needs to see a manager."

"I'll be there soon; I have business to take care of right now," William replied.

"Please," Mitch begged. "Don William, I will never use such disrespectful words around you again."

Riley stood like a statue as Mitch begged more.

"Oh, kitten," Cherry interrupted as she somehow entered the room in his daydream. "Mistress needs her feet rubbed," she continued. Riley, Mitch, the waitress and the other men in suits busted out laughing.

"Cherryyyy!" A humiliated William whined as his daydream ended.

Nah, I'd never pull it off, William thought. He was far more Tony

Montana than Vito Corelone.

"Yeah, I don't think I want to be a mob boss." William said to Buddy as he laughed at himself.

"How about president?" Buddy replied.

"No way," said William. "That's crazy."

"Yeah? That's what Reagan said. One day he's getting second billing to a monkey, next day he's Governor of California. What changed? His attitude. He took charge. So can you."

"There's gotta be more to it than just telling people I'm in charge."

"You don't tell people, you show them. For example, in Japan no one ever splits a check. The big man at the table always pays for the meal. He puts the money down to prove he can and immediately puts everyone in his debt. He's paying so he says who eats and who doesn't. People trip over themselves to do him favors so they stay in his good graces and keep their place at his table."

"Sounds kind of medieval."

"It is. The rules of power wrote themselves in the days of kings and castles, but they still hold true. Technology may have evolved since then, but human nature hasn't. We're all still barbarians at heart."

"Good thing they outlawed flails," said William.

Buddy polished off the last of his chili. "Our society conditions us to be *Yesmen*. They use the *Prisoner's Choir* against us to hold us down. What a *Leader* has to do is break that programming. He stops seeking the approval of others and makes decisions based on what he thinks is best. He doesn't care about people's opinions, or how his choices impact someone else. He doesn't worry about making mistakes, either. He knows that sometimes he has to make decisions based on incomplete information. But he makes his best guess and lets confidence make up for what he lacks in knowledge. He knows he will be wrong sometimes, but he goes ahead anyway. And if he doesn't get it right, he doesn't beat himself up over it. He learns from it and moves on."

"Prisoner's Choir?" William repeated. He hadn't heard much after that. Buddy was hard to keep up with.

Buddy waved his hands in a shooing motion. "We'll talk about that tomorrow. Pull out your phone. There's some stuff on my phone you need to read."

"I don't have a smart phone," said William.

"You gotta be kidding me?" Buddy shook his head in disbelief.

"Nope." William held up his battered old flip phone.

"Wow. Captain Kirk in the house." Buddy laughed. "Here. I'll write it down for you."

Buddy pulled a napkin out of the dispenser. He called the waitress over. She tore their check off her pad and held it out to him. Instead of taking it, he pulled a blue pen out of her apron pocket. He wrote while the waitress stood there glaring at him. She looked at William who looked at the table.

After several long minutes Buddy pushed the napkin across the table. He watched while William read what he had written.

--I don't need to be feeling this way.

--Love doesn't have to = suffering.

--Someone can only love you the way they know how, not the way you want them to.

--They will take your rights and turn them into privileges if you let them.

--We attract those we are comfortable with even if it means abuse.

--Why do I invest so much energy in things that do nothing for me?

"That's not quite what I was expecting," said William.

"It's just a starting point," said Buddy. "More traps to avoid. When you find yourself spiraling down go through this list. Then look yourself in the eye and say 'I am in charge of my own life. I'm the boss'. Once you believe it the magic starts happening."

William nodded slowly as he read through the list again.

"There you go, hon." Buddy gave the waitress back her pen and took the check. The waitress gave him another dirty look and stomped off. Buddy handed it to William. William looked confused.

"You're the big man at the table, right?" Buddy said.

"Yeah," said William. "I am." William felt a surge of energy pump through him as he said the words. He pulled out his wallet and got up. At the counter he paid with the new American Express card Cherry had helped him apply for just to show off a bit. He signed the charge slip with the same pen Buddy had used. Feeling generous, he placed a ten dollar bill on the table when he got back.

"What are you doing?" Buddy asked.

"Leaving a tip."

"Dude, never tip your first time at a new place. Especially since she was huffy with us the whole time."

"What?" Having been a server for so long, William had strong feelings about people who didn't tip. In fact, his policy at Moe's was to ban those who stiffed the wait-staff more than once.

"A tip is a gift, not an entitlement. Don't give it just because it's expected. Make them earn it."

"But--"

"No buts. This is exactly what I mean. A *Yesman* tips no matter how crappy the service is because he feels sorry for the server or because it's the 'nice' thing to do. A *Leader* doesn't because he knows that if he rewards poor performance then there is no incentive to improve."

"I don't think it works that way. If someone didn't tip me their service got worse next time, not better."

"That's because you aren't a natural *Yesman*. Even as a slave wage slob you were a *Leader* waiting to be, so you reacted like a *Leader*. But it's different for them. Trust me on this, ok? Don't tip tonight. Then we'll come back same time tomorrow and I'll bet she quits rolling her God damn eyes at us every time we need something."

William hesitated, but so far Buddy had been right about everything else. Maybe he was right about this, too. Reluctantly, he put the bill back in his pocket. He could feel the waitress's eyes burning into his back as they left.

"See ya, William." Buddy said and took off on foot.

On his way back to his car, William passed through more crowds of people. He still felt the gap he'd noticed early, but he realized it no longer made him feel lonely. It just felt natural. Right somehow. They were *Yesmen*. He was a *Leader*. No wonder he didn't fit in. He was never meant to.

William got back to the dinner just after it closed. He was surprised to find the lights still on and Riley waiting for him behind the bar. Concerned, he went in to see what was wrong.

"William!" Riley called excitedly. "You will never guess what happened tonight!"

"Do I want to know?" William asked. He sat down on one of the stools. Riley poured him a glass of scotch.

"For once, yes." Riley answered. "City councilwoman Martha Stout was in here tonight. She came to see you. You remember her right? She's the one who had the *2016 Outstanding Senior Citizen Awards* ceremony here a few years ago."

"Yeah, I remember. The old man who won was, like, sobbing all over the place."

"Well, that was quite an emotional moment for the old guy," Riley replied. "He had said it was one of the greatest awards he had ever gotten."

"Yeah," William snorted. "Bet when he dies his kids find that award and be, like, 'what the hell's this?' And throw it in the trash."

"Anyway," a turbulent Riley replied, offended by William's aloof humor. "Since you weren't here she talked to me instead."

"Oh great. Let me guess." William lit a cigarette to go with his Scotch. "Her broom broke down and she needed a lift home."

"No, William. She's putting a new proposal before the council and wants your endorsement for it."

"And what exactly does old kill-a-business Martha have in mind this time?"

"I would think you'd be more excited, William. A city councilwoman wants your opinion and your approval; that's a big deal."

William blew a cloud of smoke towards the ceiling. "Depends on what she wants me to endorse, don't you think?"

"Well, she's got this great idea for eliminating tips and just paying the servers the same wage as everyone else. She says it would make great progress in improving the dignity of servers. I told her I thought you'd love the idea. I know how you feel about jerks who don't tip."

Oh great, thought William. He looked at Riley. They had been friends for so long, but he was starting to see more of how Buddy was right about Riley overstepping his boundaries. Now he was endorsing things in his name without even asking him first. This was going to suck, but it had to be done. William sighed deeply.

"Riley, listen, I know you meant well and all, but I don't want you speaking for me. Especially when it comes to something as important as city politics. You're my friend, but I'm also the owner here and you need to let me make decisions like that for myself."

"Sorry, William. I didn't think there would be a problem."

"Well, that's why you shouldn't make assumptions. Sometimes I think you forget who's the boss around here," William protested.

Riley's face flushed. "It's your diner, William. I don't forget that. I just try to do my best to keep it going when you aren't here."

"Well, I appreciate that, Riley, I really do." William knocked the ash from his cigarette and took a sip of his whiskey. "You do a great job of running this place. In fact I'm thinking it's time I backed off and just let you do your job. God knows I pay you enough for it. I should quit crawling up your ass and trust you with the day to day operations. But for big stuff like this you need to ask me first, ok?"

"Sure, William, I'll do that."

"I do want you to hire another bartender and a couple more servers, though. Maybe a line cook."

"We don't really need them. You do all that."

"Yeah, but I shouldn't. It's not fair for me to hog all those jobs when other people need them. And I need a break, man. When was the last time I took time off?"

"It has been awhile. When you were arrested years ago?" said Riley. "Is everything ok, William?"

"Yeah, I'm fine. Why do you ask?"

"I'm just wondering why now? You never wanted to be away before. Did something happen?"

"You know, Riley, I really don't have to justify my decisions to my employees."

"I know that, William. But I am also your friend and I'm worried about you."

"Thanks for the concern, but I'm fine. It's not a crime to want to enjoy my life a little."

"I didn't realize you weren't." Riley said through tight lips.

William saw the genuine worry in Riley's eyes and knew his old friend was afraid he was once again about to melt down. Boy, was he going to be surprised when he found out what William was really up to. He hoped it would be worth adding to Riley's gray hairs. His new persona slipped a little as an old sense of guilt tugged at him.

"Nothing's wrong. I've just been working like a grunt for more than half my life now and I want to take some time and see what else is out there. Just for awhile. I've missed out on a lot. I want to catch up a little."

"Good for you," said Riley. "I'll handle things here."

"I have complete confidence in you." William tipped his glass towards Riley.

"So what are we going to tell Ms. Stout about her proposal?"

William bristled. Damn. This was going to be harder than he thought. "*We* aren't going to say anything. *I*, however, am going to tell her it's a terrible idea. Yeah, I always hated not being tipped, but I at least understood that tipping exists for a reason. Tips encourage a server to give their best performance.

"The success of an entire restaurant relies on servers delivering that performance. Having the best cook in town doesn't do us any good if we can't get an entree on a customer's table in a timely manner. And people aren't just paying for the food. They pay for the whole experience. They want to feel special and important. It's the servers who do that."

"Other businesses don't rely on tips to reward performance, though," said Riley.

"Yeah, and look at the service you get. Last week I couldn't get the kid at the grocery store to put down his phone long enough to ring up my orange juice. And why should he? He's going to make the same crap wage whether he does his job or not. Minimum wage is a dead end so why should he care?"

"I don't know. A flat wage may be a more stable living for servers."

"Only at first, but in the end they're cheated. They don't deserve to be cheated."

"How is a flat wage cheating them?" Riley wondered.

"Because they don't deserve to have the government tell them what they're allowed to make and then tax the shit out of it. They earned that money, Uncle Sam and Martha Stout didn't. You know as well as I do they don't fully report all their cash tips. If we pay a straight wage we'll have to report the new figure and they'll pay more taxes. Besides, *good servers* make more now off tips than they would under that stupid 'living wage' they want to get passed."

"But sometimes they may make less money if customers are unhappy and tip less."

"Exactly. They wanna punish hard working servers and reward slacker servers. You've seen the wait-staff we've had here over the years. They were not all equally hard working. So it's stupid to pay them all like they are. Don't you think?"

"Well, at least Ms. Stout has good intentions."

"People don't pay their rent with good intentions. That woman needs to go back to her cauldron and keep her nose out an industry she doesn't understand."

"You aren't actually going to say that, are you?"

"Why not? I got something for Martha Stout to ponder. How come if someone gets too drunk at my diner and kills someone driving home I can be sued? It's not my job to play daddy. I mean, now a days, you can be sued for someone's *potential lifetime earnings*," William said.

Riley just stood there with his arms crossed as William ranted.

"I can see it now in court," William continued. "Your honor, that young angel-face could've grown up to be president! But because Moe's Diner over-served some asshole he's dead."

"Um, William," Riley said in a disenchanted tone. "The last thing either of us needs is for you to start a feud with city hall."

"Ok, fine," William said. "But I am going to tell her the proposal is a bad idea, and I'm going to tell her why."

"Can I watch?" Riley asked with a mischievous smile.

William snorted. "You bet."

Chapter 4

Celebrations and Sorrows

William woke with a fuzzy head and ringing in his ears. He laid in bed staring at the ceiling as he played back the night before. He'd only had one drink all night, so why did he feel like crap? He wondered if lack of alcohol could give someone a hangover.

His phone beeped. He really didn't want to know, but he reached for it anyway. He sat up and rubbed his eyes before he flipped open the phone to read the screen.

"Chardonnay or Zinfandel?" Cherry's text read.

William blinked. "Huh?" he typed. A moment later his phone rang.

"Hello?"

"Hi ya, sleepyhead," said Cherry. "Did I wake you?"

"No, no, I was awake." He stretched against the sheets. "What's up?"

"Which wine am I getting?"

"Wine?"

William heard an exasperated sigh. "For the pork loin."

"Pork loin?"

"Yes, the pork loin. You, me, dinner with Paula and Jeff; remember? I said I'd make that Italian pork roast you wanted to try, but the recipe calls for white wine and I don't know which one to get."

"Oh, geez, is that tonight?"

"Uh, yeah," said Cherry.

"Damn, I forgot."

"That's ok. They won't be there till seven, so you have time to get ready."

"Right." He'd have to call Buddy as soon as she hung up. Damn, damn, damn. He had been really looking forward to seeing how the tip thing played out, too.

"So which wine?"

"Zinfandel," William answered. He loved it that even though Cherry was so smart and competent there were still some things she looked to his expertise for. He liked knowing that he gave at least a little bit back in return for everything she gave him.

"Thank you. Love you." Cherry said.

"Love you, too."

William hung up the phone. He pulled himself out of bed and pulled some clothes on. After a hurried search he found his wallet under a chair. He leafed through it, hoping Buddy's card was still in there. Had he even put it in there? Nope. Damn again. He checked his suit pockets. Not there either.

Hadn't Buddy said he had a website? Maybe William could Google him from the office computer. William grabbed his shoes and headed across the alley. As he passed his Impala he spotted Buddy's business card on the dashboard.

"Brilliant," said William. "Good move, Defreno. Advertise the fact that you're seeing a life coach to the whole damn world."

He grabbed the card and hurried back inside. As he dialed the number and waited for Buddy to answer he started searching for his comb.

"This is Buddy Richfield. I'm away from my phone right now, but leave a message and I'll get back to you. Thanks."

Another damn. William was starting to feel like a beaver.

"Hey, Buddy, it's William." He paused. He knew leaders didn't apologize but what *did* they do when they canceled an appointment? Oh well, he'd wing it. "Hate to tell you, but I totally forgot I had plans tonight so I can't make our meeting. See you tomorrow night I guess."

William hung up the phone. He had just brushed his teeth and was about to shower when it rang again.

"Defreno here," William answered.

"William, my man, it's Buddy. What's going on? I thought we

made a deal?"

"We did. I just forgot about this when we planned to meet."

"I'll see what else I got. But what exactly is more important than your own future?"

"Cherry and I are supposed to have dinner with a friend and her new boyfriend."

"Cherry? Oh good. Tell her you can't make it. Something came up."

"I can't. She'll kill me." Or at least beat him, and not in a fun way. He made a mental note to hide her oak cutting board.

"No she won't. Look, it will do you good to stand up to her for once."

"But I promised. We made these plans a month ago. Besides, Cherry really isn't the type that likes being stood up to."

"She'll get over it."

"But Buddy--"

"No buts. If you don't show up to night we're done, got it?"

"Come on, maaan, give me a break here!"

"Sorry, William, but I have my rules. The school of life does not hold make up classes."

Buddy hung up. William reflected that the best thing about sleeping past noon was that when you had a bad day at least it was short. He wondered if there were any florists around, then he realized that handing Cherry rose stems right now might not be the best idea.

With the same enthusiasm of a convict sitting down in the electric chair he picked up the phone. He stared at it a long time before flipping it open and then stared for even longer before finally hitting one on his speed dial. He cringed like he'd just pulled the pin on a grenade. Maybe he'd get lucky and get her voicemail. Nope. She answered.

"Hi," she purred.

"Hi."

"Guess where I am?"

Probably not a convent, he thought, but he knew he'd better not say it. He was about to be in enough trouble as it was. Instead he said, "No idea."

"Oh, come on, guess. If you get it right, you'll get a treat."

William whimpered. "Uh honey, listen. I have a little problem."

"Oh?" There was the steel in her voice. He was going to be in BIG trouble for this one.

"Um, yeah, uh, you see... something's come up with the diner and I have to meet somebody this evening to sort it out."

"William, are you in trouble?"

"No, no, I'm not in trouble, honey. I just have to do some business and it has to be tonight."

"And what exactly am I supposed to tell Jeff and Paula?"

William took a deep breath. "I guess just that sometimes the restaurant business can be unpredictable and things come up."

"Fine," said Cherry. That tone was a death sentence.

"I'll make it up to you and to them, too."

"You bet you will!" Cherry replied.

"Love you, honey," said William.

Cherry hung up without replying.

William looked down at his shaking hands. He went into the bathroom and took a long drink of water. He lingered in the mirror, looking himself in the eye.

"I don't have to feel this way," he told his reflection. "I am the boss. I am in charge of my own life."

William pulled into a public parking lot across from Marylou's at exactly five minutes to seven. He found a spot where he could see the diner's front doors and waited. At five after seven he saw Buddy go in. Feeling spiteful, he waited another ten minutes before he crossed the street and went in himself. Pretending he didn't see Buddy, he sat down at a booth near the door. The same blond waitress approached him with a big fake smile on her face.

"Hi there, hon. how are you tonight?" She asked William.

"Pretty good, thanks. Can I get a coke with a straw, please?"

"Sure thing."

William and Buddy sat at opposite ends of the diner, each pretending the other didn't exist. It wasn't until William picked up his menu that Buddy finally came over.

"'Bout time," William said, not looking up. Buddy sat down across from him.

"Hey, I'm not the enemy here," said Buddy. "It's not my fault if you let your girlfriend make unreasonable demands."

"Expecting me to show up for a dinner I already agreed to isn't all that unreasonable."

"Maybe not, but expecting you to always do exactly what she wants when she wants it is. You gotta learn to tell her no once in awhile. Do you even like these friends of hers?"

"I guess."

"That means no."

"Ok, Buddy I do admit I hate how Paula parades this turd of a husband of hers around. I mean, the whole time they come over all she does is talk about is how wonderful he is. He makes Google money. He was gonna quit once and Google begged him stay at any cost 'cause they would crash and burn without him."

"Wow, sounds like making a starving peasant watch the king eat a steak."

"I mean, hours of it is beyond annoying. She thinks this guy could like pick up dog shit and it would turn into a diamond 'cause *he* touched it. On their Facebook, Paula, like, every couple hours has to post what great wonderful things Jeff did today."

"Well," Buddy replied. "Bet you wish you had a woman who thought you were the greatest thing in the world."

"Oh, I gave up on the fantasy a long time ago."

"William, this is what I mean, you know why this Jeff fella has a wife like that?"

"Good luck in life? Good Karma? Maybe he didn't shoot the president from the grassy knoll in the past life."

"That was you?" Buddy replied sarcastically with a raised eyebrow.

"Well, I did get sent home from school in the 6th grade for saying that to the class and teacher."

"Really?" Buddy replied with a laugh. "And what did everyone at home think?"

"They were really pissed."

"Why?"

"They really liked JFK."

"Oh my God!" Buddy said followed by extended laughter. "Well, see you were a *Leader* even in the past life."

"How do you figure?"

"You got away, Lee Oswald got arrested. Leaders are the last to be killed or arrested."

"Yeah, Cherry is gonna kill me tonight."

"Here we are, a perfect example. You think if Jeff had to stay late at Google Paula would guilt him and shame him?"

"Probably not."

"Yes, because he is what's called a *man in his power* and she knows it. I bet he does very little for her and she worships him anyway. But you'll do anything to make Cherry happy. You and I were always taught that being a *Yesman* in a romantic relationship is good. But I'm here to tell you women will always dump *The Yesman* eventually for a *man in his power*."

"Sure, dude," William replied.

"I mean it. Today you're mad at me, but I probably helped your relationship. Cherry has more respect for you right now."

William daydreamed for a moment talking to Cherry.

"William, I can't believe you stood up to me like that!" Cherry said.

"Yeah! Well!" William said in a tough tone. Then his tone went soft as he said "Do you like it ma'am?"

"I hate it!" Cherry replied.

"Sorry, ma'am," William replied.

William awoke from his quick daydream and sipped his coke. He decided to live a little dangerously. Since he was missing out on Cherry's pork loin, he figured he might as well treat himself. He looked through the menu, searching for something good and greasy to go with his soda.

"More coke, hon?" the waitress asked.

"Yes, please," William answered.

"Any water?"

William shook his head.

"Can I get a fresh iced tea?" asked Buddy.

The waitress gave him that hateful look again before forcing herself to smile and say "You got it, sugar."

She brought their drinks and waited patiently at the table while they read the menus.

"Have you gentlemen made your selections?" Her sweet tone had started to take on a tart edge.

"Give us another minute," said Buddy. The waitress went back to the counter. "See what I mean? She's way friendlier tonight. Like you did to Cherry, we stood up to her yesterday. Now she knows if she wants a tip, she needs to show us respect."

"Yeah, I noticed that," said William. "That reminds me, Martha Stout wants to talk to me about a citywide ban on tipping."

"Oh man, no bueno."

"Yeah, I'm going to tell her why it's bad idea."

"No, man, send her a letter. Don't meet with her. She'll suck you into all kinds of crazy schemes." Buddy protested

"Wouldn't that be rude?"

"Rude is an opinion. What do leaders think of other people's opinions?"

"Shouldn't I do it, though? Always good to have a friend at City Hall, right?"

"Only if it's the right friend."

"I still feel like I should talk to her at least."

"That's your *Yesman* talking. A nice lady who seems important wants a favor from you, and you are conditioned to say *yes*. But a *Leader* has to look at it more critically. What has this lady ever done for you? What could she do for you in the future? She's never helped you a bit, and now she wants to screw up your business. Odds are she won't even be in office next year, so why is she worth your time?"

"Well, when you put it like that," said William, "I guess it does seem like a waste."

"Sad, but true, my friend. Sad, but true."

The waitress made another pass to refresh their drinks. This time William ordered a plate of chili cheese fries. Buddy did the same.

William knew Buddy was right, but he still felt uneasy. "What if she gets mad?" William asked.

"Let her. Martha Stout is not your boss."

"No, but she's in city council."

"Hark, what is that I hear?" Buddy asked. "Could it be the opening notes of the *Prisoner's Chorus*? This is the core of bullshit here! What if Cherry gets mad? What if Martha Stout gets mad? What if the waitress gets mad? What if Riley or Mitch get mad? Let 'em be mad. The second you stop seeking their approval of you, they will start to seek yours."

William bit his lip. Buddy studied him carefully. He put a hand up to his ear.

"What is the *Prisoner's Chorus*, anyway?" asked William. "You said you'd tell me later."

"Imagine a classical music concert. Picture the cello player and the trumpet player and that guy with the big drum in the back. Now imagine the conductor. A skilled conductor, say someone like Andre Rieu, has complete control over the musicians who play for him. He makes sure the right instruments are playing at the right time. It sounds beautiful as long as Andre keeps control.

"That's what a *Leader's* brain is like. He stays in control and keeps everything in harmony. But if the conductor can't stay in control, you have a real mess. The cello guy is playing too loud and the trumpets are trying to play even louder to compensate. Everyone's playing the wrong notes at the wrong time and it all sounds like shit."

"So my brain's out of tune?"

"Sort of." Buddy sipped some tea before he continued, "we all have an inner chorus that's like that orchestra. The different members do different things but they all work together to shape how you react to things and how you make decisions."

"And if they work together we do better than if they fight each other?" William asked.

"You'd think so, but it depends on the song they are singing. The choir members aren't your friends. They'll hurt you just as easily as help you."

"I was always taught that they key to being at peace was to be in touch with your emotions," said William. Then again, he remembered, he'd been told that by the same therapist who had given him the "brainwash pills."

"Yes; and no," said Buddy. "You have to be aware of your emotions, but you can't let them take you over. Let them sing, but keep it under your control."

"Who's in this choir, anyway? What do the members do?"

"The choir has five main members: *The Child*, *The Yesman*, *The Victim*, *The General* and *The Boogeyman*. Each feeds off a different emotion and pushes you towards certain toxic behaviors. It is only once you recognize them and start to understand how they impact your thinking that you fully transition from *Yesman* to *Leader*."

"You mean like that inner child all the self-help books talk about?" William wondered.

"Yeah, only you don't coddle the little brat. That's where people go wrong. They over indulge their inner child and it keeps them immature. They don't learn how to wait for what they want or pass up a smaller reward for a bigger one later. *The Child* is all about impulse. He wants what he wants and he wants it *now*. Sometimes you have to rein him in to keep on track. He wants affection, so he's easily controlled by praise and shiny prizes. He wants all the love is afraid to challenge anything that might take it away from him.

"When you see some idiot trying to bend over backwards to change who he is to please some chick, that's *The Child* running the show. He'll do anything anyone wants as long as they tell him they love him. Men who won't leave disrespectful and downright abusive relationships are the same way. They know it's wrong, but they let her do it because the women say they love them. That's *The Child* who makes them stay, because he's afraid he won't get love anywhere else."

"Some of them might not actually have a choice, though." William said as he realized it was himself he was talking about.

"There's always a choice. Some people are just too afraid to leave what's comfortable to make it."

William shook his head. How could Buddy think like that?

"Of course T*he Child's* not the only one to blame," said Buddy. "*The Victim* helps keep people trapped in toxic relationships too."

"Why is it the victims' fault? Isn't it the abusers' fault for treating them that way?"

"Being mistreated doesn't make someone a victim. It makes them a survivor," said Buddy.

"What's the difference?"

"You can't choose to be a survivor, but you can choose to think like a victim. Victims constantly seek to be re-victimized because they think they deserve it. They crave misery because that is what they are comfortable with. They seek out drama for attention and sympathy. Nothing ever improves for them because they don't want it to."

"So they create pain just so someone feels bad for them?"

"Look at all the poor shmucks out there complaining about how life keeps screwing them over. It's the same thing. 'Waa, waa, poor meeeee.' What they never realize is that by constantly advertising their willingness to tolerate abuse they invite more of it. They make themselves easy targets. It's like screaming to the world, 'hey everyone, you can treat me like shit and I'll put up with it'."

"Do you think that's why people keep coming after me?"

"People come after you because everyone always wants to shoot out the brightest burning light. But yeah, by focusing on being down you probably invited some of the ass kicking you got."

"Gee, thanks."

Buddy shrugged. "I told you I don't sugar coat things. A real *Leader* does not indulge *The Victim*. He has no need to create drama or seek attention. Instead of crying about it, he doesn't put himself in positions where he can be taken advantage of again. If he's mistreated he gets up and walks away, no looking back. He shows those he's dealing with that he's not afraid to lose them. Because no matter how valuable something may be it isn't worth more than his self-respect."

"So if someone screws you over, you don't fight back?" William asked.

"You do fight back if necessary, but only if absolutely necessary. And when you do, you do it with a cold calculating ruthlessness that gives them nightmares for the rest of their lives."

"Sounds a little extreme."

"We live in a world of extremes. Moderation is for monks."

"How do you know when fighting back is necessary? How do you know when it's better to just let something go?"

"You have to have your own set of laws. Know what you're willing to tolerate and what you're not. Set your boundaries and enforce them. *Demand* respect, don't *beg* for it. Know when to walk away."

William heard Kenny Rogers in his head '*you got to know when to hold 'em, know when to fold 'em, know when to walk away and know when to run...*'

"Are you humming?" asked Buddy.

"Yeah, I do that," said William. "Riley says it's how he knows my hard drive is writing new information."

"That Riley of yours is an odd character," said Buddy.

"I'd be lost without him," said William.

"Yeah, just don't tell him that. You need to humble that guy a little."

"I'm working on it."

"Good," said Buddy. "Anyway, why you fight back isn't nearly as important as *how* you fight back. That's where *The General* comes into it."

"He fights my wars?"

"All too well. *The General* is always itching for a fight. He's addicted to anger and is always looking for a reason to unload on somebody. All those road raging assholes out there, they all have *The General* behind the wheel. He takes everything as a personal insult and lashes out without bothering to think about the cost or the consequences. You can't give him free rein or he'll wreak havoc on your whole life. Fight when you gotta, but never take the fight personally. Use *The General* for strategy but remember to put him back in his box when you're done."

"What if you're afraid to fight?" William wondered.

"Ah, fear," Buddy wiped his mouth. "Fear is the domain of *The Boogeyman.*"

"That one's kind of obvious," said William. "What else would he be?"

"He is the most obvious, and that's what makes him the trickiest. He's always in the shadows, whispering in our ears, casting doubts, undermining our confidence. He wants you to be afraid because when you're afraid he stays in control. He's the most persistent and the hardest to pin down because there's such a fine line between exercising reasonable caution and letting fear hold you back when it doesn't have to.

"He's also the hardest to conquer because he's so prevalent. We're afraid of failing, afraid of rejection, afraid of injury, afraid of loss. We don't do the things our souls beg for because we're afraid of what other people would think. We shouldn't even care, but *The*

64

Boogeyman makes us care. Fortunately, he can be defeated. A *Leader* handles fear by analyzing a situation objectively and carefully weighing the risks and benefits. And poof, *The Boogeyman* goes up in smoke."

"That's quite a cast of characters," said William. To him, the choir sounded like a bunch of arguing relatives trapped in a room together. No wonder it drove him crazy.

"They are all bastards," said Buddy, "And they all work to keep you trapped. Together they make up the four walls of your very own mental prison. As long as they keep you distracted you'll never realize you have the power to set yourself free."

"This is all a lot to take in," said William. "I'm not sure what to do with all this information."

"Just start paying more attention to how you react to things and why. Make sure you are driving the bus, not riding it. Let them have their say, but keep them in their place."

"And what about this *Yesman*?" William said.

"Yeah, saved the worst for last. Your *Yesman* is the worst member of the choir. He's the roof on your prison. The other members push him to push you to do what he wants. He's addicted to approval. He wants everyone to like him so he never makes waves, never disagrees, never says no to anything. He wants to make everyone else happy all the time, even at the cost of himself.

"*The Yesman* really screws things up because he can't be honest with himself or others. Say his best friend has a new girl and he can tell she's going to be trouble. A good friend would warn his buddy, right? I mean if Riley brought home some skank who was going to ruin him you'd speak up, right?

"But a *Yesman* won't. He'll just smile and say she's nice and hope for the best, because he doesn't want his friend to get mad at him, even though he knows his friend's going to get hurt. Don't be that guy, William. A *Yesman* doesn't do anybody any favors."

William nodded. He's always had a hard time say no to people. Maybe it was time he learned.

"I think you've had enough for tonight. Let's get out of here."

Buddy signaled the waitress to bring the check. William picked it up without even thinking about it.

"Tonight you leave a few dollars; she was somewhat pleasant to us," said Buddy. "Now that she knows she's headed the right direction she'll do even better tomorrow night."

"Got it," said William.

Once again, William made it back to the diner after closing only to find the lights still on. This time both Riley and Mitch were still at the bar.

"Hey guys, what's up?" He asked.

"Mitch has a problem," said Riley.

Mitch looked down at the bar. He fidgeted with his beer can, carefully not meeting William's eyes."

"Oh boy, what's wrong?"

"Starla came back," Mitch mumbled. "She said she was sorry for stealing my car. She just got spooked because of how much she liked me."

"And you believed her?" William couldn't believe it.

"She was crying, man, and kissing me and hugging my neck. I thought she was telling the truth."

"Then what happened," William asked in demeaning tone.

"Well, you know, we watched a movie and things got a little hot. We were making out and stuff and well, she said she wanted to get a little kinky and well, next thing you know..." Mitch trailed off.

"She tied him up and stole his wallet," Riley said.

"Dammit Mitch! What were you thinking?"

"I was thinking she looked really hot straddling me like that."

"Anyway," said Riley. "Mitch has his car payment and his electric bill due before he's going to get paid again. He can get an extension on the utilities, but he's already a payment behind on the car because of what happened last time. So if he doesn't make this one they'll repossess."

"Wow, that's rough," said William.

"I was, you know, kind of hoping you might help me out a little," said Mitch. "I'd pay you back when I got my next check."

William almost said yes automatically before he stopped himself. This was what Buddy meant about being a *Yesman*. Would it really help Mitch to bail him out? Or would he just repeat the same mistake again and again because he was counting on William to fix his problems for him each time?

Now he finally got to see all his members of the Choir come to play. *The Child* wanted to feel bad for him and say things to make him feel better. *The General* wanted to scream and pound on the bar what a stupid son of a bitch he was. He didn't want to think that, but looking at Mitch he knew the answer.

"I don't think I can do that, Mitch," said William.

"But, why not? Come on, man. I need help."

"I think I help you most by saying no. You can't keep doing this, Mitch. You're never going to learn if I bail you out every time you do something stupid."

"What about all the times I bailed you out, huh? Who stole a body so you could escape from the cops? Doesn't that count for something? I helped you, now I need you to help me."

"I am helping you, by making you learn not to repeat your mistakes."

"That's really cold, William. I thought we were friends."

"I wouldn't be your friend if I just rubber stamped whatever stupid thing you did next. I'm being your friend by saying it's not ok and you can't keep doing this."

"Great. Thanks. That helps me a *whole* lot."

"I'm not letting you drink for free anymore, either. From now on you pay for your food and drinks like every other customer."

"Oh come on, William."

"Giving you free booze isn't helping your situation. It's making it worse and ruining your health. A real friend shouldn't let you do that to yourself."

"Yeah, how's your health?"

"I'm not the issue here. I pay for the booze in this bar, you don't. And I have to cut you off before you wreck us both."

"Glad you're looking out for me, old pal." Mitch slid off his bar stool. He could barely keep on his feet. How much had Riley let him drink? Mitch stumbled out the door, slamming it shut behind him. Riley went to lock up while William cleaned up after Mitch.

"Wow," said Riley. "Never thought I'd see that."

"Was I wrong?" asked William. He felt his General snap to

attention, but held his temper back. He didn't need a fight with Riley right now.

"No," said Riley. "It had to be done. He has been in here way too much. Poor guy. That's probably why he can't meet anybody. He's always either here, The Love House, or at work. He needs a hobby or something."

"Maybe we should get him some real help," said William.

"You mean like a therapist? I don't think he'd go."

"Well, maybe not exactly a therapist. Maybe, you know, like one of those life coaches or something."

"A life coach? You're kidding, right?"

"No. Why? What's wrong with life coaches?" William wondered as *The General* inside him was ready to open fire.

Riley shrugged. "I don't know. They just always seemed a little weasely to me. I mean if they have all the answers why aren't they off on some tropical island or something instead of selling their *top secret system* for $99.95 a pop?"

"Maybe they just aren't that selfish."

"Please. I've seen these bozo's on YouTube. The only reason they're so successful is because they can sell magic sand to people. And, when the magic sand doesn't work, they can sell them magic water too. 'Cause magic sand just doesn't work without magic water."

"Ya know, I've seen it too. Yes, they sell some hot air. But really there are just people who know how to get their way and those who don't."

"They're con artists, William!"

"I don't know, Riley. I think you're getting cynical in your old age."

"If so, I got it from you." Riley said. "But I think I'm just prudent. There's no secret key to wealth and success. There's no get rich fast selling houses or 900 lines or something. You gotta work for it just like everyone else. I don't need a coach to tell me that."

"But don't you think there has to be some answer to why some people get all the breaks? What if they know something the rest of us don't?"

"If they did, do you think they'd really tell anyone else? If you knew the winning PowerBall numbers would you tell the rest of the world?"

"Probably not." William answered. He was a little sorry Riley saw it that way, but then Riley was also a *Yesman*. Even though Riley went to a fancy college, he worked for William. Maybe he wasn't the best person to take advice from. He had felt bad about keeping secrets from Riley, but now he was glad he hadn't told him about meeting with Buddy. He knew Riley just wouldn't understand.

Chapter 5

Man in His Power

"What do you mean we're out of vodka?" William asked Riley. "How are we out of vodka?"

It was too early for this crap. He'd only snuck into the diner office long enough to try and watch a video Buddy had recommended, but he hadn't even sat down before Riley broke the news.

"Well," Riley replied. "I left Gerry in charge out front last night because I had to be in the kitchen, and he let a few folks have drinks at Happy Hour prices even though technically it was past time."

"How far past time?"

"Um, all night."

"All night? For everybody at the bar?"

"Every customer in the diner."

"Jesus," William went to the office shelf for his personal bottle of whiskey. It wasn't there. "What the crap?"

"It's in the desk," said Riley. "I didn't want it sitting out while I interviewed people."

"You put my whiskey on Skid Row?"

"It's fine!"

"Find anybody good?" William asked as he poured his drink. If this was how things were going to go he was going to have to rethink this whole stepping away business.

"A couple people. Two new waitresses start today and the new line cook started last night."

"If we hired somebody why were you in the kitchen all night?"

"Just making sure he stayed on track. He's not very experienced, but I think he'll be good with some training."

"We can't have you babysitting one employee all night. Get him up to speed or get rid of him."

"You got it."

"Anything else I don't want to know?" William said as he gulped a shot.

"We have a letter from FirstUnion. Some lady is disputing our charge on her card."

"I'll handle that one." William enjoyed the thought of taking his foul mood out on some bitchy customer. Cold, calculating... Yeah, he'd fire up the nightmare generator.

"What do you want to do about the vodka?" Riley asked.

"Fill the old bottles with magic water and sell it anyway."

"What?" Riley said really hoping this was a joke.

"Go over to Goldwater's Liquor and see if you can buy a case. Pay cash and try not to let anyone see you."

"Don't you think that's a little risky? You know we can't use liquor store booze for a restaurant."

"It's a gamble, but I think the benefits outweigh the risks. Odds are we won't get caught, but we'll be totally screwed if we lose two days of sales before our next order gets here."

"Ok. You're the boss."

Riley left to get the vodka. While he was gone, William looked over the letter from FirstUnion. Apparently, one Abigail Newton had been "deeply disappointed" when the feta cheese on her Caesar salad didn't seem fresh, and since the manager had refused to refund the full cost of her meal she was left with "no choice" but to turn to her card company for redress. She hoped for a satisfactory conclusion so she didn't have to "resort to" leaving bad reviews on social media to "warn others."

"Good grief," said William. Moe's didn't even put feta cheese in their Caesar salads. In fact they didn't use feta cheese for anything in the whole restaurant.

William remembered the woman, though. In fact he'd waited on her. He could tell she was the type that had to complain just to inflate herself and get something free. She had been rude and snotty, talking on her phone all through him trying to take her order and actually getting mad when he interrupted to ask her the questions necessary to get it right. She hadn't hung up until her food came. She'd eaten every morsel of her salad, main dish and both side dishes without mentioning any problems. Then, when he'd brought her the check, she'd scolded him like a dog, wagging her finger at him while she listed a dozen petty complaints that had made her meal "nearly inedible" and asked for the manager. William had ducked into the old phone booth by the bar, taken off his waiter's apron and put on the sport coat he kept in there just for such occasions. The look on her face when he walked back to her table and introduced himself as the owner had been priceless.

The card company had included a form to respond to the complaint. Rather than fight with the scanner he could never seem to figure out, William stuck it in the old manual typewriter he'd bought in a thrift store on a lark and began clacking away.

"Moe's Dinner takes great pride in providing the freshest, highest quality food and service possible. We take customer complaints very seriously. However, no dish in Moe's restaurant contains feta cheese. Therefore, we can only conclude that either Ms. Newton does not know what feta cheese is or does not know which restaurant she actually ate in. Security footage confirms that she was in our establishment on that date and did in fact consume her entire meal. Therefore, we cannot refund its full cost. However, seeing as she did not like the PARMESAN, we will issue her a 48 cent refund for the cost of the cheese in her salad. Unfortunately, we are unable to process such a small transaction through the card system, but Ms. Newton is free to pick her refund up at the bar any time she finds it convenient."

William printed off a copy of the menu page describing the salads and stills from the security camera that showed her shoveling food in her face as well as the empty plates she'd left behind. He stuck them into the envelope provided for his reply along with the response form and sealed it.

At first, William felt pleased with himself for handling the situation so maturely. Even if he had deliberately chosen the most unflattering frames to include with his response, he didn't feel completely satisfied. If he had to fight, he wanted a total and complete victory, not just vindication. Temptation nagged at him, he knew he shouldn't give in, but what the hell, he was bored.

What would *The General* do?

A quick internet search gave him both her home and work address. Armed with this new information he went to worldcheeses.com and ordered her three pounds of feta crumbles and a five pound wedge of parmesan. On a whim he also went to an art printing site and ordered her a poster of an old cigarette ad that said "for those who know the difference." He set it all up to be delivered to both addresses.

Ok. Now he was happy.

A short time later Riley came back with the vodka. They hurried to refill the bottles behind the bar before they opened. William had been thinking while they worked and by the time they were done he had decided something. It was harsh, but a *Leader* did what he had to, right? He motioned for Riley to follow him into the office. Riley shut the door behind them.

"Fire Gerry when he comes in," said William.

"We can't fire Gerry!" Riley pleaded with his hands. "He's been with us since we opened. He worked for free his first two months until we got enough cash flow to pay him."

"Well, good for him," said William. "It was great of him to do that, but we don't need to run the diner of charity anymore. Times have changed and we have to change with them. So tell me, Riley, what has Gerry done for us lately? I mean other than give away half the bar and potentially jeopardize our liquor license?"

Riley sighed. "I'm not saying that what he did was ok. I'll talk to him and make sure he doesn't do it again, but we shouldn't get rid of a good employee over a mistake."

"A mistake is putting vermouth in a martini twice. This is practically theft."

"Ok, well, how about this? Maria's off, Paul's on vacation, I'm on the host station, and apparently you're 'otherwise engaged' for the evening, so if I fire Gerry who the hell is going to tend bar tonight?"

"I don't know, Riley. Guess you should've though of that before letting Gerry give away everything I own."

"Don't you remember your roots, William?"

"Yes, Riley, I do. I remember that my first car cost about $500, which is about how much booze he wasted last night. You're the manager; you figure it out. That's what I pay you for."

"Really?" asked Riley. "I thought you paid me to clean up your messes and bail you out of jail occasionally."

William's eyes narrowed. He was pretty sure Buddy wouldn't think too highly of William letting a subordinate speak to him that way, but the remark was so spot on he couldn't keep a wide grin from spreading across his face.

"Nah, man, that's just your side work. Catch you later."

"You really want to fire him?"

"Well, that's what you say at first. After he breaks down and cries about mortgages and car payment, you make him an offer. He pays back the vodka bill out of his tips tonight or he's gone."

"Ok, have fun doing whatever it is you do."

William headed out the office door. William wondered if Riley could hear him whistling as he walked down the hall.

At Marylou's, Buddy hooted with laughter at the story of Abby Newton and her new cheese subscription.

"Oh man, you are brutal!" Buddy pounded his fist on the table. "I love it, I love it!"

William glowed at the praise. He had been afraid Buddy would think what he had done had been stupid or immature.

He leaned back in the restaurant booth and stretched. Over the last few evenings he'd really started to feel at home in Marylou's. He even missed their usual waitress a little. Not that there was anything wrong with the girl working tonight. She had short red hair styled in a pixie cut and an adequate, if not ample, chest. Every time she talked to them she called William "big boy" and looked up at him through her dark fluttery lashes.

"Yeah, I don't think she'll be demanding free meals again any time soon," said William.

"Well done, my friend. How's everything else going?"

"Made my main bartender pay out of his pocket for the booze he wasted last night. Riley didn't want to, but I stood up to him and made him do it anyway."

"Good for you." Buddy sipped his drink. "I have to say, William, I'm impressed. You've made progress faster than anyone else I've ever coached."

"Thanks." William signaled the girl for a refill on iced tea. She leaned in close as she poured it, giving William a clear view down her top.

"I think she likes you," Buddy said after she left the table.

William shook his head. "She's probably just trying to get a better tip. Waitresses are actually nice again since Martha Stout's flat wage thing didn't pass."

"You think so? There's *The Boogeyman* again. "Buddy beckoned to the waitress. "Hey, honey, come here a minute."

"Yes, sir?" More eyelashes fluttering.

"What do you think of William here? Do you like him?"

"I think he's cute," the waitress said, smiling at William.

"You see?" Buddy said to William. Then he addressed the waitress again. "Mr. Defreno here owns Moe's diner. He's a very prosperous man."

"Ooh. I never imagined someone so important would come in here. Everybody talks about Moe's. People love it there. I'd do anything to get a job there."

"Have you been there?"

"No, not yet, but I'd really like to."

"Well, maybe Mr. Defreno here will invite you for dinner some evening."

"Oh, I'd love that."

"You would, huh?" Buddy looked pointedly at William.

William swallowed. "Uh, may I have a glass of water, please?"

"You got it, big boy," said the waitress. She blew a kiss at him before sashaying off into the kitchen.

"Told you," Buddy said. "Heck, she'd probably let you bang her right here on the table."

"No thanks, I'm good," said William.

"How are things with Cherry?"

"Ok, I guess." William reached for his tea.

"You guess?"

"She hasn't talked to me since I blew off her friends for dinner."

"She's just winding you up. It's a power play. Shake it off."

"I don't know, Buddy. I think I really messed up this time. What if she doesn't forgive me?"

"Move on."

"Move on? That's it? Just move on?"

"No one is irreplaceable, William. Cherry wasn't your first girlfriend, and she won't be your last. There's always someone out there."

"Cherry's not just some girl. She thinks I'm just as amazing as she is."

"She thinks you're amazing because you'll put up with her abuse and mind games. There's a difference."

"She was there for me at my lowest. She pulled me away from the edge when I'd given up. Nobody else would have done that for me."

"William, that's your *Child* talking, with *The Boogeyman* singing back up. You think that just because nobody loved you then that no one will love you now. But you're wrong. It's great that Cherry saved you, it was a wonderful thing for her to do, but that doesn't mean she owns you forever. You're allowed to move on to something better."

"I don't know."

"That's where you're wrong, my friend. Very wrong. You're just afraid to let go and take a chance. You're doing great with the program but still get stuck."

"Stuck how?"

"You're still brainwashed that everyone's a winner and that you're no better than anyone else. Bullshit! There are winners and losers. Like the waitress. You're a million dollar business owner, she's a ham n' egg waitress. Stop pretending you two are at the same level. Act like the big man at the table. Let her know you're of importance and that a date with you is probably out of *her* league. Not the other way around."

The waitress came back with his water. She stood at the edge of the table, waiting for William to look at her.

"Thanks," he said with a weak smile. He took a big gulp and set the glass down.

"May I do anything else for you, Mr. Defreno, sir?" She licked her lips.

"Tell her to take off her top," said Buddy.

"What??!!"

"Tell her to take off her top. She'll do it, won't you, baby?"

William hesitated. "What about Cherry?"

"This is Cherry's punishment for playing mind games with you," Buddy insisted.

Fear whispered in the back of his mind. Should he listen to caution or send his *Boogeyman* back into the shadows? Looking wasn't cheating he told himself, and, odds are Cherry would never find out. The girl seemed to be a willing participant. The place was totally empty. Could he really do it?

"Would you please take off your top?"

"No," said Buddy. "Tell her, don't ask her."

William swallowed hard. "Take off your top, please."

Smiling, the girl removed her apron and began slowly pulling her top over her head. She wasn't wearing a bra underneath. Her large peach nipples stood erect.

"Oh, very nice, said Buddy. "You have a great rack. Look at those, William. High and firm, but totally natural. Bet they're nice and soft."

"They are very nice," William agreed.

"Give 'em a feel." Buddy said.

"I can't do that."

"Sure you can." Buddy reached out and placed his palm on the waitress's right breast. He squeezed it between his fingers. "See. She loves it."

William searched the girl's eyes for some kind of sign. Did she really want this? Why was she letting herself be demeaned this way? No girl would do all this just for a fat tip, would she? She must really like him. Maybe she enjoyed being used this way. Maybe Buddy was right that she saw him as someone of power and importance and was excited by him flirting with her like this.

He cautiously stretched out his hand and rested it lightly on her rib cage and gave her chest a quick touch. The girl gasped. He felt her breathing get faster.

"Come on big boy give them a squeeze," she said.

William shook his head. This was going too far.

"I have to be somewhere." He laid cash out on the table, making sure to leave an extra $10 for the girl. "Thank you for a very interesting evening."

William felt dirty. Who did he think he was, doing something like that? Just because some poor girl threw herself at him didn't mean he had the right to take advantage of her. Still, he couldn't deny the feeling of excitement and arousal he got from making her do what he wanted. Buddy had been right that he thought *she* was out of his league when in fact she thought the opposite. He wondered how far she really would have gone.

Back home, he showered twice, but the guilty feeling still wouldn't leave him. Caving in, he picked up his phone and called Cherry. She didn't answer. Even though he tried to tell himself it was for the best, he didn't really believe it.

The Choir started singing at full volume, telling him what and idiot he was and how he'd ruined everything. He tried all of Buddy's exercises, but they didn't help him silence the voices. William knew only one thing would. He reached for the nearest bottle and started drinking.

William woke up with another headache, but at least he'd earned this one. Looking down at the floor, he saw the empty bottle of vodka lying a few feet away from the bed. Recalling the events that had prompted last night's binge, he suddenly felt queasy. He stumbled into the bathroom for a glass of water.

Damn. He felt like he was shit. Wait, no he wasn't, that was just the choir talking. He repeated his affirmations, but he could not look his reflection in the eye as he said them. He tried again. By the third time through he finally felt stable. Once more after that and he felt downright cocky. It was good to be alive. Even if his head did still hurt.

The phone rang. He answered without looking. "Cherry?"

"No, Apple," said Buddy.

"Oh, hi, Buddy," William said feeling slightly embarrassed.

"What's up, man? Ordering danish?"

"No, why?"

"Because that's the only cherry your life needs, pal."

"Look, Buddy, I appreciate your help and all, but I don't want to argue with you about this. Cherry will forgive me and were gonna be fine."

"Ok, ok, I get it. Fine, I'll let you learn the hard way. We got bigger problems right now anyway."

"We do?" The queasy feeling returned.

"Yeah man, listen I need a favor." There was a brief pause before Buddy continued. "I was supposed to have a double date for dinner tonight but the other guy backed out. Can you meet me at The Aspen Grove tonight around 6:30?"

"I am not going on a date with another girl, Buddy. We just talked about this."

"You are not going on a date. You are just going to have a nice meal and keep a pretty young lady company while I talk her friend out of her panties, ok?"

"I don't know, Buddy. I really don't think this is a good idea."

"Come on, man. Have some fun for once. What's the point of all that money if you're just gonna hide in that shack and live like a hermit?"

"Cherry would for sure not like that."

"Thought she was still punishing you for standing up to her? What, do you have to sit at a desk with your hands on it, feet flat and not move till she calls?"

William remembered such a thing from a movie but didn't know which one. He had to admit that Buddy had a point.

"Fine, I'll be there."

"Fantastic. Oh and hey, check your email. I sent you a link. Friend of mine has a 1993 Rolls Royce for sale. You'll love it."

"I've got a car, Buddy."

"You mean that second hand go cart that looks like something a middle class dad would give his kid to help him 'build character'?"

William flushed. "Hey, that car and I have been through a lot together."

"Oh here we go. Holding on to the past again. William, man, you've worked hard to get where you are. You deserve to treat yourself a little and drive something that fits your new station in life."

"Flashy cars are a pain in the ass."

"So are women, but we need them anyway." Buddy laughed at his own joke. "I always say if you gotta have one, at least have one that makes life more fun. Just take a look, ok? What could it hurt?"

"What does he want for it?" William asked.

"Well, asking price is $30,000 but since you're a friend of mine he says he'll let you have it for $25,000. It's got the most beautiful banana yellow paint you ever seen."

William whistled. He could buy a new car for that.

"Picture it, William. You driving down the street in a classic Rolls Royce, chrome shined up, sunglasses on, wind in your hair, sunlight on your skin and the girls hanging all over themselves to check you out."

William thought he'd probably evaporate in direct sunlight since often he would never see the sun due to his late sleeping, but the image still appealed to him. He pictured the look on the faces of the members of the Gentlemen's Club when he pulled up for the next meeting in something like that. Yeah, he'd get their attention then.

"Ok, I'll check it out."

"Great. The girls are gonna love it. See ya at 6:30."

William pulled into the parking lot outside The Aspen Grove at 6:48 on the nose... in his old Impala. Buddy came down the steps to meet him. He looked at the Impala and shook his head.

"Aw, man! What happened to the Rolls?"

"No time, my friend," William replied. He tugged at the cuffs of his brand new navy blue dinner jacket. He had at least looked up the Rolls on the diner's computer, and he'd liked the look of it, but he still couldn't quite make up his mind. While debating he had searched for The Aspen Grove's address and discovered that the restaurant had a dress code. By then there had been no time to get his suit cleaned or wash a shirt so he had gone shopping instead.

A patient older saleslady had spent an hour with him at the store and had even taught him how to tie his brand new green and blue paisley tie. He didn't feel like confessing to Buddy that not having Cherry's help had caused him to run behind.

Buddy gave him a skeptical look. "Ok, pal. That's too bad, though. I'd been really talking you and your new car up to the girls. You're kinda making me look bad, here. I promised Beth Prince Charming, not Gomer Pyle."

William rolled his eyes. "I won't eat with my fingers, ok? I don't see why the car even matters. I'm not the one trying to get the girl here."

"A man is judged by the company he keeps. You just brought my stock down about 10 points showing up in that bozo-mobile. But I'll forgive you this time." Buddy jerked his head towards a pair of pretty young women standing near the restaurant's front door. "The blond with the big tits is Paula, she's mine. The cute little brunette is Beth. She's yours."

William looked the girl over. She had long black hair and wide green eyes, a short, thin, body and breasts that were a bit smaller than average. She looked beautiful in her tight fitting gold cocktail dress, even if she did seem a little scrawny. William was pretty sure the jewelry sparkling on her neck and ears were made from real diamonds.

"She's a virtual assistant," Buddy said. "She has an MBA from Vanderbilt, drives a BMW Z and volunteers at the hospice. She's from an old money family. Her mother is the president of the Historical Society. Her dad is president of Mountain State Banks."

"Oh boy," said William, remembering what he'd said to some pushy lady who'd wanted him to buy tickets to one of the Historical Society's stuffy fundraisers.

"Yeah, she's a real find. The perfect wife for a millionaire with future political ambitions."

"Well, I hope she finds one," said William. "Let's get inside. If I get spotted out here by Cherry, the only new car I'm going to need is a hearse."

"After you." Buddy bowed and stepped aside to let William pass. William could feel the girls evaluating him as they watched him climb the granite steps up to the building. Maybe buying a new suit was a good move after all. Paula's expression showed definite approval of his appearance. Beth looked excited and nervous.

"Ladies," Buddy said, "allow me to introduce the one and only William Defreno. Remember this moment. Someday you'll be telling your grandkids about the day you met this amazing man."

"Uh, hi," said William. "Nice to meet you."

Buddy held one of the double glass paned doors open. The ladies went in. William followed.

The Maitre D' approached them in the entryway. He looked at Buddy's lack of a tie and frowned.

"I'm sorry, sir, but we do require a tie," he said.

"No can do, my man. I have a phobia due to being hung in a past life," Buddy said. William laughed and wondered how far this was going to go.

The Maitre D' looked confused. "We do have a tie you may borrow."

"I just told you, it ain't happenin'. I don't wear ties."

"I'm afraid you cannot be seated without a tie, sir."

"Then I'm afraid I'll have to go outside and make a phone call. Now I don't want to have to get you in trouble, but if you're going to insist on practicing this kind of discrimination, I'm required to report it."

"One moment, sir."

The man left to confer with someone. A moment later another man came over, greeted them and led them to a table near a back corner. Buddy rejected it. And the one across from it; and the one near the window. He rejected five tables all together before finally accepting the last open four top in the place.

"Wow, Buddy, were you really hung in a past life?" Paula asked as they settled into their chairs.

"I've been hung in every life, my dear, if you know what I mean." He winked at her. "Play your cards right and I'll show you."

Paula giggled.

The waitress brought them four glasses of water. Buddy sent his back. "Make sure the glass is *clean* this time," he called after her.

William was starting to get uncomfortable with the looks they were getting from diners at other tables. He didn't like this much attention focused on him.

"So what do you do, Mr. Defreno?" Beth asked.

"Mr. Defreno here is our town's newest millionaire," Buddy answered for him. "He owns Moe's diner and is looking to purchase a few other key properties."

"Ooh, real estate is a very respectable investment," said Beth.

"Well, mostly I just run the diner," said William. "I make a really good Long Island Iced Tea."

Buddy laughed awkwardly. "This guy is such a kidder. When he's not busy with his big meetings or managing his portfolio he likes to prank people by pretending he's just a bartender."

"Do you make the Long Beach version?" Beth asked. "Those are my favorite."

"Come by sometime, he'll whip you up one, won't you?" Buddy said.

"Sure," said William. He hoped Beth never took them up on the invitation. Cherry would kill him.

The waitress brought Buddy another glass of water. He sent it back again. "Too much ice."

The waitress left again. She brought back a third cup of water The look on her face promised Buddy's imminent death if he complained again. "Wow, never thought I'd have so much trouble just getting a glass of water at a nice place like this. You know what, hon, just skip it."

Buddy pulled the wine list out of her hands and passed it to William. "Since you're the restaurant owner, I'll leave the choice up to you."

William squirmed as he read the list, aware that the whole table was watching him. Most of the wines were good, but nothing really stood up as being all that spectacular.

"Mr. Defreno here has very discerning tastes," Buddy told the women. "He's got a very sensitive palate. He's even won awards for his tasting abilities."

"Oh my, how special." Paula said. "What do you recommend, Mr. Defreno?"

"Don't rush him," said Buddy. "A place like this probably doesn't carry the caliber of wines he's used to."

William tried not to laugh to himself that Buddy may be right about them not having the wine he was used to. He didn't see Arbor Mist anywhere on the menu.

The waitress let out an impatient huff. "I can send for the sommelier if you have any questions."

"Lady," Buddy said. "This guy could answer questions your sommelier couldn't even think of."

Gee, no pressure here, William thought. He ordered a crisp Australian white to go with their first course and a hearty German red for later.

"Oh my," said Beth. She sipped her wine and fluttered her eyelashes at William. "You do have good taste."

"William has the best taste," said Buddy. "Just wait till you see that Rolls Royce. It costs more than most of the houses in this town but he doesn't care. He only wants the very best."

"I'd love to ride in a car like that," said Beth.

"Me too," Buddy said. "It's too bad the detail shop didn't get it done in time today and left you with that rental car."

"I'd love to see it too," said Paula. "What made you choose it?"

"Trunk space." William said. "It can fit three and a half adult bodies. Most luxury cars only hold two."

Paula's eyes widened in shock.

"He's a real kidder, huh?" Buddy laughed.

"Yeah," Paula answered, but she looked uneasy.

"Actually, I just got a good deal on it," said William.

"There he goes again." Buddy guffawed as he kicked William from under the table. "Come on, William. We all know a guy like you doesn't care what something costs. He bought it because it's a good investment. Classic cars always go up in value, right, man?"

"Sure, Buddy." William smiled, but he didn't really like the idea of lying about how much the car cost. To him, it seemed better to be proud of getting a good deal on something than to brag about how much he spent on it. He reminded himself that he promised himself he would give this new mindset a chance, so he didn't contradict Buddy or argue with him.

Buddy ordered grilled chicken Caesar salads for the girls.

"Do those come with feta cheese?" William asked.

"What?" said Paula.

"No, Sir, they have parmesan," said the waitress.

"Do you use feta for anything?"

"No, sir, none of our dishes use feta cheese." The waitress was now giving him the same look she'd given Buddy. William decided to shut up.

Buddy ordered the Surf and Turf for himself. William did the same.

"What was that about?" Paula asked William.

"Just kidding around again," said William. He tapped his fingers on the table and wished he could smoke.

"Where did you go to college, Mr. Defreno?" Beth asked.

"Well, I didn't--"

"Toots," Buddy interrupted. "There are leaders and followers. Most of your leaders see no need for college. William here got his education in the real world by running a business and bring down corruption and drug dealers."

"Oh, wow," said Beth. "You must be very brave."

"Not really," said William. "I just did what I had to do."

Paula looked suddenly gleeful. "That's where I know you from. You were in the paper in 1999."

"You were?" Beth looked at William.

"Yes, he was," said Buddy. "Tell 'em about it, William."

"Oh dear, well, I got a trumped up charge at school and got expelled. The newspaper head line said 'William Defreno gets the big one' and had a picture."

"Oh my!" Beth replied.

"I know, right," Buddy said. "William, you need to blow that up real big and have it right on the wall of the diner. I mean this guy's no boring dude. He's been in trouble, he's got enough life experience for five lifetimes."

"That's great, Mr. Defreno!" Beth replied.

"You can call me William."

"Ok, William, I wasn't going to call you by your first name till you said it's ok."

"See, William, Beth here is polite and has class. She knows how to treat a man like you."

Their dinners all arrived. William did his best to remember what little table manners he had and not eat too fast or too loud. He didn't finish all of his salad and remembered how that made Cherry fume. It seemed like no matter what he did, Beth would think it was great. Although he missed Cherry and hoped she would never know about this, it was like no other experience he ever had. It felt good to be part of the *in crowd* for a change.

Buddy looked at his steak. With careful deliberation, he slid it onto his steak knife with his fork and put it on his empty roll plate. He set the plate with the steak on it on the edge of the table and went back to eating his lobster.

On her way past their table the waitress noticed the plate and stopped.

"Is anything wrong, sir?"

"Is there?" Buddy asked.

The waitress looked at the steak. Then she held the palm of her hand over it, close to the meat without actually touching it.

"I'll have them cook this longer for you, sir." She took the steak away.

Buddy gave William a pointed look. William realized Buddy was trying to teach him something. He paid closer attention.

A moment later a runner brought the steak back. Buddy cut into it, frowned and then put the plate at the edge of the table again. This time the waitress came over immediately. She looked at the steak.

"This is a bit overdone, I'll have them fire you another one." She whisked the plate away.

William was really starting to feel for her, but she stayed prim and polite as she brought out another steak.

"You're an angel," said Buddy. "Listen, can you find me a beer someplace?"

"We don't serve beer, sir,"

"Aw, are you *sure* you can't find me one?"

"Not allowed," said the waitress.

Buddy gave her a pouty look. She shrugged and left. Buddy subtly shook his head at William.

They group turned back to their meals. There were a few more halfhearted attempts at small talk but they all petered out.

One of the bus boys came up to the table. He set two cans of Coors on the table along with two frosty glasses.

"My man!" said Buddy. He slipped the guy a $10 bill.

"Wow," said Paula.

"But the waitress said they couldn't sell beer." Beth looked very confused.

"They can't, but they do have it because they use it for the shrimp batter, and they can *give* you one if persuaded properly."

"You mean because of the problem with your steak?" asked Paula.

"Because I made her *think* there was a problem with the steak." Buddy tapped his temple with his fingers. "It's all in the psychology."

"I learned about that when I studied Political Science at Boston University," said Paula. "How candidates with the worst backgrounds and behavior can still get elected if they just make people believe certain things."

"Really?" said William. "I'd think some things would automatically rule someone out."

"You'd be surprised what people are willing to overlook when someone has a charismatic personality," Paula added.

"Yeah, William, even you could end up in office," said Buddy.

"I doubt that," William said.

"You never know, man." Buddy winked at him and cracked open his beer.

As they finished their meals the girls had a few more questions for William, but Buddy kept jumping in to answer them before William could. William noticed the girls exchanging puzzled glances. Several times he caught Paula glancing his direction with a look that seemed to say she wasn't sure what to think about him. Every time he looked at Beth she beamed an overly bright smile at him. He didn't know if she actually liked him and was just nervous or if she was just trying hard to pretend.

The same waitress brought out their check. "Would anyone care for dessert?"

"Ooh, dessert," said Paula.

Buddy looked her frame up and down. "You don't need it my dear."

An awkward silence fell. Buddy grabbed the check and handed it to William.

"Let me guess, I've got this?" he said, already reaching for his wallet.

"You are the big man at the table," said Buddy.

It was then that William looked down and noticed that after all that trouble Buddy *still* hadn't eaten his steak. He tried not to let his annoyance show as he handed over his Amex card.

"Next stop: *Club Marguerite*," said Buddy. "I hear their band tonight is something out of this world."

"Actually, I have an early day tomorrow, so I better get home," said Paula. She got up from the table and grabbed her purse. "Nice meeting you, William."

Buddy watched her go with a sour look.

"I think I better go, too," said Beth. "Bye, William. Hope I see you again."

William just waved.

Buddy turned a murderous glance his direction.

"Man, I hate it when a chick doesn't know she's got a good thing going."

"Sorry it didn't work out, Buddy."

"Eh, I'm not bothered." He finished the last of his beer. "That's the thing about the program. A *Leader* sees all resources as infinite. If one girl doesn't work out, another one will."

"I don't know, I've always been a bird-in-the-hand type."

"Yeah, that's why you have so many problems with women."

William didn't think that was entirely fair, after all, *he* was the one with the girlfriend, but he didn't says so.

"There's that look again," said Buddy. "I don't think you should play cards, man, because your poker face sucks."

"What look?"

"The one that says you think you know better than I do; but you're wrong." Buddy stood up. "Come on, let's go find a good bar. We got one more lesson to go over."

Chapter 6

Steak and Lobster

They ended up back at the Ale Haus, where they had first met. After settling at a booth in the back, Buddy explained further.

"Tell me the truth, you'll beg Cherry to forgive you for ditching the dinner."

"I thought we said we weren't going to talk about Cherry anymore."

Buddy shrugged. "You brought her up."

"Just to make a point."

"You made the point. Believe me, you made it." Buddy said as he set his beer bottle aside. "Listen, the way you think about women, wait-staff, employees, is all wrong, man. You act like you're some peasant groveling before a queen. Women don't respect that. They want a *Leader*, someone who is in charge and knows it. That's why nice guys always get dumped."

"But women always say they want a good guy who listens and treats them well," William insisted.

"That's because women don't understand their own psychology. Stuff like that is what society tells them they should want. You know, Mr. Sensitive who's in touch with their emotions and cuddles kittens while strolling through art galleries holding their date's purse. What they really want is that He-Man alpha male who proves he's the fittest mate in the room. They're hardwired to be attracted to that on a primal level. They can't help it."

"Do you really think so?"

"I know so. Why else do you think that waitress let you feel her the other day? You asserted dominance. You could get her fired with a

89

phone call, but she can't do anything to you. You were the Lion; she was the lamb. And, really, all it took was for you to realize who the lion was."

"Yeah, she just, like, did it without a thought."

"Yes, it's true. Some sweet, sensitive nice guy would've got slapped for asking. Remember that lousy bum, Ralph. He made his own rules and to hell with everybody else. Chicks dig it, man."

"Ralph wasn't like that, though. He just kinda drifted. I mean his biggest accomplishment was revving his motorcycle and pissing off the neighborhood. He never seemed to care about much of anything except stealing guitars."

"Yeah a guitar thief huh?"

"*He stole a guitar to punish his mom,*" William replied quoting a Pink Floyd song.

"Yeah. Not only that, but a few cops around town know of him for more than just the *Acoustic Thief.*"

"What do you mean, Buddy?"

"Never could prove it, but let's just say he's been caught around the middle school more than once with no reason to be there."

"Wow.

"See, Ralph thinks like a *Leader* even though he was a bum. You thought like a bum even though you were a lion. Ralph worried about himself and only himself. See most guys, if they go out on a date, they spend the whole night worrying about whether or not *she's* having a good time. Does *she* like the restaurant? Does *she* like how he looks? Is he making *her* laugh enough?

"A *Leader* doesn't care about any of that. He cares about whether or not *he's* having a good time and that's it. He is who he is. She can take it or leave it. He doesn't go out of his way to impress her."

"That's kind of selfish."

"No, it's just practical. Why waste time faking it? You save yourself more grief if you keep it business like. Don't get attached. Treat a date like a job interview. You wouldn't go out of your way to chat up and impress a busboy, would you?"

"No, but dating is different."

"No, it isn't." Buddy wagged a finger at him. "A *Leader* treats love and business exactly the same way. You are looking to fill a position, that's it. Don't over complicate it."

"Well, it's not terribly complicated if I already have somebody."

"Do you? I thought things were getting a bit rocky with Cherry?"

"I thought you said she'd actually want me more after all this blew over."

"She will, but are you still going to want her?"

"Cut it out."

"Oh, come on. You can't tell me having her off your back the last few days hasn't felt good."

Mostly it just felt lonely, but William did have to admit it was kind of nice to not be constantly nagged. "It's been alright."

"Just alright, huh? Listen, tell *The Child* and *The Yesman* to shut up for a minute and hear what I'm saying. You can't spend your whole life begging for crumbs of affection, otherwise someone will always have you over a barrel. You have to live for your own happiness, not anyone else's."

"I suppose that makes sense," William admitted reluctantly.

"Wouldn't you like to know what it feels like to be on top for once? To really be in charge with a lady who knows it and respects you for it."

"I don't know," said William.

"Tell your *Boogeyman* to shut up and answer for yourself."

William took a deep breath. He pictured the awed, aroused look on Cherry's face when she saw him take charge.

"Yeah, I'd like to know how that feels," William said.

"Good, because you're taking Beth out again tomorrow night."

William gasped. "You're kidding, right?"

"No, I am not kidding. You are taking that little lady out for a good time and you are leaving *The Child* and *The Yesman* at home. William, *The Leader* is taking charge."

"There's no way, Buddy. Tonight was one thing, but I can't do that to Cherry."

"She'll never know."

"But I'll know."

"So don't let on. Look, you may not realize it now, but if you don't do this you will spend your whole life wondering if you really did the best you could or if you just settled because you were afraid to take a chance."

"This seems like a lot to risk," said William.

"What risk? Either you'll find what you've been missing and break free, or you'll realize you already have everything you want and you'll love *Mommy Cherry* more than ever. You can't lose here, pal."

William was tempted to ask Buddy if he brokered deals with the devil as a sideline but figured he'd better not. Buddy did have a point.

"Ok. Do you have her number or something? Where do I pick her up?"

"You don't pick her up. You call her and ask her to meet at a place of your choosing. Let her worry about getting herself there."

"But what if she doesn't know where it is?"

"She'll figure it out if she wants to. You can't make it too easy for them. If they want to be with you, make them earn it."

"Wow," said William. He wondered what Buddy'd say if he pointed out all the things Cherry had done to earn it. Mostly likely Buddy would just dismiss all of Cherry's kind acts as pity or more attempts at manipulation, so William kept silent again.

"I'll text you Beth's number. Call her in the morning to set it up. Keep it casual. Under dress, remember, you aren't trying to impress her."

"Ok," said William.

"And buy the damn car!"

"Why do I need the car if I'm not trying to impress her?"

"You aren't buying it to impress her. You're buying it to communicate to people that you are a man of wealth and power who commands attention and respect. You are letting the world know that you are Mr. William Defreno, millionaire, business owner, and a *Leader*; a man who gets what he wants and doesn't settle for less. A car like that says that the man who drives it is not to be trifled with. Trust me, you pull up in that Rolls Royce and you will find you get treated like a whole new man."

Once again William had his doubts, but he was curious. Driving a car like that could be fun. He supposed if he didn't like it he could probably turn around and sell it. He might even make a profit.

"Give me that number again," he said. Buddy happily complied.

William woke at the ungodly - to him - hour of 1:30 PM. As usual, when awake so early, he wondered why no one had ever gotten around to outlawing mornings. Reluctantly, he rolled over and checked his phone. He had two messages from Buddy. One was Beth's number. The other let him know the guy with the Rolls Royce was expecting him at three.

He shook himself the rest of the way awake and dialed Beth's number. She answered on the first ring and sounded very happy to hear from him.

Just after seven that evening, William arrived at a popular chain restaurant just off the Interstate in the next town over. Between the crowd and the distance, he figured he was unlikely to be spotted. And, well, Buddy had said to make Beth *work for it.*

He drove his new 1993 Rolls Royce around the parking lot, looking for a space toward the back where he could park easily. This car was bigger than the Impala had been and the new size took some getting used to. William had to admit, though, he rather enjoyed gliding along behind the wheel of such a luxurious car. He finally found a spot and pulled in. Smooth as butter. Yeah, this car was gonna be a lot of fun.

Beth sat on a bench by the restaurant's front door. She stood up and waved. He waved back. She came over to meet him at the Rolls.

"Wow, you got it back from the detail shop!" she said as William climbed out. "It looks amazing!"

"Thanks." William couldn't help grinning.

They headed inside. In the lobby they immediately ran into a crowd of people waiting to be seated. Out on the floor, someone's twenty-first birthday party filled one corner of the place. In another corner a woman wearing a hot pink bridal veil and a condom necklace chugged beer straight out of a pitcher while a bunch of women in matching pink t-shirts cheered her on. A dozen or so teenagers in matching soccer uniforms took up a bunch of tables to the right. They laughed as they shouted insults and threw paper napkins at each other. Every other table in the place was full. Overhead, three TVs displaying three different channels flickered silently while loud rock music drowned out any noise quieter than a scream.

William suddenly had the feeling he had made a very big mistake. Nonetheless, they were here. He approached the harried looking woman at the hostess station.

"Sorry, folks, it's at least an hour's wait for a table," she said without even looking up.

"Oh," said William.

"That's ok," Beth said in a chipper voice. "I don't mind waiting."

"I have a better idea," said William. He dangled his new keys in the air. "Want to go for a ride?"

"Yes, please!" Beth answered. Her face beamed.

The evening was warm, but instead of turning on the AC William rolled down the windows as they cruised along the interstate. Beth tossed her hair in the wind and laughed.

A few miles down the road they pulled into a mom and pop burger stand. William ordered two classic combos and two sundaes for dessert. They drove down to the lake outside of town and found a bench near the water to sit and eat. Beth laughed with delight as she tossed French fries to the baby ducklings that came up to check them out. William supposed most men would find her behavior cute, but he just found it immature and annoying.

"Sit down and eat," he said.

"Yes, sir," Beth promptly sat down and dutifully took a bite of her burger. She chewed daintily and swallowed before speaking again. "This is so much fun. No one ever does things like this with me. Usually it's all boring dinners and stuff charity balls, or gallery openings and weird art house movies."

"Well, I'm not big on art films, but we can watch my copy of Pulp Fiction if you'd like."

"That's like a comedy, right?"

"Kind of. You've never seen it?"

Beth shook her head. "I don't have much time for movies and stuff just on my own."

"Well, what do you like to do to relax and have fun?"

"Not much, really." Beth shrugged. "I just kind of enjoy doing whatever somebody else wants to do. I'm happy anywhere."

"Don't you have any hobbies or anything?"

"Well, I help mom with her historical reenactments sometimes, mostly because I'm the only one who can fit into the clothes. Wearing the outfits is kinda fun. I mean where else does anyone wear a corset these days?"

William swallowed hard. He didn't think she'd really want the answer to that. Looking at her more closely, he realized she'd lock really cute in a tight little bustier...

Beth was no match for Cherry in any way, but still, William wondered.

"Finish eating," he told her. "It's time to put that engine to the test."

"Yes, sir."

When they'd finished their food they went for a long drive through the winding hills up the mountain. As they rode in silence, William reminisced about a drive he'd taken with Cherry along the same road a few months before. When they'd passed the sign that said *Chain Up Area Ahead* she'd teased him about needing to pull over so she could chain him up. A while later, when they'd passed the *Chain Removal Area*, Cherry had said that was no fun at all.

William saw the same *Chain up* sign ahead.

"Hey, look, *Chain Up Area* ahead," he said. "What do you think that's used for?"

"Oh I think that's for trucks and stuff in the winter, when the roads are icy."

"Maybe. But maybe that's just what they want us to think. Maybe it's really for something else."

"Like what?"

"You know, maybe it's for couples."

"I don't understand," said Beth.

"You know," William said. "Couples. People who like to play games."

"You mean like *Fifty Shades of Grey*?" Beth's nose wrinkled in distaste. "I do believe in my psychology class there was something about intense feelings that come around when someone is scared. But sometimes it's just all a person knows and they want experience emotions that are safe to them," Beth continued

William tried not to show her the emotions he was feeling. While he spent his life in the real world on the front lines owning a business, doing jail time, dating strangers, trying dangerous things and fighting corruption, Beth learned about all that in a fancy classroom.

William turned around at the next scenic outlook. He noticed it was next to the *Chain Removal Area.* Just like Beth..... *No fun at all,* he thought.

They drove back in mostly silence. Occasionally, Beth pointed out something painfully mundane to him that she found fascinating: a bird, a particular tree, a crack in the rocks. William just nodded as she chattered on.

He dropped Beth back at her car and headed home feeling a bit deflated

Halfway home his phone rang. Buddy calling, of course.

"Hey, man, how'd it go? Isn't she great?" Buddy sounded way too enthusiastic.

"I don't know," William said. "I mean she's nice and all but we don't have much in common. We didn't really click."

"Click? You want to click, I'll buy you some castanets." Buddy laughed at his own joke. "Did you talk about her business experience? Her family connections?"

"She told me she helps her mom at the historical society. I don't think playing dress up is much help running a diner."

"You're killing me here, William. Just killing me. You wanna be stuck in that greasy spoon forever? The diner is running itself. What you do next is wide open. Don't you ever think about your future? Or were you too busy thinking about the *Chain Up Area*?"

"Little snitch!" William snapped. "Is she gonna have detailed files of our date on your desk in the morning? Make sure it has a header and footer and she shows her references in APA format."

"Nah, I got the gist of it. You know if you're really into that shit, we'll take you to The Love House on the weekends. Beth won't even mind."

"I can believe that."

"Look, in my experience, William, a wife should be a wife and a mistress should be a mistress. Don't try to have one woman be both."

"It's not just about that. I don't know, she's kind of a dork. What future is that gonna be like?"

"A good one! Look, William this right here is like the core of my teachings. Guys who let their *Child* and Y*esman* run things always piss away a chance at a good wife."

"I think Cherry could be a good wife."

Buddy groaned. "Well, luckily for you, I know best. I spent my career repairing the damage that things like single mothers and divorce and just generally weak or absent fathers cause to boys. Sometimes I have to overstep my boundaries to do what best for my clients. I'm going to text you an address. Meet me there tomorrow night around six. I've got a surprise for you."

William hesitated. He had his doubts about Buddy and his surprises.

"I don't know if I can."

"Make it happen. Trust me, you don't want to miss this."

Buddy hung up. William put his phone down and hung up. What had Buddy gotten him into now?

The address Buddy sent William turned out to be an old stone building three blocks from City Hall. Like most others, this one was long past its prime, but seemed to be making a comeback. Someone had cleaned and polished the old stone steps out front and new flowers grew in the large planters that flanked the glass entry doors. A white banner with the words "office space available" and a phone number hung from the second story.

It looked to William, though, as if the bottom floor had been recently occupied. Paper on the windows blocked most of his view in. The space seemed conspicuously free of the dust and random debris usually left behind in empty buildings. Boxes stood off to one side, waiting to be unpacked.

William wondered what Buddy had in mind. He figured most likely Buddy wanted him to buy the building. William laughed at the idea of himself as a real estate mogul. He could see himself being the new Randy Casner, sitting down somewhere and pointing a finger at some sniveling underling. "I own this town, I just let you live in it!"

Buddy pulled up at the curb behind the Rolls and got out of his car. William's heart sank when he realized he had Beth with him.

"Hi, William," she said in her usual overly perky voice.

"Hey," he said.

"My man!" said Buddy. Boy, am I glad you made it. You aren't going to want to miss this."

Buddy pulled a key out of his pocket. William and Beth followed him up the steps and into the lobby. Buddy unlocked the first glass door on the left inside and motioned William through first. Once inside, Buddy turned on the lights.

Yep. It was an office. A big office. A big, empty office, except for those few boxes William had seen earlier. A counter with what seemed to be a food prep area of some kind ran along one back wall, but other than that the room didn't have many distinctive features.

"What do you think?" Buddy asked.

"Wow," said Beth.

Somehow William was not surprised that Beth was impressed by an empty room.

"Uh, it's nice, I guess," said William. "Good location. Lots of space."

"Glad you like it," said Buddy. "I rented you out the whole first floor."

"What??" William's head swung around towards Buddy. "Why??"

"For your future," Buddy said with a large, beaming grin.

"Ok." William still didn't understand. He gave Buddy a suspicious look.

"William, my friend, I have a little confession to make."

"Oh?" William wasn't sure he liked where this was going.

"We did not meet by accident, my friend."

William's stomach started to twist. Jesus. Here it came. What did Mr. Cadillac want from him…? William hoped he wasn't about to be murdered.

"Uh, why do you say that, Buddy, old pal?" William began slowly easing back towards the door. Had he locked the car?

"Because I sought you out on purpose. I was hired by some people."

Yep, William thought. He was about to die.

"Did you ever wonder why my services were completely free?" Buddy asked. "Usually I charge close to three thousand bucks for my program, sometimes more if someone's in as bad shape as you are."

"Ok, so why didn't you charge me?"

"My services were already paid for by Mr. Nichols and your good buddy Hank."

"Hank? Love House Hank? Cherry's old boss Hank? No way. That asshole hates me."

"I ain't gonna lie, he does. But he needs you and he knows it. Hell, we all need you, William."

"What for?"

"Here, let me show you." Buddy crossed the room to an easel William hadn't noticed before. Buddy turned the large poster that was propped on it around. William found himself looking at a large picture of himself with "Vote Defreno City Council District 1" printed across it.

"You gotta be kidding me," said William.

"No, man, dead serious. You're who we want."

"I don't know anything about government or politics."

"No, but you know business and they are the same thing. We need men in their power to run this city the way it needs to be run. Which means Martha Stout has to go, and we think you're the only one who can beat her."

"Why me?"

"I guess living behind a diner in the commercial area has it perks. You're the only one out of everyone we know who lives in ultra-liberal District 1 for starters."

"Really?"

"But that's not all. You're young, you're rich; the hipsters in your district love you. Every bleeding heart liberal loves a feel good story. Troubled kid makes good. They see you as a champion, a success story, and they want to be part of it."

"I don't know, Buddy. Why didn't Hank just rent a loft in the district and run himself?"

"Yeah, right, William! I'm sure all the hipsters, feminist and metro-sexuals are really gonna vote for a grumpy old man who owns a whore house. Is that you talking or your *Boogeyman*?"

William paused and thought. He honestly didn't know the answer to Buddy's question.

"You've always wanted to be somebody," said Buddy. "Here's your chance. Are you going to take it?"

"Could I win? I mean what do I have that's better than Martha Stout?"

"Yes, people in your district are all being conducted by *The Child* choir member. I mean, Hank has two successful business and knows both tax codes and building planning. You know, the kind of person you would want on city council. But because their *Child* thinks he's a big meanie, they'll vote for some witch who knows nothing about anything and has her online Mickey Mouse degree in butt scratching just because she throws them all a pacifier. You're what we need! You're gonna throw them a bigger pacifier and a rattle too!"

Beth's hand slipped into William's. She gave him a gentle, reassuring squeeze. William noticed her small hand barely covered half of his, but her touch felt warm and genuine.

Could he really do it? He'd said he wanted to change his city for the better, clean up the town and make it a better place. William could picture a shining new future waiting at his fingertips. Big cars, more money, power, respect, the dark shadows of his past finally erased by the blinding glow of his new success. He wanted that. He *needed* that. And he'd earned it. It was time to take the reward he deserved.

"I'm in," William finally said. "Where do I start?"

"Fantastic!" said Buddy. "I knew we could count on you. Listen this will be easy. I'm going to be your campaign manager. You'll meet the rest of your staff tomorrow. We've hired you the best consultants and speech writer's money can buy. All you have to do is stick to the script we give you and pour out the sympathy."

"Really?" William didn't like the idea of winning an election on pity.

"Oh sure." Buddy paused and looked at William for a moment. "Of course, uh, you'd be the most qualified candidate anyway, and we'll make that clear as well. Your story just adds a certain romance to your campaign. You are the underdog everyone loves to cheer for. Think of the example you'll set for all the kids like you out there."

William liked that idea much better. "Alright."

"Are you ready?"

"I guess."

"Whoa, ok, one little tip. A born *Leader* never says *I guess*. Say something like *you bet* or *I was born ready*. Having confidence in yourself helps others have confidence in you."

"Got it." William cleared his throat. "I was born ready."

"You know," said Buddy. "I actually believe that. It's like this is your destiny finally coming true."

"Me, too," said Beth. She looked up at him with big moony eyes. "I can't wait to help you with your campaign, William."

"Oh. Um." William looked at Buddy for help.

"Beth is a vital part of the plan," Buddy explained.

"Ok," William said slowly. He waited for more clarification.

"Yeah. She's going to play your wife."

"Uh..." Panic set little alarm bells ringing in William's head. Wife? Beth? Did he ever need a wife? And if he did...

"William, my friend, it is an unfortunate and unpopular truth that achieving our greatest ambitions requires great sacrifice."

"Right," William said cautiously. He really didn't like where this was going. "What exactly am I sacrificing, Buddy, old pal?"

"I hate to tell you, man," Buddy put his hand on William's shoulder and looked him right in the eye. "Cherry's got to go."

"I knew it!" William spun away. He paced the room angrily. "What the hell is your problem with Cherry? You've been out to get her since the first time you ever talked to me. Why do you hate her so damn much?"

"I don't hate her. Nobody hates her. But, William, difficult women like Cherry do bring large emotional highs. They're exciting and fun but don't offer shit in the long run. They drain energy and deplete men of their life force."

"What difference will it make if I have Beth or Cherry as my so called wife?"

"Cherry won't want this for you. Let's face it, she wants to keep you down so that you're too brow-beaten to find someone better. Women do it all the time. I've had my own Cherry before."

"What you mean?"

"Remember what I wrote down for you? 'They will take your rights and turn them into privileges'. That's what Cherry women are like. Everything's a fuckin' privilege! Sex, love, respect, a good meal, a boys' night out, a companion. Heck, a new tool, a beer, a cigarette, a vacation, a new car, all become a privilege that must be earned by groveling at their feet."

"Wow, was your girl really like that?"

"I remember once I wore this cool 80's jacket at the club and the girl hated it. Yet the other girls at the club loved it. For years I didn't know why my girl hated it so much."

"Why did she hate it?"

"She hated how it looked on me. She hated that I looked good in it and other girls were noticing. She never wanted me to achieve anything or look good. She always used the whole 'just be who you are' shit on me. As long as my self-esteem was in the sewer she had me. I already know if you try to do this, Cherry will make sure it fails so that you're always her little pussycat. "

"She's a good woman. She's done a lot for me. She was there when I hit bottom. Where the hell were you then, huh? Where were your program and your promises when I was on the edge and about to end it all? She threw me the life preserver. You didn't."

Buddy looked regretful. "If I had known you were that bad off I'd have come to you sooner. But I didn't know. You were too strong to let anyone see your struggle."

"She saw it."

"She saw it because she is a predator. She sensed you as easy prey and moved in for the kill. To Cherry you're just a soft target with a lot of money and little brains. As long as you kiss her ass and pray to her shoes she'll keep throwing you tidbits, but if you push back you'll see her true nature."

"I've seen her true nature."

"No, you haven't. She dangerous. A violent criminal with a record."

"I know about her past. She told me about getting arrested and her conviction."

"Yeah, but what exactly did she tell you?" Buddy stared William down. "Are you sure it was the truth?"

"She said she got in an argument with some girl in a bar. It got physical and they charged her because of her MMA background."

Buddy sighed. "I was afraid of that."

He picked up a manila folder from the counter. "Here's the police report of her arrest. If you think she's not hiding anything from you, go ahead and look at it."

William stared at the folder in Buddy's outstretched arm. He swallowed hard. A sickening pit had begun churning in his stomach. Cherry couldn't have lied to him, could she? She trusted him more than that... Right? She wouldn't keep things from him. She believed honesty was everything.

His confidence warred with his paranoia. His *Boogeyman* whispered that, of course, she had lied. All along it had all been too good to be true. Of course she was playing him for a fool. Mainly to shut off the terrible voice in his head, he reached out, grabbed the folder and opened it. As he scanned pages written by one Officer Bundy, his feeling of sickening horror grew stronger.

"On 6/23/2009 I was dispatched to a residence located at 20791 Lafayette Dr. Upon arrival, I made contact with the home's occupant, one Ms. Heather Bonny.

Heather stated that 30 minutes prior her co-worker, one Ms. Christina Pfeffer, who goes by the name "Cherry," had arrived at the home, damaged property, assaulted Heather and threatened one Wesley Roberts, who Heather identified as her boyfriend. Wesley had been dating Cherry for years and had recently broken up with her on April 13th of 2009. I smelled alcohol on Heather's breath. She admitted to consuming "3 to 4" 12 oz cans of beer in the privacy of her own home.

According to Heather, she and Wesley had been in the home's living room watching television and drinking beer when Cherry arrived. Cherry allegedly began pounding on the door and demanding that Heather come outside to talk to her.

When Heather refused, Cherry punched through the storm door at the front of the residence, thereby shattering the glass. I did observe the frame of the door with a broken pane of the glass in the top half and several pieces of glass scattered across the porch.

Heather then said that when she still refused to come outside, Cherry began to pick up the potted plants along the driveway and smash them against the pavement. While smashing the pots, Cherry was said to have begun screaming threats and obscenities at Heather and Wesley, including calling Heather a "cunt", a "whore" and a "bitch" and screamed "find your own fucking man" as well as calling Wesley to "come out here and face me!" and "Come on, come to me, come to me"

At this point, I inspected the driveway and discovered several broken pots, dead vegetation and piles of rocks and dirt in Heather's driveway. Pictures were taken for evidence.

Heather stated that she went outside to try and stop Cherry from doing further damage. Heather claims she stayed on the porch and called out to Cherry to stop damaging the plants and to leave her property. According to Heather, Cherry responded by throwing one of the potted plants at Heather. Heather ducked, and the plant smashed against the side of the house. Heather claims it missed her by only a few inches.

After the plant missed Heather, Cherry shouted "How you like that, you fucking floozy?" Heather told Cherry again to leave and Cherry shouted "who do you think you fucking with? Huh? You fuck with me, you fucking with the best." The presence of more pottery shards, dirt and dead vegetation on the house's porch appear to corroborate Heather's version of events.

Heather claimed she went back inside and Cherry shouted "I take you all to fucking hell" Wesley then told Cherry through the window he was going to call the police. Heather claims she again came outside and asked Cherry to leave, to which Cherry replied the only thing she was going to leave was Heather's body on the blacktop. Cherry then allegedly punched Heather in the face with a closed fist, knocking her unconscious.

Heather did indeed have a large contusion underneath her eye on her left cheek and her eye was swelling shut. I then interviewed Wesley separately and he confirmed most of Heather's story. Wesley didn't actually see Cherry strike Heather. Wesley admitted that he and Heather had been drinking lots of alcohol and that maybe Heather fell down the step.

Wesley also said Cherry was a Marine who "knows how to fight" and "doesn't hit like a girl" and that he "runs from her." Wesley went on to say that he and Cherry had their differences in the past. Also, that Cherry can really hit hard and stated "believe me I know."

After concluding my interviews with Heather and Wesley, I proceeded to the residence of Christina Pfeffer (Cherry) to ask for her version of events. Due to her potentially volatile state, I requested back up and was accompanied by Officer's Gracy and Feher.

When questioned, Cherry admitted to going to Heather's home. She claimed that she knocked on the storm door, which caused it to shatter due to the glass already being cracked. She admitted asking them to come outside to talk, but denied screaming or making threats.

She also denied striking Heather. Cherry then said that she was "a certified killer" and informed me that if she had hit Heather, she would be "either in the hospital or the morgue."

Cherry claimed that Heather, being heavily intoxicated, tripped over the flower pots, breaking them as she fell and injuring her face on the pavement. However, Heather had no other injuries that would be consistent with a fall.

> Based on the evidence available, I decided to place Cherry under arrest for 3rd degree felony assault and 2nd degree felony burglary. Upon being informed that she was under arrest, Cherry began to behave erratically, sobbing and struggling. She did not settle willingly or tamely to the arrest until Officer Gracy threatened to tase her."

William felt like he had been kicked in the gut. She *had* lied. He stared blankly at the pages in front of him as the image of Cherry he held in his mind began to crumble.

"I keep telling you, man," Buddy said quietly. "She isn't the woman you think she is. She's a liar, a manipulator. She's crazy and potentially violent. Sooner or later she will turn on you and destroy you. You have to get out now, while you still can."

William shook his head. "Who she was then isn't who she is now. People change."

"Yeah, well, I suggest you ask Hank about just how much she's changed. I mean, she did tell you about the night she left The Love House, didn't she?"

"I never asked," William said flatly.

"William, listen, it's not your fault you got suckered. She took advantage of you at a vulnerable time. That's just the way women like her are. There's no shame in having fallen for it. The important thing is what you do now."

"I guess I'll go talk to her."

"Whoa, no way man. If you confront her she will snap like she did with Hank. She may even hurt you."

"She's not violent."

"Not violent? The former MMA fighter and Marine with a criminal record and a weapon collection that would make Al Capone jealous?"

William shrugged. How did he explain Cherry?

"She won't hurt me," he said, sounding slightly desperate.

"Are you sure about that? I'd hate for you to be in the place of her heavy bag. That lady can do some damage."

William thought about it. Suddenly, it didn't seem exciting and sexy anymore.

"She stabbed Hank in the crotch with a pen, man. He's got a scar."

"Jesus!" said William.

"She's unstable and unpredictable. You'll go through life walking on egg shells, never knowing when she's going to explode next."

"We can get her help."

"She's had help." Buddy placed his hand on William's shoulder again. "Listen, man, I know this is hard, but you have to understand that sometimes you can't fix people. She is dangerous and if you stay with her, some day it's going to be you in the emergency room."

"I really don't think that is going to happen." William pulled away from Buddy. "The way she is with me; it's different than she is with anyone else."

"Ok, fine, so let's say you're right. Say it's not you she hurts, but sooner or later she will hurt somebody again. She won't be able to help it. And when she does, she'll drag you down with her. Your career, your investments, the diner, you could end up losing it all if you get caught up in her next outburst. It's a simple choice, William Either you stay anchored to her misery and stay trapped or you set yourself free and finally become the man you are meant to be."

"I need time to think about it," said William. "You taught me that, right? About taking time to make decisions and not doing things impulsively?"

"I did," Buddy agreed. "I'll give you 'til morning, but we have to have an answer by afternoon. We gotta get your paperwork filed right away or you'll miss the deadline."

"It'll be ok, William," Beth said gently. "We'll be here for you." She hugged him. William merely nodded.

"Right, so I'll see you back here first thing in the morning," Buddy said. He patted William on the shoulder. "Good luck, man."

"Hey, Buddy," William said as Beth and him were leaving.

"What?"

"Is it worth it?"

"No question about it, William."

They left him alone in the silence of the empty building. William stared at his picture on the campaign poster. He wanted to cry.

William left without locking up. He drove in circles around the city for hours, watching past scenes with Cherry play out in his mind. He recalled time after time when they had gone somewhere together only to have everyone fawn over Cherry while they ignored him or treated him like a pest.

There had been the restaurant that had doubted his age when he ordered a beer. The waiter had spent the whole night flirting with Cherry while acting like William wasn't even there. And the time a hotel maid had thought Cherry was his mother. It seemed no one took him seriously, especially when he went out with her.

Looking back now, he began to wonder if Buddy was right about how her past would weigh him down in the future. He realized Buddy might be right about him being at risk if Cherry did anything else in the future. He was already branded by his own past. Would adding hers to it be too much to overcome?

Back at the diner, William sat down at the bar and poured himself a glass of whiskey. As he drank, his mind continued to churn out memories of little humiliations he had suffered with Cherry. The way other men hit on her. The way Mitch teased him. The way other women looked at him like they didn't understand what Cherry saw in him.

He thought about the slight sneer on people's faces when they walked into certain businesses. The whispers behind their backs when they crossed paths with certain people. Snippets of conversations of people wondering how much he "paid" for Cherry. They had never bothered him before. Cherry wasn't ashamed of her past and neither was he. Now, though, he realized how those opinions would affect him as he put himself in the public spotlight.

He poured another drink and began to pace. This was by far the hardest decision of his life. His personal crossroads. He could either stay with Cherry and live a life of comfort but also insignificance, or leave her behind and claim the success he deserved.

As William got more and more drunk, he began to imagine Cherry there in the room with him. He pleaded with her, trying to explain his struggle.

"God damn it, Cherry, I just wish you could understand," He said to himself. "I'm tired of always being minimal. I'm tired of still being white trash no matter how hard I work. You'll never understand, you'll never really get it. I wanna have class, I wanna be important, I wanna be something - instead of a bum, which is what I am. Even as a millionaire, I'm still a bum."

The more he drank, the more he could imagine Cherry sitting right next to him.

"Come on, Cherry, remember when we went to the Spa Toscana in Reno last year? They didn't want us there. First, they asked me 'are you even old enough to be here?' and then 'we require payment up front'. Hell, they might as well have said 'pawn shop's across the street, loser'. How many years do I have to be like this? I wanted respect. I want admiration. I wanna be a city councilman!"

After a few more drinks he picked up his phone. He began to write a text. "Cherry, I'm sorry, but--"

"Oh, wait, I'm not supposed to apologize," he said aloud. He tossed his phone across the bar and began to pace again. He tried to pour himself another drink, but spilled the bottle on the counter instead. Oh well, Riley could clean it up in the morning.

William went to the shelf behind the bar to choose something else to drink. While reaching up for another bottle of whiskey he caught sight of his reflection in the mirror.

"What are you looking at, asshole?" he asked himself. His reflection returned his hateful stare, seeming to condemn him for his shortcomings.

"Is it so wrong to want to be somebody?" he pleaded with the image of himself in the glass. "That's not selfish, is it? I mean I didn't mind being her little pussycat when I didn't have anything else really. But, I could be important. I could finally be that person I was so jealous of my whole life."

His reflection shook his head. William held is hands out. "You don't understand! I could've been a contender!" He laughed at the image of himself in a boxing ring. But wasn't that his life? Hadn't he been fighting a rigged fight since day one?

Well, everything he had been fighting for was finally within reach. He could change his whole life. All he had to do was send that text.

And lose the current best thing in his life.

His reflection gave him a soulful look. "It's not that bad," he reassured himself. "Sometimes sacrifice is necessary."

But the image in the mirror seemed to be skeptical about that.

"It'll be worth it, I promise."

He picked up his phone and began to type again.

"Cherry, listen, I have had a great time with you, but I need to break things off. I can't explain why so please don't ask me to. You would not understand. Please don't call or text or come to the diner. Thank you for everything. You will always be a treasured memory."

He stared at the screen for a long moment before hitting the send button. When he looked up, he realized his reflection was sobbing. He lowered his head onto his arms and joined it.

Chapter 7

Into the Flood Again

Just after ten the next morning, William slunk back into the office building downtown. He was unwashed, unshaven and still in the smoke coated, liquor stained clothes from the night before.

Buddy, on the other hand, looked fresh and crisp in a clean, pressed button down shirt with the sleeves rolled up and a pair of well-tailored black slacks. His black leather shoes shone. He stood in the center of the large room, conducting people with grace and confidence as they hurried to carry out their assigned tasks.

Phones rang, people laughed and chatted. Pretty women walked in high heels, trailing waves of rich smelling perfumes behind them. From a banner hanging on the wall, William's smiling face looked down on it all. William shook his head. He didn't belong here. He turned around and left.

Just before he reached the Rolls Royce, he heard Buddy's voice call his name. Reluctantly, he stopped and turned around.

"Hey man, you made it," Buddy said with a cheeriness that had to be fake.

"Yeah, I'm alive."

"How'd it go?"

"Rough."

Buddy nodded sagely. "Change is hard, my friend."

"She called like eight times and has sent me about fifty texts. I haven't read them."

"That's for the best."

As they spoke, William's phone dinged again. He pulled it out of his pocket just to see if it was Riley or someone instead of Cherry again. Before he could look, Buddy grabbed the phone and chucked it into traffic. It bounced twice, skidded along the pavement and came to a stop at the edge of a storm drain. A moment later a delivery truck came around the corner and ran it over.

"Probably still works," said William. He started across the street to retrieve his phone. Buddy thrust his arm out to stop him.

"Let it go, man."

"I need my phone, Buddy."

"You need *a* phone. You do not need *that* phone. That phone is the past and so are all the messages on it. Leave it alone; get a new one. Start over."

"It's not that easy, Buddy."

"It's only as hard as you want it to be."

William sighed. "I don't have to feel this way."

"Exactly." Buddy nodded. "Go home. Get cleaned up. Go, get a new phone and come back ready to fight for your future."

"My future," William echoed. Once again the visions of respect and glory flashed before his eyes.

"That's what you're going through all this for, right? The hard part's over. Don't blow it now."

"Sure," said William.

"Then let's do this." Buddy punched the air. "William Defreno, city councilman. Here we come!"

"Here we come," William repeated.

Ninety minutes later, a freshly shaved and showered William returned to his campaign headquarters. The tan slacks and blue dress shirt he wore were wrinkled, but at least they were clean. He carried his brand new iPhone 6 Plus in a leather wallet case clipped to his belt.

Once again, he stood in the doorway watching instead of immediately entering the building. This time Buddy had everyone gathered in the center of the room while he gave a loud energetic speech.

"Remember today, ladies and gentlemen, because this is where history begins. This is the day we put America's next great leader in office. Now I know most of you have not yet met Mr. Defreno, but once you do, you will understand. He is a powerhouse of dynamic energy that is going to carry this city, this state and our nation forward into the future.

"We may start here in these humble beginnings, but those of you who stick with our winning team will someday find themselves at the very top. Make your decisions now, because there's no going back from here."

Buddy carefully scanned the eager, excited faces of the people gathered around him. "We are Team Defreno, and we are unstoppable!" The group broke into applause. Buddy's eyes flicked towards the door. He saw William and acknowledged him with a nod.

"And here he is now. Ladies and gentlemen, I give you our next City Councilman, William Defreno." The applause continued as everyone turned to look William's direction. William flushed from the sudden attention, but he confidently stepped forward and waved.

"Hello, everyone," he said. "Thank you for being here."

"Come say a few words, Mr. Defreno."

William felt something shift deep inside himself as he crossed the room and took a position standing next to Buddy. His mind calmed as the choir went silent and he felt an inner harmony take its place. While he waited for the clapping to stop, he looked over the crowd and saw, for once in his life, awe and respect instead of contempt. His usual nervousness in front of an audience left him. As he began to speak he didn't even have to think about the words.

"Our city has been struggling for a long time. We are growing, but our roads, our fire services, our utilities and our police force can't keep up. A lot of money is flowing in, but few people are seeing the benefits of it, so where is it all going? There is a dark heart of corruption in this town. As some of you know, I began fighting it clear back when I was a teenager. It cost me my education, my love and nearly cost me my life, but I put it all on the line anyway.

"And I'd do it all again. In fact, I am doing it right here and now. I, William Defreno, am promising to clean up our city once and for all. No more corruption, no more dirty deals. No more fat cats getting rich on our money while they sit and do nothing to earn it. That's what I'm committing to. That's what I'm asking you to commit to: to helping me, and other hard working people like yourselves, make the best future possible. It may not always be easy, but it will be worth it. I hope I can count on each and every one of you to stay strong and see our campaign through."

The applause began again. William made a short bow to his audience. Buddy, in turn, bowed to him before stepping forward and waving for silence.

"Ok," said Buddy. "Mr. Defreno and I have work to do, so we will be in his office. You all have your assignments. Make it happen, people!"

Buddy escorted William down a long hallway to a large office at the back of the building. The room included a huge marble topped desk, computer, phone and over stuffed leather chairs surrounding an ornate wooden coffee table. Plush rugs covered the floors. Big windows gave them a view of the street outside. William reflected that this room was a far cry from his dark, tiny office in the diner.

"You like it?" Buddy asked.

"It'll do, I guess," William said.

"Mine's across the way," Buddy pointed to a room with glass walls across the hall. It looked to William that Buddy's office had a more modern look, with all the furniture done in glass, black leather and chrome. William thought he saw what looked like a cappuccino machine.

"Where's the bar?" asked William.

"There isn't one."

"Oh." William had thought offices like this always had bars. They seemed to always have one on television. Maybe he could put a few bottles on a bookshelf somewhere.

"Have a seat, man," Buddy said, gesturing to the chairs around the table. "We have a lot of ground to cover."

"Let's get started," said William. He took a seat. Buddy shut the door before sitting down across from him.

"First of all," said Buddy. "I have some stuff I need you to sign. I got you a line of credit from the bank but they are waiting on your John Handcock."

"How'd you manage that? Cherry never finished my application."

"Welcome to the world of millionaires. You don't need an

application. I just call the bank and say 'Mr. Defreno needs a line of credit' and they say, 'yes, sir, how much?' You'll get it before close of business the same day."

"Wow."

"Yeah. Two hundred and fifty thousand, with an option for another two fifty if we need it."

"That'll buy one heck of a house," said William. Although, the idea of a real house seemed kind of hollow now that Cherry would not be with him in it.

"It's not for a house. It's for the campaign."

"It is?"

"Yeah. You and a few *loyal friends* are paying for the whole thing yourselves. No fundraisers, no special interests, no big donors. You're your own man who can't be bought. It's going to make a great angle."

"You know, that kinda makes sense," said William. He was starting to really wish for a drink. Or at least a cigarette. He looked around. Nope, no ashtrays, either. Geez. What did people do with themselves this early in the morning?

"Beth will be here a bit later, and the two of you will hold a press conference officially announcing your candidacy. Right now she is out shopping for a ring set."

"Um, Buddy, how far is this 'pretend wife' thing going to go? Is she going to live with me at the diner?"

"No, actually, you are going to move into her town house with her. It's only a few blocks away but still in your district."

William squirmed at the idea of living with a woman he barely knew. He wondered what Cherry would think. Then he remembered he wasn't supposed to care. He guessed he could always sleep in the den or something.

"You know, William, you're a very lucky man. Beth is an amazing girl. She cooks, cleans and makes a great playmate. She'll make you forget about Cherry in no time."

"I, uh, can't wait to get to know her better."

"Take her to bed tonight. She'll show you a real good time."

"I'll keep that in mind." Water? Was there at least water? William spotted a stainless steel mini fridge in the corner. He got up and opened it. Yes, there was bottled water. He opened one and chugged it down. Suddenly, William craved a banana. He looked around, but didn't see any.

"Is there any food around here?" He asked Buddy.

"Sure thing, one sec." Buddy stood up and hollered out the door. "Hey Debbie, run out and get Mr. Defreno some breakfast. Angie, baby, start a pot of coffee. Bring it in as soon as it's ready."

"Yes, Mr. Richfield," answered a high, feminine voice.

"Life at the top." Buddy turned back to William and grinned.

William tried to wrap his head around the fact that he had an entire office full of people waiting to do his bidding. It didn't seem real. It was, though. A few minutes later a tray of coffee, sugar, cream and a few pastries got brought in by a pretty young blond lady who kept smiling as she poured him coffee and asked how he liked it. Soon after that another woman with dark hair and a sparkly necklace delivered an omelet, hash browns and bacon, all still hot and fresh in a styrofoam clamshell.

"Will this do, Mr. Defreno, or would you like something else?" she asked demurely.

"No, uh, this is fine."

"Now, if you'll excuse us, ladies," said Buddy. The women exited quietly shutting the door behind them.

William sat down and dug into his omelet. Buddy picked the chocolate chips out of a muffin as he briefed William on their election strategy.

"Now we just barely squeaked you in under the deadline to get you on the ballot, but you're on there. We registered you as an independent, so you will be unopposed in the primary. Martha is also unopposed, so nothing much will happen until after the primary. There will be a couple of meet and greets and one town hall meeting, but that's about it. Closer to November you will have to be ready for a few debates, but the coaches will have you prepped long before those come up.

"Our main challenge right now is to get your name out there. We have to make people feel like they know you. We'll schedule some public appearances, a few interviews. I've got a photographer coming by later, and the boys are working on getting your website going.

"Today and tomorrow we'll walk neighborhoods in your district.

The day after that you and Beth will attend a charity dinner to give you a chance to meet the high society people."

"I'm not exactly the high society type, Buddy," said William.

"Just let Beth worry about that. She has a lot of connecticns in that circle so she'll get you in good with them. That's the kind of thing having the right wife does for a man."

William bit his lip. He might still have his doubts about Beth, but he did have to admit that Buddy was right about that. He couldn't see a bunch of high society folks rolling out the red carpet for someone like Cherry.

"I guess," he said glumly

"Hey, buck up, pal. We are on fire here. The good life is finally yours."

"Yeah, sure, I guess it's about time," said William.

The rest of the day flew by in a crowded blur. Beth swooped in wearing a smartly tailored blue dress. She kissed him enthusiastically. William noticed that she had his suitcase. Apparently, Buddy had sent her over to pack a few of his things for the move to her place. Good thing he never locked the door to his house. William sincerely hoped she had neither found nor opened that certain box Cherry kept under his bed.

At the last minute, Buddy decided it was better for them to be newly engaged than already married. Beth slipped a very expensive looking diamond ring on her left hand. William had to admit it suited her. She was beautiful with that sparkle in her eyes. He felt good about having an elegant, graceful woman by his side.

An hour later, he stood at a podium on the steps of city hall reading a speech he barely recalled into the mass of lights and cameras pointed at him. After that, another group of reporters snapped pictures of him handing the keys to his old Impala to a lady from the local Veterans' charity. Then, yet another photographer took engagement pictures of him with Beth in the garden of a local historic mansion.

Later in the afternoon, Beth went off to volunteer at an after school program while William sat down with a group of consultants to work on his platform and learn more about public speaking and debating. William found doing the things they taught him came easily. He quickly added his own flourishes to the gestures and postures he practiced, making them more his own. He saw the looks of approval he got from the men in the room.

"I told you he was a natural," said Buddy. "Poor old Martha won't know what hit her."

"We should get him some shoe lifts," said one guy with dark hair.

"No good," said Buddy. "Beth is way shorter than he is already. They'd look awkward if he were any taller."

"What about a pair of glasses?" asked someone else.

"Little late for that," said the first guy. "We already took all the pictures."

A third man studied him carefully. "He's just so *young* looking, though. Hey, William, how would you feel about growing a mustache?"

"Leave it," said Buddy. "He's perfect."

"What about his wardrobe?" said the second guy.

"We're working on it," Buddy replied. He turned to the first guy. "Have one of the girls make him an appointment with a personal shopper at Brinkley's Menswear."

"Sure thing, Buddy."

In the evening, William and Beth went out for a fancy dinner at another local five star restaurant. Buddy and a few key members of his entourage tagged along, making a noisy spectacle of their table. Buddy made a point of telling the waitress they were celebrating William and Beth's engagement. She fawned over them, cooing about the "young love birds." The manager sent them complimentary champagne. Someone sent them a sweetheart cake for dessert. Buddy snapped pictures as William and Beth fed each other forkfuls of decadent chocolate.

"Those are going to look great on your Facebook page," said Buddy.

William gritted his teeth in what he hoped looked like a smile.

After dinner, William drove Beth home. He felt awkward having to ask his supposed fiancée where she lived. Beth gave him clear, simple directions without too much extra detail. This made it easy for William to find the quiet side street where her small, cookie cutter brick townhouse stood. Seeing as the building lacked a garage or driveway, William parked on the street. He took his suitcase out of the trunk and followed Beth up the front steps.

William stepped into the stereotypical marble entryway. She showed him around the first floor, but his tired mind refused to latch on to the details of his surroundings. He could tell that the muted earth tone furnishings and tasteful abstract art were expensive, but it all seemed cold and impersonal to him. Nothing in the townhouse showed any personality. There were no mementos tucked onto shelves, no framed photos on the tables, no silly knickknacks filling up the empty corners.

Upstairs, she showed him the bathroom, home office and finally her bedroom.

William swallowed hard as he stepped inside. The dark wood furniture, soft purple carpet and matching purple bedspread seemed nice enough. He still was not comfortable sharing a room, much less a bed, with a woman who was still essentially a stranger.

"The dresser on the left is for you," said Beth. "I couldn't find any pajamas or underwear when I packed for you, so I stopped and bought you some. They're in the top drawer."

"Thanks," William said as he looked at his new underwear.

"I don't really wear these," He said.

"Why?"

"Well, 'cause I'm free, free ballin';now I'm free ballin'," William sang to the tune of an old Tom Petty song.

"What?" Beth wondered.

William didn't feel like explaining. He carefully put his shirts and slacks away. Behind him, Beth stood waiting quietly. When he finished unpacking, he turned back to face her. She gave him a bright, but slightly nervous, smile.

"Would, um," she said in a faltering voice. "Would you please undo my zipper?"

"Uh, yeah, I can do that." Jesus. William hadn't felt this awkward since his middle school days. He crossed the room. Beth turned her back so he could reach the zipper on her dress. He slid it down, catching a glimpse of her black satin bra as the zipper parted.

Beth stepped out of the dress and left it pooled on the floor. She turned around and smiled before reaching back to unhook her bra. She stepped towards him, wearing nothing but her tiny black satin panties.

"Buddy said to be extra nice to you tonight," said Beth.

"He, uh, did, huh?" William squirmed as Beth pressed her body up against him.

"Uh-huh."

"Well, um." William put his hands on her shoulders to hold her still. "That's very sweet of you, but I'm very tired. I think I just want to go to bed."

Beth looked disappointed for a moment before slipping back behind her mask. "Ok, William. Goodnight." She pecked him lightly on the cheek and climbed into bed.

"Goodnight."

Feeling shy, he went into the bathroom to change into his new pajamas. By the time he came back, it seemed Beth had gone to sleep. He slipped into bed beside her and turned out the light. If he were not so tired, it would've been impossible to sleep without lots of alcohol like he was so used to.

In the morning William woke to the sounds of breakfast sizzling and the aroma of fresh coffee. He heard the chatter of a morning news show keeping Beth company as she worked in the kitchen. So this was the American Dream he'd spent most of his life not even knowing about, he thought as he dragged himself out of bed. He wondered just how early it was. Then he decided he didn't want to know.

After a brief debate, he pulled a robe on and went down in his pajamas. Maybe with a little luck he could go back to bed after breakfast.

Beth stood in her tiny galley kitchen, hair done, make up perfect, wearing a red short sleeved blouse and tight fitting black skirt. Over them she wore a frilly plaid apron. As he stood in the doorway watching, she slid two perfect eggs out of a skillet and onto a plate.

"Good morning, William," she said. "Did you sleep well?"

"Morning. I did, actually, even though I didn't get to drink last night."

"I know, I'm so proud of you. How do you feel?

"I'm shaking like Michael J. Fox," William replied.

She set her breakfast preparations aside long enough to pour him orange juice and a cup of coffee. William sat at the counter that separated the kitchen from the dining room and sipped the rich, dark coffee while she finished cooking.

"You have your appointment at Brinkley's at 10:30," she told him as she placed his breakfast in front of him. "And Buddy called to ask if you could please be at headquarters by noon. He has some local business leaders coming by to meet with you."

"Aren't they always?" William replied.

"Imagine how hectic things are going to be once you actually get elected. I better enjoy having you to myself while I can."

William looked down at the counter to avoid meeting her eyes. He noticed the morning paper folded up next to him and picked it up.

His picture smiled at him from the center of the front page.

"WILLIAM DEFRENO ANNOUCES CITY COUNCIL BID"

The headline declared. On page six he spotted himself again, this time with the headline:

"DEFRENO DONATES BELOVED CAR TO CHARITY."

He grinned as he skimmed through the accompanying article.

"Local entrepreneur William Defreno surprised the local Veterans' shelter yesterday by handing over the keys to his cherished Chevy Impala. Defreno said he was moved to make the donation after reading about some of the transportation struggles faced by the shelter's residents. 'The shuttle service created by Councilwoman Stout was a nice gesture," said Defreno. "But it's a bit out of touch. A lot of life happens outside of typical office hours. A 9 to 5 shuttle doesn't do a man much good if his shift starts at 7 A.M., or doesn't end until 11 P.M. Real people work weekends. They work holidays. They work swing shift. They work graveyard. With access to a car, the shelter's residents will no longer be hindered by limited transportation as they seek employment." Councilwoman Stout had no comment on Mr. Defreno's remarks."

"That was so nice of you, William," said Beth. She kissed his cheek. "Look, here we are again on the society page."

Beth flipped through the paper until she found their engagement announcement. William studied it, feeling oddly disassociated again.

"The pictures came out nice," he said. He didn't bother reading the headline or the article underneath it.

"You look very handsome. My friends can't wait to meet you."

"Uh, oh, well, hm... We'll have to see. Things will be pretty busy with the election and all."

"I understand," said Beth. "Would you like more toast?"

William spent the rest of that day pretty much like he spent the one before. And the next day and the one after that. Soon, he had developed a predictable routine. He wore what he was told to, went where he was told to, did what he was told to and said what he was told to. He met people he didn't remember two minutes later and took positions on issues he knew little, if anything about.

Everywhere he went, though, it suddenly seemed like everyone loved him. They all wanted to say a word or two. Everyone shook his hand. Strangers acted as if they'd known him for life. He was finally the big man in the room and everyone around stopped and took notice.

Two days a week he worked a half shift at the diner to remind everyone he was still a "working man," but so many people came by to see him he never got much of anything done.

And in the evenings there was Beth. Always there, waiting patiently to dote on him when he returned home. She would rub his feet and stroke his hair while he told her about his day. Over the home cooked dinners she served him they made fumbling attempts at conversation, but struggled to find a topic of common interest. William always felt he had to hold back a little when talking to her in order not to shock or frighten her with his dark sense of humor. Beth covered the awkward silences by chattering away about the minute details of high society drama or sharing bits of random trivia.

On the weekends they did typical couple things. They were seen at the right parties, made sure to attend the right events. They volunteered for the right causes. One Saturday they adopted a kitten from the local animal shelter. William wanted to name the small orange tabby Chico, but he was afraid it would sound too racist. He could imagine with his luck seeing the cat in the street and saying "go home, Chico" without realizing a Hispanic couple was walking by. So they settled for "Orson."

Beth spent hours dragging string around the house and giggling while Orson chased after it. William started to wish Beth's townhouse had a garage to hide in.

Life was good, he guessed. But even with the campaign eating up his days he was just so *bored.* He missed late nights at the diner. He missed waiting tables and tending bar. He missed his bull sessions with Mitch and Riley. He missed goofing off with the staff after closing.

And though he tried hard to stop himself, he missed Cherry. Beth was nice, but something about her was just too perfect. Almost like a group of "men in their power" scientists had created her. He went through the motions with her, having finally run out of excuses not to, but he found their encounters thoroughly unsatisfying.

He doubted they satisfied Beth, either, but she still applauded his tepid lovemaking with loud moans of pleasure.

He soon found he only liked having her around if he could subtly embarrass her in front of other people. He hated himself a little for treating her that way, but there was something about the twinkle in her eye and the way her breathing changed that made him think she enjoyed her little humiliations.

Feeling trapped in his new life, William began to get restless. Long after Beth had curled up and gone to sleep each night, William found himself still wide awake and roaming around their quaint little gentrified neighborhood. Despite having early mornings ahead, he could never unwind enough to get to sleep until he'd had a few drinks and gone for a long drive. Even though Beth would surely never break his balls for drinking and driving, he still felt embarrassed that she even knew he liked to drive around aimlessly at night for fun.

One night he just was too restless to stay around the townhome. William drove with the windows down, flicking the ash of cigarettes out of the car as he cruised up and down his little town's quiet roads. Perpetually, he found himself going down Cherry's street. Each time he was tempted to stop and go up to her door, but he kept *The Child* under control and drove on.

Late one night, her lights were on. Unable to help himself, he stopped across the street. He could see Cherry in the kitchen washing dishes. He sat and watched her for a while as she gracefully moved through her home tidying up. She paused by the bookcase in her living room. Cherry pulled the anthology with his short story off the shelf. After rifling briefly through the pages, she smiled sadly and placed the book back on the shelf. She turned away from the bookcase and walked down the hall towards her basement.

William started up the car and pulled away from the curb. As he passed by, he was pleasantly surprised to see one of his campaign signs on her lawn. He knew being endorsed by a former "adult entertainer" didn't really help his campaign, in fact it probably hurt it, but he didn't really care. All that mattered was that even now she still supported him.

Chapter 8

You Opened Fire and
Your Mark Was True

The night of the big town hall meeting William showed up at the civic center well dressed, groomed, coached and ready. Beth sparkled at his side. Buddy and a few others followed behind, ready to step in with anything William needed.

As the make-up artist prepped him to be on camera for the local affairs channel that would televise the event, Buddy went over a few last points, making sure William had his quotes ready for anything he might be asked. The make-up artist frowned a bit as she struggled to cover the heavy bags and dark circles under his eyes from years of excess alcohol.

From behind the curtain, Buddy peeked out at the audience.

"Wow, man, that's quite the crowd out there. Are you ready?"

"I was born ready," said William.

They took their places on the stage. As the lights came up he got his first real look at his opponent. She was shorter in person and a bit greasy looking. She wore a dated tweed suit with a ruffled blouse that made her look silly. It looked as though she had tried to cover the grey in her hair with a home dye job that hadn't gone well. Despite being made up for the camera, she still had a wrinkled, withered appearance. Her thick glasses magnified her eyes, making William think she looked like a toad.

A short pudgy man with thinning gray hair and square horn rimmed glasses stepped out of the wings and took his place at the moderator's podium on the center of the stage. The audience welcomed him with a light patter of applause.

"Good evening, everyone, and welcome to this evening's Candidate's Roundtable. Our purpose here tonight is to help you get to know your candidates for local city offices better by learning more about both their personal lives and their platforms. Each candidate will have a brief introduction and then will have five minutes to speak. Our hope is that when you leave this evening you have a better understanding of our candidates and their positions on the important issues and will be better able to make your decision on Election Day.

"Questions will be taken later in the evening, after each candidate has had a chance to speak, so please hold them until the end. We will begin now with the candidates for City Council, in District 1, our incumbent, Martha Stout," the moderator paused to allow a few people to clap and cheer, "and her challenger, William Defreno." The moderator paused again. This time the audience clapped and cheered louder.

"Wow. They love you," Beth whispered without breaking her sparkling plastic smile.

"Per roundtable rules, incumbent Martha Stout will go first," the moderator announced.

Martha Stout's campaign manager, a tall, thin, balding man wearing a beige suit and a bow tie leaned into the microphone at their podium.

"Ladies and gentlemen," he said in a voice that was nearly a mumble. "The lady I am introducing tonight hardly needs one. For many years Martha Stout has faithfully served this community as the representative of District 1. You all know her by reputation and her record speaks for itself. Her accomplishments during her tenure on the council are far too numerous to list, but just to highlight a few..." the man paused to shuffle through some papers on the podium in front of him.

"Wow. Her own campaign manager doesn't even know what she's done for the city?" William whispered to Buddy under his breath.

"That's because she hadn't done much of anything" Buddy whispered back. "It's mostly been twenty years of hot air."

William couldn't believe it.

"Ms. Stout was the driving force behind the local bike rental program. She brought the proposal for community gardens at all the city's elementary schools to the School Board. She spearheaded the city park's beautification campaign and was an instrumental part of the pollinator support initiative. She has also being a strong advocate for the city's recycling programs, litter prevention and pollution reduction.

"Additionally, she secured expanded funding for the local animal shelter and brought the spay and neuter mobile to town. Ms. Stout is also a firm believer in social justice and economic equality and had fought to ensure equity at all levels of society. Ladies and gentlemen, I give you Martha Stout."

The crowd clapped politely as the campaign manager stepped back and Martha Stout took his place at the microphone.

"Good evening, everyone. Thank you for being here," she began. William noticed that she kept glancing down at the notes on the podium. Her hands trembled as she shuffled the index cards in front of her. William realized she was nervous.

"I have dedicated my time and effort to this city tirelessly since I took office," said Ms. Stout. "I have stood up to corruption. I have voted against mega projects that would choke our roadways, voted for stricter air emissions to protect the health of our children. I voted against the encroachment of nuclear power and its dangerous potential side effects. I have voted for stricter dumping laws to protect our waterways, and I have voted to hold our local police more accountable for their actions."

Her voice wobbled. William suddenly realized that his opponent wasn't confident she could win. Buddy must have been right that she had always won by default before. Now that she faced a real opponent, she was crumbling under the pressure. As she continued speaking, she faltered more and more.

"Everyone who knows me knows I love this city and the values we stand for," she said. "We have made solid, steady progress in the last few years, and we are set to continue making a better future as we move forward. We live in challenging times, and it is more important than ever to stick with what we know is sure and true. Friends, now is not the time for a risky gamble on our future. Stay the course. Keep focused on the world we have promised ourselves and our children.

Come November, stick with a winner. Vote Martha Stout for another successful term of prosperity and protection for our beautiful world."

William could not believe that this supposedly powerful woman had never seen a life coach and therefore did not have the advantage he did. This election was his. Martha Stout just didn't know it yet. He nodded to Buddy. Buddy nodded back and then stepped up to the microphone as Martha sat down.

"William Defreno," said Buddy. "Who the heck is William Defreno? Oh, come on now, people, don't look at me like that. I know most of you have been asking yourselves and those around you that very question. And I'm here to answer it. You want to know who William Defreno is. Well, let me tell you."

Buddy paused for dramatic effect. William could feel the tension building in the audience as they waited for Buddy's next words.

"William Defreno is a living freaking *legend*, ok? That's who he is. This guy's story is amazing. It's like something out of a movie. This guy, this guy right here," Buddy said, pointing to William. "He started out as absolutely nothing. He was the child of a single mother, left on his own while she struggled to support him. He started working at fourteen. Still, he found time to excel in sports and do well in school. He built himself a future, only to have it snatched away from him.

"But what did he do? Did he run and hide? Hell no! This tiny David took on his personal Goliath and brought down the most corrupt, evil man in the history of this city. And he didn't stop there. He came back to town and cleaned it up again. He took on the whole police force single handedly to weed out the corrupt ones. And once again, he won. You want to talk about love for this city?

"This man put his own life on the line for each and every one of you so that you could live free from fear of the thugs that turned our town into their personal playground while our elected officials turned a blind eye to their actions," Buddy said as he looked right at Martha Stout for a moment. She knew exactly what he was talking about and that she was blind to it during her terms in office.

"Then what did he do?" Buddy continued. "He turned around and bought the diner he'd spent his whole life slaving away at. He turned that around, too. He took it from a one star greasy spoon to the hottest night spot in town. He brought us the business, the attention, the popularity that put this town on the map and started our economic boom.

"You all know Moe's Diner. Would this town be our town without it? I don't think so, and I know you know so. If he can do that for one small business, think about what he can do for the city. Come on folks, give it up for the man with the plan, William Defreno!"

Thundering applause echoed through the hall as William took Buddy's place at the microphone. William looked out in awe as he waited several long moments for the noise to finally die down.

"Oh my God," said Beth.

"I told you, man, you're their hero," said Buddy.

The moderator waved for quiet, but the clapping rolled on. Finally, William held up a hand and the crowd fell silent. William felt almost drunk with power. He could sense that he held the audience captive and he set about reeling them in.

"Wow, thanks, Buddy," said William. "After and introduction like that I hardly need my speech." William comically threw a stack of index cards over his shoulder. The crowd laughed.

"But folks," he continued. "As long as I have your attention, I do want to talk to you about a few things. Things that worry me about our city, and I think probably worry all of you, my neighbors, as well."

William kept his gaze steady as he looked out at the audience. He scanned the crowd with a slow, steady gaze, making eye contact with as many people as possible. He could see people nodding in agreement with him.

"I do love this city. I never wanted to live anywhere else. Even back as a kid in the rough part of town, I believed in us. In the potential of this place. In everything it could be if we were just strong enough and brave enough to make it happen. All through school I believed. I remembered that beautiful phrase from civics class 'We the People'. I knew I was one of the people, just as every one of you out there is. And I knew together we could build a better life for all of us.

"So I buckled down. I worked hard. I scrimped, I saved, I sacrificed. Every time I thought I'd done enough a voice told me to do better, so I kept pushing, kept trying. I had a vision I believed in, and it moved me forward. Because of that vision, I found the strength to defeat the dark evil at the heart of this town, but I didn't stop there.

"I bought my business, and I worked even harder, always reaching for that brighter, better tomorrow. This city, my city, the place I'm proud to call home, is where I want to build that tomorrow. And I want to bring all of you with me. I want better, safer schools for our children. I want more economic opportunities, I want better roads and cleaner sidewalks.

"I want to see our youth coming back home after college and putting their hard earned degrees to work here in the city that raised them instead of watching generation after generation flee to the mega metropolises where they think they have to live to make those degrees worthwhile.

"Why can't we have a bigger, better hospital? Why can't we have a tech sector? Why can't we have a diverse economy that welcomes tradesmen and merchants as well as young professionals? Why can't we be the place where a new American Dream is born for a new generation?

"Well, I'll tell you folks, we can. We can be all of that and more. You just have to believe. Believe in yourselves. Believe in me. Believe in our children. Believe in our city and what we can do if we all work together."

And then it happened.... William caught a flicker of movement out of the corner of his eye and turned to follow it. He saw those long, tan, muscular legs, the black mini skirt, the tight red top, the red patent leather heels, the blond hair, the sweet, sad, smile. Cherry. Cherry was there. Her eyes met his for a brief moment and he mind stumbled. His legs went limp and his guts went to water. He forgot where he was, what he was doing. For several long moments, he merely stood there, mouth open, seeing nothing but her.

A sharp jab to his ribs brought him back to himself. Shaking his head, he cleared his throat as he grappled for the rest of the words he'd had perfectly memorized a few moments ago.

"Uh, folks, I guess that's all. I hope you'll think about what I've said here tonight. This November, vote Defreno for your tomorrow to a better ticket. Er, I mean your better tocket to timarow, oh heck, you guys know what I mean. Have a great night, folks! Enjoy the pot holes while you can, 'cause they'll be gone once elected!"

Under the cover of the audience's applause, William ducked backstage. He was sweating and shaking. He thought he might throw up.

"William, honey, what's the matter?" asked Beth. "Are you sick?"

"I, uh, I'm fine," William said. He wasn't fine at all, and they both knew it, but he couldn't tell Beth what was wrong. Buddy knew though. William could tell by the gleam in his campaign manager's eye that he had seen Cherry, too.

"Go powder your nose, gorgeous, William and I need a minute," Buddy said to Beth.

"Ok. I'll be right back, William." Beth tried to give William a peck on the cheek, but he pulled away. Looking confused and hurt, she walked away.

"When she gets back, send her home for the night. You and I gotta talk, and we can't do it here."

William nodded. He stumbled towards the refreshment table and grabbed a bottle of water. After sitting down, he opened the bottle and drank it without pausing for breath. Buddy handed him a stack of napkins. William blotted his face and neck, smearing make up all over himself as he tried to clean up the thick heavy sweat on his skin.

Beth came back, looking worried. She carried a bottle of water and a muffin.

"I thought, you know, maybe low blood sugar?" she said. "You should eat something."

The last thing William wanted was food.

"That's very sweet, but I'm not hungry." He stood up, forcing his legs to work through sheer will power. Still forcing himself through the motions, he leaned over and kissed her on the cheek. "Go on home. Buddy and I have some work we have to do. I'll be home later."

"Am I to wait up for you?"

"No, and if you do it anyway, I'll turn that pretty little bottom of yours redder than those fancy lace panties you're wearing."

Beth blushed. She bit down on her lower lip as she squirmed in the way she did when he hit a nerve. She looked up at him through her bangs and pouted. "Yes, William."

She left them again.

"Wow, where did that come from?" asked Buddy.

"I think she likes it."

"Oh really?" Buddy stared after Beth like she was an exotic animal he'd never seen before. "Damn, wish I'd known."

"Hey, get your own girl," William teased.

"No thanks. I am a professional bachelor." Buddy jerked his head towards the door. "Come on, let's go find a quiet dive somewhere and get a drink. You look like you need one."

"I need the whole damn bottle," said William.

"Maybe later, but we gotta do something about your little problem first."

"I don't think it's so little."

"That's why it's a problem. Let's go before they realize we went."

"But what about the 'Q' and 'A'?"

"It's covered. Tom will read a statement that you have suddenly taken ill and gone for medical treatment. Anyone with questions will be invited to email you directly."

"Er..." William wasn't sure he wanted his campaign aide telling the general public to email him at minigoofy69...

"At your *new* email address."

"Oh."

"Now can we go, please?"

"After you." William gestured towards the exit with his still shaky hand. He followed Buddy at a slow walk, trying to keep upright on his wobbly legs.

Buddy drove the Rolls Royce. William didn't pay much attention to the route they took. Somewhere on the edge of town they stopped at a small microbrewer set up in an old grain silo. After a few beers and a plate of a bit too greasy, but still tasty, chicken wings William began to feel like his new self again.

They didn't talk at first. Buddy just simply watched as William gulped his beer and tried to regain his composure, but after he had settled down, Buddy finally spoke his mind.

"William, my friend, I have a confession to make," said Buddy.

"I've been holding out on you."

"I knew it," said William. He dropped his last chicken wing back down onto his plate. "Go on, spill it."

"Well, you see, there is one last thing a man in his power does to make sure he stays on top. I wasn't going to make you do it because I knew it wouldn't fly with you. I see now, though, that it has to be done."

"What has to be done?"

"You have to take Cherry down. If you don't she's always going to have a hold over you."

William shook his head. "No way. I don't care how bad I want it, winning an election isn't worth hurting somebody over."

"I don't mean physically. I just mean mess with her, fuck with her head."

"Why though? I already broke up with her. I'll get over it. I just need time."

"Time is one luxury we do not have my friend. If just seeing her messes you up that bad, it's going to blow your whole campaign. You have to do something."

"Isn't there like a meditation or something I can just use to stop her effect on me?"

"I'm afraid not. Some things are primal. This is your initiation. Your trial by fire. Your own personal hero quest. Every man has to slay the monster at some point and kill the queen bee. She's your queen bee, and you need to squash her before she stings again."

"Yeah, but what good is that going to do? What does it prove to anybody if I can scare her?"

"You prove to yourself that you really are a man in your power and that nobody can hold you down anymore."

"I already know that, Buddy."

"Yeah? Then why did you fall apart up there tonight?"

William sputtered, searching for an answer. Why had he? It was just Cherry. His Cherry. The light of his world -- he cut off that train of thought. She wasn't his anything. Not anymore.

"I just got distracted, caught off guard. I was confused by all the lights and the noise, that's all. It won't happen again."

"Ah, but it will." Buddy slowly wagged a finger at him. "I've seen it more times than I can even recall. All newly minted men in their power think they finally have it on lock. Then that one chick from their past comes in, and, so help me, she *always* knocks them over like a stack of milk cans in a carnival game. Boom! Crash! It's all over before they even know what hit them.

"Once or twice, and they still think they are ok, but it happens every time they see her and suddenly all their hard won confidence goes up in smoke."

"Yeah, well, that won't happen with me," said William. "I won't even look twice next time."

"Glad you said that," said Buddy. "Because she just walked in the door."

"What?" William twisted around in his seat. In the process, he knocked his glass off the table, sending the beer flying before the glass smashed on the polished concrete floor. All around the room people's heads swiveled towards the noise. An irritated looking waitress came over to clean up the mess. William squirmed in his seat.

"I rest my case," Buddy said sadly. "Just the thought of her and you go to pieces. You're no good like this, William. You have to take that final step if you want to make a permanent change."

"I guess you're right," William said glumly.

"Have I been wrong yet?"

"No." William sulked. "It just seems like such a *Dick move*, though."

"So? *Dick move* is just a term people use when they're jealous that you had the nerve to pull something off and they didn't."

"Never thought of it like that," said William. The waitress placed a fresh beer in front of him. He took a long drink.

"Yeah, but it's true." Buddy drank from his own glass. "Men get shamed for being courageous, but they get shamed for being timid, too. You can't win, so if you're damned either way it's better to be damned for something you *did* than something you *didn't*."

"You got a point there." William finished his beer. "So what do I do?"

"Ah, see now that's the thing. This is your challenge, not mine. I can't tell you how to slay your queen bee. This is your first solo."

"So I'm on my own?"

"Think of it as your final exam. Graduation day. Make it yours."

"I may have an idea or two." Visions of devious pranks danced before his eyes. *The General* was going to war.

William dropped Buddy back at his car and then drove around for a while making plans.

Late into the night William pulled up behind the diner. After a quick trip into his old bungalow to grab a few things, he let himself in the diner's back door. Silently creeping down the dark hallway, he slipped into the office and locked the door before turning on the light. He felt silly sneaking around his own diner, but he thought would be best if no one knew he was here tonight.

William fired up the office computer. One by one he feed the stack of DVDs he'd brought with him into the disc drive. He uploaded them into the fancy video editing software he'd bought to produce the diner's commercials.

Once upon a time in California, William had made a fairly decent living as a junior film editing assistant for a small independent film company in the valley. One of the shorts he'd worked on had even won an award. He now put those highly polished skills to work, crafting the perfect punishment for Cherry.

But victory did not come easily. The anti-piracy features of the software blocked his first attempts to copy the footage he wanted. Feeling frustrated, he nearly abandoned the whole project before an idea came to him. He hurried back to his bungalow for his old camcorder.

To get around the scrambler, he played each clip on the computer screen and filmed it. The images came out grainy with an odd blue tinge, but he sort of enjoyed the affect. Like a lot of things in his life, the film industry's best anti-piracy software didn't stop him from doing stupid things. He recorded a few videos off the internet and some old news footage the same way.

And now for the music. William laughed gleefully. Once upon a time on his kindergarten summer break he had stumbled across a new Stallone movie on cable. With little parental supervision around and, despite it being well past his bedtime, he had stayed up to watch the entire violent movie.

He remembered understanding the plot pretty well for five years old. Little did his first grade teacher know the following semester it was *that* movie he was quoting when he got *In School Suspension*. Little Mitch had ruined little William's milk by putting Elmer's glue in it. The first grade teacher Mrs. Reitz, listened in horror as little William said to Mitch, "Hey dirtbag! You wasted my milk..... For nothin'..... Now I think it's time to waste you!"

He remembered the electric feeling that had surged through his little body as he watched an unknown gunman load an ominous looking weapon in the shadows while the heavy drumbeat of the background music pounded in his ears.

All summer he'd waited for the movie to come on again so that he could catch the name of the song. He'd found the soundtrack to the movie and bought it. His first record purchase of his own, paid for with lawn mowing money.

It was still a favorite. He played it now, as he worked, imagining himself as the lone gunman preparing to take aim at his target.

"Feel the heat," he sang to himself. "Feel the heat... Feel the heat."

Nothing else would do. He uploaded the song and began matching his chosen clips to the beat. For hours he sweated each precise detail, timing the clips down to the hundredth of a second. Sometimes working frame by frame as he strived to get it exactly right. It took him a dozen tries to sync the clip of a crashing airplane to the right moment in the music.

"Well, Cherry, at least I respect you enough to make this perfect," William said to himself.

Finally satisfied, William burned the disturbing video to a blank DVD. The software prompted him to enter a title. He thought for a moment. *Feel the Heat* was too obvious. On a whim he titled it "Dead Inside" instead. William tucked it away in its jewel case. With a black permanent marker he found in the desk drawer he wrote her name across the front of the case with a flourish.

And then he hesitated, unsure if he really had the nerve to leave it on her doorstep. He looked at the clock. It was too late anyway. The night was almost over. Dawn would break before he got there and back.

Screw it. He'd decide later. For now it was time to visit the diner's bar.

After drinking Patron while watching the YouTube video of how Patron was made, he gathered the things he'd left scattered around the office and stumbled back to his tiny shack behind the diner.

"No place like home," he said as he tossed the movies and the camera aside. He curled up on his old bed and fell asleep.

After sleeping most of the next day, William woke up and noticed a text message from Beth.

"What on earth are you talking about LOL"

He looked at his phone and realized he had sent a drunk text to her at 4AM last night.

"I'm not content with beating you in the daytime....... Girl I want to beat you all of the time........ The only time I feel alright is beating your siiiide..... Girl I want to beat you all of the time.... All day and all of the night...... All day and all of the night.... All day and all of the night."

William busted out laughing and decided he would spend the evening working at the diner. Just like old times, he stayed behind the bar, serving drinks and chatting with customers. They had a busy night. Riley worked beside him through the rush, enjoying William's energetic company.

William felt full of nervous energy. Throughout the evening the tension slipped out in cryptic remarks that he worked into his conversations with his customers as he mixed up his signature Long Island iced teas.

"Wow, this is so good," a pretty young blonde said. "What made you choose Skyy vodka over Grey Goose?"

"Grey Goose is way overrated," said William. "Yeah, they may filter it more, but the flavor is so *dead inside*."

"These cherries are fantastic," said an older man in a business suit. "Can I get another one?"

"You bet." William dropped another cherry in the man's drink. "Our cherries are the very best. They even send a Cherry DVD with each shipment talking about them."

Riley gave William a funny look. He was used to William saying weird stuff though, so he just kind of blew it off. William went back to mixing drinks.

As they closed down, Riley reached over to set adjust the thermostat for overnight.

"Hard to believe we still have to run the AC this late in the year," Riley said.

"Yeah, but I'd much rather *feel the heat* than be left in the cold," said William.

"I suppose," said Riley, eyeing William cautiously.

"Hey, don't forget to put those way," William said, pointing to the box of fruit. "We wouldn't want our sweet cherries to *feel the heat* and spoil."

"I'll handle it. We went through three boxes of these tonight and nineteen bottles of vodka."

"Now that's *feeling the heat*," said William.

Riley just shook his head.

"How's the campaign going?" he asked William.

"Playing like a movie," said William. "Lots of little details, but it's all coming together smooth as perfectly timed DVD."

"Just like your campaign commercials?" said Riley. "Saw one the other day. You looked pretty good."

"Thanks, man."

"Hey where did you meet Beth, anyway? I just realized you never even told me about her."

"She came with the Rolls Royce."

"Oh, come on."

"No really. I bought it from Hank over at The Love House. He runs a car lot. Free girl with every purchase."

"OK. I give up. I'll quit prying."

Pleased that he'd gotten Riley to back off so easily, William grinned as he turned out the lights.

Riley headed for home. William stayed to lock up.

As he turned the key in the lock his phone rang. Beth of course.

"Hey, sweets," William answered. "You being good?"

"Yes, sir," Beth answered. There was a brief pause. "Unless you want me to be bad?"

"Maybe later."

"Are you coming home soon? Orson misses you."

"Not just yet. Big Daddy has some business to take care of. Then I'll come pet my kitty."

Beth giggled. "I'm wearing that special nightie."

"Without permission?" William chuckled. "Now that is naughty."

"Well, I guess you'll have to teach me a lesson, then."

"Yes, I will." Thinking about the degrading things he would do to Beth later got William's adrenaline pumping. His predatory instincts kicked in, zeroing in on his other target for the evening. "Just as soon as I take care of one little errand."

William's adventure in crime began twenty miles away at a low rent department store in a suburb of the nearest mega-city. He was unlikely to be recognized here. As he walked through the automatic doors, he realized just how long it had been since he'd done any of his own shopping. Ever since he'd moved in with Beth she had taken over all of his daily errands.

While he was happy to let her most of the time, he figured this was one shopping trip he had better make personally. He knew she'd never tell anyone or question what he wanted these things for, but he still thought it was best to keep her in the dark about what he was about to do. Not that keeping her in the dark about anything was all that hard.

"Wow," said William as he looked around the dirty, disheveled store. He hadn't exactly expected five star shopping, but he didn't think even a discount store usually looked quite this bad. Apparel items littered the floor. Shoes lay about in random places, abandoned by their mates. Boxes of product sat on the floor in the middle of the half empty grocery aisles. Despite the poor conditions, the store was packed. He moved through the crowds of slow, roughly dressed shoppers listening to screaming children and arguing couples.

He got stuck behind one overweight lady who pushed her cart down the meat aisle at a pace that would make a glacier look fast. William started to wonder if there was such a thing as "cart rage." How did people live like this? He had been in some low points in his life, but he had never let himself get like the people around him. What was wrong with them? Why did they all seem so hopeless? Didn't any of them want life to be better? Maybe they were too tired to care.

Suddenly feeling depressed, William wandered to the back of the store. He laughed when he spotted a copy of the Stallone movie that had inspired his first music purchase in the $5 discount bin. On a whim, he picked it up.

He finished the rest of his shopping as quickly as he could, throwing a pair of twelve inch black taper candles, a fancy glass candle holder and a chess set into his rickety shopping cart. He had just made it to the checkout line when he realized he had forgotten gloves. Feeling aggravated, he fought his way back through the store to find some.

As he turned to head back to the front of the store, he nearly collided with a large Hispanic man coming around the corner. The guy smiled as he stopped to let William by. As he passed, William couldn't help but notice the tattoos covering the man's arms. One in particular caught his eye. It looked like a playing card, but instead of the usual king or ace, this one had a big red valentine like heart pierced by three crossing swords in the center.

"Nice, huh?" The guy said. "I always work with the best artists. They guy who did that one is the top in the state."

"It's an interesting image," said William. Something about it intrigued him. "Never seen anything like it."

"It's a tarot card, the Three of Swords," the man said. "On my eighteenth birthday my grandmother took me to the fortune teller and that was the first card she drew. She said that was me, my trial in this life. I would suffer three heartbreaks, but as they healed each would make me stronger. When I finally survived all three I would come into my power."

"A man in his power, huh?" said William. "Thanks for the insight."

"Anytime, man."

William went through self-checkout. He paid with cash and tried to keep his head down in case anyone checked the security footage later.

Feeling safely anonymous, William slipped back out to the car. As he pulled away he noticed several heads turning to look his way. He cringed as he realized his Rolls Royce didn't fit in here.

For a moment he missed his loyal old Impala. Oh well, odds are most people in this neighborhood wouldn't even know what a Rolls Royce was, even if it was a bright banana yellow. Still, just to be on the safe side, he pulled over and covered his license plates with wet rags. He didn't know how he'd explain it if he got pulled over, but he trusted his current lucky streak would hold out and he wouldn't cross paths with anyone with a badge.

William's nerves started getting to him again. He imagined being followed as he made his way to Cherry's quaint little cottage. He soon realized there was no way he was going to pull this plan off sober. He stopped at the next liquor store and bought pint size bottle of Wild Turkey 101. He popped the top off right there in the parking lot and took a large swig before taking off.

"Because nothing is as inconspicuous as driving along twenty miles over the speed limit in a bright yellow Rolls Royce with an open container," William said. "Well, better to be damned for something I did than something I didn't, right?" He toasted himself in the rearview mirror and took another swig.

William felt calmer now, but he still felt unsettled, like he was missing something. He ran over the list in his head again, double checked that he had the DVD and his lighter. What was it? What did he need? The memory of the tarot card tattoo flickered in his mind. It just felt so right. That image. Three heartbreaks. Annie, Andrea, Cherry. A man in his power. He needed that card.

Where did you even buy tarot cards? A quick Google search pointed William to a New Age bookstore twelve miles back the other direction. He got off the highway and back on, headed the other direction.

"The course of fate never did run smooth," he misquoted.

Fifteen minutes later William had a pack of colorfully illustrated cards. He looked through them, confused and fascinated by the intricate images on each card. He almost felt guilty splitting up the deck just for the malicious act he was about to perform, but did it anyway. After all, it wasn't like they were alive or anything.

Along with the three of swords, he pulled out a card with a regal looking woman on a throne that was titled *The Empress* and another card with an austere looking figure holding a sword that was titled *Justice*. He dropped the rest of the deck into the floor of the Rolls Royce.

As he got close to Cherry's house, he could hear his heavy breathing. He noticed almost half the bottle of Wild turkey was consumed. For a moment he wondered if he would stop and just throw the items out the window and drive home. He began to hear voices calling from inside his head. He knew he wasn't crazy.

They could be the voice of reason or even his conscience. He could hear them louder and louder as he approached her neighborhood. Suddenly, vanishing memories of times he'd once had with Cherry didn't seem as important as it had before.

He stopped on the far side of the park across from Cherry's house long enough to take two more swigs. Feeling nicely buzzed, he finally found his courage to finish his task. He slid his gloves on.

With slow, meticulous care he wiped down every item he had collected. The candle, the candle holder, the chess piece he had chosen, both sides of the DVD and its case, along with the three tarot cards.

"Fuck it, let's do it!" He laughed at using the word "let's" when he was the only one in the car.

He pulled onto Cherry's street and parked a few houses down. As silently as he could, he got out of the car and shut the door.

William stopped just before actually walking on to her property. *What's happening to me?* He asked himself. He stood in the street for almost ten seconds hypnotized with fear. He realized standing here only increased his chances of getting caught. This was it, he needed to make the choice at this exact moment whether to open fire or abort this mission. He made the choice to proceed.

He arranged everything perfectly on Cherry's porch and then whipped out his Lucky Strike Zippo to light the candle. When he was done, he ran like hell toward his car. Being so panicked and intoxicated he felt like he was a flying bird for a moment as he lost his balance and fell on the street. He didn't even catch himself with his hands. He got back up and noticed blood dripping on the pavement beneath him.

He got into the Rolls Royce and was scared to look at himself in the mirror. He knew he hadn't broken any teeth but his blood stained shirt and the metallic tang of blood filling his mouth frightened him. A glance in the mirror showed him he had a bloody nose, a large bruise on his cheek and that his eye fluttered rapidly as it began to swell. Due to the adrenaline flooding his system he didn't yet feel the pain of his injuries. He wasn't sure yet just how extensive the damage was. One thing was for sure, though. He'd have to clean up before he went home to Beth.

He started the car and drove away. Then he realized he needed to pull over and remove the rag from the license plates. With so much blood all over him he was pleased to have a wet rag. He drove the car out of sight and back to the diner. He cleaned himself up as well as he could. There was no doubt he would look like 'Rocky' in the morning. He changed clothes and threw his old bloody shirt away in the dumpster in the alley.

Half an hour later he slid into bed next to a sleeping Beth. She woke instantly and turned towards him. He was thankful that she couldn't see his face in the dark.

"Hi," she purred, wriggling her body up against him. William noticed that her skin was bare. She must have taken off the nightie.

"Hi," he said.

"I was getting lonely," she pouted.

"Oh, well, we can't have that." Still pumped from two days of rollercoaster emotion, he found he responded easily to her not so subtle coaxing. With his appetite raging, he suddenly grabbed a fist full of her hair. She gasped, but when he reached over to pinch her he could hear her excitement.

"Roll over and get on your hands and knees," he commanded. "I've got a use for you."

"Sure thing."

"Now, what was that about teaching my naughty girl a lesson?"

143

Whatever Beth said in response was muffled by the bedclothes. Just as well, William thought, as he imagined he had Cherry in her degrading position as well. Yeah, he'd teach her a lesson alright...

Chapter 9

A Small Regret
You Won't Forget

Cherry stood in the tiny kitchen of her old cottage basking in the early morning sunlight that filtered through the yellow lace curtains on the window above the sink as she waited for her morning coffee to brew. Still damp from her shower, she cinched her old terrycloth bathrobe a little tighter against the slight chill her house always seemed to have in late fall and winter. As the coffee dripped, she blotted her still wet hair with a fluffy white towel.

Across the road, she could hear birds chattering in the park. Further away, she could hear the sound of rushing traffic. The distance muted it, turning into mere white noise that took on a soothing quality, almost like flowing water.

She was off work and had the whole day to herself. She intended to make it a good one, dedicated to relaxation and self-care. The coffee finished. She poured herself a full steaming mug and padded out to her living room. She contemplated the idea of indulging herself with a stack of homemade pancakes and scrambled eggs for breakfast before taking a leisurely walk on the local nature trail.

The sudden break up with William had caught her off guard, and it had stung her badly, but from a practical standpoint she had understood. She missed him, but still wished him well with his new ambitions. Those first few days had been hard, but she had made steady progress in the weeks since and was feeling stable again. Occasionally she caught herself wistfully hoping they would cross paths again a little later on and at least reconnect as friends. But she had long ago disciplined herself to not let her happiness depend on someone else.

Cherry did have to admit that she had taken a moment of pleasure in the way William had been thrown off stride when he had spotted her at the candidate's roundtable. Not that she had intended to cause a disruption, but her womanly pride had thrilled at having that kind of effect. She wouldn't do it again, though. As much as she might enjoy seeing if he would react the same way, she didn't want to do anything that would make him uncomfortable or actually hurt his chances.

Annoyed with her melancholy mood, she decided to let in some light and air to chase it away. She crossed the living room and opened her front door.

Cherry froze in shock at the sight of the spectacle laid out on her porch. Her damp towel hit the floor. She didn't notice.

"Wh-what?" she said. She opened the screen door and stepped outside to get a closer look.

In a simple clear glass candle holder a long black taper candle had burned almost all the way down, leaving drips and swirls of pooling black wax on the glass. In front of the candle a white queen from a cheap plastic chess set lay on its side as if to signal defeat. Next to them lay a recordable DVD in a clear plastic case. Her name was written across the front in an eccentric old world style font.

Cherry crouched down in front of the little scene, trying to make better sense of it. It looked as though there was something in the case with the DVD. Setting aside her coffee, Cherry reached for the case and picked it up. Just as she did the heat of the candle shattered the candle holder, making a cracking noise and sending drops of wax and pieces of glass everywhere.

Cherry jumped back and screamed, knocking her coffee cup over in the process. The coffee ran along the seams of the porch like a muddy river sweeping along overflowing banks. It pooled in a low spot, looking eerily yellowish in the early morning light. Suddenly the smell of the hazelnut creamer she'd used made her feel sick.

Painful memories began dancing in the back of her head like little goblins with pitchforks ready to stab at her mind. She closed her eyes and focused on her breathing, struggling hard to stay in control and in the moment and not get swept away.

She won the fight, but just barely. Cherry took another breath and took a mental step back, putting an emotional barrier between herself and the scene on the porch.

Feeling calmer, but slightly detached, she opened the DVD case. Despite trying to brace herself, she jumped when the cards fluttered out. They hit the porch floor before she could catch them. Cherry studied each card carefully, trying to memorize as many details as possible.

The first depicted a woman in a long flowing robe reclining on a throne in an open field. She held a scepter and wore a crown of stars. A white box at the bottom of the card titled it *The Empress,* "YOU" had been written across the face off the card with marker in the same odd looking script.

The second card, this one titled *Justice* showed another figure in a robe who held a sword in one hand and scales in the other. "ME" had been written on the face of this card.

The third had nothing written on it, but the image of the heart skewered by three crossing swords was disturbing enough without words. Cherry didn't need any commentary to figure out what that one meant.

With shaking hands Cherry gathered the cards and put them back in the DVD case. She retreated back in the house, tripping over her towel as she went. Kicking it aside, she shut the door. Hands still trembling, she inserted the disc into her DVD player. She grabbed the remote. Standing back as if the TV might explode, she held her breathe and pressed the power button....

The video started out with a white man with thick dark curly hair, heavy eyebrows and a thick beard appeared on screen. He turned his head to the left, looking at someone off camera. Cherry recognized the man as Ted Bundy.

"Have you ever physically harmed anyone?" asked a woman's voice.

"Have I ever physically harmed anyone?" Ted repeated. The ribbed fabric of his brown turtleneck became visible as he turned his head away from the questioner. "No," he said, smiling, almost laughing. "Not in... not in the way that I think you're speaking of"

Next, a screech of white noise played over the image of a man jumping down onto a sheriff's deputy from a high tree out in the woods somewhere.

As a synthesizer riff straight out of the 80's rolled out of the speakers the scenes changed again, now depicting black and white footage of a man in a rage throwing a vase of flowers at a mirror. A blond woman ducked for cover and both the vase and mirror shattered.

The violent scenes that followed changed almost too quickly for the naked eye to see, driven along by the rapid fire drum beat.

A man with a black leather jacket and a smear of blood on his cheek pointed a gun at someone off camera to his right. A different man in evening clothes appeared out of the shadows and then quickly faded away. An arm moved across the screen, revealing a tattoo that read "my time is at hand" in a clumsy uneven text.

Grainy news footage depicted a cleaned up Ted Bundy in a light gray suit walking across a courtroom. Next clip was a man who screamed in panic as he was dragged along by the rope tied around his hands. The man in the stopped abruptly. He mouthed the words "Oh, Jesus Christ!" At what he apparently was in front of him.

A male musician voice finally began to sing about how all along he knew it wasn't right. At the same moment the scene changed to a pudgy, dull looking boy with dark hair that was a bit too long sitting at the defendant's table in a court room.

Cherry also recognized him as Damien Echols of the *West Memphis 3* from *Paradise Lost*. The scene changed again, this time to a man wearing a studded leather mask and full leather lace up bodysuit held a gun in his right hand.

While the singer lamented playing a game that wasn't fair, a businessman wearing a suit and tie and tan overcoat shot someone sitting at a reception desk. Cherry also knew that scene from *American Psycho*. Next clip was just a sinister looking blond man in a leather jacket smoking a cigarette while a police flashlight shined on him. Next, a dirty looking man with shoulder length hair held a framed painting up, while a drugged woman tried to attack him.

The singer wailed about dreaming alone and hearts of stone as Robert De Niro, dressed leaned up against a the wall, bracing himself on his arms while police searched him. In the next clip a man wearing an open leather vest and mask crawled backwards across the floor, shaking his head at the gun pointed at him. The gun fired anyway.

As the song lyrics warned listeners to move their chessmen right, two men, carried a semi-conscious man. As they half lifted, half dragged him down a hallway the video showed the carpet and odd ceiling lights of the building they were in through the man's warped view. It seemed he was on a heavy tranquilizer.

The singer now sang about hidden feelings. On screen, a detective in a white dress shirt up backhanded a man who sat in the interrogation chair. CONFESS appeared on the screen in white letters. Now the same man beaten up and tied to the chair was looking at a police officer in uniform tapping his baton against his palm menacingly while the detective in the white dress shirt shoved a Polaroid picture of a dead nun in his face.

Next, a hick looking sheriff in a wide brimmed hat smiled oddly as he pulled a two foot long piece off a roll of clear plastic wrap. Why would he be so happy to unroll saran wrap? Cherry wondered.

When the chorus of the song started the video cut back to pudgy Damien Echols in the courtroom who had just been found guilty. He looked off camera to his left with a sour expression on his face.

The singer chanted "feel the heat" over and over as the violent images continued. A teenage boy in shorts threw a black gaming console through a glass door into someone's brightly lit kitchen. He then stomped his feet and appeared to scream "fuck yooooou" at the people inside.

As the song's chorus warned that 'the time was turning' a giant humanoid shaped figure made of wicker reeds filled the screen. A ladder lead up to the open compartment in the structure's chest. At the base, four evil men with torches stood ready to burn it.

Cherry jumped back from the screen. Her legs buckled. She fell on her butt in the center of her living room floor. "Oh my God!" she cried.

On screen the man who was about to be burned inside this Wikerman also appeared to scream "oh my god."

The song's chorus continued while a man with a bloody cheek and a gun frantically yelled "take off the fucking mask" at someone off screen. Next, Al Pacino slumped in a restaurant booth holding a cigar. The mirror behind him revealed a dancing figure wearing a suit and tie along with an odd animal mask. The man who threw the vase earlier reappeared. This time he threw a bottle of red wine at the woman who ducked just before it smashed against the wall.

Electric guitars screamed out the song's instrumental bridge over the next few scenes. Once again it showed Ted Bundy in the courtroom looking lost in thought as he held his fist in front of his mouth. Next, the rampaging man now made it into the bedroom. The blond woman balled herself up on the floor while he threw the TV, knocked over the dresser and threw a framed painting.

When the singer resumed singing the screen showed a grey haired witness testifying into a microphone. He held a manila folder containing the picture of a pentagram surrounded by inverted crosses up to the camera. Now Robert De Niro peered through a pair of binoculars as the singer asked for answers. Another arm tattoo that said *VENGEANCE IS MINE* appeared in the same odd script as the one before.

As the song's lyrics expressed the frustration of trying to explain something the singer didn't understand himself, grainy news footage depicted John F. Kennedy slumped against his wife in the back of the infamous Lincoln convertible. Next, a man in a police uniform aimed a rifle from the grassy knoll. A close up of the man with one eye closed filled the screen.

The rifle fired in time with the first line of the chorus as it began again. The scene cut back to John and Jackie in the car. John's head snapped back and blood flew. Following that scene was the man in the leather suit, now without his mask, looking surprised and sad as blood dripped down from his curly black hair, staining his forehead.

The singer chanted on. A kid with long blond hair watched a red pickup truck crash into an above ground pool. The next frame showed the same blond kid pointing a gun at his father and crying. It looked like this young man was screaming "you made me this way!"

The guitars wailed again. More insane images rolled across the screen. Flames engulfed the Wicker-man from earlier as the people watching danced and sang. Then a bound woman lay on a bed, still dressed, for now. In front of her was yet another man in a leather hood and vest studying a table full of ominous looking instruments.

Another man in a suit and tie covered by a clear plastic rain suit swung and ax. Blood splashed across his face. More grainy news footage showed a sniper on the roof of the school during the Columbine shooting. The man in the trench coat pushed his way through a revolving door and shot someone else. A moment later he collapsed against the back of an elevator, sobbing as the metal doors closed.

"You feel there's something wrong with your life," sang the vocalist.

"Bang, bang, shoot 'em up!" The vocalist roared.

The man on the rampage threw a TV through a plate glass window. Shards of glass flew in all directions. The man put his hand on the window frame, digging his palm into the glass until blood spilled down.

The song's lyrics questioned the meaning of reality and dignity. On screen a photograph of a book titled *Magick in Theory and Practice by Aleister Crowley* lay in a manila folder in the courtroom. Now on the witness stand, the pudgy Damien Echols shook his head as he silently answered questions.

Electric synthesizers tore through another instrumental stretch of music. A car's headlights lit up an empty lot. *DEAD INSIDE* screamed in bright orange letters painted on a piece of plywood. The camera zoomed in on the neon letters until they filled the screen.

"Feel the heat," sang the vocalist. The hick sheriff held up his flashlight as he questioned someone driving a car. He pulled a half smoked joint out of the driver's dashboard ashtray and held it up to the driver's face. "Feel the heat," the singer sang again.

"Feel the heat. Feel the heat. Feel the heat."

Another grainy news clip showed the twin towers with smoke pouring out of them on the day of the 9/11 attacks. Street level footage captured debris raining down. Another camera tracked a plane as it flew into the second tower. It seemed a loud drumbeat from the song played just as the plane hit the second tower. Was this just luck? Or did the artist of this video plan it out meticulously? Cherry wondered.

The camera stayed focused on the buildings as they crumbled into piles of dust. More grainy, blurry footage showed a smiling Ted Bundy being led away in handcuffs.

The song faded out, leaving the last twenty seconds of the video totally silent. In a small room odd numbers and the words *I'm a psychopath* covered the floral wall paper in the background. The camera drew closer, showing that the words ran in many different directions and were written in many different styles hundreds of times in this tiny room. Who the hell would write such a thing over and over?

Mercifully, the screen finally went black. Cherry remained seated on the floor, frozen in horrified shock. What had she just watched?

She sat on the floor in silence for several minutes, trying to collect her thoughts. When she finally got to her feet her legs burned from lack of circulation. The sensation brought back more unwelcome memories. After a brief search she found her phone on her dining table. She dialed the local police department's non-emergency line.

Perhaps calling the non-emergency number had been a mistake, Cherry thought. Officer Bundy and Officer Bateman, who showed up to take her report did not seem to take her seriously. Bateman, a tall thin blond with two days worth of stubble sneered at her as she answered his questions while Bundy, a short, dark haired pudgy one kept trying to stare down her robe. She wished she'd thought to change before they'd arrived.

"So you don't have any idea who might have left this stuff?" Bateman asked with a hint of a southern drawl.

"No, I don't," Cherry replied through clenched teeth. It was the third time he had asked.

"Could it have been one of your former customers?"

"Excuse me?" asked Cherry.

"You did used to work at The Love House, didn't you?"

"Yes."

"Well, you know, places like that attract weirdos." said Bundy. "Could someone you saw there have done this?"

"I don't know, I mean, maybe. But none of them knew where I lived."

"Are you sure?"

"Relatively."

"Ma'am, we need direct answers here," Bateman said. "Did you ever bring a client home or not?"

"No, I did not," Cherry felt her temper starting to flare.

"Ever see any of them any place but the club?"

Only one, Cherry thought, but he was the last one who would have done something like this. There was no need to bring up William's name.

"No," she said.

"What about one of the other girls?" Bundy asked. "Any cat fights going on behind the scenes?" He seemed a bit excited about that idea.

"No. We all got along well."

"Are you still in that line of work?" Bateman said. "Taking clients independently?"

"I'm a martial arts and self-defense instructor."

"So you're no longer a sex worker?"

"I was never a sex worker. I was an entertainer."

"Uh-huh. Listen, if you can't give us more to go on there isn't much we can do for you. Now someone doesn't do something like this unless they are carrying a serious grudge. So if I were you, I'd be thinking real hard about anyone you might have pissed off."

"I really can't think of anyone," Cherry said. "I lead a pretty quiet life these days."

"I'd like to watch that video again," Bundy said.

Cherry stayed outside as the two officers watched it again. Occasionally, she could hear them say "whoa" or "oh shit" like a couple of teenage boys watching a horror movie. After the video was done they came back out to Cherry.

"Are you dating anyone?" asked Bundy.

"No," said Cherry.

"Who were you with last?" Bateman asked. "Are you sure you didn't end up messing around with some guy who has a jealous girlfriend?"

"I don't date men in relationships."

"Yeah, but what if you didn't know?" Bundy intervened.

"I'd know," Cherry replied sternly.

"We're going to need a list of all the sexual partners you've had in the past year anyway," Bundy said. "I need to know how many there were and what you did with them. If it was just sex, oral or even kink 'n fetish."

"Yeah," Bateman interrupted. "I mean from that video there sure were a lot of guys in leather outfits. This is somehow related to kink. What kind of kinks do you do?"

"I've only had one partner in the last few years," said Cherry.

"Does that include casual hook ups and one night stands?"

"I don't do one night stands."

"No *friends with benefits* or anything like that?"

"No," said Cherry. "I was in one relationship with one person and did not see anyone else."

"Did you end the relationship or did he?"

"He did."

"Had he given you money or gifts? Was he supporting you financially?"

"I support myself."

"Could he have any reason to believe you deceived him somehow?"

"No!"

"Did he know what you used to do?" Bundy asked.

"Yes, he knew," Cherry snapped.

"You didn't answer me ma'am, what kinks did you and this guy do?" Bateman said, looking keyed up to hear the answer.

"None!" Cherry barked.

"Does he know your criminal record?" Bundy asked, remembering arresting her almost a decade ago.

"Yes, he knew I was arrested."

"Why did he end the relationship?"

Cherry huffed out a breath and shrugged. "He didn't really give me a reason. He just said he needed to move on."

"Was he satisfied with your sex life?" Bundy asked.

"Maybe he wanted to do kinks and you didn't and he's mad," Bateman added.

"What does that have to do with anything?"

"Just being thorough, ma'am," Bateman said.

"Yes, "Bundy added. "A man enters a relationship expecting certain things, and if you didn't meet those expectations, he could become frustrated and angry."

"Well, I did burn the gravy once," said Cherry. "Do you think he could be mad about having to eat dry pork chops?"

"Ma'am," Bundy pouted. "If you aren't going to take this seriously--"

"I *am* taking it seriously. *I* called *you!* I'm terrified that some whack job out there knows where I live and might want to harm me."

"Why did you watch the DVD if you were scared?" Bundy asked.

"I don't know." Cherry shook her head. "I thought it might tell me who did this, or why, or that it might turn out to be a joke."

"So you're saying you think this was just a joke?" asked Bateman.

"No, I am not saying that," said Cherry. "After watching that DVD I am certain it was made to terrify and intimidate me."

"But why? Who would take the time and trouble to make something like that?"

"If I knew, I'd tell you."

"How well do you know your neighbors?" Batman continued.

"Not very well," said Cherry. "I haven't been home much until recently."

"Anyone seem odd?"

"Not that I noticed."

"Are you careful about closing your curtains when you change clothes? Making sure you're fully dressed when you go outside? Do you sunbathe in the yard or anything like that?"

"I sit outside and read in the yard. And yes, I catch some rays for vitamin D." said Cherry.

"What do you wear when you have sunbathed?" Bundy wondered.

"Like maybe shorts."

"What color shorts?" Bundy asked in a soft creeper tone.

"What difference does it make, huh?" Cherry snapped.

"Ma'am," Bundy said. "If we're gonna have any chance of nailing this creep you gotta tell me everything. And I mean every God damn detail. Was it red shorts?"

Cherry glared at him with the supreme meanest expression she could.

Officer Bateman shuffled through the tarot cards she'd handed him with his bare hands.

"Why did you pick these up?" he asked.

"Just reflex," said Cherry.

"You realize that by doing that you corrupted any evidence that might be on them, right?" He held up the cards. Cherry noticed the pad of his thumb pressed into the center of the card with the heart and swords. "Totally destroyed any fingerprints that might have been on them other than yours. You may have wrecked the one and only clue we had."

"Wouldn't there be fingerprints on the other things?"

"Not likely. Hard to dust pooled wax and shards of glass."

"I just wasn't thinking," said Cherry. "I was still in shock."

"But you had the presence of mind to operate your DVD player?"

She wanted to tell this jackass he'd be surprised just what a person in shock could have the presence of mind to do, but it was best not to go there.

"What are we supposed to think if we get all this down to the lab and the only fingerprints we find on it are yours?" Bateman continued.

"That whoever did it wore gloves?" Cherry guessed.

"Oh, right, gloves." The cop rolled his eyes.

Baffled by his reaction, Cherry turned to Bundy.

"See if they only fingerprints on anything are yours some people might think you did this yourself," Bateman continued.

"What? Why would I do that?"

"People have, for the attention. Maybe you wanted to get your boyfriend back and thought he'd come protect you if he thought you were in danger."

"I don't need protecting and he knows it."

"What was his name, anyway?" asked Bundy.

"Whose name?" Cherry asked.

"Your boyfriend. What was his name?" Bundy asked still irritated he didn't know the color of her shorts.

Cherry hesitated. She bit her lip, looking from one of them to the other. She didn't want to tell them, but she supposed she had no choice at this point.

"William Defreno," she said quietly.

"William Defreno?" Bundy laughed. "William Defreno? The guy who owns Moe's Diner? The one running for city council?"

"Yes, that William Defreno."

"You used to date William Defreno?" asked Bateman. Cherry could see the disbelief in his eyes. "Can anyone confirm that?"

"Mitch, Riley, anyone on the kitchen staff."

"Oh well, we'll just call Mr. Riley right now and ask him, huh?"

"I would prefer you didn't. I'd like to leave William out of this."

"I bet you would. Hey, did he ever take you to his townhouse?"

"William doesn't have a townhouse. He lives behind the diner."

"Yeah? Well, I'm pretty sure it's his townhouse he parks that Rolls Royce in front of. We see it every night on patrol."

"Rolls Royce?" Cherry felt like she was floating above herself. "William drives an Impala."

"Oh right, an *Impala*, silly me. The Rolls must belong to his cat."

"Cat?"

"I thought you said you didn't date married guys?" said Bundy.

"William's not married."

"Guess the pretty lady he introduced as his wife at the policeman's ball the other night was a figure of my imagination then," Bundy laughed.

"Are you sure the guy you were seeing didn't just tell you he was William Defreno?" Bateman said. "We been getting that lately. The other night we pulled over a drunk woman who said William was her sister and if we arrested her he would make sure we were unemployed."

"No, it was really him," said Cherry, thinking she wished Bundy and Bateman were unemployed.

"When did you break up?"

"Maybe a month ago."

"So," Bundy said. "In just a month he went from you to somehow being happily married and living together with this new girl."

"Lady, listen," Bateman added. "I have known William since we

157

were in high school. We were on the baseball team together. I can tell you he has been married to Becky for at least four years now, ok?"

"William ran track. He was not married to anyone while dating me I have no idea where the little wife of his came from all of a sudden."

Bundy shook his head and wrote up the report. After a few minutes he handed Cherry the report "I think we're done here. Have a nice day, ma'am."

They didn't even bother to close the door behind them when they left. She looked at the report and shook her head at how small and un-detailed it was considering the amount of time they were here.

"Investigation revealed that unknown suspect(s) left a DVD and a tarot card on the victim's driveway. The DVD case had the victim's name written on it. At the end of the video showed a wall with "I'm a psychopath" written all over it. The suspect(s) left in an unknown direction by unknown means"

Cherry sat down on the end of her couch and curled up in a little ball, suddenly unsure of what, if anything, was real anymore.

Chapter 10

It's Just a Fantasy

William woke up in the late afternoon. He checked his phone and saw a text message from Buddy.

"I'm calling the feds.....lol"

William gasped that Buddy somehow knew what he did last night and has now turned on him. Before he stressed out too much he realized Buddy was responding to the drunk text William had sent him before bed last night.

"Hey Buddy, thanks for the day pass to John F Kennedy Golf Course last week. I sure noticed a lot of grassy knolls on that golf course........"

William met Buddy for lunch at a casual barbecue chain restaurant with murals of giant pink pigs in chef's hats and bibs on the yellow walls. The porcine cooks looked down on the diners, seeming to relish the sight of their fellow porkers being consumed.

Buddy studied William's split lip, black eye and bruises. He let out a low whistle.

"Yo! Adrian!" Buddy said.

"Ha ha."

"What happened to you?" he asked William.

"Slipped on a banana peel taking out the trash."

"Ouch, man. Looks brutal. Donna's going to have hell of a time covering that up."

"I could always just tell people I got mugged."

"No bueno. City Councilman William Defreno is nobody's victim."

"I guess. I feel kinda stupid, though, telling people I fell on my face."

"Don't tell anybody anything. Just make a joke if someone asks or say it's classified."

"Fair enough," said William. "Geez, what does it take to get a waitress in this place?"

William twisted around in his seat, scanning the room. Finally, he spotted a waitress. He snapped his fingers until she looked up. He crooked a finger at her. After giving him a dirty look, she came over to their table.

"Hey guys, how we doing this afternoon?" she asked through gritted teeth that she tried to make look like a smile. Even though William could tell she was faking her friendly attitude he just didn't care as much as he once would have.

"Oh, you know, not bad," he answered. "Can we get two iced teas, please?"

"Sure thing." The waitress jotted down their drink order. "That eye looks awful, honey. What'd you do to it?"

"I think it's a bruise," said William.

"A big one, from the looks of it," she said. "How'd it happen?"

"I lost a fight with a rubber tree."

"Say what now?"

"A rubber tree. I didn't like the attitude it was giving me so I slapped it, and it slapped me back."

The waitress giggled. "Oh, come on, now, what really happened?"

"That is what really happened. Want me to make you a DVD of it?"

"Are you for real?"

"He's real as taxes, doll," Buddy chimed in. "Now how about that tea, huh? I'm dying here."

"Coming right up."

"And wash off some of that perfume, you're giving me a headache."

She walked away without acknowledging that comment.

Over lunch Buddy laid out their hectic schedule for the remaining few weeks of the campaign. William tried his best to pay attention, but his mind kept wandering. He wondered what Cherry was doing. Had she found the stuff? Did she watch the DVD? What did she think? Did she suspect he was the one behind it?

Towards the end of their meal the waitress came back to clear the table.

"Were you fellas wanting dessert today?" she asked.

"Sure, I'd love some DVD, er I mean dessert," said William

Both Buddy and the waitress gave him an odd look.

"We have apple cobbler or rhubarb pie," said the waitress.

"I'll have the cherry cobbler," said William.

"Sorry, honey, cherry's not available anymore. It's apple cobbler."

"I'll have the cherry pie then,"

"Honey, I keep telling you, cherry's gone. It's rhubarb pie or apple cobbler."

"Two slices of rhubarb pie," said Buddy.

The waitress went to get their pie. Buddy leaned in close to William, looking deeply concerned.

"How hard did you hit your head last night?" he asked.

"Not that bad, actually," said William. "Why?"

"Cause you're out of it, man. What was that with the pie?"

"My mind was just on something else."

"Yeah, I could tell." Buddy sipped his tea. "You, uh, took care of your little problem, right?"

"Sure did."

"What'd you do?"

William shook his head. "Sorry, Buddy, that's classified."

"Oh, ho, ho," Buddy chuckled. "You really are a man in his power today, aren't you?"

"Sure am, a real *man in his power* today," William said half sarcastically.

"I live to serve," Buddy made a mock bow across the table.

The waitress brought their pie.

"Careful now, honey, it's steaming hot."

"How do you know? Did you take a bite out of mine?" asked

Buddy.

"Oh heavens no. I can feel the heat coming off it from here."

William's stomach sank at the phrase, *feel the heat.* Was Cherry *feeling the heat*?

Still home in her little cottage, Cherry sat alone in the dark, too afraid to open her door or curtains to let in the warmth of the sun. Her whole body shivered both from the cold of wearing her still damp robe and the fear from earlier events. She knew she should get up, she *had* to get up, but she couldn't make herself move.

Out on the road a car backfired, causing her to flinch. The jerky movement actually physically hurt, which made Cherry realize just how tense her body had become. From somewhere deep inside herself a voice called to her to snap out of it, reminding her she was stronger than this. Just get up. Just get up. GET UP!!!

She took a deep breath and planted both feet on the floor. Yes, she could do this. Gathering all her strength, she pushed herself up off the couch onto her wobbly legs. She took one step and then another.

"That's it," she told herself. "One at a time. You can do this." As she walked the memories flowed in, taking her back to the weeks in the hospital so many years ago. The warm, gentle voices of her nurses and physical therapists as they coaxed her to learn to use her damaged body again. Her muscles had gotten stronger, her scars had healed, and step by painful step she had come back to herself.

She had been good for a long time. Other than her dramatic arrest, the one time she let the rage take her over, she had done well. She'd put the past behind her, closed off the memories and moved on, making a life for herself. She had learned to trust, learned to love, and even after losing that love, she had still been ok. She wasn't going to let herself lose it now.

First, she turned up the thermostat. Next she found a dry towel and took it in her bedroom. She shed her wet robe and blotted herself with the towel, removing the last of the dampness from her skin. She pulled on underwear, sweatpants and a thick warm sweater she'd bought at a ski resort years ago. She put on a pair of thick fuzzy socks with rubber treads on the bottom.

Back in the bathroom, she blow dried her still damp hair, deciding the resulting frizz would be worth it this time. On a whim, she paused long enough to put on a bit of tinted lip gloss and eyeliner. "War paint," she called it, a commitment to herself that she would keep fighting and not give up.

She blew her unknown enemy a kiss in the mirror. "Hit me with your best shot," she sang to herself. So someone out there wanted to hurt her? That was ok. She didn't want to have to hurt them back, but she would protect herself, and if they tried to harm her she would do what was necessary.

One last thing. Cherry removed a lockbox from a secret compartment in her built in bookcase. In it was a black 9mm handgun, her shoulder holster, two clips of ammunition and a small pouch containing her old meds. Carefully she loaded the gun and strapped it on. The BuSpar, Xanax and Celexa would wait for now, but she took them out of the case and put them in her bedside table, along with the second clip of ammunition.

Whatever came next, she was ready.

After a week or so, William's injuries finally healed up. He filled the time making speeches and having lunches with community organizations that all seemed to have the "perfect plan" for the city's bright new future. As hard as he tried, he couldn't make himself get excited about variegated chrysanthemums and composite fiber utility poles.

Being constantly surrounded by people and stuck on a schedule the complete opposite of what he was used to left him constantly tired. At first the excitement of the campaign had carried him through but over the months the repetitiveness of his routine had started to wear him down even more.

One particular afternoon, after three interviews, two speeches, another long boring luncheon, two monotonous campaign briefings and a particularly awkward photo op with a group of kindergartners at the local petting zoo, he was just done.

Yawning and rubbing his burning eyes, William got into the Rolls Royce and headed home. Driving on autopilot, he headed for the diner instead of Beth's house. It wasn't until he came face to face with the poster of Tony Montoya on the wall that he realized he was back at his old home and not Beth's house. He looked around the dingy little one room bungalow and, noticing the dust collecting in the corners, he sighed.

Deciding he was too tired to care, he sat down on the bed and pulled off his polished black loafers. He groaned with relief. He stripped off his black socks and stuffed them into the shoes. He removed his sport coat and tie and hung them on the door. After rummaging around a bit, he found a ratty old t-shirt and a stained pair of jogging pants that seemed reasonably clean. He changed quickly and went back to the bed for a nap. A few minutes later he was sound asleep.

Just after dusk, Cherry left the dojo where she taught martial arts and self-defense. She paused in the doorway, carefully scanning the parking lot before heading to her car. Still with her guard up, she stalked across the asphalt, every nerve and muscle pulled tight and ready to react to sudden attack.

She heard the crunch of gravel behind her. Out of the corner of her eye she noticed a person walking around the outside of building and stopping for no reason to snap pictures. She walked toward her car. He seemed to be following her. She whirled around and sprayed mace at the dark clothed male figure that had come up behind her.

He gagged and spit before dropping the camera and screamed.

"Cherry?" a woman's voice called behind her. She turned to see her boss, a tall, slender, light skinned African American woman wearing teal spandex, a few feet away.

"Evelyn..." Cherry began.

"Well, this is certainly great advertising, but I think Fire Marshall Paul is going to need some soap and water."

"Fire Marshall?!" Cherry did a double take. Sure enough, there was his shiny badge splayed out on the blacktop. "Oh no!"

"What the hell is this?" Paul coughed.

Cherry cringed. She backed away from the prone figure and put her mace away. "Guess I kind of overreacted."

Evelyn took Cherry aside as Paul went inside to use the bathroom.

"Look honey, I understand if a man you don't recognize

approaches you in the dark, nothing you do, short of maybe shooting the bastard, is an overreaction. Except when it's the Fire Marshall."

Something about this gave Cherry and odd sense of déjà vu. Her head began to hurt. The florescent lights in the building seemed to warp and wobble. She suddenly felt sick. They had barely gotten Paul to open his eyes in the first aid room before she had to run off to the bathroom.

"Hey Paul," Cherry said shyly from the doorway. "Sorry about that."

Paul just moaned in response. Cherry cringed and ducked back out into the hallway.

Fifteen minutes later Evelyn followed her out.

"Are you alright?" she asked Cherry.

"Yeah, just a little queasy," Cherry said.

Evelyn gave her an appraising look.

"You've been through a lot lately," Evelyn said.

"Yeah, I guess, I mean kind of," said Cherry. "I have been a little edgy."

"I've noticed. Is there anything you need to talk about? Like, oh I don't know. Maybe why you did that!"

"No." Cherry shook her head. "I think I'm just worn out."

"Do you also know that our self-closing devices on the fire doors don't work well? Paul usually lets it go cause it's not that big of a deal. But, thanks to you, they have to be repaired and I got a $100 fine."

"Oh no, I'm so sorry," Cherry replied.

"Yeah, well, be glad he's not having you arrested, my dear."

"I really didn't mean it. I just been edgy 'cause of something at home."

"Well, it'll be quiet around here for a while with the holidays coming up soon. It would be a good time for a vacation."

"Oh no, I can't do that," Cherry said, feeling panicky.

"Cherry, listen," Evenlyn put a hand on her shoulder. Cherry flinched. They both pretended not to notice. "You are a highly valued member of our staff. You've turned this place around and contributed more to our success than I can tell you. You've worked hard, and I can't even begin to tell you how much I appreciate everything you've done for us. But it is ok to need a rest. Life gets to all of us sometimes. So go ahead and take some time. Come back refreshed and better than ever."

"But--"

"No buts. Girl, I'm not asking! You more than deserve a break and you've certainly earned it. It's just two weeks, we'll be here when you come back."

Another load moan from Paul made Cherry cringe again. Maybe Evelyn was right. She couldn't go on like this.

"Ok," said Cherry. She hung her head, feeling defeated.

"Even the mightiest warrior rests," said Evelyn. "It's not a failure. It's just necessary sometimes."

She hugged Cherry tightly. Cherry hugged her back. She felt the tension start to melt away from her muscles.

"See you in two weeks," said Cherry.

"See you in two weeks." Evelyn waved. Cherry turned away and left the building.

William woke sometime after the diner closed. He cringed a bit, realizing he had missed yet another important meeting and dinner with Beth. He lied in a text explaining he was being interviewed at the diner by the high school newspaper staff. Truthfully, he regretted missing dinner more than the meeting. His stomach rumbled. He grabbed his keys. Rather than try to go get something he decided he'd just raid the diner's refrigerator.

He frowned at the state of the diner's kitchen. Fingerprints covered the stainless steel fridge and freezer doors. A thick layer of old grease coated the tops of the fryers and the wall behind. He would have to have a talk with Riley about stepping up the kitchen staff's cleaning. Lord knows he paid them enough to keep the place sparkling.

In the walk-in cooler he found several pans of covered leftovers stacked haphazardly on the shelves. Dry looking mashed potatoes half-filled one. Wrinkled, overcooked whole Italian sausages swam in thick greasy marinara sauce in another. Two more overflowed with rock hard biscuits. Why were they saving this stuff?

William was definitely going to have to have that talk with Riley, but for now he was somewhat glad the stuff was here. Grabbing a plate he went about filling it up, choosing the most appetizing bits from the buffet of leftovers. He threw the plate in the microwave and waited for it to heat up. He frowned again when he noticed the stains and scorch marks on the hot glove he used to pull his plate from the microwave. He put it on his mental list of complaints and grabbed his food.

Rather than take it back to his bungalow, he decided he'd eat at the bar. After all what was a midnight snack without something to wash it down with? He popped a can of Coors and settled down on a bar stool. Despite being hungry, he found it hard to concentrate on his meal. All around him echoes of the past seemed to leech out of the walls and play out before his eyes.

He recalled his days working in the diner as an awkward kid as young as fourteen. The multiple times he'd gotten fired, only to get rehired when his old boss, Lois, was desperate. The day he'd finally bought the place. The day that Roger kid had been arrested in the middle of the lunch rush. The night they gave Roger a job. The good bye dinner they'd had the night before Roger had left for college. The day Cherry walked in after he'd spent months thinking he'd never see her again. All the bull sessions at the bar with Mitch and Riley.

It seemed that wherever he went in life, it all came back to this place. This humble little greasy spoon had made him a millionaire and it might be about to put him in office. Yet he still missed the "good old days" when all he had to worry about was getting through his next shift and making enough in tips to put gas in the car.

Briefly, he wondered what member of the Choir was responsible for getting stuck in nostalgia. Buddy had never talked about that. He would have to ask him about it one of these days.

Deciding just beer wasn't going to be enough, William pulled a bottle of whiskey off the shelf and poured a glass. He noticed several of their liquors were out of stock behind the bar. Rolling his eyes, he wondered what other problems he was going to find tonight.

He grabbed his drink and began to pace. The more he looked, the more flaws he spotted. Stains in the carpet, scratches in the tables, dust building up on the windowsills, lights burnt out in the fountain. He shook his head in disgust. He had thought he could trust his best friend to run his diner, but obviously not. Did he have to be here fourteen hours a day seven days a week to keep this place running? Wasn't he ever going to have a life?

In the back of his head he heard Cherry's soothing voice telling him not to worry. He knew she'd tell him there was nothing wrong with working a humble job until he retired.

"Sure, Cherry," said William. "I don't need to be rich, or famous, or powerful. I can just slave away at the diner all my life."

He poured another drink and took a long gulp. "Heck, you didn't mind if I was nothing. You liked it that way, because as long as I hung my head low and was covered in grease I was always your puppy dog. You never had to worry about me being snatched away. But you sure always wanted me to worry who could have you."

Deep down, he knew Cherry hadn't really been bad to him, though. She had, in her way, been loving and caring and had never insulted him. Beth might be the perfect politician's wife, but William felt that maybe he'd needed the firmer maternal guidance Cherry had provided in order to keep him from self-destructing.

Or maybe that was just the Choir talking. After a few more drinks he had drowned them out.

"I know you thought I should just be a simple man, Cherry, but I can't," William said to nobody. "I need this. I can't be a nobody forever. I can't be trapped in this diner for the rest of my life. See, so I had to cut the cord. I had to get away from you. You were keeping me down."

He stopped and stared out the window. He had a perfect view of the gas station across the street and the bench dedicated to Annie, his late first girlfriend. He felt that old pang of regret. He hoped that once he got elected he could turn the old gas station into a proper memorial so she would get the honor she deserved instead of being just a long forgotten name among the rest of the collateral damage from his past wars against the town's corruption. He shook his head sadly.

"I don't know what made you ever think anything of me, Cherry. No one else in my life ever has. Heck, I probably did you a favor. Even as the city's newest millionaire and maybe councilman, I still suck. If I could only tell you how fucked up it really is, then maybe you'd understand."

But he couldn't tell her. He didn't think the words existed and she would not agree. Maybe, though, just maybe, he could show her.

William went back to the office and fired up the video editing software. He picked through his movie collection for the most brutal, graphically violent footage he could find. Fiery explosions, men jumping from buildings, chainsaws roaring, blood spattering; the more revolting the images the better.

He added news footage of people holding signs outside of Ted Bundy's execution and the assassination attempt on Ronald Reagan. He put in men loading rifles and a white hearse driving by. There were car windows being smashed and an angry father destroying his son's room with a baseball bat. William set his Ode to Chaos to Pink Floyd's *Run Like Hell*. The final result gave even him goosebumps.

Although he still wasn't sure he would actually use it, he burned the video to a DVD anyway. He carefully set it in its protective case. He rifled through the remnants of the tarot deck and pulled out three cards with violent, frightening images on them.

William gathered the disc, the cards, a full glass of whiskey, a fresh pack of cigarettes and his keys and headed out into the night. He drove back to the same run down discount store, remembering to park further away this time and bought a few more supplies.

On his way to Cherry's house, the song *Fantasy* by Aldo Nova came on the radio. William sang along with the high energy lyrics.

"Can't you see what this crazy life is doing to me? Life is just a fantasy. Can you live this fantasy life? So forget all that you see, it's not reality, it's just a fantasy."

William wished it really was just a fantasy. He recalled the night he had first met Cherry at The Love House and how he had spent the whole time talking about how much he was reminiscing the past. And now here he was reminiscing about reminiscing. He laughed at the thought. Maybe people were right when they said he didn't cherish the moments he was actually living in.

"I did cherish them," William said to himself, "but the clock ticked anyway. The time passed, and the good times ended whether I wanted them to or not."

On the radio, Glen Frey's *Part of You, Part of Me* began. A mix of alcohol, his guilty conscience and Glen's soulful voice made him break down like never before.

"Whatever time may take away, it cannot change the way we feel today," Glen sang plaintively.

William wondered if that was true for him. Would the good memories he had never fade away regardless of what he did tonight? Would they be locked safely in his heart regardless of any fallout from his actions?

He parked down the block from Cherry's cottage and tried to collect himself. First thing he noticed was the glass of whiskey was empty and that he smelled like a distillery. He had realized after the fact that last time he had left DNA evidence behind in his blood. This time he would leave the DNA of his tears. He took one more deep breath and proceeded to do what he had come to do.

Cherry slept restlessly. Terrifying nightmares haunted her sleep. In one in particular scene she heard a noise outside and went to investigate. She found a man wearing a black studded leather suit like the one in that hellish video standing on her porch. A black leather mask covered the upper half of his face. He held a black candle in one hand and that damn card with the heart and swords in the other.

Cherry calmly told him to "take off his mask" but he refused. Suddenly her gun was in her hands. She pointed it at the man and screeched, "Take off the fucking mask!" Again he refused. Angry, Cherry reached out and snatched the mask off herself. Underneath there was a gaping black hole where the man's face should have been.

She woke up screaming. Sweat drenched her hair and skin. She fought her way out of the tangled sheets and got to her feet. She kept telling herself that it was just a dream, but her hands shook anyway as she dressed. She took up her meditating position and did her breathing exercises. Afterward she felt calmer but the feelings of dread and terror would not leave her.

"Normal," she said to herself. "Normal is good."

She went to the kitchen and started coffee. It had been over a week since the incident and nothing else had happened. The threat had likely passed. She actually smiled as she went she went to the front door to let in some light and air.

Instantly, she froze in her tracks when she spotted the flickering black candle on her porch.

"Noooo," she moaned as she sank to her knees. "Noooooo. No, no, no."

Hot tears ran down her cheeks. Who was doing this? Why?

Steeling herself with a few deep breaths, Cherry got back to her feet. After carefully strapping on her gun, she opened the screen and stepped out onto the porch. The scene looked the same as before. Black candle burnt most of the way down, the DVD case with her name on the front in the odd eccentric script and three tarot cards fanned out between the DVD and the candle.

The first card showed a woman sitting up in bed with her hands covering her face. The second showed a man lying face down in a pool of blood. Multiple swords stuck up out of his back. The third depicted people falling from a tall stone tower that was breaking apart after being hit by lightning. No chess piece this time though. Just a folded note. Carefully Cherry used just her fingernail to open it. It had the word *VENGENCE* written across it in wobbly red letters.

"Wha-what the Fuck!!! Cherry blurted as she saw it was signed: *From Master Crowley.*

She leaned over and blew out the candle before it could shatter the glass. Leaving everything else just as it was she went inside and called the police again.

Unfortunately for Cherry, the same two officers showed up to take her report.

"Hey, how's it going? I guess your secret admirer came to visit you again," Officer Bateman said.

Cherry just glared at him. He quickly looked down at his shoes.

"You still dating Brad Pitt?" Officer Bundy asked. He didn't even bother to look at her.

"I never said I was dating Brad Pitt," said Cherry.

"Oh, sorry. Who was it then? Richard Branson?"

"William Defreno. I used to date William Defreno."

"Right. Who isn't married and doesn't drive a Rolls Royce."

"He didn't drive one when he was dating me."

"Hey, Chevy Impalas are cool cars," said Bateman. "There's a song about 'em and everything. You ever heard it?"

"Um, no," said Cherry. She had the feeling this was a mistake.

Bundy picked up the DVD case with ungloved hands.

"Did you watch this?" he asked.

"Uh, no. I didn't touch anything except the note. I left the rest of it just how I found it."

He popped the DVD out of its case, leaving a big greasy thumbprint on the front.

"Well, let's have a look-see shall we?" Bundy said. They all went into Cherry's living room and put the disc in her DVD player. "Come on, fire it up."

"I'd rather not," said Cherry.

"Ma'am, I need your full cooperation here."

Cherry turned on her TV with her remote and pressed play to start the DVD.

The video started out with Charles Manson saying to the court, "I feel good feelings toward everything. I feel no bad and I know no bad." Cherry knew this video was going to be bad news. Sure enough she was right. Many senseless violent clips played along to Pink Floyd.

"Whoa," Bateman said. "This is even cooler than the last one."

"Love me some Pink Floyd," added Bundy.

They all watched the music video more. Cherry just stood is shock at the terrible images being played out before her eyes.

"Hey is that JFK in Dallas again? What's this dude's obsession with JFK?" Bateman said.

"Damn. This guy is good." Bundy said as he bopped his head to the rhythm of the song and tapped his foot as they watched the rest of the video.

"How do you know it's a *male* who made this?" Cherry asked, hoping their years of school, training and cop instincts were seeing something the spoke to the gender of this film maker that she wasn't seeing.

"A female wouldn't be this creative," Bundy replied.

When the screen went black, they turned back to Cherry.

"And you still have no idea who's doing this?" Bateman said.

"No," said Cherry. "I can't think of anyone."

"Been sunbathing lately in the red shorts?" Bundy asked.

"No," Cherry said through gritted teeth.

Bateman popped the DVD out of the DVD player, leaving more big fingerprints on the back.

"Aren't you worried about damaging evidence?" Cherry asked him. She still remembered the humiliating lecture he had given her last time.

"Nah. A guy this meticulous would have worn gloves. There won't be prints to find."

"I see," Cherry said tartly.

"Seems like whoever you fucked with, you fucked with the best," Bundy said remembering her statement in her police report in 2009.

"Just keep your door locked," Bateman said. "And if you see anything suspicious call 911 right away."

"Yeah, usually guys who do this don't actually harm anyone," Bundy added.

"Thank you for the suggestions, officers," Cherry said as she shook her head. "I guess if next time you come over and I'm dead and *Helter Skelter* is written on all the walls in blood over and over, you guys can be like *oops, my bad, we should've listened to her* or something."

"Oh God, lady," Bateman said. "It's probably some little gothy thirteen year old."

"It seems too sophisticated for some teenager," Cherry replied.

"I agree," Bundy added. "Whoever did this is has resources and is sophisticated like a thirty-some year old."

"But as mature as a thirteen year old?" Cherry added.

"Bingo!" Bateman said. "We'll do extra patrol in this area and if we see any thirty year olds, who have the maturity level of a thirteen year old, we'll nail 'em, ok?" Bateman said as he handed her the freshly written report.

"Comp. related that during the listed dates and times, unknown suspect(s) left the following on her driveway: a candle and tarot cards along with a note with "Cherry" on the outside and on the inside was written "vengeance" in red paint. This is the second time tarot cards have been left along with other items on the driveway. The suspect(s) left in an unknown direction by unknown means."

Cherry fought down the urge to be sick. Waves of panic washed over her, causing her body to shake uncontrollably. Shadows swooped in, clouding her vision. Her head spun. She fought to force a breath into her tightening chest.

Feeling like the floor might collapse under her at any moment, Cherry scampered into her bedroom. She opened one of the medicine bottles in her nightstand and swallowed a tablet from it. She curled up on her bed and waited for the attack to pass. When it finally passed, she went back to sleep.

At least this time there were no nightmares.

William sat in his office at his campaign headquarters, watching cat videos on his computer and trying to look like he was busy with something important. Buddy walked in, grinning from ear to ear.

"Guess what I've got!" he said, smacking a bundle of papers against the palm of his hand.

"Something that isn't contagious, I hope," said William.

"Funny, pal, real funny." Buddy tapped the papers against his hand again. "What I have is our latest poll numbers."

"And?" said William.

"You're ahead twelve points. Twelve! Can you believe it? You got this thing in the bag!"

"Well alright, then," said William. "Nice work, Buddy."

"Glad to be of service." Buddy made one of his quaint little bows. "Hey let's celebrate. Go get Beth and we'll have a nice dinner somewhere, ok?"

"Sounds like a plan."

On their way out the door a pretty blonde lady in a sleek red dress stopped them.

"Mr. Defreno?" she said, extending her hand. "Hi, I'm Rachel Grey from *Small Business Weekly*, I was wondering if you had a few minutes for a quick interview?"

"Um," said William.

"Sorry, doll, no interviews today," said Buddy. "We're on our way to a very important dinner. But there's room for one more if you know of a lovely lady whose free this evening." Buddy flashed her bright smile.

"I think I might," said Rachel. "But only if I can bring my husband."

"Maybe some other time," said Buddy.

He shook his head. Once they were outside he vented at William.

"I don't know what's wrong with women these days," he said. "Used to be a woman like that would be smart enough to take advantage of any opportunity a man gave her to advance her career."

"Maybe she loves him," said William.

"She can love him all she wants. It's not like I was gonna make her sleep with me. Just accompany me for dinner," said Buddy. "Whatever, Come on. Let's eat."

Later that night Cherry heard a noise coming from the back of her house. She debated calling the police. The fear that *dumb and dumber* may also work night shift made her decide not to. She would handle whatever it was herself.

Opting for her sawed off shotgun rather than her 9mm, Cherry quietly slipped out her front door, gun in one hand, long heavy aluminum flashlight in the other. She circled the house, keeping close to the wall to be sure no one could sneak up behind her.

The sound seemed to be coming from a basement window well at the back of the house. Taking a deep breath she aimed her light at the window.

"Whoever's down there, come out now!" she ordered.

There was no response, but the odd noises continued.

"I said come out. Now!"

She waited a few more seconds but there was still no response.

"I'm warning you, I'm armed and I will use force if necessary. Now come out of there!"

She waited again. This time when she got no response she approached the window well, gun aimed and ready.

"Alright, hands up!"

Two beady little black eyes stared up at her. She recognized the fluffy black and white animal in the window well a moment too late. She yelped and jumped back just as the skunk sprayed her. Cherry screamed and then began to gag. The skunk jumped out of the window well and ran off into the night.

Leaving the gun and flashlight where they were, she headed for the sliding glass door that lead into her living room. The horrible stench followed her, clinging to her skin and hair. She would just stink up the place even worse if she stayed inside. She grabbed a can of tomato paste and a can opener and went to her garage. She wished she had actual tomato juice but she wasn't getting in her car or going out in public smelling like this.

In the garage, she took her clothes off and threw them in a garbage can with a lid. Standing naked in the center of the concrete floor, she began rubbing the tomato paste into her skin and hair. In her head she kept hearing the mocking voice of Officer Bundy asking her about what she wore outside and if her neighbors ever saw her undressed. She wondered what the big creep would think about this particular incident.

Luckily, she got back to the house and inside without being seen. Despite the frigid temperature, she opened all the doors and windows and huddled under a blanket while she let the house air out. As she shivered on the couch, she imagined just what she was going to do to this *Master Crowley* if she ever caught him. She thought locking him in a room with a rabid skunk might be a good start.

Chapter 11

In the Jealous Games
People Play

That night William's dreams ran deep. He forded rivers and swam oceans. He climbed over mountains and walk through ancient forests. Near the edge of the tree line he heard the sounds of joyful humming and laughter that rang like wind chimes. He let the happy sounds coax him out into the wide green meadow spread out before him.

A few yards away he saw a young blond girl in a white dress dancing to a song she was singing to herself. A warm orange glow flickered around her as she moved. Her skin shone like polished metal in the sunlight.

William moved closer, carefully circling around until he approached her from the front. When he was within a few feet she finally turned to look at him. He gasped in surprise. The girl had Cherry's face, not the face she would have had as a child, the face she wore now as an adult. She smiled at him.

Up close, he could see that the orange light actually came from beneath her hard, translucent skin. Glass, not metal like he first thought. She was made of glass that was lit from within like a lantern. She blew him a kiss.

Suddenly, William held a sledgehammer. He tried to stop, but his arms moved on their own. The hammer swung towards the girl's head. She screamed. William turned his head to protect his face from the flying shards of glass.

The phone rang, jarring William just enough to snap him out of the dream. He answered it automatically.

"Hello?"

"I know all about," a voice said.

"Yeah you know about what?"

"About that girl," a woman's voice whispered on the other end of the line.

For a moment William wondered how this woman knew about his dream.

"What?"

"We know about the girl," the woman's voice repeated.

"What girl?" William was awake enough now to start getting annoyed and worried.

"The girl at the diner. Maisy. The waitress. We know what you did to her. Drop out of the race or we'll go to the press."

That did it. William had had enough of crazy phone lady.

"Look, lady, I don't know any waitress named Maisy, and I don't have any idea what you're talking about. Now buzz off!"

William snapped his phones case shut.

"Who was that," Beth asked sleepily.

"It was nothing; go back to sleep." Beth snuggled back into the covers.

William, however, found himself unable to take his own advice. He got up, dressed quietly, grabbed his keys and headed out to the Rolls Royce.

For hours he drove around the city aimlessly, choosing right or left turns based on the flip of a coin. As he drove, he thought about recent events in his life and reminisced about his past. How did he ever get in this mess? All he'd ever wanted was a little respect for a change.

William watched the sun come up over the river, still feeling moody and wondering who the crazy lady on the phone had been. Who the hell was Maisy? What was Cherry doing now? Could this thing with Beth work out after all?

He had everything now, so why didn't he finally feel happy?

Pulling a six pack out of the trunk, he popped the top of a beer and took a swig. He made a face at the taste, but drank the rest anyway. There in the early morning quiet he finished the beer.

Sometime later he realized he was hungry, so he headed to the only place that ever seemed to bring him peace of mind.

William stumbled into Moe's Diner and sat down at the bar. The place was slamming busy for lunch. A young waitress with short black hair cut in a bob style hurried over. William didn't recognize her.

"Excuse me, sir," she said. "Do you have a reservation?"

"Do I look like a freakin' Indian to you?" William replied and then laughed at his own joke. He lit up a cigarette.

"Sir, smoking isn't--"

"Tell the cock to get me some scrambled eggs with a double side of bacon. Wheat toast."

"We don't serve breakfast, sir."

William gave her a cold stare. "You do today. Now can you just tell the cook I want scrambled eggs and bacon?"

The waitress hurried away. William smoked in silence.

Riley came out of the kitchen. He started speaking before he even looked up to see who he was speaking to.

"Sir, I'm very sorry, but--"

"Good morning, Starshine," said William in loud obnoxious voice.

"Oh hey, William, hi."

William noticed the mousy little waitress hovering in the kitchen doorway. He continued to stare at her as he began his conversation with Riley.

"Tell me something, Riley. Do I still own this diner?" William was pleased to see the waitress's shocked expression.

"Yes, William, you still own this diner."

"Then why the hell am I having such a hard time getting some goddamn eggs around here?"

"Sorry. Amy didn't know who you were."

"Well, she should have. Now am I getting my breakfast or what?"

Riley turned to Amy "Would you please tell Ernesto to make Mr. Deferno some breakfast?"

Amy ducked into the kitchen. William shook his head.

179

"Where did you find that one? The Soviet Union?" William asked.

"Job fair at the college. She's a nice girl."

"When she isn't trying to lecture your customers about their bad habits. And when she's not telling them where they can sit and what they can eat." William flicked cigarette ash into an empty highball glass. "How does an employee not recognize her employer?"

"Well, to be fair, William, she only started here last week, and you don't come around much anymore."

William shook his head. "No excuse. I'm not going to put up with a snotty attitude from someone who works for me. When I was running thing we used to listen to what customers wanted, not tell them what they want."

"Come on, William, give the girl a break. This is her first job. Give her time to learn."

"I'll give her the same thirty days I give anyone else, but I better see a change in that attitude immediately."

"I'll make sure she understands."

William grabbed the remote and turned on the TV behind the bar. He flipped through the channels until he spotted the sour expression of his opponent on one of the local talk shows.

"Let's see what Ol' Battle Axe Martha has to bitch about today, someone probably ran over a bullfrog," William said. He turned up the volume.

"It's disgusting, just absolutely disgusting that things like this are still happening to women. It's sick," old Martha was telling the pudgy middle aged host. "To think that a man like that thinks he's entitled to treat a woman that way just because he has money. It's horrific. You can't imagine what it was like for this poor girl."

"No, no," said the host. "I don't think any of us truly can."

Something about the petite redhead sitting next to Martha Stout seemed familiar. Then the camera zoomed in on the girl's anguished face. William realized she was the young waitress from Marylou's.

"Awww shit!" he shouted.

"Can you tell us what happened in your own words, Maisy?" the host asked her gently.

"He," the girl's voice broke. "He, uh, he was there with a friend.

They, they were talking and I guess had kind of been well, they'd been saying things, like how nice my r-r-rack was and how I had a nice tight little butt."

"Who is 'he'?" the host prompted. "Look right in that camera and tell us."

Maisy looked right into the lens. William saw the heat and malice in her eyes. He knew he was a microsecond away from *feeling the heat*.

"William Defreno," she sobbed.

"What else did William Defreno do to you that night?"

"When I dropped of the check," Maisy paused to snivel and blot her eyes, "he, Mr. Defreno, he made me take off my top, and he- he-he t-t-touched me. He fondled my breasts." The girl broke down into sobs.

Riley looked at him in horrified shock. "Please tell me you didn't."

"It's not what you think," said William."

"The sad thing is, I'm not even all that surprised," Martha Stout said to the host. "We all know Mr. Defreno has a history of playing fast and loose with the law. He thinks he's untouchable and above having to answer for his actions."

"Well, yes, he does have a history," the host agreed. William's old mug shot came up on the large screen behind the trio on camera. A moment later the image shifted to the twenty year-old newspaper headline "William Defreno Gets the Big One!"

"Oh, God dammit!" William groaned. Riley just stood there shaking his head.

"Well, William, it was a nice try," said Riley.

William's phone went berserk. Texts, emails and tweets flooded his phone. He got eighty-seven chat notifications all at once. The phone at the bar started ringing. So did the one at the host's station. Even the one in the phone booth rang.

Buddy's number popped up on his cell screen. William answered his call.

"Buddy!" William yelled.

"I saw it," said Buddy. "Keep calm. I've got it handled. Get down to the campaign office and don't talk to anyone from the press. Tell everyone at Moe's to refer all questions to me."

"On my way." William hung up. He headed for the door. "If the press calls refer them to Buddy. Other than that it's business as usual."

"William, wait, what's going on?" Riley followed him to the door.

"Just relax."

"Should I call your lawyer?"

"Just run the diner, I can trust you!"

"Whatever you want, boss."

William chose to ignore the *doubt of his innocence* in Riley's voice and headed for the car. He was halfway there before he realized he never got to eat his eggs.

Buddy had the troops rallied. Everyone worked briskly, juggling multiple tasks as they hurried back and forth. They all stopped when William came in. Everyone's head swiveled in his direction.

"Oh man," Buddy said. He looked at William and shook his head. "Get in here."

Buddy pulled William into the room he used as his private office space.

"Dude, what have you been doing?"

"Just driving around."

"You look like you lost a fight with a mountain. And you smell like a brewery."

"You're starting to sound like Cherry." William giggled.

"It ain't funny, man. You cannot go to pieces on me now."

Buddy stuck his head out the door and began barking orders. "Axton, get down to Brinkley's and get Mr. Defreno a suit, shirt and tie. Shoes and socks, too. They should have his sizes on file. Suzy, get a pot of coffee going. David, run down to the drugstore, get shaving cream, razors, all that stuff. Becky, get on the phone to the Hilton, tell them we need a room, put it under your name. Garrett, start setting up a press conference for 2 P.M. Carly, run out and get some food. Let's go, people, we have a campaign to run here."

"We do?" William asked. "I figured all that was left was for me to make a graceful exit."

"Like hell," said Buddy. "I've been waiting a long time to take down that bitch. We aren't stopping now."

"Are we going to have a choice?"

Someone banged on the door. "Buddy! The Associated Press just picked up the story. It's gone national."

"Wouldn't be the first time I was on national news," William said, remembering that his arrest almost twenty years ago had also made national news including USA Today.

"Good," said Buddy. "Order extra chairs for the press conference. Maybe Tom Brokaw will show up."

William laughed. "We're screwed."

Just then Carly came in with a plate of lasagna for William to eat.

"Hey, hey, the William Defreno I know does not give up."

"Only because until now I couldn't afford to. Face it, Buddy, I blew it. I screwed this up just like every other good thing in my life." William replied as he tried to eat his lasagna.

"William, tell your *Victim* to sing her aria later, right now I need my conductor at his podium."

"He's out having a smoke." William flopped down into a chair. "What happened Buddy? I didn't mean to hurt her. I thought she liked me."

"She did. You know and I know she fully consented to it. In fact, she was feeling hurt that you were being so hesitant. Martha's just messing with her mind to get an edge in the election."

"Martha's a bitch!"

"Yeah, I'm adding a new member of the *Prisoner's Choir*. It's call *The Loser* and that's whose running Martha's Choir right now. This is what losers do when they know an opponent is superior to them and that she can't beat you fairly. Be glad she didn't Photoshop you at a KKK rally or something."

William looked around. "Got anything to drink in here?"

"Just water. And plenty of coffee."

"I'm going to need more than coffee."

"No can do, I need you sober."

"Wow, you really do sound like Cherry," William said as he accidentally let the lasagna slide off the plate onto the floor. A hungry and angry William started to think of a DVD for Buddy's doorstep.

"You fucked up my lasagna!" William protested.

"William?"

"Yeah, Buddy?"

"Shut the fuck up."

William and Buddy went back out to the main office. Buddy handed William a cup of strong black coffee and a sandwich.

A crowd of reporters began to build outside the building. The bodies packed in tight, fighting each other for a glimpse through the windows.

"Jesus, it's like The Birds," said a male staffer.

"They must have found the car," said the woman sitting next to him. "They know he's here."

William groaned.

"Ok people," Buddy said. "Operation Bugout begins *now*!"

The staffers all sprung to their feet and gathered around William and Buddy. A black trench coat appeared from somewhere. William pulled it on along with a wide brimmed hat. Someone handed him a pair of sunglasses.

"Go, go, go," said Buddy. The cluster of people began moving towards the back of the building, all of them constantly shifting position while still keeping William and Buddy in the middle of the circle of people. The moved down a long hallway to a loading dock that opened up into the alley.

One guy slipped outside, pretending as if he were just stepping out for a smoke. A few moments later he came back inside.

"All clear," he said.

Buddy made a call on his cell phone. "Yeah, now," was all he said before hanging up.

A few minutes later William heard a loud engine rumbling outside the dock door. Someone opened it. A nondescript white van had backed up to the dock. Another guy wearing a hat, coat and sunglasses like William's got in the back. The van drove away.

"What the hell?" said William.

"Wait for it," said Buddy. Sure enough, several of the press vehicles tore off to follow the van.

Buddy made another call. Shortly afterward a 1986 Lincoln Towncar with tinted rear windows pulled up to the dock. The driver hopped out and opened the door.

"Alright, let's go," said Buddy.

After some coffee, a meal and a hot shower at the hotel, William looked and certainly smelled much better, but he still didn't feel any better. He had been accused of a lot of things he hadn't done, but this one kicked him right in the gut.

As he sat on a leather bench in the suite's dressing area lacing up his shoes, he began to regret running for office. He had been a fool to think he could ever escape his past. No matter how he learned to talk, act or think he would still be the same old schmuck he'd always been. No magic program was going to change that.

William struggled with his tie. The more he fought with it the madder he got.

Buddy popped his head in. "How's it going, man? They're about ready down there."

"I'll be ready for my execution as soon as I finish tying my noose," said William, holding up the ends of his tie.

"Oh, no problem." Buddy stepped over to William and tied his tie.

"What's the matter with me, Buddy? Twelve year olds know how to tie a goddamn tie."

"Those twelve year olds are spoiled rich stuck up brats whose mommies and daddies have the money to send them to private school. You were busy learning more important things. No one can fault you if you didn't have time left over to pick up social niceties."

"You have a point," said William.

"Now, I know you prefer to write your own speeches," said Buddy. "But since there wasn't time in this case we wrote it for you. Look it over and see if you're comfortable with it, but make it quick, ok? We only have a few minutes."

William scanned the sheet of paper Buddy handed him.

"Yeah, this is fine," said William. Buddy could have handed him the Gettysburg address to read and he wouldn't care. He sure as hell didn't have anything better himself.

Buddy gave William a pep talk in the elevator on their way down.

"You are still William Defreno, don't forget that," Buddy said.

185

"This girl is nothing. She's just some desperate attention seeking slut. Don't let her into your head. You didn't do anything wrong, so don't let yourself think you did. You've faced bigger and badder than her and come out on top. She's nothing. Martha Stout is nothing. That room full of reporters is nothing. You are *the* champ. The one, the only William Defreno. No one is gonna take you down, ok?"

By the time they reached the ground floor William almost believed it. Buddy was right. This was nothing. Just some pest trying to get her fifteen minutes of fame at his expense. William would make sure she regretted every second of her time in the spotlight.

"Ready?" asked Buddy.

"You know it."

William burst through the door, walking tall and proud. He stared down the bright lights and the cameras as he made his way to the podium at the front of the room. Cameras flashed. People shouted questions. William ignored them and took his place behind the microphone.

He had a moment of panic when he realized he hadn't brought his speech with him. Then he looked down to see a copy waiting for him on the podium. Lifting his head high, he looked out at the crowd and began to speak.

"Good afternoon, everyone," he said. "Thank you all for being here. I wish we were gathered for a better reason, but I have never been one to shirk away from a difficult situation. We are here today because of the statements that were made about me this morning. I have every intention of addressing them openly and honestly because the people of this city deserve the truth."

William paused for effect. The entire room had gone still. No one talked or made noise. Every eye remained fixed on him. The crowd followed his every word as if they were hypnotized.

"Let me start by saying that any time an accusation of this kind is made it should be taken seriously, and this one is no exception. Now, I have never hidden my past from any of you. Long before I ever even considered running for office I was always open and honest about the young man I used to be and the actions I had taken to protect myself and clear my name.

"You've also seen my mug shot, so you all know I've done things most people would disagree with in order to fight a greater evil. I will not attempt to justify my actions, as they need no justification, and I will ask you not to judge me or my past. Before you do, however, please keep in mind how often freedom fighters throughout history have been labeled as criminals simply because they refused to stand by and let evil go unchallenged.

"An arrest record is not something to be ashamed of if it's acquired for the right reasons. Many of the world's greatest heroes have one and I'm proud to count myself among them. They, and I, stand as living proof that the law is not always what is moral, and what is morally right is not always what is legal. I would far rather have a checkered past and know I had remained on the side of justice than have a lily white record at the expense of turning a blind eye corruption and cruelty.

"And while I have spent far more time than I would have liked on the opposite side of the past law enforcement officials of this town, I do still believe in justice."

He paused for a moment as his brain thought of the tarot card *Justice* on the doorstep. He quickly dismissed that thought.

"Therefore I openly invite an investigation into the accusations brought against me and intend to give our police department my full cooperation if they choose to look into the matter.

"It is an unfortunate fact that mudslinging and personal character attacks of this kind have long been part of the American political process. I wish it weren't, but it will always be the tactic of lazy minds to aim for the easiest way to discredit someone when they lack enough substance to face campaign issues head on or wish to distract people from how little they have to offer.

"I hope that as a city we can rise above this and stay focused on our mutual goals instead of letting ourselves get bogged down in a tedious game of 'he said, she said'. All I ask is that you let the police do their job, keep an open mind, and let the facts speak for themselves so that we can all keep moving forward towards our better, brighter future. Thank you all and God bless."

Loud applause erupted around the room. William looked stunned. Even now they loved him.

Buddy stepped up to the podium and took William's place at the microphone.

"Good afternoon, folks," Buddy began. "In order to preserve the integrity and objectivity of any potential police investigation of the allegations we are unable to disclose too many details about the events of that evening at this time. However I will answer as many questions as I can.

"Before I take those questions, though, there are a few facts I would like to bring to your attention that the honorable Ms. Stout seems to have neglected to mention during her television appearance this morning. The first is that there was an eye witness present at the time of the alleged assault and that witness is also prepared to make a full statement to the police. I can't disclose all details, but I will say that the waitress in question had asked Mr. Defreno for a job. When he didn't have any opening she asked if there was 'any other way of getting that job'.

"The other is that the restaurant where it allegedly happened has security cameras. A copy of the tape from that evening has been made available to our local police. A copy has also been provided to us and while we cannot distribute it, I have been granted permission to show you parts of it."

The lights in the room dimmed. A still image of the interior of Marylou's diner appeared on the projector screen above Buddy's head.

"First, let me draw your attention to the design of the building. Notice the large windows, notice the glass door. Notice the open layout and the large pass through window that allows anyone in the kitchen to look out into the dining room. Does this look like the kind of place where someone would commit a sexual assault? Notice also that the front door is unlocked and there is nothing obstructing the door into the kitchen. There is nothing preventing anyone from leaving this room."

With the sound of a click the picture on the screen changed to a view of the restaurant's kitchen.

"Second, this frame clearly shows three male employees working in the kitchen at the time of the alleged incident. Help was only a scream away at any time, so why didn't she scream? Also, why were the police not notified until today?"

The picture changed again. This time it showed a close up of Maisy's face. She had her eyes closed and her mouth parted in an ecstatic smile.

"Lastly, there's the alleged victim *smiling* as she is supposedly being victimized. Smiling! Not crying, not cringing, not showing the slightest bit of fear. Now, I'm not exactly an expert, and it isn't my place to tell anyone what to think, but does anyone see any signs of trauma here?"

Buddy stopped talking for several long seconds while Maisy's picture lingered on the screen.

Finally, the lights came back up. The projector switched off. Buddy leveled a calm, cool look at the reporters out in the audience.

"Does anyone have a question?"

The room remained quiet. Finally, a hand in the back went up.

"But you will admit Mr. Defreno was at Marylou's diner the night of the alleged incident?"

"He was. Mr. Defreno often visits competing restaurants in town to evaluate them."

Another hand went up. "Did he touch the girl?"

"That will be up to investigators to determine."

"Did they know each other previously?"

"They did not."

"Has Mr. Defreno hired a lawyer?"

"Mr. Defreno has had a business attorney on retainer since he purchased Moe's' Diner."

"How soon to you expect the results of the police investigation?"

"Truthfully, I don't expect an investigation at all. The video speaks for itself. But that will be up to our fine local officers. It is not my place to tell them how or when to do their job."

"Do you think this is a character attack designed to damage your candidate's chances in the election?"

"I don't want to think Ms. Stout would be that underhanded, but we have to remain open to all possibilities."

"Do you think the waitress is after money?"

"Again, that will have to be up to the police to determine."

"Is Mr. Defreno willing to take a polygraph?"

"He'll take one if his alleged victim takes one."

"Are you implying that the young lady is lying?"

"I am not implying anything. I am simply stating that all avenues need to be explored."

"Is there a reason Mrs. Defreno isn't here today?"

"The future Mrs. Defreno has a prior commitment today and she didn't feel like disappointing a room full of school children to address a matter she considers immaterial."

Buddy looked down at his watch. "I'm afraid that's all the time we have, folks. See you all next time."

William and Buddy stepped out into the hall.

"You still got it," Buddy said, grinning from ear to ear.

"Of course I do," said William. "I'm William Defreno."

But William's confidence was short lived. A moment later he spotted a uniformed police officer marching towards them. William swallowed hard, already dreading the humiliation of being arrested in front of the reporters streaming out of the conference room.

"William Defreno?" The officer asked.

"Yes," said William, holding his hands in a surrender position. The loud voices silenced, the lights swirled as time slowed down. He could already feel the cold steel of the handcuffs closing around his wrists. It was all going to crumble to the ground. Another trip to the county jail, possibly The Department of Corrections and having to register as a sex offender for life. He wanted to screech at the fact he didn't actually want to touch her.

"The chief sent me down to tell you that after personally reviewing the security footage of that evening he sees no evidence of a crime being committed."

"Thank you for taking the time," said William.

"Thank you, sir. Have a good evening."

The officer left. William shook his head in disbelief.

"I've never seen the cops in this town work so fast in my life," said William to Buddy.

"Um, the police chief is out of town this week. He's testifying at the state capital about the *New Laws Program.*"

"Wait, so you mean he hasn't watched the video yet?"

"I'm saying he's not going to. They have been asking for a budget increase for the last five years straight but old Battle Axe Martha keeps voting no. They figure getting her out of office is their best chance to get the funding they need."

"So I got a free pass?"

"Wouldn't be the first time. That's how things work in this town. Only this time you really were innocent."

"Don't I know it," William said glumly. Still, it was nice to be the one to catch a break for a change.

Despite being cleared of all charges, the scandal still lingered in the days leading up towards the election. Everywhere he went William seemed to overhear someone talking about it.

"I don't believe it. A guy doesn't do something like that when he has a good woman like he's got waiting at home," he heard a guy say one time.

"I bet he paid her off. He must not value women much. I feel bad for his fiancée," a woman said into her phone as William waited in line behind her to buy cigarettes.

"That Richfield guy has some nerve, suggesting that an assault victim should have to take a lie detector test. What a scum bag," said guy working at the donut shop.

"It's sad how some girls lie to get attention like that," a teenager girl said to her friend as they walked in front of him in the park.

All the talk hurt him in the polls as well. He didn't lose all of his support, just enough to wear his once comfortable margin down to a nail-bitingly thin razor's edge.

"We'll bounce back," said Buddy, but as Election Day drew closer William's numbers remained ominously flat.

William kept his momentum going, lunches here, speeches there, but where he once saw unwavering admiration he had begun to see the occasional doubting glance or hesitation in someone's eyes.

"We need something else for people to talk about," Buddy said one day over lunch. "That's the problem. Nothing ever happens in this town."

The next day Buddy popped into William's office at the campaign building.

"Grab your coat There's a sick kid at the hospital who needs visiting."

William didn't argue.

When they got to the hospital a nurse made William, Buddy and the photographer Buddy had dragged along all put scrubs on over their street clothes and funny net caps to wear on their heads. They were required to cover their shoes with paper booties, but oddly enough they did not have to wear masks.

The nurse ushered them into the hospital room. A young gaunt looking boy lay passively in the bed, staring up at the ceiling. All around him machines beeped. Tubes of all sorts ran in and out of his thin arms. He had another in his nose.

William shook hands with the boy's parents. Then he turned to the boy himself.

"Hey kiddo, how are you feeling?" asked William.

"Not so great," the kid said in a weak voice.

"He has a chronic condition," said his mother. Tears welled up in the corners of her eyes. "It's treatable, but we don't have insurance. We make too much for Medicaid, but not enough to buy our own insurance. And we don't qualify for state supplemented insurance, either."

"I thought the city offered 'bridge coverage' for people who fell into the gap between public assistance and private insurance," said William.

"It doesn't cover pre-existing conditions," said the boy's father. "Or treatments considered 'experimental'. We filed an appeal but it got denied."

"We've called Martha Stout's office a dozen times begging her to intervene of his behalf," his mother said tearfully. "But she never calls us back."

"Probably too busy pulling weeds and building squirrel feeders," said William.

"Mommy, I feel dizzy," said the boy. He began an extended coughing fit. William watched with horror as the boy turned red and then purple as he struggled to catch a breath. One of the monitors started beeping louder and faster. Finally, the boy seemed to pass out. The coughing stopped and the monitor quieted down.

"This is disgraceful!" said William. "No child should be suffering this way. If I get elected the first thing I'm going to do is push through an amendment to make sure your son and all the other kids like him get the treatment they need."

"Thank you," said his mother. "It's good to know somebody cares."

The photographer packed up his equipment and left. As soon as he was out of sight the kid sat up, took out his oxygen tube and got out of bed.

"I thought he was dying," said William.

"So will all the suckers that read about it in tomorrow's paper," Buddy said.

"I knew it," William shouted. "I didn't think even that old prune would let a kid suffer like that."

"William, you worry too much about facts. People are too stupid to figure anything out. They just see a sick kid that the government is gonna let die. A government that, as far as they're concerned, is run only by Martha Stout. People don't think with their brains. Their stupid emotions vote for them. It goes back to the choir member *The Child*. A child will think with his heart, not his head."

"Wow, a fake hospital story. Can't wait to see what else I have to do to win this."

"Just be thankful the press finally has something else to talk about, ok? We gotta get your numbers back up. This will do it. So will the local TV news story about Moe's Diner donating all their leftovers to the local homeless shelter."

"Better than having them stock up the cooler," said William.

"And from now on you and Beth go everywhere together. You are so in love you can't bear to be apart. Get caught holding hands, kissing in public, doing cutesy couples things."

William rolled with the punches, doing what he had to do to remind everyone he was the good guy they all knew and loved.

He and Beth went shopping. They went out for ice cream. They went out to dinner and strolled through art galleries. They even bought Orson a leash and harness and began walking him around the neighborhood. He kissed her so often his lips got chapped. Everywhere they went they had their hands on each other.

Still, it wasn't enough. It was never enough. William's poll numbers came back up, but they stayed far short of the pinnacle he had once reached.

Buddy pulled one last *Hail Mary* in the days just before the election. In their official statement, the police department had said they would not be releasing the full surveillance video from Marylou's in order to "protect the dignity of the alleged victim and her family" but suddenly very carefully cherry picked clips of the footage appeared online. People watched over and over again as the waitress appeared to tease and taunt William with her body before willingly taking off her shirt. The story that she was flirting with him to get a job was more believable than not.

The tactics worked. William's numbers slowly rose, but, as of the night before Election Day, they still weren't strong enough to ensure a solid victory. All William could do was hold tight and hope for the best.

Chapter 12

The Winner by a Knockout

Election Day dawned bright and clear, with just enough of a breeze blowing to send a charge of electric excitement through the air. Weathermen predicted the first hard freeze in a day or two, and some promised a chance of snow.

William got up early at noon so that he and Beth could be photographed casting their ballots down in the high school gym in time to make the afternoon news. William found some amusement in the fact that he ended up using the voting booth positioned right under the spot where the plaque commemorating his record breaking mile run used to hang.

He still felt a mix of sorrow and pride that Roger had finally broken it legitimately. He wondered if his honorary godson was following the election from his college in California. Full ride scholarship. He could still hardly believe how well the kid had turned out, even if he had been directly responsible for most of the change.

Local ordinance forbid campaigning on Election Day itself, so technically the candidates had the day to themselves. The paper ran a story about how Martha Stout planned to spend the day volunteering at a local women's shelter. A reporter asked William for a comment on it as they left their polling place.

"Well, it's nice that she has the luxury of doing that," said William. "But some of us still work for a living."

To prove his point, William spent the day waiting tables at the diner and occasionally tending bar.

"Wow, so you really do still work?" asked one slightly overweight middle aged man with graying hair and bloodshot eyes.

He wore a dress shirt with faded stripes that strained against his spreading gut.

"Every day of my life," said William.

A woman with frizzy dark hair and thick tortoise shell glasses frowned at him.

"Why?" she asked. "I mean you're pretty rich, right?"

"Yeah, but if I didn't keep working I wouldn't be rich," William replied. "See what most people don't understand is that not all wealth is the same. Some people have passive incomes. They live off trust funds and investments so they just have to sit back and the money rolls in. The rest of us actively make our wealth. We generate our income by working for it.

"When we work for our money, we also spend it, pumping it into the economy and making money for everyone else. We keep the wheels turning. The others are just takers who skim off the top without putting anything in."

"Never thought of it that way," said the middle aged guy.

"Most people don't," said William. "But what it comes down to is that I have to make good, responsible decisions because my livelihood depends on it just a much as my employees' do. If I screw up we're all out in the cold. We don't get to pass a bond measure and make the public foot the bill if we blow our budget."

"Ain't that the truth! There are three different tax increases up for a vote this year."

"I know," said William. "I can't tell you how I voted, but let's just say I don't approve of spending money that hasn't been earned yet. You can't pay bills on wishful thinking."

"Hmmm," said the middle aged guy.

"Wow," said the frizzy haired lady. "You've really put a lot of thought into this."

"Like I said, I had to," said William. "You don't pull yourself out of the gutter without thinking through every move."

"You must have had it tough," the woman said sympathetically.

"Yeah, but the way I see it, if a steel beam doesn't complain about its time in the forge why should I? It may have been a trial by fire but I wouldn't be the man I am without it."

As the afternoon wore on, William just kept up doing what he did best, talking to people while keeping their plates and glasses full. He carefully avoiding discussing the campaign directly, but still managed to make an impression on his potential voters.

"Do you get a tax deduction for the leftover food you donate?" a perky blond asked him.

"Actually, we don't," William answered. "We can count food we throw in the trash as a loss and get a break on it, but food we give away comes out of our pockets. That's why more places don't donate it. I mean, we can afford to do it, but not many small businesses can absorb the cost."

"That's messed up! It shouldn't be more affordable to throw away good food than it is to give it to someone who needs it!"

"I know. As a kid who grew up not always knowing where his next meal was coming from, it makes me sick to see a business forced to waste food when so many people are going hungry. Hopefully it will change someday."

William saw in the woman's eyes that what he'd just said had clicked with her.

"Yeah, maybe it will." She soon left. William could only hope she was on her way to a voting booth.

About an hour before the polls closed William turned the diner over to Riley and headed down to his campaign headquarters to watch the results come in. Beth greeted him at the door with a glass of sparkling cider and a kiss.

"What, we can't afford real champagne?" William muttered to Buddy.

"Save it for the win," said Buddy. "It'll taste sweeter."

A pair of buxom blondes in black waitress uniforms moved through the crowd of campaign workers, passing out soft drinks and tea sandwiches. People stood in groups around TVs and computer monitors, watching the election coverage on different channels.

Someone had put red white and blue streamers around the walls. Bunches of matching helium balloons filled the corners. Paper lanterns hung in the windows.

"It's like Christmas Eve!" said Beth. "Imagine if it actually snows!"

"If I win the first thing I'm going to do is outlaw snow in

November," joked William.

"Can you do that?" asked Beth. William didn't answer.

"Hey, honey," Buddy said to Beth. "Why don't you go get William another drink and something to eat? He's gotta be starving."

"Okay." Beth dutifully trotted off to fix William a plate.

William marveled at how easily she obeyed any order given to her. Sometimes he wondered if he ordered her to do something to hurt herself, if she would do it.

"She's a great girl, isn't she?" asked Buddy. "Polite, dutiful, organized, quiet, cooperative."

"She's ok, I guess," William answered.

"You ever think about actually getting married for real to her?"

"Say what? I thought we were just faking it for the election."

"Well yeah, but it doesn't have to stop there. She's the perfect wife for a budding politician like yourself. She has the education, the breeding, the class. She's completely submissive, dedicated to fulfilling her husband's every need and keeps her mouth shut, well unless she's giving head, but then you know about that by now."

William looked away from Buddy. "Uh, yeah."

"What's the matter, pal?"

"I don't know," William sighed. "She does a lot of things very well, and I like her, she just... well..."

"No passion?" said Buddy.

"Not really. I mean she kind of so easy to please I guess. Like nothing exciting comes from her."

"William, I've told you, men in their power live by a separate set of rules. They have their wives for practical matters and mistresses for fun."

"So I should marry Beth and then cheat on her? Won't she mind?"

"Of course she won't. You could completely neglect her for years and she wouldn't complain a bit."

"Wow, really?"

"Really. See women like Beth are kind of competitive with each other in their own way. They pride themselves in having successful husbands. Unlike so many other women that more pride themselves on how well they emasculated their men. So they're willing to make certain compromises if that's what it takes to make him happy."

"Seems a little hard to believe."

"It just takes getting used to. It's like when older people work their whole lives and become millionaires like you, but can't accept it. They still save car parts and shoe strings and cereal boxes like they did when they were poor, because they're not used to having infinite resources."

"I guess I'm not used to her yet."

"That's because you're used to selfish, demanding women like Cherry who pitch a fit if they don't get their own way or have to share your attention, but Beth is different. She's not full of restless *Child* energy that demands constant appeasement. She knows she can't give you everything you need. Heck, no woman can be 'everything a guy needs'.

"Marriages like this are the ones that last. Well educated women like Beth don't try be something they're not. They think with their brains more than their hearts. They don't have the divorce papers stuffed in their bra, ready to go, in case their man looks at another woman. They don't expect you to be like 100% all about *them, them, them*. She has realistic expectations of what a man's needs are. But, best of all, she knows you're the boss. She respects you as a man. She'll let you do whatever you please."

"Even have another woman behind her back?" William wondered.

"William, you could fuck another chick right in front of her face and the only thing she'd do is fetch you a towel to clean up with. For your own sake, though, keep it discreet. Common people don't understand the world we live in. That's why we have places like The Love House."

"I thought that was just for guys who can't get dates."

"Nope. It's for men who need a safe outlet for less than conventional needs."

No wonder Hank was the center of power in this town. William wondered what kind of dirt he had on those who used his establishment. William made a mental note to be sure that if he did do things Buddy's way, he wouldn't do it at The Love House.

Beth came back with William's food. She looked up at him with a devoted smile as she offered him the plate.

Someone in the back of the room shouted. Buddy turned up the sound on the Big screen TV at the front of the room.

"Here we go, people!" he called out.

"Oh boy," said William. Beth squeezed his hand.

Sitting alone in her dark living room, was a very zoned out Cherry watching the election results roll in. City Council District One came up on the screen. Even with only one percent of the precincts reporting they already showed William Defreno ahead 55% to 45%. Some distant part of Cherry's brain knew she was happy about that but she was too deep in her drug induced fog to remember exactly why.

The anxiety medication wrecked her ability to concentrate and right now other things occupied her thoughts. In the dark corners of her mind memories gathered, pushing her to think back on where she had seen odd hand writing like the font on the DVD case before. Every time she almost had the memory it slipped away into the shadows again.

The news anchors said "William Defreno" and a different memory broke through. This time she saw the first time William had come to The Love House. She remembered how young and vulnerable he'd looked, and how she had fallen for him at first sight, even if it took her months before she realized it.

She missed the ordinary William who drove an old car, lived behind the diner, worked hard every day and was never was unpleasant to her.

Then the memory was gone again. She hated these damn pills. She wished she didn't need them, but without them she immediately turned into a shaking, panicky mess. She might function more slowly under the influence of the medication, but at least she was functional.

Deciding to let the mystery of the handwriting go for now, she picked up the book containing William's short story "One More Year" and began to read it....

As they waited for the rest of the precincts to report, a few key "friends" dropped by the campaign office. William noticed that the higher his numbers climbed the more people seemed to want to come by to congratulate him. He ended up seeing just about everyone from that first business association meeting that had started it all.

Shortly after that, he found himself meeting the Police Chief and the Fire Chief. Even the Mayor stopped in to say congratulations, all before half the ballots were even counted.

As the night wore on, William found himself trouncing his opponent nearly two to one in the polls. He reached just over 66% of the vote while Martha Stout lingered at 34.5.

"Where do the missing votes go?" asked Beth.

"The same place socks go in the dryer," said Buddy.

Cherry sat with the short story anthology, tracing the letters on the cover with her finger, trying to remind herself of how it once felt to love and be loved. She opened the book, suddenly wondering if there were pictures of the various authors somewhere inside. Cherry paused at the cover page, smiling at the odd curlicue writing William had used to sign the book "To Cherry from William Defreno." The odd handwriting seemed familiar somehow, but she couldn't quite place it.

Disappointed that the book didn't have pictures, Cherry reached for her phone instead. For awhile she simply flipped through her picture galleries, looking back on her happier times. Somewhere she had a picture of William standing in front of an old civil war statue, mimicking the old soldier's pose. It had always been her favorite picture of him. There had been something magical about that moment. The light, the air, their laughter, everything had fallen into place to make it absolutely perfect.

Where was the picture? She went through the galleries again and again, but she couldn't find it.

Something else caught her eye, however. She paused at the pictures she'd taken after the second time the strange items had appeared on her porch. She zoomed in on the DVD case. Cherry cropped the picture down to just the writing and zoomed in again. She dropped the phone and went to get the actual DVD case. One glance at the word "Cherry" written on the case in magic marker is all she needed to realize exactly where she knew that weird eccentric handwriting from.

"With over 90%of the precincts now reporting, election officials have called the race for city council District 1 in favor of William Defreno, with a final vote tally of 67% to 33%."

Buddy let out a loud whoop. Williams' staffers cheered and applauded. Someone popped a champagne cork. A moment later Beth put a glass in his hand. William blushed and shed the first tears of joy he could remember shedding in years. He had actually done it.

He took a deep breath and cast his mind back to his years of struggling, intentionally calling up as many of his bad memories as possible just to show himself how far he had come.

William recalled being arrested at gunpoint and dragged out of school. After a receipt from a cigarette purchase provided him with an alibi for the bank robbery they tried to frame him for, the police unapologetically tossed him out on the curb without even being offered a ride back to his car.

He also recalled being pulled over for no reason other than driving through a nice neighborhood. The cops had told him to get his loser car out of the good part of town and not come back. William also remembered how one Officer Marshall had crossed the city limit line into the next town to assault him and arrest him on another trumped up charge.

He recalled the hard days he had working at the junkyard for a guy nick named *Redneck Roy.* Although he liked Roy very much, the work was very hard and low paying. Another memory of the Drama teacher in high school giving the part in the play to Timmy instead of him because Timmy could afford to donate money for props.

Lastly, he thought of the many *many* times Melissa had degraded him as human being by telling him over and over how stupid, ugly and pathetic he was. Everything he did she had to scream and yell and try to ruin it for him. She would rub it in his face that she never had to work and still to this day got to live free at home at age thirty-eight.

He was always angered that her years of verbal abuse had actually caused him mental distress and that she lived unpunished for it all. First thing he thought he should do is approve the new sewage treatment plant right next door to her house. Maybe even a garbage incinerator on the other side of her house.

William shook his head and laughed as he thought about how all the cops who had given him such a hard time were now either dead or imprisoned. For the first time ever he could think of all these terrible things and not be hurt or angry about them anymore.

William imagined celebrating his victory by dressing up as a sheriff and prisoner with Cherry and-- William snuffed the idea quickly. Beth. He would celebrate his victory with Beth, although he wasn't sure exactly how.

"Excuse me, Mr. Defreno," said a young wide eyed female reporter from a local lifestyle magazine. "Sorry, I mean, Councilman Defreno, what are your thoughts at this moment?"

William smiled. Not wanting to reveal his true feelings, he decided to make light of her question.

"I think you're working way too hard, sweetheart. Take the night off and have a drink. I'll give a statement later."

Drunk off the champagne and the euphoria of winning, William, Beth and Buddy all piled into the Rolls and drove through town, cheering loudly and blaring the horn as they wove in and out of traffic. Buddy popped open another bottle of Dom Perignon and poured it into plastic glasses held by Beth. Some of the bubbly liquid spilled over onto the Connolly leather seats.

"Oh man!" said William.

"Don't worry about it," said Buddy. "I'll call my carpet guy. You can use it as a tax deduction."

William drove at random, as usual, paying no attention to their surroundings.

"Wow, look at that house!" said Beth.

"Somebody's a little paranoid, I think," said Buddy.

William looked around and suddenly realized that he had once again driven into Paradise Cottages. Even worse, they were in front of Cherry's house. William stared in horrified shock at the bright halogen lamps illuminating the porch and yard and the heavy iron bars on the windows. He spotted tiny black security cameras hanging from the eaves. He suddenly felt sick. She had even parked her car across the walkway from her driveway to her house so that no one could go past it without bumping the car and setting off its alarm.

This wasn't his fault, he told himself. She didn't do this because of him. What he did wouldn't disturb her this much. His *Choir* was just overreacting.

But no matter how much champagne he guzzled, he could not drown out the accusing voice in the back of his mind.

Cherry opened the front cover of the short story anthology once more. Her eyes flicked back and forth from William's signature on the title page to the DVD case. She checked again and again, darting her eyes back and forth for over a minute, trying very hard to deny the obvious truth in front of her. Then she laid the case on top of the book and slowly compared every detail. She could no longer deny that the letters matched.

The knowledge pounded at a mind and body already made weak by stress and exhaustion. She felt the last of herself slip away as she strained to hold on to the last bright spot her world had held.

William. The person who had come to her for help. The one she had brought back from the brink of oblivion. The one she had saved from self-destruction. The person she had grown to trust and then love. The one she had let into her darkest corners and her most private thoughts. He was the one who had attacked her. For no reason she could understand.

It was more than Cherry's fragile mind could take. She slumped over into a faint. When she woke she would find that the gun strapped to her side had bruised her ribs.

Buddy took a turn at the wheel of the Rolls. He donned a chauffeur's cap and put on an exaggerated English accent as he drove William and Beth from party to party around town.

As the night wound down, they drove towards the mountains, away from Beth's townhouse near the heart of the city.

"Where are we going, Buddy?" Beth asked.

"Just sit tight, cutie pie, I have a present for the two of you."

Beth gave William a questioning look. He gave her one back. Neither of them knew what Buddy had up his sleeve. William stared out at the dark as their car rolled through the country silence, but couldn't see much of their surroundings.

Sometime later Buddy pulled up in front of a luxury hotel

attached to the new casino that had been built a short distance away. William stared dizzily at the lights flashing around sides of the high rise tower.

Beth stood silent, mouth hanging open.

"You have the presidential suite til' Friday," said Buddy. He handed William a pair of key cards and tossed the keys to the Rolls to a nearby valet. "Have fun and if you do anything illegal don't get caught."

He gave William a back thumping hug and kissed Beth on the cheek before stepping on the casino shuttle back to town.

A bellhop came out to unload the bags Buddy had apparently packed or had packed for them. They followed the young clerk up to their suite on the top floor.

"Oh my God," said Beth as she took in the elaborate decorations and luxurious furniture. She pulled open the drapes. "William, I can see downtown from here!"

"Only the best for you, sweets," said William. He gave her a light kiss.

After washing up and changing clothes, they decided to check out the hot tub. William carefully set his fancy phone down with their towels and sandals before stepping into the water. He slipped into the water next to Beth and leaned back with a sigh.

"Would you like me to take my top off?" asked she.

"You do fully consent to doing this right? Maybe I should have you sign a waiver," William said, sadly, only half kidding.

"Yes, silly."

"Sure. We have the tub to ourselves, so why not?" Inauguration day would be here before he knew it, so William figured he'd better get any reckless impulses he had out of his system while he still could.

Beth reached back and untied the strings of her bikini. She gave William a mischievous smile as her small, firm, breasts popped free.

"We should celebrate your victory," Beth said, grinding herself against him.

"Oh, we will," William replied.

"Why wait?" Beth's had slipped under the waistband of William's swim trunks. He moaned again as she put her quick little fingers to work. "Touch me," she pleaded.

William had just begun to stroke the tiny black triangle of fabric at the front of Beth's swimsuit bottom when his phone's notification tone sounded. And then sounded again. And again.

"Goodness," said Beth. "Someone must really want your attention."

"Probably just another reporter," said William. He reluctantly climbed out of the tub to check the message and turn his phone off. When he saw the message though, he froze in shock. The expensive phone began to slip through William's suddenly unsteady fingers. He caught it just before it fell to the wet cement at his feet.

Chapter 13

Cherry Bomb

"William I KNOW it was you who left fucked up shit on my porch. I'm sure you were too drunk to understand me when I told you why I was once suicidal too. After what happen to me in the Marines I wanted to die. Instead I swore to live and KILL anyone who ever deliberately hurt me again. Looks like that person was YOU!!! I HATE YOU!!!!! You ruined my life. I was off the meds and had a stable respectable job. Everything was amazing for me till you decided you had nothing better to do than scare the SHIT out of me to the point of sleeping with a sawed off shotgun in MY OWN FUCKING HOUSE!!!!!! You are deplorable. You're just an INSECURE, PATHETIC, PETTY, DISGUSTING HUMAN BEING!!!! Hate is not a strong enough word to describe how I feel about you. DO NOT THINK YOU WILL GET AWAY WITH THIS!!!!!!!!"

William stared at his phone with his mouth hanging open for so long that Beth became concerned. She gave him a puzzled look as she shook his arm to get his attention. The angry messages from a number he recognized as Cherry's tore at his conscience like angry dogs, making him wish he had let the phone smash. How the hell had she had finally figured out he had been behind the DVDs?

"William?" she asked. "What's the matter? Are you alright?"

"Uh, I'm not feeling well," said William. "I think I need to go back to our room."

"Okay. Do you need help?"

"No, no, I can walk."

"Do you want to tell me what's wrong?"

"Not right now."

Beth gathered their things. She hastily wrapped a towel around herself rather than taking the time to retie her bikini top. They walked back to their room in silence. Beth kept giving him concerned looks and trying to find some way of comforting him, but William just stared straight ahead and didn't respond.

Back in their room William went out on the patio for a smoke while Beth dried off and changed. While pacing back and forth he reread Cherry's text several times, trying to decide what to do. He had three options, one, he could confess everything and throw himself on her mercy. Two, he could try to intimidate her back into silence, or three, he could play dumb and deny the whole thing. He knew Cherry was not easily intimidated, and he had a feeling she was fresh out of mercy, so he opted for number three. After smoking another cigarette to steady his nerves he began to type out a carefully worded reply.

"Cherry what on Earth are you talking about how did I ruin your life?"

"By leaving that fucked up shit on my porch." she fired back. "That ruined everything! Nothing has been right since!!!."

William had a feeling she wouldn't believe he was innocent. She must have pretty damning proof if she was willing to confront him. He wanted cave in and confess, but his new programming wouldn't let him give into weakness or apologize, so he bluffed it out instead.

"You are unbelievable," he texted back. "I mean do you have any idea how hard I had to work to get anywhere? I been working since I was 14 serving people like a fucking peasant. You on the other hand had every advantage in life I never did. Being a sexy, white, female you NEVER suffered. Money was easy, sex was easy, love was easy, attention and admiration was easy. You never knew what it was like to be some depressed, unprivileged loser who had to work his ass off for peanuts. Who had to kiss the ass of women like you just for a little affection."

"Only in the last few months have I got to see what being on top of the world is like – ya know the feeling you've had since the day you were born. Now you wanna falsely accuse me of stupid shit just to bring me down. What's the matter? Can't you stand to see me on top for once? I don't know who fucked with you but whoever it was I'm sure you did something to them to deserve it, so stop whining. What you considered a ruined life is just having to spend a few weeks at the level of life I was stuck at for YEARS. I don't like to hear that things are bad for you, but at least you had a prime in life. I NEVER did. I was the dog who gets beat from day one!!"

As he waited for her reply, he gulped down a shooter of whiskey from the mini bar and had another cigarette. His hands shook from rage as he tried to hold the lighter up to its tip.

After a few minutes his phone pinged again. He could feel Cherry's fury through the screen as he read her latest response.

"You have no idea what you're talking about you FUCKING psychopath. Do you think it was fun to have to sexually entertain a bunch of perverted pigs at the love house? Yeah, it's great being pretty, 'cause guys think you're some conquest to win. Also that it's ok to sexually assault me because I was only born to give sexual pleasure. To smile at them and pretend I wanna hear all about their pathetic cocks. I had an abusive mother and ran away to the Marine Corps at a young age. I've told you all this, but I guess you were too busy drinking yourself into oblivion every day to drown out the fact that you can't stand what a miserable person you are."

William lit another cigarette. He suddenly realized he had gone through half a pack. He pulled another shooter out and drank a swig as he replied.

"Cherry I enjoyed our time together, I have no regrets and I thank you for caring about me. But let's be real, you always looked down your nose at me. Like that thing women do where they intentionally date some loser so that he'll never leave and never be able to do better and always must realize she's better than he deserves. You made it seem like being around me was *charity* and deserving of points for the afterlife. I always had to feel less around you cause there was always *10 guys waiting in line for me to screw up*"

Another message beeped just as he swallowed the last drop of whiskey.

"I could've had any guy I wanted but I went out with you cause I thought you were a decent person who was just lost. I would've loved you. But you decided being around your plastic pal that's fun to be with and fake girlfriend was better. You think that bitch loves you? She'll love anyone. I HATE YOU!!!! I will make you pay for this!!!!! SUCK IT BITCH!!!!"

William decided not to reply again. He knew he had nothing to gain from it. He figured with some time to cool off and calm down Cherry would back off. Surely she wouldn't do anything crazy. She was probably just blowing off steam.

He drank two more shooters then called room service to bring up a bottle of whiskey.

Beth finally came out of their lavish bathroom. She looked sick with worry when she saw how fast William was drinking.

"William, honey, is there anything I can do?"

"Just shut up and go to bed," William said, knowing he would regret talking to her like that. He knew she would not be able to help at all.

"Yes, William."

Beth slid under the thick covers of suite's massive bed and curled up with her back to him. After finishing half the whiskey and the rest of the pack of cigarettes he stumbled over to the bed and collapsed next to her, still wearing his wet swim trunks.

The next morning a hung over, still exhausted William left Beth at the hotel and drove into town. He stopped at a red light near the center of town. A moment later three flamboyantly gay men in a flashy red Cadillac Escalade pulled up beside them. The driver looked down at William and smiled.

"Oh! Hello -- cutie!" he said to the backseat passengers. He looked in his rearview mirror. "Hey gurl, check out the hottie in the Rolls. He looks like your type."

"I don't think so," said the woman in the backseat.

"Flirt with him guuurl. He's cute."

"I can't even see him." She replied.

"Well, we'll fix that," The Escalade pulled up a little more to let the woman in the backseat get a look at William.

"Come on now, gurl, he's way too hot to get away. If you don't get his number, I will."

She turned her head his direction and froze in shock. William's eyes met hers for a second. Cherry was the woman in the back seat of the SUV.

William's eyes widened as his icy breath whispered screams of pain.

"You gotta be kidding me!" Cherry said. "A yellow Rolls Royce? Really? Fuckin' jackass!"

Cherry realized at that moment that a lifetime of being an alpha female meant she was surrounded by guys that would be worthless in defending her. She did her best not to ruin the mood of her friends.

"What's the matter guuurl?" asked the guy sitting next to her.

"Never mind, just let him go. I'm not interested." Cherry replied.

The light turned green. William floored it. No matter how fast he drove, though, it still seemed like he could feel Cherry's eyes boring into the back of his neck.

He arrived at Moe's diner about an hour before lunch to find Riley up on a ladder taking down streamers and some sad looking half deflated balloons.

"Hey there, Mr. Councilman," said Riley. He climbed down from the ladder and shook William's hand.

"What's all this?" William asked.

"Well, the staff thought you might stop by last night so they kind of had a congratulations party ready for you."

"Oh," said William. "I figured the place was busy," he lied to cover up his sudden guilty feeling. "I was afraid I'd be too much of a disruption."

"We weren't that busy," said Riley. "We maybe did half our usual volume for a Tuesday. That new place over on Elmwood has started offering two for one entrees on Tuesdays. It's taking a real bite out of us."

"So bite back! That's what always happens. Someone like me does well and now every shit-for-brains in the city wants to be the next William Defreno." said William.

"I know what you mean, William. It's like everyone wants on the boat and it's gonna sink. But you know what? We've got a well-established place, twenty-five years in business, I think the new *flash of the pan* place will blow out soon."

"For sure, even though the place has only been popular the last five years I owned it. Hey, uh, listen, has anything usually happened around here today?"

"Define unusual," said Riley. "We don't really have a usual to judge against."

"I mean like anyone snooping around, asking questions, meddling with stuff? Maybe like old friends of mine like the Casner family or maybe, I don't know, Cherry or something?"

"The health inspector came by. We passed with an eighty-nine. Other than that the only people asking questions have been reporters covering the election."

"Eighty-nine?" asked William. "We usually score a perfect hundred."

"Not this time," said Riley. "Someone forgot to date some prime rib in the cooler, and there were a few other minor things."

"Yeah, about that," said William. "I came by the other night after close and things seemed kinda sloppy. What's going on?"

"Well, you have to remember that you did most of the extra cleaning yourself after hours. When you stopped you didn't factor anyone else to do it into our labor budget. Also, between you being gone so much and the election reporters, I am doing the work of three people and I can't be everywhere at once. I only have so many hours a day, William, and so do the staff. Things have started falling through the cracks."

"We really can't afford more labor," said William. "Couldn't you maybe promote someone to assistant under you?"

"Well, there's that girl Amy."

"Um, no," said William.

"She's the best we've got. The kitchen guys are good, but she has the best head for numbers."

"Best head, huh? Ok, I'll give her a two week trial period, if she passes she gets to be your new assistant, if not she's back in the kitchen."

"Sounds fair."

William felt for his pack of cigarettes, then remembered that he had finished them last night and why. He looked at Riley cautiously, trying to figure out exactly what to say to get what he wanted without alarming his longtime friend.

"Listen Riley, I've heard some things about that new place on Elmwood. The owners over there play kind of rough. They've been known to stoop to some pretty underhanded things to drive their competitors out of business in other towns, like copy recipes, steal employees, even make threats and commit acts of vandalism."

"Do you want me to hire some security?" asked Riley.

"Uh, no, we don't want to be that obvious. It might tip them off. Just keep an extra eye out, ok?"

"You got it, boss."

"Now that the election is over, I'll be around a bit more. Beth and I need a little vacation time, but as soon as we get back I'll start coming in again, ok? Just hang in there a little longer."

"I'm hanging," said Riley. "This place is my second home. Heck, I'm here so much it's more like my first home. I even slept in your old place last night."

William gasped hard at that. Would his best friend be in potential danger if Cherry mistook Riley for William some late night? What was one more lie if it might protect his longtime pal?

"Oh man, don't do that! I found some black mold in there I haven't had a chance to get rid of yet. That's why I moved in with Beth so suddenly. I'll get it taken care of, but in the meantime stay out

213

of there, ok? I don't want you getting sick."

"Oh, wow, ok, sure thing."

William left the diner and drove aimlessly through town. After stopping for a pack of smokes and a twelve pack of tacos he hit the open highway and floored it. He took solace in the fact that taking a long drive while smoking and blaring 80's rock could still calm his nerves and even bring him a small amount of joy.

The city only had one 80's rock station and it was William's favorite. The DJ came on after the song.

"Ok, that was *Queensryche* with *The Thin Line*. We at K-Zay radio want to congratulate our newest city councilman William Defreno.

"Thank you very much," William said to the radio.

"A very lovely lady in town made a song request in honor of William," The DJ continued. "Here is *Pink Floyd, Run Like Hell* on K-Zay radio."

William dropped the cigarette he was smoking and coughed.

"No fuckin' way! No fuckin' way!"

After thinking about what just happened he persuaded his paranoid brain that it was an awesome coincidence. No way! No way! He kept telling himself.

Somewhere in the midafternoon his phone beeped. William flinched at the sound. Although he dreaded the possibility of seeing another message from Cherry, he checked his phone anyway. The text was from Beth.

"Hi William. Where are you? Are you ok?" the screen read.

"How many times are you gonna ask me if I'm ok?" said William. "Yeah I bet you're worried, sweetheart. Wouldn't want your rich fiancé to go and kill himself before he wrote you into his nice fat will now, would you?"

Sighing, he reluctantly typed out a reply. "Urgent business. Will be back for diner." He added and XOX at the end just to make it seem less dismissive.

Her reply came instantly. "Ok. Love you!"

He typed out "OK" and sent her a kissy face emoji.

As William drove on Aerosmith came on the radio. He sang along with a few lines of *Janie's Got a Gun* before he realized he had unintentionally changed the lyrics to *Cherry's Got a Gun*. The thought made him squirm. Cherry did indeed have a gun, and a powerful one at that.

He had gone to the shooting range with her once and her accuracy score had left no doubt in his mind that she was very skilled in using it. He remembered her laughing wildly when she got to fire the big automatic weapon they had there.

Trying not to think about Cherry smiling wickedly as she loaded her magazine, he turned off the highway and drove through the hills and valleys back toward the hotel. Now being daylight, he laughed at the odd roadside signs he passed. One assured him that "God's Hand Moves In America." Another promised him raw honey, goat milk soap and other *tasty treats*.

William had never considered the flavor of soap to be all that tasty, but then again what did he know. His only experience with soap tasting had come from having his mouth washed out by his childhood babysitter. She had told him to "sit still and quit running around" to which he replied, "yer mother what?" He smiled as he wondered where Mrs. Carrick was these days. Probably terrorizing the orderlies in her nursing home with the sandpaper covered ping pong paddle she kept hanging from the back of her closet door.

William made it back to Beth at the hotel. They went for a quiet dinner at the seafood restaurant on the hotel's main floor. Unfortunately a group of loud drunken men shouting about sports and joking about going gay for each other if they lost their respective bets spoiled the mood.

"Let's go back to the room," said William. They didn't even wait for their main course to be served.

Once back in their suite, after Beth went to sleep he went out for a walk and a cigarette. On the way back to the room he picked up another bottle of whiskey. Sitting across from Beth as she slept he drank himself into another unconscious stupor.

Friday morning William dropped Beth off at home and went down to city hall to meet the other Council members. He was the only newcomer to the group. Despite having his usual urge to hang quietly on the sidelines and try to go unnoticed he dove right in and introduced himself. He even made small talk and a few jokes.

"How many Martha Stout supporters does it take to change a light bulb?" William said to Councilman Scott Smith.

"How many?" Scott replied.

"None, they like being in the dark."

Scott laughed just long enough before Martha Stout showed up for a briefing on what projects William would take over from her when she left office the following January. William thought to himself that if he'd known how much work would be involved in holding the office he never would have run for it.

At the end of the meeting she shook his hand and wished him "all the best," but she didn't quite sound sincere.

Mind buzzing, he didn't pay much attention as he crossed the street to his car. He got behind the wheel and turned the key, but nothing happened.

"Oh, come on, now what?" he said as he popped the hood and got out to have a look. William immediately noticed that one of the battery cables was detached. He reached for it to put it back in place and found a note tied to the end. He unrolled the scrap of yellow paper and read the spiky red handwriting inside.

"Unlike you, I learned useful things in life like how to wire a car to make the gas tank explode when the person tries to start it. Too bad all you learned in life was how to be a jackass. Right now the fire department could've been sweeping up the smoldering ashes of their newest and greatest councilman. I'm sure all the alcohol in your veins would only make you burn faster. AS OF THIS MOMENT YOU'RE ON BORROWED TIME!!!! SUCK IT BITCH!!!!!!"

William stared at the note in shock. He reread it a few times, trying to make it sink in. Jesus, had he really just almost died?

With shaky hands, he carefully reattached the battery cable. Still moving cautiously, he got behind the wheel and turned the key. He flinched, waiting to see if he would explode. When nothing happened, he put the car in gear and slowly eased out into traffic.

William lit a cigarette. He took a long drag while he tried to figure out what to do next. As his nerves settled he began to be able to think clearly about what had just happened. He knew Cherry was angry but he could not bring himself to believe that she might seriously mean him harm. She probably just meant to scare him. A little bit of payback for his own stupid pranks. He supposed that was fair enough. He threw his cigarette butt out the window and drove on, trying his best to just forget the whole thing and move on.

After hours of driving around William finally went home to Beth. As he walked through the front door a heavy feeling of despair settled over him. He looked around at her tasteful designer furniture and bland colored walls and sighed.

What did normal people do in the evening? Up until this point in his life he had always been working at this hour. Now, though, with the campaign over and Riley running the diner, he didn't know how to fill his time. The idea of spending it cooped up with Beth in her small townhouse suddenly made him feel claustrophobic. He had to get out of there or he would go crazy.

Thinking he would sneak out again before Beth realized he was home, he began easing himself quietly toward the door. Just as he had his hand on the knob, though, Beth popped her head in.

"Hi, William!" she said brightly. She gave him a coy smile. "You're home early tonight."

"Uh, yeah," said William.

"I wasn't sure when you'd be home so I haven't started dinner yet, but I was thinking I'd make that shrimp scampi you like. It won't take long to cook."

William closed his eyes. It was all just too much.

"William?" Beth said in a concerned voice. "What's the matter? Are you alright?"

"Just fine, babe." He flashed her a fake smile, relieved that unlike Cherry, Beth never seemed to know the difference. "I was just thinking maybe we should go out."

"Okay," Beth said blankly.

"Go on up and put on something pretty. I'll be in the car."

"Yes, William."

As he waited for Beth to do her hair and make-up, William smoked a cigarette and watched the traffic go by. Despite the deep chill in the air, it seemed a lot of people had decided to be out tonight. William scanned the cars parked on the street. At the end of the block on the opposite side he spotted a blue Toyota Prius that he didn't remember seeing in the neighborhood before. Something about it looked familiar, though. Feeling paranoid, he leaned out the window to try to get a better look at the license plate, but it seemed to be obscured by mud. From here it looked like the car was empty, but its presence still made him nervous.

Beth climbed into the car and dutifully buckled her seatbelt. William glanced at her sparkly dress and supposed she looked lovely, but he still wasn't all that impressed. As he pulled away from the curb he kept an eye on the blue Toyota. Sure enough, it pulled out right behind him.

Trying to keep his cool so Beth wouldn't realize anything was wrong, William cautiously put the car through a series of random turns on the way to the interstate. The Prius stayed on their tail. William sped up, shot past the on ramp to the interstate and doubled back. The blue car followed his every move. In the seat next to him, Beth looked concerned, but she didn't say anything.

"Darn GPS," William laughed. "I keep losing my signal."

"Oh," said Beth. William thanked his lucky stars that she was dumb enough to believe whatever he said. William got on the interstate. The car followed. Two exits later he got off again. His tail did the same.

William made a few more random turns through the obscure back streets of a middle class suburban neighborhood, watching as the blue car stayed close behind.

Finally, he took a main street towards downtown. A few blocks later the blue car turned off. William sighed with relief. He got back on the interstate, only to find that the blue car was now ahead of them. He shot past it and didn't look back.

"Let's see if that little piece of shit can do ninety," William mumbled to himself.

There was no way that crappy little Prius could keep up with the Rolls at the speeds it could reach on the open highway. Just to be sure, he overshot their exit by a few miles and then doubled back again. The blue car was nowhere to be seen.

By the time they pulled up to the restaurant on Elmwood, Beth looked pale and grim, but she still did not utter a word of complaint. As the valet opened her door, she beamed her usual smile and thanked him.

William scanned the room carefully as they followed the Maître D' to their table. No one looked out of place, but he still asked for a corner booth near the back.

"This is cozy," Beth said as they took their seats.

"I wanted us to have a little privacy. More romantic that way."

"Ooh," said Beth.

William looked at his menu without really reading it. When the waiter came by he ordered wine by merely guessing what they were likely to eat and picked his entree by asking for the soup of the day and the night's special.

"I always thought you weren't supposed to order the special," said Beth, looking genuinely curious.

"Most places it's a bad idea, but at a really high end place it's ok. At Moe's we use the special to try out new menu items to see if they'll be popular. I want to try this one to see how creative their chief is. Word has it that we may face some stiff competition from this place."

"Oh, I see," said Beth. "Is it ok that I just ordered the Cobb salad?"

"It's fine," said William.

They ate their meal mostly in silence. Despite what he'd told Beth, William didn't pay much attention to the food on his plate. He more drank his dinner than ate it. Beth picked at her salad, looking more and more concerned.

The waiter brought them dessert.

"We didn't order that," said William.

"Complements of the house, sir," the waiter said as he laid the plates in front of them. "Enjoy your cherry cheesecake."

William gave a raised eye brow at the slice of cheesecake on his plate like it was a snake that might be about to bite him. Laughing a little out loud at his own paranoia, both him and Beth enjoyed the fine dessert.

The waiter laid the check in front of William. He opened it and realized their dinner had been comped.

The valet met them at the door as the left. He examined William's claim ticket with a serious expression for a moment before speaking.

"Chevy Impala?" the valet asked.

William gave him a murderous look.

"Just kidding," the valet chuckled. "I'll be right back with your Rolls."

"Idiot," William muttered under his breath.

When the car came back a note was on the windshield. William snatched it before Beth could. He opened the note.

"The cheesecake may or may not have been laced with Botulism toxin, which may or may not be fatal. May the odds be forever in your favor."

William said a silent prayer that his war wouldn't hurt Beth. He already had one girlfriend who died as a result of his wars; he didn't need another.

"What is it?" Beth asked.

"Ad from a car detail shop. Apparently, they can't see this car has, like, ten coats of wax on it already."

William slept until nearly two in the afternoon but, after a shower and a shave, he went down to the diner to keep his promise to help out more. After an hour behind the bar, though, his mind began to wander. The more the customers' conversations droned on, the harder he found it to concentrate on his work. Orders for the tables began to back up as he just stood staring out the windows. Realizing that he wasn't doing anyone much good like this, he let Riley take over the bar and went for a drive.

As he turned onto the highway, after picking up his twelve pack of tacos, William reflected that it was a good thing he paid Riley well, considering all the extra work he kept having to take on.

Somewhere in the foothills, William stopped at a tiny hole in the wall bar with a row of snack vending machines out front and a dark, dingy interior. As he sat down at the worn, rustic bar, he noticed that all the men around him were twenty years older and forty pounds heavier. They all wore faded jeans and well-worn t-shirts. Most wore some type of grungy old ball cap. Everyone seemed took look sullenly down into their beer, drinking in silence except for the occasional grunt or murmur as they shifted their weight on the bar stools. For a moment William had the eerie feeling he might be looking into his own future -- provided Cherry didn't kill him before then.

"Johnny Walker," William said to the bartender.

The old man shook his head. "Sorry, son, this is a dry county. We only serve beer."

"Coors, then."

The bartender opened a bottle and set it in front of him. William took a long pull to quench his dry throat. He followed his first beer with a second and, as the old familiar buzz kicked in, he finally felt himself starting to relax a little. His stomach rumbled. Realizing he hadn't eaten yet, he got up to check out what the vending machines had to offer.

As William perused the candy bars and bags of chips he kept noticing a little red dot appearing and disappearing on the glass in front of him. The dot came and went so fast he wasn't sure it was even there. Then the dot appeared on his chest. Or he thought it did, by the time he looked down, it was gone.

William shook his head. It was probably just a reflection or some kids playing with a laser pointer, if it was even real at all and not just a product of his paranoid imagination. He bought a bag of chips and took it back to his seat at the bar.

A moment later the bar's phone rang. The bartender answered it with a gruff hello.

"Excuse me?" The bartender said into the phone. William watched the poor man cringe at whatever someone said at the other end of the line. "Ok, geez lady. Hold on, I'll ask."

The bartender set the receiver down and looked around the bar. "Is there a pathetic loser named Mr. Crowley here?"

The bar patrons looked at each other in confusion. William casually sipped his third beer and tried not to choke.

The bartender picked up phone again. "Sorry lady, not here." He cringed again as the female voice unleashed another wave of vitriol.

"Ok, ok, God." The bartender put the phone down again.

"Is there a walking bag of horse shit with an out of whack ego and serious daddy issues named Master Crowley sucking down liquid courage in here?"

William squirmed. A few of the other men in the bar had caught on by now and turned to look his direction. The bartender stared him down.

"Over here," William said reluctantly. People around the room began to laugh. They probably figured it was just his wife or girlfriend telling him to get his ass home.

William reluctantly put the receiver to his ear. For an absurd moment he imagined a bullet shooting out of the speaker and lodging itself in his brain. "Mr. Crowley here," he said.

"Borrowed time," Cherry said sweetly before hanging up. William handed the phone back to the bartender and ordered another round.

Late that evening William drove through town with a blood alcohol level well above the legal limit. As he passed two cops parked on one of the side streets having a bull session, he braced for trouble, but they just waved as he passed. William thanked his good driving skills and his new position of power and respect for making him as untouchable as his old rival, Randy Casner, had once been.

William pulled up behind the dinner and looked inside. Riley stood alone at the bar, drying glassware and putting it away. Even from this distance, William could see how worn and haggard his old friend looked. Feeling guilty, William slipped inside to offer help.

"Hey, man," William said. "How did tonight go?"

"Not the best," said Riley, "But not the worst either. Just kind of average I guess. Amy got on one of the kitchen hands for taking an overly long break, so he quit."

"Dammit!" said William. "I knew she was gonna cause problems. Why didn't you call me?"

"I did," said Riley. It was then that William realized he'd turned his phone off. He reached down and turned it back on.

"Sorry," said William. "What do you have left to do?"

"Just wiping down the kitchen counters and hauling the trash."

"Go on home," said William. "I'll take care of it."

"If you insist," said Riley. He gave William a long look. "You sure you're ok though?"

"I'm always ok," said William. "Go get some rest."

"Ok, goodnight, William."

"Goodnight."

After Riley left, William went behind the bar and poured himself the glass of Johnny Walker he'd been craving. As he savored the burn of the liquor he wondered how much longer he could keep up under this strain.

With the glass in one hand, he began hauling bags of trash out with the other. When he got to the dumpster he set his glass and pack of cigarettes on the nearby grease trap so he could use both hands to throw the bag in. Mid swing, the glass suddenly shattered. Its broken pieces fell on the cement at his feet. Thinking he must have just hit it with the bag, William tossed the trash. A moment later it the pack of cigarettes flew off the grease trap.

"What the hell?" William looked around frantically. He didn't see anything that could have caused the cigarettes to go flying.

He picked up the cigarette pack with a hole now in the center and put them back on the grease trap and waited. A moment later it flew off again. There was a ping and a crack as something hit the cinder block wall surrounding the grease trap and dumpster.

William looked down at the shattered glass and cigarette pack and spotted a small lead pellet like the type an air gun fired among the shards. His phone beeped. He looked at the screen. "BORROWED TIME!!!!!" read a text from the spoofed number '867-5309'.

"Jesus Christ," said William. Suddenly realizing that Cherry wasn't playing around anymore.

William ran inside his old bungalow and locked the door. Shaking from head to toe, he pulled his emergency bottle of Jack Daniels out from under the bed and poured a glass. And then another... and another before finally drifting off to sleep.

The next afternoon William woke up dry mouthed and fuzzy headed. He drank down a glass of water and grabbed his toothpaste.

"Dammit!" He yelled as he realized the tube was empty. He threw it across his tiny bathroom. The pipes began hammering. A moment later the faucet ran dry. "Stupid pipes, you gotta be kidding me!" William said as he reached under the sink to turn the main valve. "Million Goddamn dollars and I can't even get pipes that work."

Shaking himself off, he straightened up and reached for his cigarettes. After a moment of searching he remembered just what had happened to the cigarette pack and everything else that had happened the night before.

"Stupid Cherry!" William yelled.

He still figured that if Cherry had actually wanted him dead he would be, but he could no longer pretend she was only playing harmless pranks.

An idea formed. He wondered how soon Buddy could get a room ready in Canada.

Chapter 14

Runaway Train

"This is so exciting, William!" Beth chirped as they wound through the narrow two lane highway towards the Canadian border. "I've never just run off on a road trip before! It's like we're spies fleeing the country or something."

William laughed. If she only knew.

"Buddy told me this resort is really nice," said Beth. "He said that even though it's up north it's not really cold there or anything. It should be a lot of fun."

"Yeah, I figured we could use some time away since we've been so busy." William replied as he threw a cigarette butt out the window and kept driving as he lit another. As he took the first drag the smoke drifted across the car into Beth's face. He could tell she didn't like the smell, but instead of complaining she just waved the smoke away and smiled.

As the border approached, William began to reminisce about the last time he had tried to cross the border with Cherry. By sheer bad luck Glen Frey's song *Smuggler's Blues* had come on the radio just as the border agent had approached their car. Even though William had hurriedly turned it off, he could tell the agent had not been amused.

Before William had known it, they were singled out for closer inspection. First they brought out the drug dog. When he didn't find anything, they searched both the car and their luggage. The young man X-raying their bags had tried to remain professional, but could help to drop their jaw at some of the more interesting items in Cherry's bag. Even more humiliating, he had had to call a supervisor who had had to call another officer over as they debated whether or not some of the items qualified as dangerous weapons.

In the meantime, yet another agent had run their passports to search for outstanding warrants or past charges. After an hour, they revealed that Cherry and William were "too dangerous" to enter Canada. Rather than argue they had turned around... only to have to repeat the whole degrading process over again with agents from the American side of the border.

Somehow, William doubted Beth had packed anything more dangerous than a hairdryer. Just to be on the safe side, however, William turned off the radio as they pulled into the line of cars waiting to cross the border.

With a flash of a smile William handed over their Passports. The agent barely glanced at them before handing them back and waiving them through.

William supposed that counted as yet another victory but the lack of excitement left him disappointed.

As they crossed the border William felt like Michael Corleone hiding out in a different country till things cooled down. He could imagine himself hiking through hills and drinking wine for lunch every day. Didn't sound too bad at all.....

After settling into their room, they went down to the resort's spa for a few hours. The stone massage he got from the blond female therapist was exactly what his tight body needed. Although she did a fine job of getting out all of his knots, she was not as strong as Cherry was. Still, he enjoyed himself and was pleased that Beth would get to spend some time with him.

After their massage, they went to the tranquility room.

A man who looked straight from India approached them with a small menu and said nothing more than "Drink."

They looked at the drink menu and, before long, they were sitting in their bathrobes and enjoying champagne and a weird cucumber and vodka drink. William smiled for the first time in a while. Even though he had some money he hadn't had a real vacation in years.

"I enjoyed my massage, William," Beth said.

"That's good."

"You seem more relaxed, too."

"Well, honey, I've had a lot going on."

"Has something been bothering you William? Ever since you got that text on election night it seems like something's been wrong."

"Oh, Cher--- Beth, it's hard to explain. But don't ever ask me about my business," William said indulging his fantasy of being the runaway *Michael Corleone* he'd been imagining all day.

"Ok I won't ask," Beth said.

"Wait Beth Wait," William said in an Italian accent. "Just this once Beth. Just this once you can ask me about my business," William continued.

"Ok," Beth said confused. "What was the text you got on election night?"

"Yes Beth it was."

"What was the text?"

"Oh geez, you're not gonna believe this. Fucking Mitch! I didn't want to tell you, 'cause I didn't want to involve you, and I didn't want to involve Buddy. I've known him since kindergarten and now he's in a world of shit." William replied apprehensively.

"Oh that's terrible! What happened?" Beth replied concerned.

William laughed to himself how easy it was to lie to her. She never doubted him and didn't even demand to see the text message. He knew Cherry would stare him down till he cracked. His new mindset reminded him this was what any man would want in a woman. Yet, he almost hoped Beth would demand to see the text so he would be forced to tell what's really going on.

"Ok, Beth, Mitch was dating some girl from The Love House and he messed with her and got caught."

"Oh no, what did he do?"

"He made a psychotic music video and left it on her porch along with a black candle and tarot cards."

"What! Why would he do that?" Beth asked with a laugh.

"I asked him the same thing. Mitch has been hanging on my every word about this idea from Buddy of being a *man in his power* and he got this stupid idea he needed to prove to her that he was a *man in his power*."

"Wow, the people you meet, William. I'm glad you're normal."

"Oh, for sure," William said with a panicky laugh. "He really

227

needed to purge and now she's, like, gonna kill him. I asked about this music video he made."

"What did he say?"

"He described it as a disturbing video that expresses emotions and ideas that cannot be expressed in words."

"Wow, that kinda creepy."

"Well," William said as he clinched his teeth. "I think he's just the creative type. I mean he says normal people don't understand. What if *he* is the normal one and everyone else is crazy?"

"I don't know, black candles and tarot cards seem pretty weird."

"Yeah, for sure. I mean what a screwball. But what if he did it without really thinking about it, like just a momentary lapse of reason? Maybe something he regretted doing later?"

"I have no clue. I know people do things they regret. But they still must suffer consequences for it." Beth said sharply.

"Really?" William replied. This was the first time Beth had actually taken a stand on anything without his approval. "Ok, but even if the guy gets punished, what does it accomplish? What does it achieve?"

"Well, he needs to be punished so he learns not to do it again."

"Well," William snapped. "How the hell is he gonna learn anything if she kills him? What does he learn from that?" William blurted out in a louder than usual voice that seemed to startle Beth.

"I don't know, William, What do you think?"

"No, no, please," William said softly. "I wanna know what you think. I already know what I think. I mean, you're the most normal person I know. What does a normal person think should happen to someone who does something like make a psycho music video and leave it on some girl's porch with a burning black candle and tarot cards? Oh and just to be a real creep a note said it was from *Master Crowley* or something."

"Who?" Beth wondered.

"It's from this old video game called *Uninvited* we used to play as kids."

"Well, honey, if you ask me, Mitch should have to do community service and seek professional help. I mean, he did something bad and there always needs to be something that happens to them for it."

"You think so, huh?"

"Yes, otherwise he might make a second music video," Beth replied with a little laugh. William just gave a nervous smile and thanked his stars Beth didn't have that same sixth sense that Cherry did. Beth excused herself and went to use the bathroom. William sat there alone and talked to himself while he daydreamed.

Casting back his memory, he thought about the time he had gone to the local elementary school to observe the local police department's presentation of the *New Laws Program* and the cops' over the top reactions to the penalties for the various crimes listed.

He remembered vividly sitting in the classroom full of young teens and watching this presentation aimed at making them behave. Three idiots named Mike, Ike and Booker ran this program and would go from classroom to class room screaming the kids about how penalties had been increased for crimes in the city.

Mike and Ike were wearing their blue police uniform and hat but without their police duty belts that would normally have had their gun, cuffs and weapons on it. Both of them were tall, white, clean shaven and looked like brothers. They must have been from back east with their bright wrinkled Irish faces. William laughed inside that their faces looked like a pig's.

The third one was a short black guy with corduroy pants, dress shirt and bow tie. His short buzzed hair and intellectual eye glasses screamed total nerd. Each time Booker would read a new law and its new harsher punishment, either Mike or Ike would get mad and say "it's not enough; it's not enough." in a rough eastern accent.

He remembered the new penalty if someone played a game called *The Knockout Game* in the city.

"Alright Booker," Mike said. "If these moron kids decide to play *The Knockout Game* how much time can we give em? How much time? How much fuckin' time? How much fuckin' time?" Mike shouted.

"If one plays this game it is to be punished by up to three years," Booker said.

"No way!" Mike said as he grabbed Booker and shook him. "You gotta be kiddin' me."

"Hold on, hold on," Booker insisted. "If it is determined in a court of law that the assault was part of *The Knockout Game,* an additional punishment can be added."

"Okay, great," Mike said and released Booker. "*Additional*, that's my favorite word when it comes to punishing you little peckerwoods. Additional, additional, additional; I love it. How much *additional* time can we give 'em?"

"Additionally, another three years can be added if *The Knockout Game* was a factor."

"Oh, man, this is-- oh you gotta-- I'm outta here!" Mike said as he walked toward the door.

"Where are you going?" Booker demanded.

"What, it's not enough; it's not enough," Mike said as he turned around and left the classroom.

William always laughed that after Booker read the new penalty, Mike or Ike would act so surprised. If their job was to do this every day, all day long, you would think Mike and Ike would know exactly what the new penalty was and not be too surprised. He figured this was all an act to intimidate the kids, but he felt they just looked like jackasses.

Now his mind twisted the memory to include his own crimes.

"Leaving a psychotic DVD on someone's porch," Mike screamed. "How much time can we give em' Booker? How much fuckin' time?"

"Leaving a DVD on someone's porch is now punishable by--"

"What!" Mike Interrupted. "That's it? That's all the time we can give him? That's bullshit Booker. It's not enough?

"What penalty do you think is enough?" Booker asked Mike.

William's daydream went outlandish when instead of Booker asking Mike, he was asking Cherry.

"Kill em!" Cherry replied with a sawed off shotgun in her hand.

William was glad to have Beth disturb his daydream by handing him more champagne.

"I'm sorry I took so long in the bathroom," Beth said.

"Oh, sure, whatever, I mean, taking too long in the bathroom. What should the penalty be for that?" William replied.

"I don't know," Beth said nervously.

"It's not enough! It's not enough!" William replied with a foolish smile.

"Okay, I'm sorry," Beth said having no idea what William was talking about.

The waiter approached them.

"I hope you two enjoyed your complimentary bottle of champagne. Would you guys like an additional bottle this evening?"

"*Additional*," William said. "My favorite word when it comes to alcohol. I sure would," William said.

He realized he didn't even ask Beth if she wanted more. Once they got their additional bottle they went back to chatting.

"Beth do you believe that *additional* punishment deters crime? Do you think that excessively punishing someone like Mitch would be a good thing?"

"I don't believe in just punishing someone excessively is the answer. I do think Mitch needs to pay some sort of penalty for scaring that girl. But also he needs psychiatric help. I hope Mitch realizes what he did was wrong and that he gets the help he needs."

"Oh, for sure. I mean, it's just that easy," William responded. "One day I can just--- I mean – he can just wake up and not have anything wrong with him. I mean have you ever done any mental health counseling?"

"I did as a teen when some kids at my school got drunk and crashed on the highway. The school counselors were very kind in making sure all the students had a professional to talk to."

"I see. I was forced to do mental health counseling during my years of fighting for the rights of this city."

"Did you find it useful, honey?" Beth said with a smile.

"Not at all. I mean she was some prissy little college twerp who had amazing mommy and daddy. She got to go to college and throw keggers every night and bullshit her way through school. I'm sure she never did any hard labor in her life and never suffered for anything. No one ever degraded her or mistreated her. Her parents baked cookies for their church and they lived in some McMansion. Daddy would drive them all the church every Sunday to pray to their fake God in the big SUV."

"What does that have to do with anything?" Beth wondered. "If she qualified to be a professional counselor why does it matter where

231

she came from?" Beth said in the sternest voice William had ever heard from her.

"Because how is this girl gonna understand me or someone like Mitch? Or understand anyone who struggles? To me, it's like the difference between someone who studied Vietnam in college and someone who went to Vietnam."

"I guess, but she may know what a person's mental disorder is and help them."

"Sure, meds. I mean, do you think Mitch asked to be this way? Do you think he enjoys it? Do you think he can just turn it off whenever he wants?"

"I don't know; maybe medication can help your friend."

"What do you think of Buddy?" William said, wanting to redirect the conversation.

"Buddy is a good life coach. I think many guys feel down on themselves when they don't need to. I know so many girls who would love a boyfriend, but guys are too timid to just ask them."

"Sure, but he is another one who doesn't understand. I mean how can you make someone a *man in his power* when they don't know how. I mean his favorite choir member is *The Yesman*. Imagine people who survived Auschwitz. They were held at gunpoint and forced to work. You think they can simply one day be like 'I'm not a *Yesman* anymore I'm *man in his power*.' If someone is just raised to be a *Yesman* they can't just turn it off by simply realizing they're one."

"Well, Buddy can show them the steps they can take. I think a person can completely change who they are if they try. It seems you learned a lot from him. At first you seemed like you didn't believe in yourself; that you thought you could never be a councilman and be free from an obnoxious girlfriend. But you did it; you changed who you are." Beth replied.

"I don't know. I feel like they can *fake it* and morons will believe they are something they're not."

"Well, maybe *fake it till you make it* works," Beth replied, unaware that William was referring to her as the moron who believed he was something he wasn't. "William, honey, I know things were rough for you and years of being arrested for doing the right thing hurt you. It's ok that you needed counseling. There is no shame that you needed Buddy to relight your fire and help you be the great person you are today." Beth said in her usual silky tone.

"Yeah, I'm really sane and normal minded," William said sarcastically.

"I know you are," Beth replied unaware of his sarcasm. "William do you ever think about children?"

"No! I'm not a pedophile!"

"Oh, William," Beth said with a laugh, "I mean having your own kids."

"No, I never did," William replied. He wondered for a moment if he could even have kids. He was worried that years of Cherry, drinking, smoking and stress would make that impossible.

"I think kids are a necessity, William," Beth said.

"Why?"

"To create and mold a life. To give children the chance to enjoy existence."

"Yeah, cause this world is so great. Everything's a lie and that's a fact! I would worry my kids would be cursed like me."

"What you mean?"

"What if he ended up like me? Just over-worked and persecuted. I would never want another me in the world."

"You would be a great father, we could give the kid so much love," Beth insisted.

"Yeah, sure, I could teach the kid how to be a *man in his power* and stuff."

"I'm not asking right away, but children are a gift from God," Beth insisted again.

"God?" William replied. This was the first she ever mentioned religion.

"Yes, didn't you go to church?"

"I think to do community service once or twice."

"Ha ha. I was raised Catholic. Children are God's gift."

"Is He gonna pay for them? I'm not kidding when I say I don't want them to suffer like I did."

"Even if our kids had struggles. God has a plan for them and would love them."

"Yeah, God's gift. Did God love all the people that were

disintegrated at the World Trade Center?" William said as he thought of the clips from *his* music video.

"I can't believe you had no religious upbringing?"

"None at all. We just thought it all was a lie to control people and keep them working and paying taxes and feeling like their meager existence mattered."

"Wow, William, I didn't know. Don't worry, I sure won't push it on you. But I would like you to come to Wednesday night services with me once."

"Do I have a choice?"

"Of course, you never have to do anything you don't want to."

William was used to Cherry not giving him a choice when he was told to do something for his own good.

"I'll think about it," he said.

After a few days relaxing around the resort, William began to feel like his old self. He still drank, but the hunted feeling left him. Even Beth began to seem less annoying. He began to think that they just might be able to make this work. It seemed it was time to come out of hiding.

As they lounged by the pool Beth's phone rang. Strangely, she hopped up and scurried away before answering. When she came back, she wore a solemn expression instead of her usual vapid smile.

"I'm sorry, William," Beth said sadly. "We need to go home. Auntie Kelli is in the hospital."

"Oh no," said William.

Beth spent most of the trip home staring out her window and brooding. William tried more than once to start a conversation but she mostly gave just one word answers. She would still get animated for a moment here and there, but she seemed hollow. When they got home, Beth left her bag in the hallway and sank down on the couch.

"William?" she said plaintively, "Is it ok if I want to be alone for a little while?"

"Sure," he said. "I'll go see how things are at the diner." He paused in the doorway, wondering whether he should hug or kiss her, or? In the end, he just left her there.

Riley greeted William at the door of the diner with a smile and a hand shake. "Well, well, look who's back. How was the trip?"

"Too short," said William. "What have we got going on?"

"Well, we're short wait-staff, so Amy has two sections and the Ladies' Auxiliary is here for their weekly lunch and are as charming as ever." Riley rolled his eyes. William laughed.

"Well, I'll pitch in wherever you want me. I'm yours for the day."

"Um, could you take over the bar? I have some book keeping to do."

"You've got it."

William watched with dread as the mousy little waitress, Amy, who had given him such a hard time, struggled to keep up with the demands of her tables. The girl got more and more flustered as the stress piled up. He noticed she didn't use tray jacks even though it was the diner's policy. She brought one table's entrees only to have them immediately rejected.

"Oh my God, there's no difference between Ranch and Italian dressing. You're really gonna make me re-make the salad?" Amy said to a family of four.

After what seemed to be a few heated words, she stomped back into the kitchen with the tray. A few moments later, William heard a heated argument in the kitchen.

"That's not the right way to wash those dishes," She barked at the dishwasher.

He thought of intervening, but Riley beat him to it, so he just poured more drinks for people and watched the show.

Amy came marching back out of the kitchen, spine straight and face puckered as she once again approached the complaining customers. William noticed her trying to text on her phone while serving the food.

Once again a heated discussion began between Amy and the customers.

"Here's your stupid salads," She said as she continued to text on her phone. Amy twisted her tray to the side to type and then watched with horror as it tipped, spilling two plates of hot pasta all over the already angry customers.

Immediate silence fell. Heads turned towards the spectacle. Amy dropped the tray on the floor. She covered her face with her hands and groaned.

Riley and another waitress rushed out to help clean up the mess, apologizing profusely as they assessed the damage. William heard him make promises about free meals and paying the cleaning bill. Amy's eyes caught his. William pointed to the office door.

"Do you care to explain yourself?" William asked the waitress as she cowered near is desk.

"It, it was an accident!" she said.

"Well, obviously. What I don't understand is how you could be careless enough to let it happen. Why were you texting while holding a tray of food?"

"My friend is sad today, but I guess you don't care do you? I was tired, and we'd been busy and I just... I don't even know. This place sucks."

"We always use tray jacks, we *never* text on the job but you decided to do it anyway cause your friend is sad."

"My friend was sad today and I need to calm her down. That's more important than stupid people's food."

"Amy, how much restaurant experience did you have before this job?"

"I went to college, I have Bachelor's degree. I should be making at least sixty grand a year with my degree. This place doesn't come close to that."

"In what?"

"Women's Studies," She huffed.

"So what made you think you were qualified to tell everyone what to do?"

"Like, everyone here is stupid. I'm doing everyone a favor."

"I really think this isn't the job for you."

"I was, uh, actually thinking that myself," Amy replied. "I was actually going to put in my notice Friday."

"Oh, well, that's settled then. No hard feelings. What do you plan to do next?"

"I've accepted a position as a women's advocate at Martha Stout's new non-profit for sexual assault victims."

William's eyes narrowed. He could have happily choked the little bitch. "Oh, I'm sure that will pay very well. You'll be out of your parents' basement in no time. Now get out."

"Excuse me?"

"You're done. Now. Leave. Don't bother to return the apron. We don't need you to finish your notice."

"But--"

"Bye."

William followed her out of the office. Riley watched with confusion, then shock and then horror as Amy gathered her things and left.

"Well, that's just great. Now what?" Riley wondered.

"Relax, I've got it covered."

William pulled an old napkin out of his desk and dialed the smudged number written on it.

"Hey there," he said when the waitress from the gentleman's meeting answered. "This is William Defreno, remember me?"

"Of course, Mr. Councilman!" Sherry replied. "Congratulations, by the way."

"Thanks. Hey listen... how would you like a job where creeps keep their hands off you and you get to keep your clothes on?"

"Sounds great."

"Fantastic. Get here in an hour and it's yours."

"I'm on my way."

William looked a Riley's pale face and shook his head. "You know, buddy, I think you're the one who needs a vacation."

"I'll settle for a drink" said Riley. William poured him a double.

In just one week William was able to clean up the diner and bring it back to the way it was before he ran for office. What was once waitresses like Amy was now waitresses like Sherry from the meeting, who enjoyed the opportunity to make as much as a stripper without removing her cloths. The carpets were professionally cleaned, the kitchen power washed and the old food removed.

William decided to go ahead and take Beth to church on a Wednesday since he didn't know what else might help her feel better.

"You look pretty," He told her as she got in the car.

"Thank you," she said sadly.

For twenty minutes the church band sang such adorable songs like 'Isn't the name of Jesus Beautiful' and 'Lion and the Lamb.' Beth sang along with the other thirty to thirty-five people in the church. William couldn't help thinking of his music video and all the news clips and terrible thing in it that this Jesus they all loved let happen to the world.

Finally, the pastor came out. He stood six feet tall, wore thin glasses, looked in his sixties and was half bald, but slicked his hair back.

"Can you all feel Jesus?" the pastor said to the standing crowd who was absorbing the last notes of the beautiful song. William could hear a few say "yes, I can" and "I feel you, Jesus."

"Can you all feel Him?" the pastor asked again. "Can you all feel the love, warmth and forgiveness of Jesus? Can you feel the heat of Jesus in the room?"

William just rolled his eyes and wondered why he had to say *feel the heat.* Everyone seems so absorbed into this feeling. It's like in their minds they really were feeling the love of their creator, whether it was real or not. Finally, everyone sat down and William realized he had never stood up and Beth sure wasn't going to correct his rude behavior.

"Thank you, all," The pastor started. "Before we begin I would like everyone to meet and greet each other and share the love."

Without even asking Beth, William snuck off to the bathroom to avoid shaking hands with the other church people. Finally, when meet and greet was done he came back in.

"Thank you all again," the pastor said. "And a warm welcome to William Defreno, the city's newest councilman."

William's jaw dropped. He hadn't realized anyone here had noticed him. He hoped the pastor and his congregation would not want to push their agendas onto him. They all clapped for him as he stood with a fake smirk on his face until the pastor motioned for silence.

William sat back down, still feeling eyes on him as the pastor began to speak.

"Ok everyone," The pastor began. "Before we start on Exodus, I wanna tell you a little story. On Monday someone came up to me and asked 'why is God important?' Why do we need Him in our lives? I responded that God is everything. We don't exist without God. He is not just a being we say *hi* to now and again like a distant high school friend. He is everything you see. I told this man do you know why Jesus died on the cross?"

William suddenly remembered Cherry telling him that Jesus died on the cross because He forgot his *Safe Word*. He struggled not to laugh out loud at the memory.

"He died for our sins!" The pastor passionately continued. "He died so we could all be here today. And why is God important? I told this man look around. Families without God do things like divorce. Families without God have siblings that hate each other instead of loving one and other. Children that hate their parents and are prone to depression and crime. Parents and children without God get sucked into devilish temptations like alcoholism, drug abuse and marital affairs."

William gulped when he heard the world "alcoholism."

Finally, the sermon started. With almost no religious background William had no clue what was being said.

"So Moses told them, 'this is the bread the LORD has given you to eat,'" the pastor said.

"Bread?" William said to Beth.

"Yes, William," she responded.

"What a cheapskate! I mean He can create the universe but all He gives them to eat is bread? How 'bout some sushi or T-bone steaks."

He sat through the next forty-five minutes. Although the story may have been interesting to hear he just didn't understand what this had to do with anything. How does this mean God loves them? How does this prove God's existence? He didn't understand what anyone got out of this. He just settled back in his seat and tried not to fall asleep.

On the drive home Beth seemed a bit happier.

"Thank you for coming with me, William, that really meant a lot."

"Oh, you're welcome."

"You're so supportive. I'm so glad I have you," Beth said with a smile.

William suddenly felt guilty.

"Um, how's your aunt, he asked.

"Not good." Beth frowned again. "Actually, I kinda need to talk to you about that."

"Oh?" said William.

"Uh, yeah, they are releasing her tomorrow but she can't really be alone so I'm going to have to stay with her for awhile."

"How long?"

Beth sighed and shrugged. "However long it takes her to get better, I guess."

William reached out and awkwardly patted her shoulder. "It'll be ok."

"I hope so," said Beth.

The next morning William helped Beth put her bag in her car and waved her off. He hung around for a bit, but found he couldn't stand being alone in a house that wasn't really his, so he packed up his own bags and the cat and headed for the diner.

After a few hours of working, he felt like his old self again. He happily tended bar until close and then stayed to help with clean up. It felt good to be back. As he took out the trash, he kicked something. Looking down he saw a shard of glass from the night Cherry had shot his whiskey glass with her pellet gun. He suddenly realized she hadn't bothered them since they'd come back from Canada. Maybe she was finally over it.

He poured himself one last drink for the night to celebrate and curled up with the cat for a nice peaceful sleep.

Sometime in the early morning William woke to the sound of loud banging on his door. At first he ignored it, but then the sound started again. Finally, he got up to see what it was about.

Chapter 15

The Fool

Opening his door just a crack, he spotted a long black taper candle burning in a clear glass holder. Next to it was *The Fool* card from a tarot deck and a DVD case with "From Mistress Crowley" written across it in bright red Gothic letters.

William shook his head. "You gotta be kidding me? What the hell's wrong with that woman? Normal people don't do this shit," he said as he blew out the candle and brought the DVD inside.

Well, so much for Cherry being done with him.

Since he was up anyway, he put on the DVD to see what it was about.

Beck's song *Loser* thumped on his TV speakers as he watched a politician in some other small town give a speech, with a girl who looked oddly like Beth at his side. The tape gave the date as four years ago. He recognized the next man in the video as Robert Hayduke who had run for city council two towns away few years ago. He stood at a podium... next to yet another girl who looked exactly like Beth.

Clip after clip showed her next to one politician or another. She was introduced as the wife of Angelo Scott who was running for State house of Representative. Finally, when the main chorus of *Soy un perdedor I'm a loser baby so why don't you kill me* came on it showed Beth and William at his big speech against Martha Stout.

William knew Cherry timed that clip just right to go along with the song lyrics. Another clip of Beth giving an introduction speech for her so called husband Aleister Wesson who was running for Crowley County Commissioner.

Even though the music didn't allow him to hear what she was saying. Her passion was clear that she really loved and supported her *so called husband.*

The video moved on to her listings on an elite escort site.

William was hypnotized with rage. The remote slipped out of his hand and he didn't even bother to pick it up.

"Oh my God!" William yelled as he knocked over the drink he'd left on the table.

The end of the song and video was William smiling for the camera while the lyrics *I'm a driver, I'm a winner, things are gonna change I can feel it.* Then it was him shaking hands after his speech with Beth by his side and the lyrics *Soy un perdedor I'm a loser baby so why don't you kill me* being said over and over.

Still shaking with rage, William picked up his phone to call Beth. It went to voicemail, so he called her again. Then again, then again. Finally, after seven, tries her tired voice answered.

"What is it, William?"

"So you're an escort, huh?"

"What?"

"Don't you *what* me! Robert Hayduke, Angelo Scott, Aleister Wesson? How much does Buddy pay you for this shit?"

"William, you don't understand--"

"Oh, I understand. It's like I said: I wouldn't want kids cause everything's a lie and that's a fact!"

"I wanted to make some money. Just listen, I--"

"Yeah, I know, the all mighty fucking dollar! Did you even care that maybe guys like me or any of the other suckers might have thought you really loved us? That you were really proud of me and wanted to be that so called *dream wife* Buddy insisted I wanted."

"I'm sorry, William, but it's just how it is. I did really enjoy being with you."

"Yeah, as long as Buddy's paying you and we're doing fun things. How much did he pay you for your conscience?"

"William, what was the harm? I mean these guys were single anyway. They got to win their elections and have a good time."

"Maybe, but they were single. But I had Cherry!"

"I enjoyed being with you," Beth sobbed. "I even told Buddy I didn't want to do this anymore because you were special and I wanted to stay with you."

"Yeah, bet you said that to Aleister, the Crowley County Commissioner so what bullshit was gonna happen next? After we get married Buddy makes sure I accidentally die and you get the diner?"

"No, I would never participate in something like that."

"How many of these assholes did you sleep with? Do I need to get tested for STD's or something?"

"No, it's not like that," Beth said continuing to sob.

"Whatever, goodbye, Beth!" William said as he hung up and threw his phone across the room. He went back to his desk. On the shelf was the bottle of Evan William's Cherry Reserve Kentucky Whiskey. He knew he would use it when he was either so happy he needed to celebrate or when times were at their worst. Even if this wasn't the very worst, he figured he it was close enough.

By 4AM the bottle was almost gone and a drunk William picked up his phone to send a text message.

"Cherry, it's William ;(;(. You win, you win. I DID IT!! I made the Fucking music videos. I drank the full bottle of Kentucky whiskey you bought me tonight. I already fell once tonight and fucked up my face again.

'You wanna know why I really did it? Here it is…… here is why…. I'm fucking nothing, you're better than me, your strong, tough smart, pretty, nice, lovable, respectable. You're everything I wish I could be. I know, what a fucked up reason to do it, but it's true. I don't know why I let those guys try to turn me into them. I not a *man in his power*, I never was. I could hardly fake it anyway. The stupid public has no idea what *Yesman* they just elected to run the city. You should've just let me do my plan years ago instead of saving me.

'Cherry, I am on my fucking hands and knees, with tears in my eyes am I am begging you for forgiveness for what I have done. Please God Cherry forgive me and don't do anything more to me

Please DON'T ….. don't do it!! I'm coming to you admitting I
made a mistake and begging you to forgive me. I'm so sorry
Cherry, I'm so sorry Cherry, I'M SO SORRY!!!!"

William woke well after 6 P.M. Even though he could hear how
busy the diner was, he stayed in bed until well after they closed
instead of going in to work.

As he scrolled through his phone he saw a number of missed calls
and texts from both Buddy and Beth, but no word yet from Cherry.

Since he was now thoroughly detoxed, William figured it was
time to *Retox*. He slipped into the bar and helped himself to a bottle of
Rockin' Rye from behind the bar.

It really wasn't that bad, he told himself. So Beth was a fake. He
could get over it. He could get over Buddy lying to him. He could get
over losing Cherry. He still had his money, the diner and his new
political office. He'd be ok.

And the local little league team would win the Series next year.

Shaking his head in disgust, he grabbed his keys and went for a
drive. He was already on the road before he realized he'd never
finished his drink.

As he drove in circles the Rolls began to act strangely, sputtering
and choking as he drove, then starting back up after he hit the brakes.
Feeling uneasy, he turned around to head for home. When he parked
behind the closed diner he wondered what could be wrong with the
car.

"Well, shit," said William. He climbed out of the car to have a
look. A loud click echoed in the night. He turned around to see a hot
barreled 45 pointed at him.

"Don't move!" A pretty voice said.

From the dark shadows he could see it was Cherry aiming the gun
at him.

"Oh my God!" William said, much more calmly than Cherry
expected. He looked around their isolated surroundings and realized
any chance of help was unlikely. He would have to face her on his
own. He calmly accepted he would be shot behind his own diner with
so many memories surrounding him.

He remembered when he was eighteen and still working for the old owner, Lois. He came to work drunk and slept in the dumpster. He remembered she called him asking where he was and had no idea he was there all day, just not inside working. He next remembered smoking out back with his late girlfriend, Annie, 'cause Lois didn't allow them to smoke in the hotel room that was now his house. Next was fighting with Roger, years later, after he bought the place.

He laughed and shook his head and wondered how it would feel to go back and tell the past him that this spot was where he was going to die. Would it be weird to the old him? Would it change anything? He knew he would die somewhere but expected it would be in a car crash or by his own hands. This was not the plan. He also pondered that Cherry once saved him from killing himself and now was going to be the one to do exactly what she begged him back in the day not to do.

He realized he had three choices. First, he could try to fight the gun away from her. He was tired, hung over and unarmed and not ready to try to snatch a gun away from her. He looked at her solid and sharp black leather boots. If he fought her and were to let his guard down for even a second, those shoes and her strong legs would make sure he regretted it.

Next, he could try to pretend he had a gun too or a bodyguard nearby with one.

"So, William," Cherry said. "Even after all the things I've done to you, you still don't carry a gun or have security in the place. Heck, you still leave the door to your house unlocked."

"How do you know that, Cherry? Did you try the lock? Why not shoot me while I sleep?"

"Oh, William, honey, I didn't have to try the lock or stalk you to see if you carry a gun or have security. I just know you. I know your attitude."

"Attitude?" William pondered.

"Yeah, since you were a kid you've always had the attitude that nobody could hurt you," Cherry said as she stared him down. For almost ten seconds she stared at him with a cold terrifying stare. She didn't even blink. "I think you were wrong," she finally continued.

William gulped and realized number two was just snuffed out. All that was left was option three, throw himself on her mercy.

"Cherry, I'm sorry I--"

"Shut up, ok? Geez!"

"Okay."

"You always thought you were untouchable, huh? Even as a little punk eighteen year old you thought you could take down the criminal elite. You thought you could never go to prison. You broke into a corrupt cop's house to steal evidence. Never once did you think you could be arrested for it. You thought you could steal drug money and fake your death and nobody would ever figure it out."

"I didn't want to; it just sort'a happened."

"Oh, of course, you wanted it. You figured you would somehow slip through the cracks. And, you know what, you did! So, good for you for cleaning up the city for a day. But, all it did was confirm your idea that you never think you would have consequences for your actions. You got your old girlfriend, Annie, killed in the crossfire."

"I really didn't want that to happen!"

"No, no, you never wanted it happen. But you do things and you always say *I didn't think this would happen.* You think because you didn't *want it to happen* it won't? I'm sure one of these nights when you're driving around drunk and plow into a minivan with a family in it you'll be sure to cry to the judge about how you *didn't mean to do that.* And then you expect to just get away with it because of that."

"Cherry, I can't help who I am. I wanted one life; I had to have another. I actually was really thinking about the idea of being with Beth and having kids and doing the whole suburbia thing. But it was lies and bullshit!"

"Yeah, I know. She was so perfect wasn't she? Never complains, never doubts anything you do, never corrects you when you're wrong. I doubt she would take your keys away when you're too drunk to drive. Or would tell you that it's not ok to leave scary shit on someone porch just to prove what a *man in your power* you are. I was actually wondering if the problem with you was just ignorance or arrogance. But now I know. It's both!"

William's eyes widened for a second. He didn't know how to respond.

"Yeah," Cherry continued. "I know you never got an equal share. Everyone else always had more opportunities than you. And you know what? Maybe you're right. You did work hard you did have it rough and you did do the wrong things for the right reasons. But do you think because of that you have this like stack of *get out of trouble free* cards that you can use anytime you want? "

"I don't know," William said as his voice cracked.

"You know why you said you're jealous of me even though you're the millionaire and powerful city councilman? Because I'm not addicted to the idea that I need to prove my worth to the world. I don't need things like trophies and fake relationships and newspaper articles to prove I'm worthy of existence. I don't do bad things just because I want to prove how *powerful* I am."

"But I really wanted to be part of city council."

"Maybe you could've won without all the tricks and crimes and bullshit. Maybe without scaring the fucking shit out of me! You're actually *not* a *Yesman* except to Buddy. I find it funny how Buddy tells his clients not to be a *Yesman*, yet he expects them to do just what he says. It's like teaching a child not to smoke by making him smoke."

"I guess, but I wouldn't have won without him."

"Sure, but maybe if he hadn't insisted you show that Maisy bitch what a powerful man you were by grabbing her you would've never needed all the bullshit hospital stories and Beth helping to sell girl scout cookies to overcome it. I was at your big speech remember?"

"Yes, I do," William said sadly.

"It was all you. You gave a true passionate speech and had more sense than Martha did. It was you William, you won it fair and square; it wasn't Beth or Buddy. They set you up for success but it was you that did it. Why do you think they choose you out of everyone else in town to coach and run? Because he knew you could do it."

William pondered why she wanted to make him feel better, yet still had the 45 firmly aimed at him.

"Thanks, Cherry. Maybe put the gun down now?"

"Not yet, There's not gonna be a *get out of trouble free* this time, William," Cherry said sternly.

William hung his head, fighting the urge to weep.

"You do need to be punished." Cherry held out her left hand, palm up.

"Keys," she said. William fished them out of his pocket. Thinking it would be smarter to keep his distance from Cherry, he lightly tossed her the keys. Cherry caught them easily. She opened the car door, put the keys in the ignition.

Relief washed over William. He was fine with her taking the car. It was acting up anyway and insured. If that was all this cost him he knew he'd be getting off easy. From the driver's seat Cherry lowered all the windows slightly and raised the radio antenna. She climbed out of the car to face him again. William's heart raced faster.

"Phone," she ordered.

"It's just my personal phone," William protested.

"Hand it to me!"

"Please don't break it!" William begged.

"Hey, shut the fuck up!"

Realizing that arguing would only enrage her, he handed it over. With a wicked gleam in her eyes, she deliberately dropped the expensive device on the ground. William winced as he heard the glass screen shatter. Not content to stop there, Cherry stomped on what was left of the phone with her boots, crunching it into pieces. When she was done she picked up the fragments and tossed them into the car.

"Wallet."

William hesitated, but her eyes warned him that he had better cooperate. He pulled out his billfold and held it out. She took it and threw it into the car as well.

"Lighter." William surrendered that as well. Out of everything, he was most sad about this because he had had that Lucky Strike lighter for almost twenty years. He was surprised when she tucked it into her pocket instead of destroying it.

"Lean on the car and drop your pants"

"Excuse me?" William wondered

"Is English your second language? I got yet one more bucket list item that I want to cross off. But this won't be nearly as fun for you as the last bucket item you helped me with," Cherry demanded as she aimed the gun right between his eyes. Too intimidated to resist, he began slowly leaning against the car. She snapped the antenna off the car.

William stared at her in shock. This had to be a dream.

"Now, William." As quickly as his shaky arms and legs allowed he assumed the position. Fear made him lightheaded as he was bent over the truck of his beloved Rolls Royce. He prayed for mercy from a God he still wasn't sure he actually believed in. She wouldn't... She couldn't.

She did.

"Oh God!" William yelled as the first blow landed on his bare skin. A second followed, and a third. "Christ!" he exclaimed as a particularly hard lash hit the tops of his thighs. He wanted to beg her to stop, but he didn't. He suffered the onslaught as stoically as he could, hissing his breath through clenched teeth and only occasionally shouting out another "Oh God" or "Good Christ" when the pain became overwhelming.

He didn't have to take this. *Just get up*, he told himself. *Just get up. Run away. You are a man in his power.* But he stayed in place, holding himself up on trembling arms as the blows rained down. *You are a man in his power*, he told himself again. *Fight back*. Yet, still, he stayed put. *You are a man-* He screamed. *You are a-* He screamed again. She was going to beat him to death. *You are-* "Ohhh Gooooooddddd!"

"Didn't know you were so religious," Cherry shouted. "Thought you didn't believe in God. Maybe you should pray to a scientist, huh?" She continued.

The entire county had to hear him screaming. She wasn't going to stop. *You- can fight this.* The thought didn't even pass his mind that this was undeserving to him, just that he didn't want it to happen. William finally broke. He collapsed onto the trunk, coughing and howling.

What felt like centuries later, Cherry finally tossed the antenna aside.

"Get up," she said in a soft tone. Slowly and stiffly William pushed himself up. His flesh burned from his waist to his knees. It felt like glass shards cut away at his muscles every time he moved.

Never in his life had William felt so broken. He wished she had just killed him.

Cherry pulled a can of lighter fluid and two white hand towels out of her bag. Oh good. If she sets him on fire he wouldn't have to live with the agony in his skin.

He wouldn't be so lucky. Cherry doused the inside of the car with the lighter fluid. Then she soaked the two rags, lit them and tossed them into the car. She kicked the driver's door shut.

"Better clear out," she said.

They moved a safe distance away. William watched helplessly as the flames ate away at his car. He was too numb to feel anything.

"Well Mr. *man in his power*, now I forgive you." She gave him a quick peck on the cheek. "See you around, Councilman."

She left him standing alone in the falling dark. He didn't even know what to do but watch the flames engulf his car.

A few days later, William lay in bed. He flipped through the TV channels, trying to find something to watch that didn't remind him of Cherry or other recent events. His flaming Rolls seemed to be in the news on every channel.

Buddy had released a statement on his behalf saying that it was a shame that even city politicians could no longer travel the streets in broad daylight without being assaulted by roving gangs of thugs. He'd turned it into a pitch to increase police funding and cracking down on the area's *dangerous inhabitants* and had made it sound like anyone opposed was leaving the average citizen at the mercy of total anarchy.

The door of his little shack swung inward. Cherry walked in. William wondered where was his new bodyguard.

"Paul's taking a little nap so we can talk," Cherry said, answering William's unspoken question.

"Oh."

"Yeah, I mean, I realize a lot of what you did you did because other people manipulated you into it. They played you, and they're still playing you. Buddy and his pals are using you like a puppet, and that's not right. Granted, you're getting a better deal than I did, but you're still a victim in this, too."

"Wait, are you apologizing to me?"

"Well, kinda, you still deserved it. Jesus, William, if you had any idea about even half the hell you put me through you'd beat yourself even harder."

"I don't think I could reach."

Cherry rolled her eyes. Despite herself, she laughed. "The thing is, I miss you, William. Nobody's ever made me feel as alive as you do."

"Wow." William said.

"You're the only person who I've ever felt like I could be my whole honest self with. Even at my darkest, my scariest, you still want me. And you want me be because of it, not in spite of it."

"Well, you know," William shrugged. "I suppose you're hot when you're angry."

Cherry hung her head and sighed. "I'm not ok right now. I'll have to get into therapy, take the meds for awhile. It may be a long time before I get back to good."

"I understand," said William. He put a hand on hers.

"It's a dark road, but I've come back before, so at least I know the way." she smiled at him. "And moral support is always welcome."

"I'm with you all the way."

She kissed him lightly. Even that was enough to electrify ever nerve he had.

"I'll call you in a few days," she said. "Stay out of trouble, ok?"

"Sure, I'll behave. I got my insurance check for the car."

"Oh good, you know those cars have terrible electrical problems anyway," Cherry said.

William smiled at Cherry. She smiled back before she slipped out the door and disappeared.

William shut off the TV. He reached for a bottle of liquor, but then put it down and smiled. For the first time since he could remember he actually felt at peace. Maybe it was a good time for a nap before dinner shift started.

DID YOU ENJOY THIS BOOK?

SEND QUESTIONS OR COMMENTS TO THE AUTHOR:

DAVE AQUINO
P.O. BOX 741351
ARVADA, CO 80006-1351

Books by Dave Aquino

Personal War

Personal War Part 2

Personal War Part 3

Counselor

The Slot Machine

Personal War, William's Triumph

Stress Management

for Adult Children of Alcoholics

How to manage everyday life without being
overcome by childhood trauma

Lolita Ščesnavičiūte Guarín

Published by Lolita Guarín Publishing

ISBN (paperback): 979-8-9881415-0-1
ISBN (ebook): 979-9881415-1-8

Illustrations by Lolita Scesnaviciute Guarin
Book Design by Maggie McLaughlin

Printed in the United States of America

Contents

Before We Start   1

Chapter 1: Difficulty Expressing Emotions   7

Chapter 2: Being Pessimistic   18

Chapter 3: Difficulty Dealing with Anger   28

Chapter 4: Fear of Abandonment   39

Chapter 5: Need Validation   5_

Chapter 6: Relying on the Opinions of Others   62

Chapter 7: Need to Control the Environment   74

Chapter 8: Difficulty with Intimate Relationships   85

Chapter 9: Extremely Loyal   96

Chapter 10: Difficulty Setting Boundaries   108

Chapter 11: Anxiety and Hypervigilance   119

Chapter 12: Eager to Please   130

Chapter 13: Being an Empath   141

Chapter 14: Feeling Not Good Enough   152

Chapter 15: Difficulty Having Fun   163

Chapter 16: Difficulty Trusting   174

Chapter 17: Blind to Red Flags   185

Chapter 18: Grief   196

Chapter 19: Can't Stand Criticism   206

Chapter 20: Codependency 217

Chapter 21: Difficulty Finding the Right Mate 228

Chapter 22: Need Immediate Gratification 238

Chapter 23: Feeling Lonely 249

Chapter 24: Taking on Too Much Responsibility 260

Chapter 25: Difficulty Forming Healthy Relationships 272

I dedicate this book to my parents.
I love you both.
No matter what.

Before We Start

When the stress made me physically ill, I learned how to manage it naturally without getting a handful of pills to swallow. I learned about meditation, yoga, proper nutrition, breathing exercises, and other things I needed to do. But it felt like I was missing something. I was still stressed. And even if I removed myself physically from some situations, emotionally it felt like I was still there. You know the saying, "You take yourself no matter where you go?" That was true for me. Stress is not like a switch that, with one flick, you can turn it off, and you're good to go. Instead, the stress lingers from hours to days to years.

Then one day, I came across a book about Adult Children of Alcoholics (ACOA), and I immediately recognized myself! Suddenly, it all made sense. The environment I lived in from an early age many times was unbalanced and chaotic. And I know my mother, who is not an alcoholic and never had any substance issues, tried her best to stay normal and keep me safe and sound, but there was not much she could do. She did her best on top of dealing with her own trauma. My dad's alcoholism derailed all her good wishes. Of course, there were periods of times when my father would stop drinking, but sadly the damage was already done. If you are reading this book, you probably had someone in your household who was an alcoholic as well, so you know what I am talking about. I realized that I was stressed already from day one. Although not a healthy state, it was my normal one.

Facing the Pain of Your Past

I discovered that most of my problems were associated with my childhood trauma because my dad was an alcoholic. I come from a country that does not necessarily care about the mental health of children who have addict parents. It wasn't unusual where I came from to have a parent who was an alcoholic. I realized suddenly that in today's world, there is so much time, energy, and money spent on addicts. But nobody talks about what happens to the families that house those addicts. It took me years to realize that.

The truth is, children live at least 18 years of their lives as hostages of addicts. Did that sound too harsh? Well, it's not like a child can leave a dysfunctional family environment. She or he can't leave, so they are hostages. It's no surprise that many wounded children who can't cope with their pain become addicts. What would happen if we addressed that issue early on?

As with any other post-traumatic stress disorder (PTSD), a smell, song, or anything that reminds us of our terrifying childhood days can trigger us. Any situation between a coworker, partner, or someone on the street can derail our day by reminding us of the hurt, mistreatment, and pain that we experienced growing up. Suddenly, while we're triggered, it feels like it's happening right there and right now, although it is just echoes of the original trauma. Sure, you can do lots of yoga, eat healthy, meditate, read affirmations, and knit sweaters. Still, if you grow up with childhood trauma that distorts your understanding of the world and relationships with other people, no yoga will help you. It is like a bandage that helps you cover the wound but does not heal it.

Understand Your Childhood Wounds

I like Dr. Gabor Mate's comparison between mental trauma and the actual physical wound of the skin. The triggers that keep on causing you pain are unhealed trauma from your past. Understanding those wounds is significant. You can start healing them very gently, with time, patience, and compassion toward yourself. You can compare your emotional trauma to the physical wound; for example, let's say you cut a finger and you have an open wound that's bleeding. It gets infected, and it keeps hurting even after it is healed. That is your mental pain that feels raw even years later. With time, a scab—a disconnect from your feelings—forms to protect the wound.

And as you know, the scab on a wound is still in the middle of the healing process. When the wound is healed, the scab falls off and exposes healed skin. This scab is not a soft, flexible tissue, so it does not grow and move with wounded skin. And those scabs can be carried from childhood to adulthood. Adults can act like children when triggered because they are not protected by adult skin. They only have childhood wounds covered by scabs.

You must understand that what happened in your childhood doesn't have to define your future. Forgiveness is the way. For some people, forgiveness can be a physical act. But for others, forgiveness heals the wound slowly, step by step, over time because when you heal the trauma, you heal the pain, and there's nothing left to forgive. I have forgiven my father, but it didn't happen overnight. Only when I understood that he is also the victim of childhood trauma inflicted in a dysfunctional family was I able to find compassion, patience, and forgiveness.

There are three types of ACOA. The first type is someone who claims the alcoholic in the family didn't affect them. And he may behave that way. He handled his childhood experience very well. He is fine as soon he leaves the house all grown up and never to return.

The second type of ACOA is aware of his childhood trauma but doesn't want to heal. He would rather not talk about or remember it and act like nothing happened because it hurts too much. It makes him feel too vulnerable, and he is afraid that the memories will get out of control, and that's scary. He can't understand that he is an adult, not a small child, who can take charge of his life, trauma, and healing.

The third type of ACOA is someone who's been through lots of pain and is courageous enough to look at it. He is on a healing journey, has faith in himself, and is willing to examine himself and take time, patience, and forgiveness towards himself and others. He has tremendous passion for life, is creative, and open to self-discovery and healing. He may still be affected by the past, but he has adopted a healthier way to deal with it. He learned childhood trauma is an opportunity to grow and learn about himself and others.

So which type are you?

Empower Your Adult Self to Heal

Change can happen in two ways. First, when someone inspires you and you want to change your life. And second, the most common, is that change comes out of pain. When you cannot take it anymore, you have to change. And you have to accept yourself the way you are, with your pain, and have time to sit in it, recognize it, and wish to heal and honor it.

Seeing and reliving what happened to you will be painful, but you will come out of it a new person, healed. It may be horrifying initially because it will not feel natural. Our survival will dictate and demand that we stay precisely where we are, no matter how painful it is. But as with all things, the more time you spend on something new, the more natural it will feel. Eventually, you will feel safe and in control of your life.

It does not mean that after the healing process, you put all your childhood traumas behind, and they will never reappear in your life. They may still trigger you, but you will know how to react to them. You will recognize them, and you will choose in that moment to control them rather than have them control you.

Let's agree on something first. Don't be ashamed of yourself or your reactions, because you reacted normally. You endured trauma, and this was how your body and mind helped you survive. You did nothing wrong. Don't be ashamed of your trauma. Trauma is not what happened to you but how you reacted to it. Different people interpret the same events differently. Hence trauma is different for them as well.

This book is about stress management, but you will not find a yoga routine here or instructions on how to eat healthy, though I agree that stress management must incorporate your whole body. I will address mental stress that comes from different triggers. I will share my opinion about how to approach different situations and help yourself heal. I am not a doctor, and this book is not medical advice. It would be best to consult your doctor and therapist on what best suits you. This book is just a compilation of my opinions and experiences. I am not claiming that reading this book or doing the exercises will significantly change your life.

The change you want to see will ultimately depend on you and your inner work, and there are plenty of other books, online programs, and resources for you to get help and support for your healing. It's best to remember that nothing will change in your life if you do not implement what you learn or take action. Just because you bought a cookbook does not mean dinner will magically appear on your table.

If you search online, it might lead you to a laundry list of ACOAs and their problems and struggles. As you can see, I touched on some of the ones I read. I did not mention and talk about every "character flaw," as I also don't believe in those flaws. We all react to situations differently. Our reactions are just a state of mind, and emotion, that can be changed. I touched on 25 characteristics, things that ACOAs may struggle with. Each chapter consists of my opinions and lists of exercises that I recommend. I also invite you to look at your "flaws" from a different point of view. Look at them as your superpowers, which not everyone has, something you can use to your advantage. Every chapter also contains a joke because we should not be sad about the healing process. We have already been sad enough. Let's rejoice and celebrate the healing!

At the end of this book, you will find information on how to reach me and access my online membership, online programs, and other educational sources.

And remember, you can do this. You deserve to live a happy, healthy, and fulfilling life.

Difficulty Expressing Emotions

Most of us have emotions and feelings, which are part of the human experience. That experience can be happy or not so welcome, depending on what kind of emotion we are feeling. Maybe we're still unsure how to approach and handle emotions the right way.

Some silly jokes about emotions come to mind. For example, a son gets home and tells his mother, "I got 62% right on the emotional test, but I am not sure how I feel about it." Another joke: "Regret is a useless emotion. I wish I had known that a long time ago!"

Emotions Are Energy in Motion

Let's start by clarifying what emotion is. Emotion is a wave, like everything else in the universe. It is energy in motion. You should understand your emotions as your inner ocean, and if you have ever seen the ocean, you know that it is very vast and deep. One moment can be calm and in flow; the next can be raging in a storm. If you have ever seen a huge wave coming at you while standing on the shore, you should know that you cannot just stand there. You will drown if you do nothing. It would help if you learned how to manage it and surf the wave so it will carry you and not harm you.

Ask yourself what is your relationship with this inner ocean. Do you see the wave coming and run to the mountains because you are afraid of it? Or are you just standing there and waiting for it to come over you and drown you? Or you know what the wave is, how fun it is to ride it, so you surf it? Your answer may come from your personal experience of growing up in your family. Others showed you how you should act toward emotions.

If you grew up in a family where emotions were feared, ignored, and invalidated, you may be unable to recognize emotions for what they are and how to exploit them. You may be one of those who run to the mountains in fear. And have nothing to do with it. You may also have grown up in a family where you expected the wave just come and overpower you, making you feel hopeless and helpless standing there on a shore, even if you saw the wave coming. It may be that you are someone who likes to surf the waves but were born into a family of those who run to the mountains. Then your way was invalidated and frowned upon by others.

You may also have grown up in a family of surfers, but something happened to you that taught you that wave coming at you is not safe, so you had to run for the mountains. We all have different perceptions of emotions and how to navigate them.

It is imperative to understand that you cannot suppress your emotions. You have to let them flow. Emotions, like the ocean, are impossible to control. You cannot make other people not feel things, not act on things. So, you cannot deny your feelings without entering a destructive storm. But, when you know how to surf and allow your emotions, you can create a better life for yourself. Emotions are just energy in motion that flows through us, and it's imperative to let them out, or we will get physically sick. The intention of your mind influences your emotions. Only that can influence the vibration. The only way to change the way you see what is outside of you is to change the perception of the world from inside of you. I'm sure you heard many times that things change when you change how you see things. It is all inner work.

Don't be afraid of your emotions and feelings. Emotions show your personal truth. Emotions are trying to convey something and will show up until you make some subsequent change. Here is a list of emotions if you ever need to refer to it:

Amazed	Eager	Inspired	Resentful
Angry	Embarrassed	Irritated	Sad
Annoyed	Energetic	Jealous	Satisfied
Anxious	Envious	Joy	Scared
Ashamed	Excited	Lonely	Self-conscious
Bitter	Foolish	Lost	Shocked
Bored	Frustrated	Loving	Silly
Comfortable	Furious	Miserable	Stupid
Confused	Grievous	Motivated	Suspicious
Content	Happy	Nervous	Tense
Depressed	Hopeful	Overwhelmed	Terrified
Determined	Hurt	Peaceful	Trapped
Disdain	Inadequate	Proud	Worried
Disgusted	Insecure	Relieved	Worthless

Why We Fear Emotions

For many Adult Children of Alcoholics (ACOA), emotions are something horrifying to talk about. That itself may be very stressful to deal with. Because when you express your emotions, you make yourself vulnerable. And for ACOA, being safe is the most important thing. It's a survival instinct.

And if you grew up in an environment where you were not allowed to express your feelings, managing stress is very difficult. You can do as many yoga classes as you want, but if you feel anger inside that you are not allowed, or in reality, you are not allowing yourself to express, you will get physically sick. The other day I watched Dr. Gabor Mate's movie "The Wisdom of Trauma," where he states that people who get cancer are mostly good people with unexpressed anger. Think about it. Just thinking about me not being able to express anger makes me angry.

As a child, I was only allowed to express feelings that my parents found acceptable. As a result, I often felt scared, afraid, betrayed, and abandoned. I wouldn't say I liked that, so I tried my best not to feel them in the first place. I would ignore them. I grew up expecting others not to comfort me or understand me. I learned that if I am feeling bad, nobody will comfort me. I carried that into my personal relationships, expecting others to undermine my feelings. I grew up with "don't talk, don't feel, and don't think."

I would explode with emotion when I couldn't keep my feelings in. It would get me in trouble when I expressed it as being angry, frustrated, teary, or clingy. I learned I couldn't display my anger or any other "bad behavior" because it would not be tolerated. Often, those feelings were met by my parents with scolding, undermining my feelings and concerns, and slapping me on the butt or the cheek when I grew up bigger. Although my mother described me as a quiet kid, I remember those instances when I was not. Of course, someone can say that I probably deserved to be slapped because I was misbehaving or throwing a tantrum. But the child in me experienced that as abuse, leading to a childhood trauma that my adult self had to heal.

I thought of my feelings as complaints that annoyed people around me. I grew to believe that I had no right to feel that way. My feelings were not valid. I also learned not to trust my feelings because the authority told me what I felt was false. I hated to disappoint my parents, and I felt guilty for even feeling bad; I would punish myself for feeling bad by hitting myself. No matter how hard I tried not to feel it, no punishment against myself worked. I had anger issues. If I did something unsuccessfully, I would get angry at myself. Then I would get angry at myself that I felt angry at myself.

Someone who grew up in a dysfunctional family can go from one extreme to the other. For example, they may be very quiet and hide emotions, ignore them, and then suddenly explode because they can't hold them in anymore. Or they could be someone who constantly lets all their emotions out and doesn't know how to regulate them, hence looking like they are constantly stressed, anxious, and in fear.

I had several clients who couldn't answer simple questions about their feelings. Those that came from dysfunctional families had difficulty identifying their emotions. They would answer that they feel nothing about a situation. They felt numb because they learned from their childhood to numb themselves, not feel anything. They were even afraid of themselves, and only by creating an environment where they felt comfortable and safe could they open up and recognize their emotions. That meant going through a valley of pain and remembering what happened to them to identify, label, and release the emotions. But it was worth doing it.

Ways to Deal With Emotions

In a healthy family environment, a child should learn self-regulation and emotional surfing from their caregivers and by interacting with other children. The frontal cortex is part of the brain that controls impulsive behaviors, flexibility, and reactivity. It takes time to develop, almost 25 years, lasting into adulthood.

But with a dysfunctional family with an addict, the child has difficulty learning emotional self-regulation because that was not exercised in their family. In addition, extreme stress hindered the prefrontal cortex development and the ability to control emotions.

I love this easy, simple, and effective way of dealing with emotions. It is a surprisingly simple practice: labeling your emotions. Research shows it is highly effective at helping us respond rationally amid stressful life experiences. Apparently, the unassuming act of putting a label on each of our feelings, called "affect labeling" by psychologists, lowers arousal and puts us back in the driver's seat of our lives. To the extent that you can name your big and overwhelming feelings, you will begin feeling safe in your skin again. By labeling the feelings, you separate those feelings from yourself. And when they are outside of you, you can let them go.

ACOAs might grow up not having someone to talk to about their feelings and resolve their emotions. If you are unsure how well you can manage your emotions or have an issue, answer a few questions yourself. Do I hide my emotions from everyone? Do I not want them to see what I feel? Am I afraid of my own emotions and resisting identifying them? Am I splitting off from emotions and don't want to feel them in this situation? Do I dissociate from pain? Do I deny, intellectualize, and minimize my emotions rather than deal with them? Do I make my emotions and feelings the fault of someone or something else? Do I push my needs and emotions away because I learned that if I display them, nobody will love me and accept me how I am?

Suppose you answer yes to any of those questions. In that case, you may have difficulty knowing how to listen to your feelings, putting them into words, naming them, even talking about them to others, and dealing with them in general. Learning how to move from feeling helpless towards feeling empowered, being balanced and self-centered, without self-medicating yourself or succumbing to addiction, is essential.

You should be able to learn how to work with others, hear their emotions and feelings, listen to your own, and express them without yelling or being upset. With practice, you should keep it cool in complex situations and have compassion towards yourself and others suffering. You can learn how to tolerate fear, become self-reliant, listen to your gut, see the good things in any situation, and come to creative solutions to get out of any situation. It takes time and practice, but it is possible with intention.

Here is another excellent practice that can help you to deal with emotions. Start the process by taking a deep breath in and out with intention. Know that this emotion shows you something you need to pay attention to. There is a message within, be grateful for it. Sit into it, feel it, don't run away from it, surf.

Make a conscious intention that you want to reroute that emotion.

When you are feeling an emotion, ask yourself, do you resent it? So many times, we have expectations and then jump to conclusions that invoke more negative emotions. Pay attention to pride, resistance, anger, fear, bitterness, and judgment.

Don't fall into the ego's trap of "they did this to me." It is important to forgive ourselves and others; if we don't, we will keep those negative emotions and create more trapped ones. When we resist, we attract more resistance, and then we are angry because we manifest more of it.

Then, attempt to recognize what the emotion is. Read the list of emotions if you can't identify them. Ask yourself, how did you arrive at this emotion? Did it come out of the blue, or are you reacting to some situation? Did you get triggered by something that happened to you in the past? Is it an overreaction? Permit yourself to feel this emotion. Ask yourself, "Which will serve me better, the negative or positive emotion?" Then continue by asking yourself, "How can I change it?"

The answer is acceptance and being in the flow, responding slowly but thinking about it by attracting less negativity. Being acceptant of the past helps to release trapped emotions. Release the past expectation. If you have a problem apologizing, you must ask where "being right" comes from. Do you rather be right or happy? Allow others and yourself to be wrong. Do you believe that emotions help you to create your life? So pay attention to what you think. You decide how you want to feel. Set yourself free.

Suppose you get triggered by someone or something coming and you are used to approaching that by drowning in the ocean. In that case, stopping yourself from overreacting and exercising self-regulation is very important. It is the ability to control your emotions, thoughts, words, and actions. The lack of this regulation can be seen as a child throwing tantrums because he's not getting what he wants. It can also be seen in an aggressive teenager or impulsive young adult. But with ACOAs, it can carry on into adulthood.

Emotional self-regulation requires self-control, which may be very difficult for an ACOA since they have not seen self-control while growing up. The good news is that it can be learned. This process also includes reframing disappointing experiences and challenges positively, hence, taking control of the situation and reacting towards it.

Understanding that emotional self-regulation does not eliminate sadness, disappointment, agitation, and anger is essential. Instead, it is just creating a framework for managing those negative emotions. And since emotions tend to multiply the longer you pay attention to them, this process can help from making things worse by stopping it before it gets out of hand. So, the true purpose of self-regulation is emotional well-being, control, and calmness.

To learn to regulate your emotions, start by recognizing that you have emotions regarding something happening to you. Then decide that this experience will not throw you into emotional chaos, and take a pause. Breathe in and out a couple of times. Center yourself. Remind yourself that you have yet to be taught how to act the right way in situations like that. You thought the opposite, to overreact. Understand that you learned this from your caregivers, but they were not necessarily correct. Give yourself a break knowing that your nervous system is primed to react in ways that you already know in order to keep you safe. It would help if you acknowledged that even though your nervous system sometimes signals you that you are in danger because previous experiences trigger you, give yourself a break. Have faith that you can safely navigate stress, fear, on any other intense negative emotion to keep yourself safe. And with practice, you will get better and better at it.

Exercises

Below you will find additional exercises to help you acknowledge and deal with your emotions. Some exercises seem pointless or painful. Just do them anyway. It is painful to face the pain, but that is the only way to heal.

Exercise #1. Practice mindfulness. That is a perfect practice that helps you to focus on the moment of now rather than feeling like you are thinking about the past or looking into the future. This practice should let your brain relax and let go of guilt, stress, anxiety, and worry. Mindfulness is just a simple practice of observance of your body in the moment of now. Pay attention to every part of your body and feel it. Do you feel comfortable? Does it hurt somewhere? Observe your body, feel the energy flowing through it, and enjoy it.

Exercise #2. Use cognitive reevaluation when you're being triggered. It is the ability to change your thoughts and react to a potentially stressful situation. Changing your point of view about stressful occurrences has been shown to reduce anxiety and feelings of hopelessness. If you are dealing with a stressful situation, cognitive reevaluation is when you mislabel a familiar occurrence as something different, preferably valuable. For example, you are a stay-at-home mom who is stressed every day while caring for your children. Instead of thinking that you don't have energy for anything else, not even 5 minutes to sit down and take care of yourself, remind yourself that you are growing into a healthy, responsible, and successful individual who will impact the world. So all that stress and suffering is not in vain. Instead, it serves a higher purpose.

Exercise #3. Name your emotions by writing them down. When you feel stressed out in the situation, worry, or feel like you can't take control of your anxiety levels, take a notepad and keep writing whatever you have in your mind at that moment. Remember that nobody will see this piece of paper, you will finish writing it and then throw it away. But the goal is to get out all of your emotions on paper. You may even write illegibly as long as you pour your frustrations out. It is the same as venting to someone, just writing it down. If you want to use something other than paper, type it into a Word document. But your goal is to get your emotions out and to feel better.

Exercise #4. Lead a healthy lifestyle. Yes, the same thing that you heard multiple times before. Eat balanced healthy foods, hydrate, get enough sleep, exercise plenty, please go for a walk every day. Practice some meditation that helps you to relax and center. Write down the activities you would like to do every day that include all of the above. And then make a schedule, how long you will sleep, when you will eat, how long you will exercise. Remember to pencil yourself into your busy schedule. If you do not make time for yourself, nobody else will.

Exercise #5. Find someone to talk to about your emotions. Find a friend that you can vent to, or find a therapist. Acknowledge that men and women handle stress and emotions very differently. If you are a woman, have plenty of estrogen-driven activities, including talking, sharing feelings about your day, having physical touch, gathering with others, serving others, and feeling valuable. Knowledge of being yourself who can make a difference in other people's lives. If you are a man, when you feel stressed and anxious, implement testosterone-driven activities that help you unwind, go for sports or other physical activities, or be yourself to contemplate.

Your Superpower

Since you are not afraid of diving deep and being overflown by emotions, you are outstanding in performing arts and expressing yourself. You are also not afraid of intense emotions and can reach emotional heights. Therefore, you can understand others who display those emotions.

CHAPTER 2

Being Pessimistic

It didn't surprise me when I read that ACOAs in general are pessimistic. What did surprised me was that I thought pessimism was a common occurrence in the Soviet Union, where I grew up, because of poverty and oppression. As it turns out, pessimism is also very common in the countries considered wealthy. So, I concluded that pessimism comes from your personal environment, no matter how rich or poor you are. Specifically with ACOAs, this pessimistic outlook on life comes from a more profound level, reflecting the sadness children experience due to the loss of a connection with their parents and neglect. In addition, it is accompanied by sadness, shame, guilt of that parent's behavior.

And I am not just talking about general negativity. Small things also come up, like, "Oh, the sun is shining now, but wait, it will get cloudy soon," or "This new government will do no good, same as the last one." I am talking about pessimism that touches people personally and clenches the soul, making a person tremble with fear, even if there is no ground for being fearful. In the eyes of an ACOA, everything is a big deal. Anything is tragic and can end badly. Many can look at that person and laugh at their fears without understanding where that pain is coming from. I am sure that an ACOA created the story of Chicken Little being afraid of the sky falling and blowing something unknown out of proportion.

Survival Instinct: Expecting the Worst

I remember being seven years old, looking through the window of our tiny apartment, waiting for my mom to come back home, my heart pounding in my chest. Usually, she would be back by six, but sometimes she would be late. I could not stop staring at the corner of the house where she should walk up at any moment and imagining the worst: that she had died and would never come back. Pair that with fear of abandonment, and you have a terrified kid. Sure, many kids are afraid of their parents leaving them, but for an ACOA, that was especially hard. I realized later in my life that I would assume the worst in many situations, with little or no evidence, no matter how old I got.

On the surface, it looks as if ACOAs just prepare themselves for the worst to save themselves from disappointments. And don't get me wrong, I think it is essential to prepare yourself for the worst. As a matter of fact, I recommend doing an exercise where you look at something that is bothering you right now and prepare for the worst-case scenario. Usually, nobody likes to plan or even look toward something uncomfortable or even painful. But preparing mentally and even taking physical action to prepare for something unseen in the future helps to lower your stress. Moreover, by preparing yourself for the worst-case scenario, you feel in control of the situation. Hence, you calm down.

That reminds me of a joke. The husband is getting ready in the morning to enjoy his weekend. He is looking forward to watching football all day. As he is hums in the shower, he hears his wife calling him, "Honey, come here!" Her voice sounds alarming, so he jumps out of the shower as a good husband would do to rescue her. However, when he pushes the shower door closed, he hits his head. Annoyed that the door was in the way, he rushes to the room, slips and falls. The wife sees him on the floor and excitedly shouts, "Look, honey, they have a Downton Abbey marathon on TV today!" He just responds, "Bad things do come in threes!"

Did you laugh? It is a weak joke but shows that we laugh at things like this story because we believe that bad things do come in threes. Many ACOAs believe that if they start the day on the wrong foot, the whole day will pass on a negative note or even end tragically. And if the things that happen are genuinely bad, we will make it that way, totally overreact, and label it as the end of the world because we don't know how else to act. But, from experience, we learned that an unfortunate event won't stop there. It will continue to the grand finale until someone gets hurt. This kind of belief was instilled by an alcoholic parent that randomly stopped and reassessed himself or changed his behavior. So, the best preparation for that child is to expect the worst every time.

As a matter of fact, ACOAs react to the environment very differently from others because they expect the worst all the time. It is a never-ending state of mind that comes from survival, from the experience of life that was constantly changing from positive to negative in the blink of an eye. Good moments often bring disappointment because it would turn into something sad, harmful, or violent. One moment you think your parents are having fun, enjoying company, laughing, looking peaceful, and in a good mood. And then the situation suddenly turns into yelling, arguing, and breaking things. Joyful celebrations such as Christmas, New Year's Eve, anniversaries, or at worst – a child's birthday party, would turn into a power struggle, broken glass, and police escort.

One of my clients was very hard to work with because any idea that I would give her to try in her daily life she would reduce. Even for easy things, such as writing in a diary every day, she would give some "logical" explanation as to why it would not work. Usually, clients come to a coach for help and expect to follow directions. But she was different. If I recommended exercise, or at least walking around the block before bed, she would answer that it hurt her knees, which would cost her money to go to the doctor. On top of that, she heard of a lady who had unsuccessful knee replacement surgery, and she was sure the same surgery would go wrong for her. She was looking for a job and I tried to cheer her up for an upcoming job interview, but she responded with, "Been there, done that, and still no job!" Obviously, her pessimism was more than just trying to keep her expectations low and prevent her from disappointment. It was intertwined with a feeling of being a victim and more.

Pessimism is common for ACOAs when it comes to themselves, everything around them, and even other people. I once overheard a conversation while in a check-out line between two women discussing an upcoming date. One said that she hoped he would take her somewhere nice. The second responded, "I hope he pays for both of you, not like my cousin who had to pay the bill when she met a guy." The first said that the guy looked like a nice guy and she was sure that it wouldn't happen. The second added, "Sure, all of them look nice until they use you and leave you." Well, that is a complicated conversation to listen to, but it serves its purpose to show how pessimism might look like something very negative. If those two ladies were family members or friends who cared for each other a lot, this might be a conversation filled with love and concern.

Moving From Pessimism to Optimism

ACOAs have experienced so many disappointments that we expect the worst out of the situation, but we also don't believe when something positive happens. Is that resonating with you? I remember days when I was a kid and would hear my father tell me that we would do something fun. But I learned at an early age that promises rarely came true. They just stayed promises. I carried that experience into my adulthood.

If something positive happened, I would immediately stop myself from celebrating or being happy about it. I would prepare myself for the "other shoe to drop." I just didn't believe that a good thing could happen to me. If something good did happen, I would expect it to be taken away from me. When I think back, it was a self-fulfilling prophecy. If

I was happy about something, and someone would spoil the moment, I would say, "I thought so." But if there were nobody around, I would stop myself from being happy. In the end, a lot of my happy moments were killed. I just learned to squash any happy feeling as soon it showed up in my heart. Of course, all that sabotage did help me survive, not to be disappointed if the situation went sour. The sad part is because I was expecting the worst, I got the worst.

In addition, ACOA are afraid of authority figures, and they are unconsciously reminded of their alcoholic parent or a close caregiver. A call from their boss ignites immediate anxiety as adults anticipate that the boss will demote or fire them.

While I was working at a small firm, I remember my immediate supervisor asked me to follow him to the conference room. I stopped whatever I was doing, stood up from the chair, and glanced at my desk, anticipating what I would take when they fired me. As I was walking with him to the end of the hallway, I kept replaying my workload and my conversations with other coworkers in my mind. He was a tall guy and walked fast, and I barely kept up with him, almost running after him. I was very confused because I couldn't think of anything I had done wrong.

As we sat down, he started with, "I had a conversation with upper management…" And I thought: "Well, yeah, that is why I am here." He continued, "We looked at our profits last year…." And I thought, "Here we go…" And he ended with, "We are giving you a raise. Not as big as you deserve, but at least something to show you that we appreciate your work." He named the hourly rate that I would charge from now on, and he didn't say a word more for a few moments. I was sitting in silence, staring at him. I couldn't believe it! Finally, I thanked him, went back to work, and continued thinking about what had just happened.

Did any of this sound familiar? The good news is that all the negative things you think aren't true, so you can relax a little! Honestly, it is not that bad! Don't despair if you have to ask yourself how you can make yourself less stressed in situations with no control. Don't despair. It will take time and practice, but it is possible.

Exercises

Below are a few exercises that will help you build a support system to use anytime you expect the worst to happen. The tools will help your mind into calm down and take control of the situation. Be patient with yourself and count every time you catch yourself being pessimistic a victory. Make a habit of correcting yourself, and you will be more at ease sooner or later.

Exercise #1. Ask yourself what the odds are of something negative happening to you. Next time you hear something that makes you fearful and invokes negative thinking, just ask yourself: "How likely is this to happen to me?" We often hear from other people about some disease, an accident, or crime and get worried that this can happen to us or to those we love. And you know, most of those fears never come true. If you hear about a criminal escaping from prison, don't get into a panic. Ask yourself, "What are the odds of him coming to my house?" We hear a lot of fearful messages on TV and radio, like the advertising that starts something like, "Four in five Americans suffer from..." Naturally, you think of four other people in your life that don't have that, and then you assign that illness to yourself! If that doesn't calm you down, then go a step further and ask yourself, "What will I do if the worst happens?" Then make a plan of how you will react IF it does. And at last, no matter how big of a worry and fear you have, ask yourself, "How much benefit is likely to result from me worrying about this?"

Exercise #2. Don't take things too seriously, no matter what happens to you. Especially, don't spend your energy on something not worth your attention. Don't make things worse for yourself by thinking and fearing something even worse than it is already. If it is a small thing, like being stuck in traffic, don't jump to conclusions that you will be late for an appointment and get upset at yourself. Don't be pessimistic and expect the worst. Maybe sitting in traffic saves you from the crash ahead, the person you will be meeting will also be late, or maybe you will get into an elevator and meet the love of your life. One time I arrived at a meeting and the parking lot was full. I got irritated that I was already late and there was nowhere to park. As I moved through the parking lot, I came across an expensive convertible with people taking selfies. At first, I was patient, but after a few minutes realizing that they wouldn't move and I was late, I honked. Of course, at this moment, I was already getting angry at myself for waiting so long. When the people noticed me, they gestured for me to go around them. And as I passed by them, someone just pulled out of a parking lot to leave right in front of me! I was able to park very close to the entrance of the building and make it to my meeting. Looking back, I realized that the car that stopped the traffic helped me get that parking spot. If not for that stop, I would have left the parking lot and had to search for the other parking lot!

Don't worry ahead of time, and don't assume the worst. Act when there is a need to act, not when you jump to conclusions by habit. Catch yourself when you start exaggerating things. For example, don't start telling yourself, "I am always late; I am such a loser!" Instead, reason with yourself and prove that you are not late every time. There were plenty of times when you arrived to something on time. Pay attention to that. Talk to yourself: "Things are working out for me, I can't see that yet, but things are good. No matter what situation I am in, it will improve. This shall pass." Also, evaluate any situation that scares you or makes you angry, and ask yourself, "Will this make a difference in my life five years from now?" If it won't, let it go and keep on thinking something positive, be grateful for something that you are already happy about.

Exercise #3. Reframe the assumption. This is one of those exercises that isn't about you writing things down, rather you should do in your mind. This exercise should be done when you are in a situation already assuming a negative outcome. The first step is to notice your adverse reaction to something, and that is done by noticing feelings of sadness, disappointment, anger, and any other emotion that makes you feel bad. When you identify the emotion, ask yourself, where is it coming from? Why do you have those feelings? Then it would help if you thought about different situations, the things that actually can happen, and reason with yourself.

Let's say you are waiting on your loved one at the coffee shop, and they are not showing up. Instead of imagining the worst – that he got in a car accident and died, he left you all together and has a new girlfriend, or he doesn't care about you at all and forgot to come, or anything else that is radiating a negative outcome – think of something positive.

Maybe he is late because he is buying flowers for you or a small gift! You would probably immediately stop being angry or fearful if you saw him coming with a token of love, wouldn't you? Or maybe he is late because he is a nice guy who stopped to help an elderly lady to cross the road. If you think he is helping someone else, you would probably stop thinking badly about him. Try to come up with other reasons why the person you are expecting to come didn't come. Play a game with yourself about how many positive situations you can imagine that may be why that person is not here. The point is to create possible positive outcomes and stay away from the negatives. And same goes for any situation in life, no matter how bad it might look initially. Usually, there is an explanation for any situation. Not all circumstances might end badly, so don't fear every negative thought you get about your surroundings.

Exercise #4. Keep a list of outcomes where you were wrong about people or things that happened. It is hard to remember previous experiences like that, but try adding them to the list. Even if you don't remember any at the moment, just start a new list and keep those instances registered for the future.

For example, this just happened to me last week. I posted a video on my social media, and I received many comments. As I glanced at them in a hurry, pretty much just eyeballing them and not reading them, one of the comments seemed to me as if it was a critique of the words that I spelled in my post. Being a true ACOA, my blood started boiling, and I thought: "So here we are, this lady is criticizing me, and she is not making any videos herself! How dare she!" But because I know that I overreact and have been wrong with reactions many times before, I paused a second and reread her comment. And it turned out that she was apologizing for her previous comment where she misspelled a word! If I had not stopped myself when I expected the worst of the situation and I had written her back with harsh words, I would have looked like a complete lunatic! So, I put that story on my list! So many things in life are not as they seem at first! And don't get angry at yourself, just have a good laugh!

To calm you down when you get in doubt or in fear about things that are unfolding, just read the list or remember some instances when your expectations about people or situations were wrong. So next time when someone doesn't come home on time or doesn't pick up the phone, or your doctor asks you to return a call to discuss your blood test results, read this list to calm yourself down and prove to yourself that your negative thinking is probably wrong. And when it turns out that your fears were baseless, add this proof to your list.

Your Superpower

Because you are more pessimistic than other people, you expect things to go wrong and prepare yourself for the worst-case scenario. If the worst happens, you might handle that better than those who didn't anticipate that.

CHAPTER 3

Difficulty Dealing with Anger

Most everyone is familiar with the feeling of anger, also called displeasure, hostility, or annoyance. It is hard to find someone who has never gotten angry in his life, which is a part of the human experience. But not all of us deal with it the same way. Most anger is caused by fear and lack of control, which threatens survival. Many things in modern times don't threaten our survival, but the brain still recalls when we felt helpless and vulnerable. Today many are not allowed to express and heal anger, which causes more anger and depression. As with any emotion, you should be allowed to be address it and not ignore or dishonor it. Unfortunately, managing anger quietly has become a virtue in today's society.

Consider the wife in this anecdote. A husband observes that his wife never fights back when she is angry with him. Instead, she keeps her cool during their arguments and lets him express himself his way. Impressed, her husband asks: "How do you control your anger?" She responds: "I clean the toilet." That surprises the husband: "That is interesting! But how does that help?" She answers: "I use your toothbrush."

Break the Chain of Anger

The truth is, no one can make you feel angry unless you let them. As with any other emotion, it is up to you to observe and change it if you don't like it. It arises as a knee-jerk reaction because we are wired that way to keep us alive, sometimes not even being aware of it. Changing your automatic reactions to irritants is possible. Although as an ACOA, it might be harder to do that due to the trauma you experienced growing up.

Anger raging with uncontrollable intensity might have been highly frightening to you. You see anger as something terrible that can hurt you or others. Anger was very present in my house growing up. I expected to see it every day. If not from my father, then from my mother. I knew that it didn't feel good, and it terrified me. I still remember the angry outbursts from my dad when he would come back home drunk. I would pray that he would be too drunk to be angry and collapse into bed, but there were plenty of days when he was not quite drunk enough. He would come home already angry, telling his stories using his hands, raising his voice, exaggerating every word he said. Sometimes he would throw things on the floor, fight invisible demons, struggle, and collapse on the floor.

I will never forget when I was seven-years-old and my dad came home drunk, but not drunk enough to go to bed right away. We lived in a small place then, and I slept on the sofa in the living room where the dish cabinet and dining table were located. I know it was in the middle of the night because it was already dark when my dad opened the window. He fought with my mother and was "dividing the property" by throwing dishes from the cabinet outside the window. He didn't even spare small porcelain figurines bought a few months ago. He was throwing plates out the window one at a time. Some plates would not make it through the window but hit the windowsill and break inside the room, so the broken porcelain pieces spread around us. My mother sat with me in bed and held me. I was as terrified as she was. We were both shaking. She tried to plead with my dad, yell, and cry, but nothing helped. We both waited until my dad threw all he could outside. The only china set that was left on the shelf was what my grandmother gave my mother as a wedding gift. That one my mother managed to save from his outburst.

I don't remember what else he did, but I still remember the terror and the sound of breaking dishes falling into the street from the second floor. The following day, I left for school and passed the broken dishes on the sidewalk as other kids were looking at them and wondering how that happened. I pretended that I had no idea.

Different Ways We Approach Anger

So no wonder I had anger issues for a very long time. I would deal with anger differently depending on what situation I was in or what people I was dealing with. Like any ACOA, I had a limited set of emotional and psychological tools that were necessary and available to recognize and deal with my own negative emotions. I would get upset and angry very quickly if something wasn't going my way. Even a slow driver would make my blood boil. Or a computer not processing something fast enough. I couldn't deal with anger and hostility effectively due to a lack of examples of how to manage them. I thought that I needed to overact and protect myself immediately in any situation since I didn't know what would be coming at me. As a defense, I would overreact to comments from other people, see situations from very different points of view, hear different meanings, and get offended easily. Act angrily and then feel ashamed that I did.

I would also go in a different direction and try to solve the uncomfortable angry feeling by ignoring it with people I thought my life depended upon. I couldn't stand up for myself when needed, and I just took in the anger from other people and swallowed it all up, which only deepened my emotional trauma. I was afraid to face it because I didn't know how to deal with it. Authority figures who displayed anger would paralyze me because it would remind me of my dad's anger. I was a people pleaser because I was afraid. I knew what damage it could cause, so I would try to avoid it however I could. I learned early on that my father is stronger than me, so I had to appease him or else I was in trouble. All my childhood friends with alcoholic parents had the same aversion to anger. They all gave in to anyone or any situation to stay safe and avoid conflict. We were bullied and couldn't stand up for ourselves.

None of the ways I was approaching anger worked. I would ignore it, or I would overreact to it. That left no opportunities to learn appropriate strategies to deal with other people's or my own negative emotions. I would abandon myself because I would not allow myself to feel angry, or I would jump into overreacting with anger. In my defense, not all of us know how to deal with anger, so I think everyone should be taught that.

An Integrative Approach Addresses Anger Issues

Luckily, it is possible to change your response to conflict and learn how to deal with anger through different behavior methods, including relaxation techniques, systematic desensitization, and self-monitoring of emotions. The goal is to maintain the presence of peace when you are faced with an emotionally charged situation and when stress levels rise. Only by experiencing new, highly charged emotional situations is learning possible. When presented with a new situation, and you react differently from previous patterns, you create new neuron paths, interrupt the pattern, and allow desensitization of the fear that has been strongly conditioned.

To change that, it takes an integrative approach to solve anger issues. First, you must revamp your mindset and habits by observing and making intentional changes. Observing it first teaches you how your mind and body work. It would help if you approached situations differently without a negative mindset. Instead of letting negative expectations drain you, you should try different ways to change your attitude and help yourself and others to overcome anger. It is worth the time for you to learn how to deal with anger effectively.

Honoring yourself and staying by your side regardless of your emotions is essential. Since anger causes violence and harm, many are afraid of expressing it. Many people frown upon someone who is expressing anger. On the contrary, any emotion should be allowed to be expressed. There are a lot of people who are suppressing anger and are in a place of depression. They have been taught not to express anger because people around them don't like it. They might even be medicated to suppress anger. But it should not be ignored, like ignoring a wound without applying a bandage, hoping it will go away with time. There is a reason why someone is angry. Perhaps their needs are not met, or they feel unsafe or unloved. If that wound is addressed, then there is no need to suppress the anger. Studying the emotional scale and healing the original wound are essential to move forward.

It took me time to stop being angry at my dad because he treated me the way he did. It took a long time to forgive my father for being an alcoholic. I understand that I was not allowed to be angry when I was a kid because my parents had no idea how to address it. They didn't know how to deal with anger within themselves either. All they wanted was a well-behaved kid while being a kid inside themselves. I understood that they also held childhood traumas from broken trust. Although they were doing their best, they didn't learn how to be a loving, supportive parent to their kid. My father was drinking because he was wounded inside. Alcohol was his way to escape. He didn't wake up every day to hurt my mother or me. I bet it hurt him even more when he would sober up and see what he did the day before. That would cause him to plunge into shame and self-hatred again, so he went back to the bottle.

Do you find yourself angry sometimes? Do you allow yourself to be angry? Do you express it? How has anger influenced your life? Do you know how to handle anger? Are you still angry at your addicted parent or caregiver? Why do you think you find difficulty in letting go and forgiving them? Take time to heal and allow yourself to be angry. Don't get angry at yourself because you are angry; that is the worst thing you can do to yourself. Work on it every day, but be kind to yourself.

Learn to be assertive instead of aggressive and be kind to yourself and others instead of weak and defensive. Learn to be wise instead of forceful. It's not about learning how to scream louder to be heard or move faster to make it there. Instead, it is about looking deeper into yourself and your patterns, seeing your anger's root causes, and befriending it to heal it. This healing will make your life more enjoyable and happier.

Exercises

It is vital to get anger under control. It causes stress and negatively impacts your health. Please make up your mind today to go through it with courage and conquer one small step at a time. Change is slow and might be painful and gradual, so please be patient with yourself. Below are a few exercises you can try when dealing with anger that will help you heal and take control of it. Be proud of yourself when making every step towards healing and celebrate small successes.

Exercise #1. If you are in a situation where it is hard for you to control anger when faced with disturbing people, remember that not everything around you is about you or your business. When someone cuts you off in traffic or yells at you for no reason, it is hard not to take it personally. You probably feel threatened because you experienced the damage of anger. It can bring memories of when you were a child and your drunk parent acted out. You also learned that reacting with anger might have kept you safe. When faced with a display of anger, assess the situation and ask yourself, is this anger needed right now? Did that person in the car mean to do this to you personally? Probably not. Then ask why you think they are doing this. They might be in a hurry because they are late for a meeting or have some type of emergency. If the person yelled at you, ask yourself why they felt that way. They might react the same way you want to, with anger. Keep on passing that hot potato from one hand to another. Have empathy for that person; you don't know what happened to them today. Let that anger stop with you. Don't pass it on. You, the one who chooses to feel it, let it go.

Exercise #2. We tend to hold our breath when upset. When faced with a situation where you feel anger, help yourself by breathing in deeply a few times. Breathe in deeply a few times, in and out from your belly. You might feel lots of discomfort in your body, so keep breathing into that place and relax your body. Look into the eyes of anger, like any other emotion, and put a label on it. Admitting your anger is a great way to get a grip on what is happening. After identifying the feeling, don't judge yourself. Just observe it. If you have been working on yourself, this anger might make you even angrier at yourself. Stop there. When you calm down, ask yourself where this anger came from. What triggered it? Are you afraid? Fearful? Angry because you can't control or change things? And the ultimate question is, will it make a difference if you just let yourself be angry? Allow yourself to feel angry and do something that will not cause harm to yourself or others. Write about it, and put all you are upset about on the paper. You can even write all kinds of stuff you would like to do with those who made you angry. Just write your anger out, punch the pillow, or run as fast as possible. Let it all out until you are inspired to move or do something constructive that will change the situation, and you won't feel hopeless.

Exercise #3. Identify your anger patterns, and face them to heal them. Take time to write down instances when your anger damaged your life. Identify that anger in your relationships, your work environment, and how it has affected your health. Look deep into yourself, and be honest with yourself no matter how painful. It takes courage to remember moments like that when we are not proud of what we did, such as yelling at someone to express your anger because the person triggered some old wound inside you. Or you might have written an email to the coworker and told them how incompetent they are by making you miss your deadline. Or you might direct your anger towards your spouse, partner, kids, or close friends, and those you love might seem like little things. Do you feel like you shouldn't have done that? Do you feel shame about what happened? First, don't feel that way. You did it out of self-preservation. You probably overacted in the situation, but that is your survival instinct trying to save you. Look deep, trace it back years before if you must, and put as much on paper as possible. Name those emotions, and acknowledge them. Start a journal where you write your anger outbursts and how they happened. Keep a daily log and identify the pattern, so you can deal with and heal it. And be kind to yourself. Remember, it takes time to develop destructive habits, and it takes time to heal.

Exercise #4. Prevent angry outbursts or any response to situations that can cause you anger. It is easier said than done, of course, but when you identify your patterns, it gets easier to find ways to deal with them. If you did the exercise above, you already found a pattern that sets you off. It might be minimal like someone moving their leg monotonously. Or maybe when your mother asks a particular question, it just makes your blood boil. Learn to identify the frustration early on so you can plan how to deal with it. If you know what question ticks you off, prepare the best answer for it. If you get annoyed by other people's shallow comments, tell yourself next time: "it's just an opinion, and it doesn't have to be the same as mine." If another person is angry or upset, remind yourself that it is probably not about you, so let it go. For example, I can't stand it when someone says, "Just relax," when I am stressing out. So if that happens, I tell myself, "They didn't mean anything negative. They are not criticizing me. They just want to help me." Be in control of what you feel as soon that comes into awareness. Feelings are like a train: it takes a few moments to gain strength, but when it is rolling at full speed, it is hard to stop. As soon you feel anger, stop yourself.

Exercise #5. Practice feeling good. The simple fact of life is that happy people don't feel angry as often as those that are unhappy. We can say that a situation or other people made us get upset. But we all know that's not correct. We choose to react to situations. Do something that makes you feel happy, be grateful, and enjoy simple things. Learn to bring positive things into your life. If you see a pattern that watching the evening news upsets you, stop watching it. Watch something uplifting. Stop hanging out with negative people that invoke negative feelings. Stop listening to depressing songs; put on something uplifting, dance, and move your body. Decide to lean towards positive instead of negative. So, when the situation triggering you to react with anger arises, you will be more equipped to weather that with grace.

Exercise #6. This, too, shall pass. Remember how often you were upset, angry, or did something in the past that didn't turn out well in the end? Stop blaming yourself and forgive yourself. It is over now. Remember that when you're in a situation that you want to react to, this will pass. It won't matter a year from now. It's not the end of the world. Don't get into arguments about who will wash the dishes with an angry tone of voice—you don't have to raise it to the level of an angry outburst like someone is attacking you. You can address the situation with a calm tone of voice. Next time try that and see how the other person reacts I bet they will listen to you more about what you have to say when you speak with a calm tone.

Your Superpower

Although anger might not be seen as a strength, feeling anger in some situations might help you to protect yourself or your loved ones. The key is to channel that anger towards a noble cause.

CHAPTER 4

Fear of Abandonment

One of the fears that I have struggled with for the longest time, especially in close relationships, is abandonment. Unfortunately, this fear is widespread in ACOAs because they never have a chance to establish a sense of self and worth. The early messages about who you are from your parents, especially the parent or caregiver who was an addict, were very confusing. One day you were loved and wanted. The next day you didn't exist and were invisible no matter what you did. Those mixed messages created the majority of beliefs about you and your values.

The funny thing about abandonment is that it starts with others abandoning you and then you end up leaving behind your true self. A story I once heard makes light of that fact. A monkey once died in a zoo and there was no way to find a new one, so the management decided to hire a man to do a monkey's job. A desperate man assumed the role and sat in a costume. Days went by, and all was well until an accident happened. The poor man fell into an enclosure where lions lived. Out of terror, the man started screaming and saw the lion running at him.

The lion opened his mouth, the man closed his eyes to meet his maker. Suddenly, he heard a voice say: "Stop screaming, you fool, or you'll get us both fired!"

How Abandonment Issues Start

I feared abandonment from an early age because of growing up with an alcoholic father. In addition to that, my fear grew worse due to other circumstances when my parents left me alone or with someone who didn't care for me. I will never forget the time I spent with my grandmother. No, she was not the loving and caring type. When I hear someone say, "Remember those days when your grandmother would bake you some cookies and rock you on her knee?" She wasn't any of that. I had to spend summers there because it was popular to send kids to the village where there was clean air and fields to run wild.

Sadly, going to my grandparents for summer felt like going to the gulag. From a young age, I tried to run away from them and go back home. One day my grandpa followed me as I snuck out of the house, walked all the way to the train station, and bought myself a ticket. (My grandpa nodded in agreement when the cashier glanced at him standing behind me). I was about to get on the train when my grandpa caught me on my elbow and yelled at me asking what I was doing.

Obviously, there was a reason why I wanted to go home: because I didn't like to be at my grandma's, simple as that. And the worst part about that is that my parents knew it but still left me there. Usually, when they were about to leave, I would hold on to my mom, not letting go and crying my eyes out. But she had to leave. So, they would do it a different way. When my mom was about to leave, they would send me for something upstairs. When I came back down, I would see that my mom had already left without even telling me goodbye. I would see her already far in the distance as she rushed through the field to the train station and hoped I didn't see her. I would cry and yell for her, and my grandma would hold me back until I gave up. Those were my summers. I would experience that abandonment over and over.

I now understand why my parents wanted me to spend summers

with my grandparents instead of in the city. That was the way I learned and connected to nature. I played with my cousins, built relationships with my neighbors, drank fresh cow's milk, went fishing, made castles out of hay. My parents wanted me to enjoy my freedom as a kid. Sadly, I didn't see it that way at that moment. Because of my fear of abandonment, I wasn't used to fully appreciating things in life; I just waited for the other shoe to drop at any moment. And that changed, but it took time and work.

You might relate to me because your parent or caregiver didn't give consistent care and attention in the ways that a child needs. You had to do a lot of self-parenting because you were left by yourself with your feelings. Obviously, you did the best you could, but that left you in constant doubt about yourself and your accomplishments. Lots of things were never explained to you, so you guessed a lot. You also didn't know how to take something that was happening around you and deal with your and other people's emotions. You just had to wing it and act like you knew what you are doing. That is what helped you survive, which is why you can find a solution to any situation. You are the person that can think outside the box. If you believe you are not that person, I invite you to take a closer look at how you react to problems in your adult life now.

Putting on an Act to Cope

Many ACOAs think that if other people found out about that acting and who they really are, they would stop loving the ACOA and abandon them. That is where the fear of abandonment comes from: you think you are a horrendous person because you were not loved for some reason. You might feel anxious about other people's opinions of you, and to win others' love, you might try to act like the person you think they want you to be. Just as in your childhood, you adjusted to being someone else to survive.

When I got divorced and stepped back into the dating arena, this fear of abandonment was very hard for me. A simple "unmatch" on a dating app? I would take it personally with never-ending "What did

I do wrong? What did I say wrong?" Common sense was telling me that maybe it had nothing to do with me. It had to do with them, but I still would take the blame. I would try to be perfect on dates and have no idea why I didn't get the second date! If I went on a few dates with the same person, I would check my phone every five minutes to ensure I didn't miss a message from them. It was like an obsession! I was the example of what not to do while dating. And God forbid if I sent a message and the other person didn't reply right away! A few times when I messaged, the guy never responded and just left me hanging forever. These experiences became full-blown crying, depressive episodes. Now, I knew where all that was coming from, but I could not prevent it from happening. I tried common sense and reasoned that there would be someone out there, and maybe I was saved from someone who is not a good fit for me. But still, it hurt tremendously until I learned how to deal with it.

Little Miss (or Mister) Perfect

ACOAs often try to be perfect children to avoid being abandonment. As you know, there is no such thing as perfection. There is the belief from early childhood that "If I am perfect, they will keep me." Sadly, no matter how well you behaved, as soon the drinking started in your family, you were not important—alcohol was. Your needs were not met no matter what you tried to do. There are different ways children react when their needs are not met. Some give up entirely and grow up not that anxious, as are those who still hold to the fantasy that maybe one day, just perhaps, things will change for the better, and they will be loved.

In my neighborhood, I knew twin boys. Let's call them Kyle and Sam. Kyle would try to be perfect, was always on top of things, never late, always cheerful no matter how bad the day was, studied hard and got good grades, pleased his parents no matter what. The younger brother (yes, thirty minutes younger) was the complete opposite. He didn't obey any rules, did the opposite of what he was told to do, always got in trouble for getting into fights, and almost dropped out of high school. I don't think some people can be so close and different in the situation. Both grew up in the same family under the same roof. Both of them had the same rules, wore the same clothes, ate the same food, had the same lack of affection and lack of support. The difference was that they decided to process things and respond to them differently. One brother tried to be a saint, and the other didn't give a damn.

Twenty years later, I found out that the perfect son got married early on and got himself a job but lost it all to alcoholism himself. And his younger brother, who kept himself at a distance, created his own company and traveled the world. Remember, no matter what situation you grew up in, you are the only one who makes the ultimate choice of how to react to it. When you were a child, you didn't know how to, but now, being an adult, you can heal from that.

The Control Conundrum

Obviously, the fear of abandonment doesn't disappear on its own, just because you know you have it. It sits there in your head and waits to show its ugly face any chance it gets. This fear of abandonment arises every time there is a conflict that needs to be resolved, and an ACOA overreacts to something small. Because you had those experience of being abandoned in your childhood, you already expect that from your relationships with other people. Many times, there is no reason to believe some things, but you might take it the wrong way. Because we see what we want and what we expect, we get the worst. Sadly, since you believed things could get better, but they never did, you project this belief towards your friends and partners. And the situation can get better, but you still can be hesitant to see it.

Naturally, you want to have control of the situation. That is just the survival instinct in you. I invite you to remember times when you doubted someone else. Have you ever caught yourself demanding something and trying to control others, questioning another's whereabouts, falsely accusing infidelity, misinterpreting statements and situations in your relationship as evidence of their desire to leave you? Does it make you feel ashamed that you did that? Nothing to be ashamed of. You did this out of fear. You were trained to react that way, to prepare for the worst.

All this might potentially lead to a self-fulfilling prophecy by pushing away people who love you. I have heard multiple times that one partner accused the other of infidelity without evidence. They kept accusing the partner of cheating, which creates mistrust and resentment by the other person. Eventually it gets so ugly that the accused goes on and cheats with someone because "I was accused of that already, so it might as well be true!"

Recognizing Abandonment Trauma as an Adult

I am an adult now, and so are you. Adults deal with issues no matter how hard or painful they are. You might have painful experiences yourself that are hard to think about, but you did your best at the given moment. And even now, you are doing the best you can. Although you may behave like you have your life in order, and you portray yourself as a funny, upbeat, and cool person, you may be pushing a deep sadness down that nobody sees. You might be surprised that Bill Clinton and Carol Burnett, among other very charismatic people, grew up in that kind of environment and use humor as a coping mechanism to survive.

Sadly, since you were a child, you might have been told indirectly and even directly that your existence caused all the unhappiness in the family. You tried to be the best you could be to prove your value to the family, so they would keep you. You might always try to be on your best behavior no matter what, and keep your sadness, anger, and disappointment to yourself. You didn't let yourself be you. So, you are afraid that if someone truly knows you, it will expose your dark side and show the lie that you have been living. And obviously, that will negate the positive side that others love. It is tragic because a lot of ACOAs don't even allow themselves to get close to other people. They might think that they let others get close to them, but they are indeed not. And because of that, many are very lonely and suffer isolation even if they are in a crowd.

Thankfully, it is hard to keep acting like someone else in front of other people, especially those who love you. Did I just hear you say, "Nobody loves me." Yep, that's the voice that was born out of trauma! It is time to heal that. The truth is that people who interact with you every day might know you even better than you know yourself because you pay attention only to the "bad" side of you. There is no reason why you should be someone else, and you are good as you are! More than that, there is nobody else like you in the world, and that should be appreciated.

Now, take a moment and think logically. Can you blame yourself for what happened to the family when you were a child? Even if someone told you, "I got pregnant with you, had to get married to your father, and he is an addict who's hurting all of us." Imagine watching a movie, and the mother tells this to her child. What is your reaction? You will probably think: "That is insane. The kid has nothing to do with it!" Well, you are this kid who keeps on punishing himself for things that he didn't do. Ask yourself, was that newborn able to control and influence adult lives to the point of causing family problems? Probably not! Your parents made their own decisions based on their childhood traumas! Drop the guilt already!

Exercises

The good news is that all this can be explained and healed. Below is a list of a few exercises that might help you deal with a fear of abandonment. It all starts with acknowledgment and then with actions to change it. Remember, only by doing exercises can you see progress, not by just reading them.

Exercise #1. Try to remember those times when someone left the house and didn't come back on time. Times when you were worried that they left and would never come back, but they did come back. Remember those times when your boyfriend/girlfriend didn't write you back or call on time, and you were worried that they were done with the relationship, but later you found out that there was a reason they were late. Write those facts down, and keep that list close by when you have another anxiety attack thinking that someone is done with you, they abandoned you, or you are not wanted. Read it a few times to prove the brain wrong.

You can remember those times when your heart was broken because they truly abandoned you, but that is not the moment you should recall. Statistically, you will have someone break your heart on this planet, and such is life. But we are looking for those times when the alarm that sounded in your head was incorrect. List those instances and read them often.

Exercise #2. Start creating a new list of things that happened in your life having to do with abandonment by the people you care about. Catch yourself feeling the fear when someone you care about doesn't call or text on time. When someone is not responding to your phone calls, it looks like they are ignoring you. Then when they call or come back, make sure you write it down, with a date and as many details as you can remember to recreate the feeling when you were anxious however everything was resolved. Keep that list close and read it with the list I mentioned in the previous exercise. You need the proof, and I know, even if you have 10 pages of the evidence, you still might be anxious. If so, then you will need to use other stress management techniques mentioned at the end of this book.

In addition, I would recommend you imagine that the person you worry about left and isn't coming back. Imagine that, and sit with that devastating feeling. Then think about what you will do. Ask yourself, "And then what?" Answer yourself. And no matter how bad you feel, no matter what terrifying action you need to take, keep on asking yourself, "And then what?" Until you get to the exhaustion point, to the peace of the worst-case scenario. And then you will see the solution, and you will feel that you can handle that too. And you won't die because you have not died from someone abandoning you so far. I believe you're not a ghost reading this, so give yourself credit. Remember that you are stronger than you think!

Exercise #3. Pay attention when, out of fear, you feel as if you can't get a grip on other people, and no matter what you tell them to do, they are still not listening to you. You can't control them. Do they call you too controlling? Or do they think you demand too much? Do you nag other people, trying to coerce them into doing something? Take time and write down your feelings and ask yourself where this is coming from. Obviously, when you want to control others, you want to go into a place of safety. That came from your childhood, and it needs to heal. When you have the urge to control, nag or demand, write what you want to see and ask yourself what it would take to make you happy. Ask yourself why you need to control the situation. Then imagine if what you want won't happen. Assess how important it is to get your way. If what you want or demand makes no difference in a week or so, let that go. If that makes a difference, then find a safe place to approach the other person to explain how important that is to you.

Exercise #4. Pay attention when you get suspicious about other people's whereabouts, especially those that you love. Do you get suspicious and then falsely accuse them of infidelity? That comes from the fear of abandonment, and you should take this with a cool head instead of escalating the issue.

Again, I am asking you to make a list of things in the past that you were paranoid about, but it turns out your anxiety was baseless. Read that list to remind yourself that you were not right every time, your fears are childhood trauma-based, and it is time to heal them. If you have a suspicion, be brave to nip that thought in the bud as soon you start thinking something negative. Then, you should go to your partner and ask what is going on. Someone in a relationship with you should be prepared for questions like this and understand that you have childhood trauma to heal. They should be supportive and explain the details for you to get clarity.

Exercise #5. Make a list of things that other people who love you do for you, how they take care of you, and how they show their love for you. Put down little things that you notice. Keep that list updated, and read it when you think you are not loved and not appreciated. It could be anything from something small, like making you breakfast, to big, like planning a surprise trip.

If you can't find anything, or you think that they don't do anything special, ask them, "How do you think you make me feel special?" You may be surprised that it turns out that your partner washing dishes for you is one of their love languages, and by the acts of service, they are showing their love for you, but you don't see it because your love language is touch.

I highly recommend taking a test online to find out what type your love language is and talk with your partner, friend, or those in your life to understand yourself and others better. It is important to find the courage to discuss this with the people you care about. And if they don't care what your love language is, it is time to find people who will care.

Exercise #6. If you are feeling lonely, search for volunteering opportunities in your community. It has been proven already that those who volunteer achieve better states of mind, peace, acceptance, and happiness. Just remember how you felt when you helped someone. Do you remember that feeling? Get more of that! Volunteering is also something you can do to blend in with other people, get to know them, meet new friends, and the best part of all, you will not be the subject of attention. You can blend in and reap all the benefits. Brainstorm what you like to do. If you like pets, go volunteer in animal shelters. If you want to be around people, volunteer in kindergartens, schools, churches, homeless shelters, or retirement homes. Your hands are needed, you are needed, so get going.

Your Superpower

Because of your fear of abandonment, you always strive to be your best, treat others well, and please others. People like you. You are a good friend and partner.

CHAPTER 5

Need Validation

Do you post a picture of yourself on social media and then keep on coming back to see how many likes you've gotten? Well, don't feel bad about it. Many seek validation that way since they don't get validation in other ways. At first, this might seem like something wrong to do or pathetic, but being validated is essential to us, like being accepted by the group. It's a survival instinct.

It reminds me of a joke about the client who comes to the lawyer's office and asks the secretary to validate his parking. She politely answers him with a lovely voice: "You did a pretty good job, Mr. Thompkins. You placed the car between two lines and left plenty of space for your neighbor to get into his car."

All jokes aside, seeking validation is something we all do, no matter what household we grew up in or how long ago that was. And we do remember how much – or how little – validation we got as a child. Some things don't go away that easily, no matter how much water has gone under the bridge or even if you left the town where that bridge was.

Growing Up Invalidated

Validation still plays a big role in my life, and like many, I need to be validated to feel accepted into a group. No matter how hard I try, and I do try a lot, it still ticks me off when something happens that upsets me, and I hear from a friend encouraging me with, "It could be worse," or "I'm sure she didn't mean that." My blood would boil when my ex-husband would tell me that I was overreacting, or I had made a big deal out of everything. And it still drives me nuts when I tell a story about something that hurt me in my childhood and my mother says to me, "That didn't happen."

I believe one of the most crucial things that a child needs from his or her parent is validation. When you are a child, you begin to form ideas in your mind about how the world works, and your view of the world takes shape. As an ACOA, you might still constantly yearn for your parents to accept your feelings, emotions, and thoughts even though they cannot give it. This feeling stems from growing up in an invalidating environment and might not learning how to handle your own stress or anxiety. You learned to distrust your own emotions and feelings. Invalidation can affect anyone, and it can be very upsetting, painful, and harmful, especially to a young child growing that is being formed into a functioning adult.

If you didn't get validated while growing up, you might feel worthless, unimportant, irrational, and not undeserving of things in your life. As a result, you might have difficulty managing your emotions, feeling chronic feelings of emptiness or impulsiveness. This can affect your relationships, work, and reactions to life in general.

I had a client once, let's call her Tracy, who suffered from childhood trauma induced by her alcoholic mother. When she was a child and felt sick, Tracy was always told that she wasn't sick and there was nothing wrong with her. No matter how bad the headache or the fever was, her mother would feed Tracy with, "No, you don't have a headache, you are not sick, you are going to school." And sure, some kids pretend to be sick to miss school, but Tracy would actually have excruciating pain and fever. Her feelings were totally brushed away, invalidated by the person who should care the most about her daughter's well-being. Her mother cared only about Tracy leaving the house. Her feeling was" get out of my hair," so she could drink herself peacefully to sleep.

During her teenage years, my client learned how to medicate herself, and she learned not to complain or tell anyone how badly she felt, emotionally or physically. She felt that nobody would believe her, no matter how bad she felt. She felt as if something was wrong with her. Sadly, during her adult years, Tracy learned to brush off how bad she was feeling and kept pushing forward without taking care of herself. Not even a cancer diagnosis stopped her from working hard until her coworkers had to stop her and force her to finally do what she had neglected, take care of herself.

Being invalidated when you're a child has a huge impact on your future and creates long-lasting effects that can continue into adulthood. If your need for validation was not met when you were a child or even right now, you might be having problems with managing your emotions. It is simply due to doubting what you are feeling since you were always told that what you were feeling was invalid or wrong. With repeated exposure, you began to distrust the validity of your own personal experiences. Sadly, what you feel is what you feel, and no matter how much others tell you that you are wrong, pain is real. So, you learn how to hide your emotions. You might be looking so calm, collected, and in control when you are dying inside. Some can diagnose ACOA as borderline personality disorder with emotional instability that affects any all kinds of relationships. Emotional invalidation leads to the a hole inside that you will try to fill in. This feeling can contribute to someone developing anxiety or depression.

Much of my experience in growing up was constantly being invalidated. No matter how painful my experience was, all I got back was, "Your feelings don't matter. Your feelings are wrong." My father would roll his eyes at me or ignore me altogether while I needed help and felt crushed. The many times when he would come home drunk and would have another episode of yelling and banging fists on the table, and I would start crying, he would yell at me, "Stop crying!" I even had no right to express my fear, and I had to swallow it.

Now I understand that it wasn't that he didn't care how I felt. It was more like he could not care because he was immersed in his own pain. I bet in his mind he understand why I would be crying. He distanced himself from his role in my being upset. Since he couldn't control his own emotions, he thought that controlling mine would make him feel less. By validating his behavior, I could let my anger subside and discover a way to validate myself. I finally understood that I didn't need him or anyone else to validate me. It was easier for me to say that when I was 40 years old. But when I was a child, all this made no sense, and I took invalidation very personally because I didn't know any better.

At this point, I have forgiven my father, but the wound of abuse is still there to heal. And by no means am I telling you that you should forgive someone for hurting you or validate their actions. The main point that I want to make here is that no matter whether or not you grant forgiveness, there is a wound that needs to heal. It is up to you to take care of yourself now.

Heal by Validating Yourself

The solution might not be easy to do, but it is worth it. First, you need to stop looking for validation from others and validate yourself. Because you are the only one who knows you best. And the most critical part: you need to stand up for yourself. You need to be there for yourself because your parents and caregivers abandoned you then. You should accept and understand emotion or perspective for what you are. Accept yourself fully now. You are the adult child of an alcoholic parent, of a mother or father who is incapable of dealing with his or her own emotions let alone to validate those of his or her child.

Like any childhood trauma, lack of validation can be healed. The solution is to deal with a problematic situation. When something makes you uncomfortable, identify it. Talk about it and then decide on what to do about it. Tell yourself, "My feelings and emotions are completely valid. It is ok to feel the way I feel right now. I am letting myself feel this way because I don't need to make myself feel happy every day."

It might be challenging when you plunge into validating yourself, but that is the only way to counter every negative perception you have brought into your adulthood from childhood. It would help if you accepted what you feel and what you think as true. That way, you love yourself more. As an ACOA, you feel very intensely how other people feel very intensely, and you would never tell your friend, "You are overreacting!" That is your superpower, to feel and understand what other people are going through. So be your best friend and validate yourself.

Simple things that can help with validation: you can start by talking to yourself as a best friend, tell yourself the things that you would say to a friend when they are going through something painful, like, "That must have been really hard, I am here for you, this must be so painful. You did the best you could. Everything will be ok."

Validating your feelings is also allowing yourself to feel those feelings. I get angry sometimes. And I used to get mad that I was angry because I was not allowed to feel or express my emotions. So now I let myself feel emotions, and if I am angry, I go all out, yell, and honor my emotions. I realized that I use humor as a defense mechanism to numb my own feelings. Now I catch myself doing that, and now I can address that.

When you feel upset, imagine your feelings like a child with a tantrum who doesn't want to tell you why they are upset. Patiently ask that child to tell you what you can do to help. Wait for the child to open up, especially if there is something that you feel shame or guilt about. That wounded child can look very abused in your imagination. It can look hurt, not only physically, but also emotionally. The child might be tranquil or maybe crying. Hug that child and ask why he or she is upset. It might take time, but don't give up. Keep asking the child what they need, assure him or her that this is a safe place to express yourself. When you discover what made that child upset, then comfort it, hug it and say you won't invalidate him or her anymore and you won't ever leave.

One of my favorite self-love meditations is Marisa Peer's "I am enough" meditation. She guides you through the relaxation and then instructs you to listen and say positive affirmations about how amazing you are. It is accessible online, and you won't have difficulty finding it. She is not giving me anything for this recommendation, but I am so passionate that it helped me with low self-esteem that I have been telling anyone who would listen about her for years. As a matter of fact, when I started the self-love journey, I had a sign, "I am enough," on my phone as a screensaver to remind me of that every time I glanced at it. People have pictures of their family or pets, and I had the "I am enough" sign. And if you have not heard about her, please, check her out and get the "I am enough" meditation and listen to it. It will change your world!

Exercises

Here are some of the exercises that can help you gain some control and sanity when validating yourself. Be kind to yourself, start with small steps, and do one exercise at a time.

Exercise #1. Make a list of your accomplishments. Obviously, I didn't come up with this genius idea myself. I borrowed it from Jack Canfield. It would be great if you could write it down by hand on a piece of paper, but if you like to use a computer, that is acceptable as well. Spend some time remembering your accomplishments, and you can talk with family members to help you remember your early days. You also can look at old photographs in your diary. List all achievements no matter how big or small they look to you. Please write down big accomplishments such as when you graduated high school, got a driver's license, got your first job, got married, divorced, bought a house. Don't discard small personal accomplishments, such as learning how to ride a bicycle, learning how to grill great steak, making your first "A" in algebra class, or just asking someone for a date! Your list should be long. The longer, the better - a few pages at least. Don't forget to add to this list any victory that you foresee in the future! What's the use of this list? Well, when you feel like you need validation or feel like you are not good enough, you can't achieve things, or the whole world is working against you, read this list. Better yet, every morning, before you start your day, read this list in front of the mirror to prepare yourself for a joyous day.

Exercise #2. Reward yourself when you achieve a victory, no matter how small or big it is. It can be something you have been working on for months, years, or days! Even if you were afraid to speak up during the monthly staff meeting, but now you have finally gathered enough courage to vocalize your great idea, it is a victory! And accomplishments like that should be rewarded! Have your "rewards list." Brainstorm and write the list of things you will give yourself when achieving something.

A word of caution: don't give yourself something that will sabotage you in other goals you are trying to achieve. For example, don't eat a piece of cake every few days, and at the same time try to improve your figure. Or don't buy yourself a Porsche and drown yourself in debt just because the boss gave you a great yearly review. You sure can have piece of cake but use it as a big reward that took months to achieve and buy that Porsche if you became a partner in a prestigious law firm. If you can't just come up with more than a few things on the list, look around, see what others are doing, turn on the TV and get ideas there! Prepare for the future and write the list down right. Keep at within arm's reach so you can revise it as soon you achieve something.

Exercise #3. Ask your friends to write you a letter about how much they love you and how wonderful you are. You might be thinking that they will laugh at you, and there is no way you will be asking for that. Just tell them that you are reading this book to help yourself, and there is an exercise where a friend needs to write a letter to you about how much they love you. That simple! If you ask someone for the letter who can't even write a few sentences because they can't come up with anything excellent about you, it is time to reconsider the friendship and move to the next exercise.

If you don't have that many friends or family members that would write letters, then you can ask your coworkers, neighbors, or those people who know you. You should know at least three people personally that you can ask to do that for you! And don't be afraid to get the letters back. Even if there is something that you don't want to hear about yourself, you can still can use this as something to improve on. Read those letters when you feel down, doubtful in your abilities, and need a simple pick-up.

Exercise #4. Please make a list of your friends and evaluate how good they are as friends. Next to their names, write whether they support you or put you down. Remember how they make you feel when you are with them. Remember how they react when something happens to you. Are they there to help you, or are they there to tell you that you should have done better? Naturally, like an ACOA, you might have friends who will invalidate you and say things like, "That was stupid what you did, you're always making big deals out of small stuff. Relax, it's not the end of the world." If you just realized that you have and hang out with friends like that all the time, please, don't get upset at yourself. That is your "normal" to be around people who invalidate you since that is what you have been accustomed to since you were a child. That is why we are doing this exercise, evaluating where you are right now, so we can change things around.

Other friends on the list are always there for you and believe in your abilities and talents even if you don't believe in yourself. Some friends might be neutral, or they sometimes support, sometimes don't, and it's okay. A true friend will point at things that you can improve but will do it because they love you and support you, not to hurt you and invalidate you to make themselves feel better. A true friend will cry with you if you need crying, they will encourage you on a new adventure, they will believe and tell you that you deserve the best.

After you are done, we will mainly concentrate on those friends that put you down and make you feel badly. Those are toxic people you need to let go of and hang out with them less and less. If you can stop seeing them cold turkey, even better. You might be asking, well, what if one of those toxic people is my sister that I can't just get along with, but she needs me? It is time to realize that you need to take care of yourself first and, for the time being, heal first before you can handle being in the same room with her. Grow a thick skin, so to speak. Don't answer her calls, don't see her, tell her you are busy, sick, or have to bathe your dog. Come up with something!

Exercise #5. Stand in front of the mirror, compliment yourself on how you look, and make detailed observations. If you just thought to yourself that there is nothing that you like about yourself because there is nothing beautiful about you, you are very wrong. If you can't find anything, ask your friends. They will point out a few things that you didn't notice about yourself. Well, it is time to notice that now. If you are trying to improve your look, pay extra attention, and point out to yourself that you are moving in this direction. If you are working on losing weight, look at yourself and say, "I look better than yesterday. I am doing so good!" Give yourself extra love when you get a haircut or buy new clothes or style a new hairdo or something else new. Adore yourself in the mirror, be happy, celebrate this moment! At the end of the day, give yourself a high five for the things you accomplished that day. And it might be silly at first, but you get used to it. Smile at yourself every time you pass a mirror!

Your Superpower

Because you seek validation from others, you are more open to hearing feedback from others about you to fuel your personal growth and betterment.

CHAPTER 6

Relying on the Opinions of Others

It's hard to find a person who doesn't care what other people think about them or never asks for anyone else's opinion. Listening to other people's opinions is something that we spend time on almost every day by listening to the news, conversing with friends, or having discussions with coworkers. Opinions are simply one person's take on something. Sadly, not everyone has a right to express or hear others' opinions, depending on the social situation. Beliefs can split the closest family members and unite enemies against a common cause. We all care about other people's opinions of us, and many decisions we make in our lives have to do with the opinion of others.

Once I heard Dr. Daniel Amen's 18/40/60 rule that goes something like this: "When you're 18, you worry about what everybody is thinking of you; when you're 40, you don't give a darn what anybody thinks of you; when you're 60, you realize nobody's been thinking about you at all." When I first heard that, I giggled because I found that very accurate. I was already in my forties, but still, I remember how other people's opinions were detrimental to me when I was in my twenties.

In part, it had something to do with the fact that I was in my twenties, but it also was because I was from a dysfunctional family.

Valuing Others' Opinions More than Your Own

Expressing your opinion cr listening and taking action based on others' opinions can be stressful, especially when it makes you feel compelled to do something that you don't want to do. Hearing different opinions than yours also can feel stressful and threatening because we feel unsafe. For some, expressing an opinion is not at all stressful. It is more like the right in the free world, but for an ACOA, it can be very stressful, as it was for me.

Growing up with an alcoholic father, I learned that definitions and boundaries are blurred. For a child to grow into a healthy adult, they need care, support, and safety, among other things, none of which I received. One day I was wanted and loved. Another day I was ignored and disapproved of. The definitions were not clear, and the messages were mixed: "Yes, no, I love you, go away." I interpreted the affirmations I didn't get on a day-to-day basis as negative. If they didn't say that they loved me, I assumed they didn't say that because they didn't love me. I had no chance to determine what was true and what was a lie. What worked one day didn't work the next. One day I did something right, and the next day it was not good enough. So, I grew up with confusion about myself. I could never get it right, and I was not good enough.

More than that, I distrusted my feelings and opinions about every-thing, damaged my belief in myself, and doubted any judgment about myself. I was seeking constant approval from others, no matter how important or insignificant a decision I had to make. It could be some-thing significant about what type of people I should hang out with. Or it could be the simplest thing, such as what type of shoes I needed to buy. If the other person didn't like the shoes I had picked for myself, I would not buy them. If they told me that the other pair looked better on me, even if I did not like them, I would wear them. I believed that someone else's opinion was probably better than mine. Sadly, I listened to other people's opinions long into my adult life.

At the same time, I was taking other people's opinions about me or what I did very personally. Any negative remark would affect me greatly, and I would feel threatened by it. It reminded me of when I was a child and I made a wrong judgment about something and behaved in a way that displeased my caregivers. The fear of getting it wrong felt deeply life-threatening to me. Any similar situation, even as an adult, caused me fear, and I would quickly become defensive.

Learn to Listen to Yourself

Maybe you grew up in a similar environment. I don't know how you coped with that until now, but I hope you are an adult who understands that every person has an opinion, and not necessarily the same one. A person from a balanced family, or at least not from an abused environment, would be able to express it and listen to other peoples' opinions without taking them personally. However, if you grew up as ACOA, you might find that the inner message about things you think are right and wrong is very blurred. You might also tend to value other people's opinions more than your own due to the belief that your opinion is wrong or just to agree with others to please them, as I did.

Only much later in life did I learn that it matters a lot whose opinion you are asking. For example, I heard a joke about a patient going to the doctor. He told her that her diabetes is causing her to be overweight and suggests she lose weight. She felt offended, didn't like the suggestion, and told the doctor she would need to hear a second opinion. He answers with: "Sure, and you have an ugly haircut, too!"

To gain confidence in yourself and your own opinions, you should listen to yourself more than others and be sure where you stand compared to others. Or course, that is not that easy, especially when you grew up in an environment where your opinion was worth nothing. If you have been working on healing yourself, and I am guessing you are since you are reading this book, you might be threatened by getting involved with other people. Others have their opinions, so out of habit and to feel safe, you want them to agree with you. It might feel unsafe to have a different opinion than others, and you might feel as if you are afraid to lose yourself.

Have you ever had an opinion about something, and you changed it? Does that mean anyone's opinion can change, yours or another person's? When you have an opinion about something, please pay attention to where it is coming from. Pay attention to how you reason, and analyze your opinions, responses, and perceptions to see where they are coming from. For example, are you forming an opinion from your own beliefs, values, and previous experiences, or are you just agreeing to agree?

Express What You Really Think

One of my friends complained that she doesn't feel appreciated at work and is constantly overlooked for a raise. She described herself as a hard worker, always coming on time and leaving after work hours, helping other people with their workload, and delivering hers on time. I recommended she talk to her supervisor. Turned out, she was seen as someone who doesn't care much about her team. Many thought she would be leaving the company soon. My friend was shocked. Apparently, she kept silent and didn't express her opinion about anything, whether it was on what show she was watching last night, or where she wanted to go for lunch, or to give her opinion about how projects were handled. Others saw it as a lack of interest and antisocial. Knowing her, I knew that her keeping to herself came from being an ACOA and her lack of ability to trust that her opinion matters. She thought if she did what she needed to do and kept everyone pleased, it would work the same as being a child in a dysfunctional family. But it worked against her. After discovering what was at stake, she opened up more and voiced her opinions more often about both important and silly things. A year later, she was acknowledged like she wanted and got a raise.

But just voicing your opinion about something can help you or harm you. It would be best if you took the time to form your opinion, and decide when it's the appropriate time to share it. This funny story illustrates my point: An old man comes to the pawn broker holding an old guitar in his hands and asks, "I would like your expert opinion on this guitar. How much do you think it's worth?" The pawn broker looks it up and down and says: "Well, I can tell it's been played a lot. It has some scratches and dents, and the lacquer is faded. For that reason, I think it is worth twenty bucks." The old man cheers up with, "If that's what you think it's worth, we have a deal!" The pawn broker excitedly shakes the older man's hand. "Here is your twenty bucks," says the old man. The broker stops, confused: "What do you mean?" The old man flips the guitar to show the sticker price of $100 and adds, "It was labeled as a hundred dollars, but now that you gave me your honest opinion, I think that twenty dollars is a great price!"

So, before you share, weigh what you truly believe. Have three choices to decide on by keeping the original opinion that you started with, then change that opinion to the other people's, or just come up with something totally different from the previous two. The third position can be the best opinion and serve you the best. And remember, your opinion about something should serve you the best, not others. So overall, don't discard another person's opinion and don't see it as a threat, but listen to it, see where it is coming from, what evidence is there. Then you can decide who you will listen to, yourself or the other person. And ultimately, the decision is yours, so you are still in control and should feel safe.

Like in the previous story, you may not have the same opinion as others, but that's okay. In a conversation, allow yourself to have a different opinion than others. Voice a different opinion than anyone else and see what happens. Listen to your true self; don't be afraid to voice it out loud. Don't be scared that others won't like your opinion. It's just an opinion. If someone disagrees with you, don't immediately change your opinion without evaluating their point as they might want you to. You might change your opinion because you see that their point is valid, not because you are afraid they don't like you. Also, when someone tells you their opinion, don't get unhinged because it is a different opinion than yours. Ask yourself where that is coming from.

What background and experience does this person have to think that way? Be curious. Analyze it. And if you still think you have a different opinion, that is okay. Honor the other person's opinion as you honor your own. Agree to disagree.

Exercises

Here are a few exercises that can help you with working on expressing your opinion safely.

Exercise #1: Write down your earliest memories of what you thought others' opinions were of you. What would you say if I asked you to tell me what your family or friends thought of you growing up? Especially pay attention to the authorities in your immediate circles like parents, caregivers, and teachers. If you can't remember what authorities in your life thought about you, then have a daily journal and keep recording what triggers you. When you identify what "truths" about yourself you have learned from others, identify who those people were that gave you those "truths." And then judge them. Yes, judge them! I am sure you already got scared just by thinking about that! How dare you judge your grandmother, who locked you up in the closet to punish you! Ask yourself whether they were models of mature and loving support or the same scared and wounded children that grew up without healing their own childhood trauma.

Most of the time, people who gave you a low opinion of you were not qualified to condemn you in the first place. Give yourself permission to forgive those people and let your opinions go. Especially let go of the opinions of others in your life who didn't even know who you were. Neighbors, friends, and even family members think they understand who you are, but they don't. You are the only one who knows yourself. So, by default, if they don't know you, how can they judge you and be right about who you are? Think about that.

Exercise #2: Create a list of things in your life that you are doing because someone else said it is good for you to do. How do you identify that? By making a list of things you do but don't want to do. Of course, going to work every day might not ignite passion in you, and you still need to, but I mean things that you feel you are obligated to do, but it won't cause damage if you stop. For example, maybe you have a mother you need to see every weekend and don't feel like doing it. Maybe you are walking in the morning because your partner told you to, but you would rather sleep in. You might be doing that because you believe those actions are good for you because someone else told you to do them. Or you might be doing it like a sacrifice and hope one day they will appreciate it, see your value, and you will be loved. Obviously, it would help if you were not doing things you don't want. When you come up with the list, brainstorm how you can improve that.

Maybe you can stop doing something that you don't like doing and nobody will know, only you. Then stop doing that or find a different way to achieve a similar goal. If the situation involves other people, then brainstorm how you can have a conversation with them and express your dissatisfaction. Get prepared for this conversation and have answers ready if they ask you something. Even better, have a solution ready if they contradict you. If there is something that you want to stop, like walking in the morning, then have research showing the evidence that you can do a workout at night and still achieve the same result. So you can solve the uncomfortable situation and feel like you didn't let them down, but simultaneously, you took control in your hands and stood up for yourself.

If you identified a situation you couldn't change, are uncomfortable with, and don't like doing it, come up with something that fills your soul with joy. Then, do something in addition that makes you happy, so you don't feel as if you constantly need to do something against your will. Fulfill yourself in other ways.

Exercise #3: If you have difficulty forming or expressing your opinion, keep an opinion log daily and collect the opinions of others around you. While in any situation, whether at home, at work, standing in line at the checkout, observing other people and their opinions, ask yourself why they formed this opinion and what are the reasons. Is their opinion essential and makes a difference just because they expressed it? By this observation, you see that everyone makes their opinions heard, but it doesn't mean that those opinions are valid. Those are just opinions and don't mean anything until they are acted upon. When you collect enough opinions on things and people, you should feel confident that you can also form and voice your own opinions.

Exercise #4: Remember when you listened to someone's opinion, took action, and it turned out not to work out for you or even work against you? It might have worked out for them, but because you are different, it didn't work out for you. Like a movie someone recommended but you didn't like. Or a diet your friend told you to keep wasn't the right fit for you. Could you write it down no matter how big or small the outcomes are? Focus on when you listened to the authorities in your life to please them or because you thought their opinion was better than yours. Make a list of those occurrences. If you don't remember any from the past, start creating a list of ones in the present. Please pay attention to whose opinion you listen to, what action you take based on that opinion, and write its outcome. Keep that list handy like other lists I recommended in this book and read it when you have doubts. And of course, you have a right not to make this list and not listen to my suggestion.

Exercise #5: Make a list of the people that you listen to their opinion almost religiously. Those probably will be the opinions you count as an authority in your life, such as your boss, partner, family member, or someone you respect or are afraid of. Evaluate your previous behavior with them and list the instances when you agreed with them because you thought their opinion was better than yours or because you wanted to please them. Do you see patterns in your behavior? You should be able to voice your different opinion in front of them, and the sooner you do it, the better. Especially if there are things that you constantly disagree with them about and it makes you feel uncomfortable.

Next to the person's name, write a few things you are afraid to disagree with and write a sentence about how you would like to voice yourself. Practice in front of the mirror a few times before you say it in front of them for confidence. Next time this subject comes up in the conversation with them, make that statement. Don't be afraid. They might take it well, giving you the confidence to voice yourself honestly in the future.

Exercise #6: One of my favorite tools that I learned from Teal Swan (I recommend you check out her stuff) is how to determine your opinion in any situation by asking yourself this question: "What would some-one who loved himself do?" What I like about this question is that you are asking yourself, so you need to come up with the answer. You can't find someone else to take responsibility for your situation. Naturally, we know the answer and what is best for us so that we can answer the question. The trick comes in two parts: you need to take the first thing that comes to your mind as accurate. And number two – you need to take action. Being ACOAs, you might not believe your own ideas, well, because you grew up in an environment where your opinions, thoughts, and anything that you can produce were not supported and were discarded, invalidated. But if you take time and pay attention to what you feel and what comes to your mind when you ask yourself this question, you will be able to come up with an answer. Also, give yourself the feeling of control and tell yourself that, even if you come up with an idea, you don't necessarily need to take action. You are just asking about this out of curiosity, so you don't put so much pressure on yourself. Now, when you decide that the idea you got in your mind is something that you believe and is what a person who loves himself would do, and you think it is a good idea for you to do too, you need to take action. And as ACOA, you probably will be afraid to take action because you were not allowed to do that in the past. Stop doubting yourself and just do it. If your answer is big, then take small steps and break it down. But use this question for anything: when you are changing lanes on the road to work, when you are wondering what shoes you should buy, when you are wondering if you should go to a party, what food you need to eat or movie to watch, what offer you should take. Don't be afraid to listen to your own opinion. Remember, if you love and care for yourself, you can be more caring and loving towards others.

Your Superpower

Although being afraid to vocalize your opinion can be a shortcoming, it can also work in your favor. If you mostly agree with other people's opinions and follow their lead, others see you as agreeable and easy to be around, more friendly and likable. So make sure you are not a total pushover and still meet your needs. On the other hand, if you voice your opinion quickly, you might be taken as someone who can see every situation from a different point of view, which is very valuable for other people. So just make sure you don't get offended if other people don't follow your advice.

CHAPTER 7

Need to Control the Environment

Being in control of your life sounds like a positive thing, and in most cases, it is very welcomed. Parents are proud of kids who plan, have their lives in order, and stay on top of things. In our society, control is seen positively and as something to be proud of. There are even jokes about how spouses control each other for everyone's amusement. Like this one: A pastor asks the congregation, "Men who are controlled by their wives, please step forward." Almost all of the men moved forward. Just one man kept standing in place. The pastor was excited to see at least one strong man in the crowd and asked him, "How come your wife is not controlling you?" The man answered, " It was my wife who commanded me to stay in place and not to move."

If you laughed and thought to yourself, "Oh, so true," then you have someone in your life who is controlling. Like everything, there should be balance. It is good to take care of yourself and your family. But for some, controlling everything can be all-consuming. Obsessive control of others becomes annoying and frowned upon. All-consuming control comes from feeling unsafe. Feeling out of control can be scary for most people, but even more so for Adult Children of Alcoholics. Living in an environment with an addict is scary and unpredictable. It takes strength to survive in this environment when you are an adult; imagine how scary it is to be a child in this type of uncertainty.

Coping with Chaos as a Child

ACOAs try to control people and situations in their environment as a coping mechanism that they developed as a child to deal with a terrifying and dysfunctional family situation. To feel safe, one wants to control everything in life as much as possible. If things don't go their way, they get angry. Anger is actually a product of believing there is no way out of a situation that they can't change. Unfortunately, this anger is often misunderstood in our society, and the one who gets angry is not even allowed to express it. Worse, they are punished for it.

Sadly, many children believe they can control their parent's or caregiver's drinking or any other type of addiction. From an early age, I begged my dad to stop drinking. I was afraid of him when he was drunk and caused scenes, and I begged him to stop being dangerous and embarrassing while under the influence. Obviously, that made no difference. I was vacillating between trying to control his drinking and feeling completely powerless to do it. Looking back, I feel sad for that child who thought she could make a difference.

I grew up with an alcoholic father, everything felt out of control, and I felt helpless about that. I was afraid to go home after school. Most of the time, I was pretty sure that my dad would come back drunk, but I never knew how drunk and how bad things would get. I would see my mother yelling at him, begging, ignoring, and even taking him to hypnosis sessions to help him with alcoholism, but nothing worked. He was drunk, and nothing was stopping him. So I grew up knowing there is nothing I can do and there is no help for things to change. The only thing I was waiting for was to grow up and leave the house so I wouldn't have to deal with it. But even after I grew up and left, I was still stressed because I was wondering how my mother was dealing with my drunk dad when I was not there. More than that, there were plenty of relationships in my life that didn't include my parents but mirrored their situation, and those made me feel stressed out and anxious. If the anxiety kicked in, my need to take control of the situation and others would kick in. I couldn't stop myself.

You might have felt similar feelings growing up or even right now. You might still try to control people and the situations you are in and force the outcome you want. Things need to be your way, or you can unravel emotionally and find it hard to cope. You might seem controlling in very subtle ways. For example, you might like to set up your desk in a particular way and get angry if someone moves your stuff.

Or you might be bullying your family and friends by behaving in a way that makes you feel safe. For example, you might be demanding that everyone in your family tells you where they are going, when they will get there, what they are doing there, and what time they will be back. You might even control what others eat, how long they sleep, and even small things, like their opinions and liking the same things you do. The reason is you feel unsafe and think you need to control things and the way they go to feel safe. Because you care for your family and friends, you feel there is security in knowing about them and their actions.

Control and Codependency as Adults

I had a client, let's call her Marsha, who was obsessed with knowing where her children and spouse were at all times. If the time came for them to be home and they were ten minutes late, she would go out of her mind fretting that something terrible had happened to them. Marsha would throw a fit if she called any of them and they didn't answer. Her kids would rebel and not pick up the phone when she called. She felt like she was failing as a mother because she couldn't take care of her children if something happened, and she felt helpless to change anything. Seeing that her obsessive control came from the childhood trauma, I recommended she keep a diary to note when she worried about her family. On later days when she would get worried, instead of calling them and asking why they were not home, she could look back at the diary and notice that there were other days when they didn't come home on time but still came back home safe and sound. In addition, we worked on her understanding of where that was coming from and on healing childhood trauma.

This type of control is not something so easy to get rid of, even if you understand that you are too controlling of everything. I still want to control my environment, and if I can't, I feel uncomfortable with the uncertainty and get upset when things don't go my way. Depending on the situation, I might be inflexible. Obviously, I tell people what they should think and do. I am better at being spontaneous and changing plans, but I hear it is hard for some other ACOAs. I still might give ultimatums and be nagging, especially in intimate relationships. However, I am much better at limiting my control now that I am more aware of my shortcomings.

Controlling other people and the environment is very stressful. It might feel like we can't get things in one place because they keep moving. It is stressful to feel unsafe. And it is not like we chose that on purpose. It is all unconscious. As a result, we are often accused of being controlling, rigid, and lacking in spontaneity. This is probably true. It doesn't come from wanting to do everything your way. It isn't because we are spoiled or unwilling to listen to other ideas. It comes from the fear that if we are not in charge or if a change is made abruptly, quickly, without our being able to participate in it, we will lose control of our lives.

From outside, it might look like controlling behavior is based on an ego-driven belief that our way is the "right" way. Trying to control people and situations gives us the feeling of power, that we are not victims and don't depend on others. That is why we hold control so tightly. We are afraid that if we let go of control, something scary and awful will happen to us.

Letting Go of Control

As adults, we know we can take care of many things and don't have to feel like scared, helpless children anymore. It is hard but doable. Since the feeling of unsafety is often exaggerated, we need to learn how to surrender control, relax, and take care of our stress levels. We should let things happen naturally. We should take responsibility for our own feelings and how we react to things. That way, we can feel in control of something. Instead of forcing others to do or be what we want, let them decide, and follow with changing our attitude and being more open to the outcome while remaining flexible and calm.

In addition, we should allow others and ourselves and others to make mistakes and accept that things will not always go our way, and it is okey if they don't. We should take responsibility for our own problems and mistakes, not other people's. New things will bring new experiences that will lead to our healing, growth, and happiness. Instead of stressing about things, we should be enjoying things!

More than that, we must understand that control is not necessarily all or nothing. We can control some things, and others can take care of the rest. We for sure can control our feelings, thoughts, and behaviors, but not other people's feelings, thoughts, and behaviors. So instead of stressing how we can stop our caregiver from substance abuse or our partner from bullying at a job, we should pay attention to how we understand that. It might be the situation that we can't control is not as life-threatening as we think. Assess the situation to figure out when you need to let it go or when you need to start to worrying and act.

You might think that controlling things is your nature, and there is no way you can change who you are. You can say there is no way a mother will stop caring for her children, and it is ridiculous to let go of "knowing what's best for them." If you think there is no way to change your controlling side, you might be right because you don't even know the allowing side. Control is all you know.

A child in an unstable family takes up lots of parenting responsibilities, depending on who in the family is an addict and who is helping to raise the kids, and how many kids there are. You might be one of the kids. They overreact to changes over which they have no control. The heightened sense of responsibility lends itself to the belief that we are responsible for fixing other people's issues and that we need to be in charge. And if you grew up a very independent child, and those who should have taken care of you didn't, you grew up knowing that if you don't take care of yourself, nobody else will. You may constantly feel you need to take care of others. Instead, concentrate on your own problems and responsibilities. Ask yourself what those indeed are. More than that, share your responsibility with others in your family, communicate your needs and make the load not so heavy.

Many ACOAs end up in a codependent relationship and try to solve everyone's problems. As we know, that is impossible, and it often leads to more stress, dissatisfaction, and resentment in the relationship. Allow others to make their own decisions, and don't bully them into what you want. Letting them do what they want and trusting them to do so will make the relationships stronger. Detaching from other people and their problems is not uncaring. It allows others to figure out their problems for themselves, and it is a loving and trusting act that enables others to grow and learn from experience. Imagine you come to an amusement park and pay for a ticket for a rollercoaster ride; you want to experience the rise and fall, to be excited, scared, and amused. What if someone comes up to you and tells you shouldn't do that because they think it is unsafe? You would probably think they are crazy and would still go on the ride. The same goes for the experience of other people. They have lives to experience on this planet, so let them experience what is theirs, and allow yourself to experience what is yours.

Exercises

Here are a few exercises you can use to help you with letting go of control and enjoying your life, even if just a little.

Exercise #1. Keep a diary of situations you want to control during your day. Even small things like how you wanted people to react to what you said, how you wanted them to take action. Did someone suggest a restaurant for lunch? Did you agree with them or suggest some other place to control them? Then take a closer look at your everyday habits and ask yourself how things would have changed if you had agreed with others. Contemplate how much of an impact that made in your life. Why be stressed about other people's actions if there is not much difference?

Exercise #2. Record instances when you went along with other people's suggestions and were pleasantly surprised. Maybe you learned something new by letting someone else take the lead. Maybe by going along with a suggestion to visit a new restaurant, you discovered something new that you now enjoy very much. Keep the newly discovered things you love and do them often or when you are sad or bored to lift your spirits.

Exercise #3. When you feel threatened in a situation and feel like you need to take action, ask yourself what will happen if you don't take action and how that will influence your life. Evaluate how important that is before imposing your opinion and making them do as you want to do. Will it matter in five years? Maybe you should let your child decide what color shoes they want to buy because it doesn't matter what they choose. But you for sure should have a say, and take action in saving money for your retirement and tell your spouse "No" to that Porsche that he wants for Christmas.

Exercise #4. Pay attention to all-or-nothing thinking that leads to only one way to solve problems. If you are in a situation and would love to have an input, brainstorm ways you can help and present them to the other person. But don't have an expectation that they are obligated to do things your way. They might decline your ideas, and you should be good with that. Remind yourself that you often make decisions without listening to other people's opinions, so they have a right to do things how they choose.

Exercise #5. Do something out of or the ordinary, something that is outside of your habits. For example, drive a different route to work, try a new place to eat, do an activity you usually don't do, or invite other people to join you. Join a club. Get a hobby. Do something that will push your boundaries. You can do tiny things that make no difference, such as rearranging your desk or going to get coffee at work by using walking the other way through the office. Do something new every day or once a week, depending on how much you are afraid to change things up and give up your control. It should give you confidence that changing things up doesn't need to end tragically. Notice how scary it is not to control something but then find joy in it. Of course, don't just jump into extremes, especially in the beginning; make yourself comfortable with letting go or controlling small stuff, and then try out more essential things in life.

Exercise #6. If you think that you let other people control you and barely have your say in things, start recording every day how much control you had with those you interact with the most. Record details so that you can compare later. You can use even different colors to see the patterns over time. Let's say write in red pen when you did what someone else wanted you to do, and in blue when you insisted on your own way. So next time you think, "I am always doing things the way they want me to," you will look at this list and see the truth. But you must be honest and write things down as they are, not as you want them to be. If you notice that you have more control than you thought, it may be time to let others control the situation. If you see that others are running you over, it is time to introduce healthy boundaries and insist on them.

Exercise #7. If you are not sure how much control you have in your life with your family members and friends, ask them. It might be daunting to do that, but if you already think you might be controlling, that is already a good start, so why stop there? You might be pleasantly surprised that you are not controlling at all. Or you might find out a truth that you didn't expect. But it is so worth it if you want to improve your relationships with others and yourself. So the only way to find out is to ask. Discovering your wounds and healing them shouldn't be shameful. It might even inspire your friends to look into themselves and heal. Simply ask them, "Do you think I am a controlling person?" If they just give you a one-word answer, ask them to elaborate on it and give examples. Take notes and pay attention next time you do something that you think you should change. A word of caution, ask this question only to those in your life who you think will give you an honest answer. Don't ask narcissists, as they cannot see you as you are nor give you proper feedback.

Exercise #8. When you identify that you are too controlling or not controlling enough, now is the time to do something about it. The best way to make change is to have an accountability partner. It can be your significant other, your friend, or coworker, to point out when you are overly controlling or letting go of too much control. You need to know how you want to improve your patterns and explain them to your accountability partner. Keep a diary and write in detail about daily situations you faced with your family, friends, and coworkers. Agree to talk to your accountability partner once a week and review your notes. Your accountability partner should be interested in detail and ask you to describe the situation more in-depth if it is unclear. I bet there will be situations in which, even though you had a chance to do things your way, you let the situation go. Or you might be too harsh on someone showing too much control. Your partner should be comfortable pointing out your patterns and calling you out about how you reacted so that you can improve. Having a partner who just agrees with you won't help you. If you tried out one partner, and it didn't work out, change the partner!

Your Superpower

Since you always need to be in control, you do many things for your family and friends, such as planning trips, parties, and overall day-to-day activities. Other people rely on you to be organized. You are a leader in your environment. Just be careful not to go overboard and control every step they take or every breath they make.

CHAPTER 8

Difficulty with Intimate Relationships

It's time to talk about intimate relationships. Intimacy can be simply described as "into-me-see" and means seeing into oneself or the other person, accepting them as they are, loving them the way they are, and connecting to them deeply. To have genuine intimacy, we must be willing to become an expert on someone by seeing, feeling, listening to, perceiving, and understanding the person without judgment. If you are an ACOA, any intimacy can be complicated, especially intimacy with yourself.

This joke comes to mind. A man comes to the restroom. As soon he sits down, he hears another man's voice from the stall next to his saying, "Hi, how are you today?" Surprised, the man answers, "I am fine, thanks." The next question is: "So what are you up to?" The man gets uncomfortable and answers, "I guess I am doing the same as you, sitting here, doing my own business." The conversation continues with, "Can I come over?" The man gets annoyed and snaps back with, "Well, I am kind of busy right now!" The next stall answers, "Look, I have to call you back later. There is a fool sitting in the next stall that keeps answering all of my questions."

How Trauma Becomes a Trigger

The joke might be funny. But the intimacy issue is one of the hardest ones for someone with childhood trauma. As soldiers who have experienced post-traumatic stress disorder (PTSD) may duck at a loud sound, unconsciously fearing that it is the sound of gunfire, ACOAs similarly fear intimate relationships and all that it encompasses. Because they were traumatized in their home and by the people who they depended on for care and basic survival, their terror-filled scenes from their previous experiences reemerge in normal relationships. Being intimately involved with someone, becoming a partner to someone, falling and love, and having a family is deeply terrifying to the ACOA, even if one is deeply reaching for it in order to be loved and accepted.

As adults, when we are confronted with similar situations to ones that we experienced as kids, the fear gets triggered, and we behave from the place of self-preservation. The memories throw us back into a state of hypervigilance, and all of the confusion we experienced as kids seem to come up to the surface. Many times, we erroneously link the feelings of fear to whatever triggered us at the moment. Actually, it is not the situation itself that caused us discomfort. We are just afraid that those situations will trigger underexposed, unprocessed, and unconscious feelings that we are not able to control. In those situations, we become a scared child all over again, and we behave like the child does, trying to become "invisible" until the feeling of danger passes. This immobilization is a self-preservation mechanism. If no one can see me, no one can hurt me.

I had a client, let's call her Soledad, who complained to me that she wasn't feeling seen by her partner and her own kids. She thought that her feelings weren't seen as important, and nobody paid attention to what she did. I asked Soledad if she felt overwhelmed from working and taking care of the house and the kids. I asked Soledad if she ever asked for help with housework or had a conversation with her partner expressing her feelings. Turned out she hadn't. She was afraid to express her own feelings and ask for help, and she was afraid she would get punished for her needs. Being "invisible" and acting like nothing's wrong was the only way she knew how to operate in the family environment. I also asked her to track everyday activities and how her family interacted with her by keeping a daily diary. I asked her to record any action towards her she encountered. After a few weeks of observation, she saw that her family was helping her in many ways, but she hadn't seen it. And she realized that when she asked for help, they would respond to it. So, in the end, she wasn't "invisible" to them.

Another extreme result of childhood trauma is that the ACOAs' response is aggression or withdrawal. When triggered, ACOAs may either intimidate people or shut them out by expressing rage and blame in an attempt to avoid feeling vulnerable. Seldom is there a middle ground. They have trouble translating feelings that lead to resolution. I have been guilty of that many times.

Poor Connections Start with Parents

The first and most obvious reason why ACOAs take things is that they have no frame of reference for a healthy intimate relationship. The only model they have is their parents, who would fight about drinking No matter what the level of intoxication would be, it would still create a very stressful situation.

I remember no matter how little or how much my dad would drink, there would be a problem when he returned home. My mom would not be happy and would lecture him and question why he was drunk again, or she just wouldn't say anything at all, but I could feel the stress and frustration hanging there. My dad's late arrival home after work would indicate that he was drunk, and that meant a very stressful situation for me because no matter how bad the fighting would get, I couldn't leave the house. I was terrified to say anything, so I would just hide in my room, afraid to breathe. When I was little, I remember being afraid even to use a bathroom because it would mean that I needed to cross the hallway and would see my parents arguing.

You might have been in a similar situation or, even worse, had to deal with both caregivers or parents being addicts. You might have been hit, humiliated, ignored, felt helpless, numb, frozen, or pulled away into your imagination while your body was still standing there. The worst part is that the people you would generally go to for comfort and solace were the ones who were hurting you! And as all of this was happening to you, you were a child who was trying to figure out what went wrong and how to fix it. You might have even blamed yourself, thinking that somehow it had to do with you.

Since you couldn't make sense of it and couldn't change it, you took the whole scene as truth and was frozen in there, making this long-lasting imprint in your memory with all the feelings surrounding you. It lives in your psyche, where it becomes exposed to other similar scenes and feelings and creates the frame for how you see the relationships in general. When we grow up and have relationships, those inner traumas and the pictures of how we imagine the relationships can reemerge with incredible detail. We might be in an adult body, but we return to this child inside of ourselves as soon as something triggers us.

In a healthy relationship, no matter what happens, you are loved and accepted. But if you grew up in an unhealthy environment, you might have been confused by the experience of coming close, going away – the inconsistency of a loving parent-child relationship. You might have felt, just like me, one day accepted and loved and the next day rejected or ignored. Not knowing what it is like to have consistent day-to-day, healthy intimate relationships with another person makes building one very painful and complicated. You might see any relationship the same way, expecting the relationship to go bad, even if it looks promising.

In addition, you might have a fear of being abandoned, and that certainly gets in the way of any relationship. The development of any healthy relationship requires a lot of give and take and problem-solving. There is always some disagreement that gets very big, very quickly for ACOA because the issue of being abandoned takes precedence over the original issue. Because of your fear of abandonment, you don't feel confident about yourself. You don't feel good about yourself or believe that you are lovable. So, you look to others for what it is that you cannot give yourself in order to feel okay. You feel okay if someone else tells you that you are okay. You give away a great deal of power. In a relationship, you give the other person the power to lift you up or knock you down. You feel wonderful if they treat you well and tell you that you are wonderful, but when they don't, these feelings no longer belong to you.

Because you felt as if your parents or caregivers hurt you for who you were, you learned to hide your true self from them, and worse, from yourself. The ultimate loneliness is when you don't feel that someone knows you, and they say they love you, but you know it is not possible. Because you feel ashamed of who you are, you are not showing yourself fully to the other person. So when they say they love you, you don't count that as true because they don't know you. There is this flawed belief that "You don't know me, so how can you love me. And if you do love, then it is not me."

Healing Your Relationships with Others

Of course, the same intimate relationships can bring the path to healing as soon we learn how to identify the triggers, understand where they are coming from, and how to deal with them. It reminds me of this situation that I just had the other day. I felt as if I wasn't getting enough attention from someone that I was in an intimate relationship with. I got angry and felt as if I was in a relationship where I just gave but got nothing in return. Obviously, I was catastrophizing the situation that wasn't even that bad.

Then I said something and had a tantrum that, right now, when I think of it, was not necessary at all. But at that moment it felt legitimate and, for a second, made me feel better, made me feel righteous. I got an answer back to my remarks that I should not behave like that because what I am complaining about is not true. I immediately stopped myself and, to be honest, I am very proud of myself for actually being able to stop and think about what happened. And after taking another look, I realized that my inner child, that was threatened and didn't feel safe, threw a tantrum out of self-preservation. So, I lashed out to defend myself. After I realized that, I felt ashamed of myself. Why would I act like a child when I am an adult? What's wrong with me!

Then something else happened. I started to apologize, and the feeling of the need to punish myself came to mind by telling myself that I don't deserve a loving relationship at all in my life. Then I went to another extreme in thinking that maybe I just shouldn't be with that person because it is causing me pain to be in an intimate relationship where I get hurt by others. Or do I actually hurt myself? If the intimate relationships cause me pain, why be in one? That is where I abandoned myself in that situation for the feeling of being safe when I craved a deeply loving relationship to begin with. Obviously, I needed to find a solution and accept my needs. I needed to stand by myself, stop abandoning myself and meet my needs. The need to be seen and the feeling of abandonment started the whole rollercoaster, and my inner child reacted to it. So, I took it as a lesson and the opportunity to heal by revisiting the whole thing, accepting it, and forgiving myself and the others. I went back with, "I acted out of my fears. Thank you for pointing this out for me." In return, I got more assurance that I was not being ignored, that I was safe and loved.

I learned from this experience and healed a little part of me by opening up and going that route. And I came back to this resolution the next time I felt abandoned, I would remind myself that I was acting out of a place of fear. I was not threatened, so I could relax and not react. Of course, this healing would not have been possible if I hadn't seen the situation from the outside, didn't investigate where all that came from, didn't take action, and most of all, didn't meet the person in my life how my behavior right from the beginning and acted with patience and love. Not everyone has a person in life that can support them. But it doesn't necessarily need to be an intimate partner. It can be a friend, a therapist, or someone to talk to you when you are riding a rollercoaster. And it starts with allowing people into your life and not being afraid to be vulnerable and intimate with yourself and others.

As soon something happens that triggers your withdrawal or lashing out in your intimate relationship, stop yourself and ask where that is coming from. Does it remind you of something? Translate the feelings into words, and talk about your emotions that trigger you before projecting them into your relationships. Use triggers in new relationships as a path to healing rather than an arena for reenactment.

A flawed image of how relationships should look influences not only your relationship with other people but also with yourself. You might be afraid to look inside yourself and acknowledge that you have particular feelings and needs. Because you feel unworthy and guilty about your needs, you are afraid to look deep inside yourself.

What is your relationship with yourself? Are you also abandoning yourself? Are you ignoring your needs? Are you courageous enough to acknowledge the truth and feelings about something? Are you honest with yourself about things? If you are not, you have to start changing that. You can change your relationship with yourself and with others.

Exercises

Here are a few exercises that will give you a start towards better relationships, or at least make getting into a relationship less stressful.

Exercise #1: The first step in any healing process is connecting with your true feelings. This can be a nerve-wracking and uncomfortable experience, especially if you were not allowed to feel or you were afraid to connect to your feelings because it hurt too much. However, it is a very powerful tool and can help navigate walls that we put up even to ourselves. Pick a time when you won't be disturbed. Stand in front of the mirror. It can be a handheld mirror as well. Look at your face, your eyes. What do you feel? Are you afraid to look at yourself? Does it make you uncomfortable to see yourself? Do you immediately start criticizing how you look? Do you remember the others' comments about your appearance? Ask yourself, where is that coming from? Then look at yourself with compassion as if you are looking at a friend who needs your help. If it were your friend that you were talking to right now, what would you say to the face in the mirror? Talk to yourself every day.

Exercise #2: Have a section of the notebook dedicated to intimacy triggers that come up while you interact with other people. Write them down to identify the patterns. Come to an agreement with yourself that you are writing them down, you are still paying attention to them, and you are honoring your feelings. But you will make a decision about what you will do with them tomorrow. Let yourself cool off. Read it the next day, and if you still think that acting will do you good, act, and mark what action you took and what results you received in the notebook. After a while, read your triggers. Is there a pattern? Address that pattern, and heal the trigger.

Exercise #3. If writing in a notebook just doesn't help you, find a therapist, a friend, a confidante that you can talk to as soon as you get triggered. Someone who can be there for you before you start acting out on your fears and ruining the relationship you are in. You should ask for help and talk to others not only about friendships or partnerships. You should ask for help in your relationship with yourself as well. Find someone that you feel comfortable opening up to, and they will support you and comfort you no matter how insecure you feel. You also should be able to be open with yourself before you contact someone else. What's the use of a conversation if you are afraid to face the truth?

Exercise #4. After getting triggered, take the notebook and divide the page into two areas. On the left, write down the trigger. On the right side, brainstorm your action steps and how you can approach that trigger next time. Ask yourself, how is that serving you? What does it remind you of? What situation does the trigger bring you to? Then think of an action that you will take to soothe yourself and heal that trigger by letting yourself feel the emotions. I would recommend doing tapping, shadow work, or any other healing technique.

Exercise #5. Keep a list of your relationships with people and make a mark when that relationship is over and why. Pay attention to if it was you who ended the relationship or someone else. That way to prove to you that not only do others abandon you, but you also have that right as well. So you can't tell yourself, "Everyone abandons me." Make a list of all the relationships you have right now, the most important ones. As time goes by, list new people that you meet, and then observe where the relationship goes. You will see that plenty of people on your list came and left your life without a big impact. Or they left an impact, but you decided to leave them.

Exercise #6. Introduce yourself to new people and build new relationships, whether friendships or romantic relationships. Gain the practice with people, and see how different the relationships can be. Have the courage to enter an intimate world with new people and give them the benefit of the doubt in order to build trust. Even if you are in a place like an elevator and you see someone for the first and the last time, start a short conversation and ask how they are doing.

Exercise #7. In order to deepen a relationship that you are in right now, whether a friendship or a romantic relationship, take time to acknowledge something very personal and intimate, like a fear, phobia, or something very emotional that you can open up about to the other person. At the beginning of the conversation, tell them that you want to share that with them and see how the other person reacts. They might share something about themselves as well. Remember, a lot of people out there have childhood traumas and want to be heard and loved the same as you. Open up to someone and you might be surprised that you helped someone else to open up and heal as well. If they don't want to open up or listen to you, that's okay. They might not be ready for it and have their own childhood trauma. Honor your and their feelings. Find someone else to open up to.

Your Superpower

Because you are very careful of getting involved with people and opening up, being intimate, you protect yourself from people who are unworthy of you. New people in your life that truly want to know you and care for you need to take time and patience and prove their worth for you to open up. Just be careful not to close yourself off to all the people and be afraid to be intimate with anyone.

CHAPTER 9

Extremely Loyal

There are reasons why one doesn't want to leave the familial relationship even though the unhealthiness is obvious. For example, a physically abused woman doesn't stay with the abuser because she likes to be beaten. She stays because she fears him hurting her more. Hence, staying with him in a domestic violence situation is better than being dead. I read in The Guardian that about 50% to 75% of women who left their domestic violence abuser were killed by them at the point of separation or later after they left. That is horrifying to me.

Another reason why people stay in abusive relationships is money, children, or just nowhere else to go. Overall, everyone does the best they can with what they have.

Remaining Loyal in an Abusive Family

The alcoholic home appears to be a very loyal place. Family members live with an abuser for very long time, sometimes forever, after reasons dictate that they should leave them. Those families are more loyal to each other than an average family with no abuse problems.

The loyalty is driven more by fear and insecurity, the survival instinct, than by love and commitment. Many times, behavior like this is learned from the previous generation. No one walks away just because the going gets rough. You can't leave. Faithful families don't abandon anyone, no matter how bad or embarrassing it gets. That was the philosophy of my mother, my grandmother, and my great grandmother. My grandpa was also an alcoholic, so I perceived this disease as something normal that just ran in the family...

I grew up fiercely loyal to my family. It served me as a form of survival and protection for all of us. My dad's drinking problem wasn't a secret, and all the neighbors knew about it. We also knew of other alcoholics as well. It is hard to find a family that was not impacted by alcoholism where I come from. It wasn't openly talked about. We all just acted like none of this was happening. I was told, "This is private to our family, and we don't talk about it to strangers." So, I kept pretending that everything was alright in our family. And since it was alright, I couldn't complain to others.

I was afraid to talk about my dad's drinking, my fear of him, and my fear of others because I believed I was being disloyal to my family. I am still fearful of what he will say when he reads this book! And here I am in my 40s, and I am as afraid as a little girl of being punished or harmed for revealing the secret.

The sense of loyalty to the alcoholic mother or father can be important and extremely difficult to change. Sadly, I took abuse as something normal, and it influenced my relationships with other people, especially romantic relationships. This childhood trauma made me believe that living in an abusive environment is normal, so I grew into a very loyal individual. It took me years to leave an abusive marriage.

When I look back, it makes me sad to remember that when my ex-husband emotionally abused me, I thought it normal. After all, he never hurt me physically. I still remember myself telling my best friend that other husbands drink and are violent or beat their wives. Some don't have jobs or always stay in trouble. My husband was none of that. So I would tell myself and others, "It is not that bad!" I remember that close to the end of our marriage, I would tell my best friend how my husband behaved with me, and I would see how she would react. Finally, at some point, I noticed that what I was describing was abuse. As soon I was able to see that, I was able to move on.

Why did I stay that long? Because I felt worthless and saw no better option for me. I was playing the same song that I learned from my family. No matter how hard it gets, I need to keep at it. Also, I didn't know much about good relationships. How can you understand something you've never seen? So I stayed with what I had, not knowing there could be anything better or different.

The fact that the abuser may have his or her reasons for behaving badly with you does not matter. You can rationalize and excuse his or her behavior. Even now, I think that my father had a reason to behave this way because he was also emotionally abused as a child. And somehow, no matter what my ex-husband did or said, I would find myself at fault. This reinforced my negative self-image and enabled me to stay in the relationship. When I made the decision to get divorced and told people I knew, they were shocked to hear it because, from the outside, everything looked great in my marriage.

What made things worse was not being able to talk to other people about my family problems. It made me feel ashamed and very lonely. Nobody in the family taught me how to cope with my fear. I wasn't even able accurately judge that those behaviors were neglectful and abusive. I didn't talk about my abusive marriage either. That was embarrassing!

Children whose parents neglected them most definitely had no help to process their feelings while growing up learned to disengage with them. They shut down their feelings and do not even remember very traumatic experiences. If the standard rule was to act like abuse or neglect is not happening, then the feelings that arise from that must be false. One of my friends grew up with two other siblings. After many years out of the house, they shared their experiences while growing up with an alcoholic father. The younger sibling took the alcoholism problem as just being sick. She argued for a long time that there was no alcoholism problem at all. It was just sickness that made her father behave the way he acted.

More than that, she didn't remember any of the harrowing incidents that other siblings remembered very well. She refused the truth and stayed loyal to her dad as he "would never hurt mom or us. "This friend, once a loyal daughter well trained in keeping family matters private, grew up to become an adult who transferred that unconditional loyalty to her friendships, romantic relationships, and job until she learned why.

Staying Loyal to False Friends

ACOA are also very loyal to friends. And since we hide our feelings and the truth of who we are, once we open up and they are still with us, we are surprised that they want to stick around. Since making friendships work takes time, energy, and effort, we keep them very close to the heart. We will do anything for the people we love, no matter how much they hurt us. We understand how hard it is to form a relationship, and since that person made an effort to know us and to spend their time with us, we feel obligated to stay loyal to them forever. We are the friends that will give the last shirt off our back to save a friend and expect nothing in return.

One of my clients, let's call her Trisha, was involved with people who used her repeatedly. She grew up with a neighbor's daughter and has been friends since they were five years old. My client was sharing all she had with the friend from a young age, such as cookies, Barbies, and lunches. As they grew older, Trisha gave her clothes and make-up to her neighbor because her parents could not afford to buy lots of clothes. They were inseparable till high school. Then, the neighbor's daughter got involved with a shady crowd and started doing drugs. Trisha would not get involved with drugs herself because she was afraid of her parents. Obviously, you need money for a hobby like that, and the neighbor's daughter didn't have any. So, she turned to my client, who had a part-time job at McDonald's.

You can guess what happened next. The friend would ask for money from Trisha, and her whole salary would end up going to drugs. The friend, of course, would swear that was the last time she would ask for a loan – a loan that, by the way, was never repaid. It got so bad that my client would go to her mother to ask for cash to give to her friend. When the mother started asking where so much money was going, Trisha stole a credit card from her mom's wallet until she was caught. Eighteen thousand dollars later, my client had to tell her parents what had happened. Her mother forbade her to meet with her closest friend, and my client felt so depressed that she was sent to see me. That is how I found out that my client's father was an alcoholic. The whole world was falling apart for Trisha, and we had to heal the wound so she would pick and maintain healthy relationships in the future.

Dedication to a Toxic Workplace

Overall, it's already been proven that you are more hesitant to leave something behind if you spend more time on it. It can be with relationships, projects, or work environments. If you are ACOA, it can be even harder to leave a workplace where you are not happy due to your loyalty to the company. You can think of any little thing your boss told you or gave you over the years. If someone even compliments you about your excellent work, most of the time, you doubt that. "Are they sure they're talking about me?" comes to your mind. It just sounds so weird! And the more you work in the company, no matter how ungodly the hours they ask you to work. Because you are so loyal, they can ask you to do work that you shouldn't even do, and you still will do it!

It reminds me of an old joke. The factory owner decided to increase the profit line by lowering employees' salaries. He expected some to complain and protest it, or at least have questions, but after he announced it, they all were silent and went back to work. The employer, happy with the victory, decided he would push for more, and the next day announced that he would increase working hours and those who were not happy could leave the company. And again, they looked at him in silence and continued to work. At that point, the factory owner thought about how far he could push those poor people. From his point of view, someone should have rebelled already. So, he declared, "Tomorrow, we will do mass hanging. Anyone have a question?" There was a long silence, and one hand raised. The employer, happy that someone was finally standing up to him, asked the man to talk. And an old man that raised his hand asked: "Should we bring our rope, or will the company provide it?"

Now, this is an unfortunate joke. But I bet those factory employees were ACOAs or other childhood trauma survivors who were loyal to the provider no matter what. So many stay because they are loyal to relationships, friendships, or work environments out of survival instinct.

Another client of mine let's call her Chris, who worked for a small company for five years before she came to see me. Chris got paid an average salary but had to endure abuse at work. The old lady running the company would call Chris stupid many times a day. She would complain to other employees about how incompetent Chris is. If something went wrong, my client would get yelled at every week. The owner's husband, who also worked in the same company, would ask Chris to dress down to come to work and encourage her to wear tights or yoga pants. He would constantly order her to his office, make her get on her knees, and get under his desk to untangle the cords since, allegedly, his internet wasn't working right, while he would be sitting at his desk gawking at her. If you have your eyebrows raised at this point, I did the same when I heard that myself!

Chris was an accountant who was ordered to drop off and pick up dry-cleaned clothes, go to the owner's house to turn the alarm off and let the maid in the house, and then stop by at the end of the day to turn the alarm on again. She had to drive the owner to work multiple times as a chauffeur and do other errands. You get the point: she was an accountant also treated as an errand girl, and nobody paid her for that.

One day Chris was ordered to feed the cats at the owner's house, and apparently, upon leaving, the alarm system got set off by mistake. The owner was unhappy with Chris because the loud alarm drove their cats wild, and nobody should hurt their fur babies, so the owner fired Chris. I think that is the best that could have happened to Chris because if not for that incident, she would still be working in the workplace where she was abused!

The sad part is Chris came to me for stress management since she wasn't able to find a job, and she was stressing out about it. She didn't see anything wrong with the actions of her former employers. More than that, she felt terrible for being fired. She kept on blaming herself for it. It turned out she grew up with a single alcoholic mother who abused her. So we had to work on Chris healing her childhood trauma and learning to set boundaries.

Many of us remain in toxic relationships because it keeps us safe. We know what to expect in life, and we are terrified of making a change that will lead to the unknown. We have a saying in Lithuania: "Even the dog that has been hanged every day gets used to it." But if you genuinely evaluate how happy you are, you see that the situation you are in doesn't serve you, and it is time to move on.

Exercises

If anything in this chapter resonated, it's time to change that. Below you will find a few exercises to help you.

Exercise #1. Write the names of the people that you spend time with. Include anyone from your roommates to family members, neighbors, coworkers, poker buddies, scrapbooking group, those you talk to at your dance classes... you get the point. It will take some time, but it will be worth it in the end. Read each name and remember how you behave when you are with them, as well as how they behave with you. Allow yourself to feel and name the feelings. Do you like to talk to them, do you like to spend time with them? How do they make you feel? Do you feel calm, empowered, "at home"? Or invalidated, abandoned, and unhappy?

If you think of that person and feel joy, write "Yes" next to their name. That "Yes" means you should continue the relationship. On the other hand, if you evaluated the feelings and the interactions with that person, and realized that there is not much joy, write "No" next to their name, which stands for ending the relationship. You might have some people on the list that you are unsure about. Perhaps you spend little time with them, or they are not so important that it wouldn't make a difference if you kept talking to them. Those people are neutrals, and they should stay in your life because they already are not making a huge impact either way. Now, some of those "neutrals" can become your close friends, and then you will need to keep an eye on your feelings and then decide if they are worth investing your time and energy or if are they toxic people.

When you identify what impact people make in your life, and you have the group of people that make you feel good, keep them in your life! You want to pay attention to the group that is toxic for you. What can you do now? Simply put, stop hanging out with them! If there is an environment where you must see them, like a coworker that keeps on bothering you with useless complaints about their life, then tell them that you don't have time for that, say you are working right now, and have due dates that can't miss. If your relative keeps calling you and dumping all kinds of negative energy, don't pick up the phone. Make conversations short by telling them that you need to go or someone important is calling you. Be busy. Tell them "no." It will be hard at the beginning, but you get there!

Exercise #2. Since you grew up in an abusive environment, you are probably not sure how healthy and happy relationships should look like. However, if you read this and already said, "Oh, I know what the relationships need to look like, and I am in a happy one now," then you don't need to do this exercise. If you took time to describe happy relationships, especially romantic ones, and are unsure about the specifics, you should do this exercise. Every day spend some time observing people around you. If you see friends, observe them. Are they happy? How do they behave with each other? What do they do to stay happy? Do you like what you see? How do they interact and support each other? Please pay attention to how your happy coworkers spend time, who they hang out with, and their interactions with other people. Watch romantic movies and observe how characters behave. Evaluate their behavior and identify what you like and don't like. Please pay close attention to how they interact using words and body language in their actions. Can you imagine being in a situation like that? Would you like your life to be that way?

Take time to write out what your happy romantic relationship would look like. Then what your perfect friendships would look like, then your ideal coworkers. Read the descriptions often to keep you on track, identify good relationships, and build the vision for your life as you want to be in the future.

Exercise #3. This exercise might be painful, but always remember that you can stay with someone in the same room as long you feel safe.

When you go see your family, or talk to them over the phone, pay attention to your family dynamics. How are your parents behaving with
one another? Please pay attention to the tone of voice they communicate with and their body language. What are they saying behind each
other's backs? Are they critical to each other? If they argue, is there a
common theme? Or do they ignore each other? This all might be very
difficult to do because you will be exposed to painful button-pushing,
but it is totally doable with time and practice.

Before you go to see them, tell yourself, "I am an observer today. I
will try to do my best just observe and not to get involved." Imagine
a bubble around you before you go inside it. Like a mirror, it reflects
back every attachment, all this negative energy just bounces off the
bubble without hurting you.

That is a great practice to do and identify the patterns you probably
have. Not that you wanted to learn that kind of behavior, but you were
destined to endure the same since children learn from what they see
around them. So, as you see more of the patterns that you inherited
from your parents or guardians, be kind to yourself and remind yourself that you are working through this, and you are changing. Their
life doesn't have to be yours.

Make observations and write things down for yourself and then
look at yourself and see if you are doing the same. If yes, and it does
take courage, try to change your behavior. After some observation,
you will be able to identify some behavior that you think you want to
change, and as soon you do it, you will see it as inherited behavior. That
is where most of the change happens! The more you identify things
you want to change, the more you will change!

Exercise #4. If you realize that you live in an abusive environment, it
is time to move out. It you are being abused physically, there are plenty
of resources in your state to start a process of leaving the relationship
as soon as possible. If you are in an emotionally abusive relationship,
start planning an exit soon. And if you are living with an abusive
spouse and can't leave because you want your kids to have a parent,

then that is just wrong because kids see the abuse and learn from it. They see your pain, teaching them to be submissive and not stand up for themselves. So, if you think that you are doing good for your kids, you are wrong. When I asked my mother many years ago why she didn't leave my dad, she answered: "I wanted for you to have a father." To that I replied: "I would rather have not grown up with my dad under the same roof than see him every day and be terrified."

Prepare for the exit by saving money, getting another job, asking help from your friends and relatives, church, coworkers, non-profit organizations. Please make a list of people you think can help you, approach them, and ask for help. If you don't want to deal with any people that you already know, call an organization that helps people like you. There is something so much better for you, and you just must believe, take a leap, and get going!

Your Superpower

Because you are very loyal, employers love you for your dedication. Likewise, your friends love you for being an amazing ally and standing by their side no matter what.

CHAPTER 10

Difficulty Setting Boundaries

A boundary is not a simple definition that separates you and others. A personal boundary is a unique property line that defines who you are, what you are afraid of, what you are responsible for, and your limitations. This cartoon comes to mind that depicts a woman sitting in her underwear at the doctor's office, and the doctor is standing in front of her, about to grab her, and says: "Great to see you! Give me a hug!" That is funny because we all know that doctors should not behave like that. There are boundaries! The bottom line: boundaries should keep you safe.

Internal Struggle

If you are ACOA, you struggle with setting boundaries. And if you don't know how well you are doing with that, here are a few questions to think about. Do you sometimes feel overwhelmed? Or feel resentment towards people that you love or work with? Would you like to avoid phone calls and interactions with people you think might ask you for something but can't deliver? Do you feel guilty about not having enough time for yourself? If you answered yes to any of the questions, you need to set boundaries in your life with the people that you live with and work with or know off.

Many get their boundaries violated all the time, and many are okay with that for different reasons. If you are ACOAs, the boundaries are broken by other people so often that it causes you emotional or physical pain. You will let those boundaries be crossed over and over because of people-pleasing and feeling unworthy.

Sadly, the biggest issue is that we let other people violate our boundaries. More than that, we also violate our own set of boundaries because we don't believe that our boundaries are valid. We are willing to change them at any moment when we feel the need to please other people or are afraid of them. We let others hurt us over and over to survive. The first time, you might promise yourself that you won't allow that person to hurt you or cross your boundary, then you think, I can let them just this one time. You immediately promise yourself it won't happen again, but eventually you let them again out of fear, and with that, you hate yourself more every day. We feel bad that our boundaries are broken, we feel bad for not being able to stand up for ourselves, and that way, we let ourselves down. When we violate ourselves, we feel abandoned by ourselves, and then we just hate and resent ourselves even more.

So many times, while being married, I put up with the emotional abuse because I was afraid to say something. I was afraid to "rock the boat." Since my childhood, being emotionally abused has been the norm. I was terrible at setting boundaries and thought it was how my life should go and I just had to deal with it. I would promise myself that I would speak up the next time, but the next time would come and I couldn't bring myself to confrontation. Then I would hate myself for being so weak and punish myself by beating myself up. For many years I felt angry at myself for not being able to stand up for myself, but when I look back now, I did the best I could. I learned in early childhood that I am not capable of making boundaries, and let's face it, what boundary can a child impose on a parent? And in my family, it was impossible to learn setting boundaries with an alcoholic father.

Identify Broken Boundaries

How to identify when you break your boundaries? Here are a few examples. The simplest example is when you say yes to others but mean to say no. Or the opposite, when you wanted to say yes, but you said no. You betrayed yourself in that situation because you didn't have enough courage to voice your preference for something.

The next step is when you say no to something or someone, but you feel guilty about that. In that situation, you corner yourself with no way out. You would have felt terrible if you had said yes to something you didn't want to do. So, you had enough courage to say no but then felt guilty because you think it hurt others' feelings. For example, I had a client, Anna, who would see her mother every week. At some point, she became very busy with her own family. She did not feel she had enough spare time to see her mother but still agreed to it every week. Over time Anna grew more resentful of her mother and herself for not being able to just say no once in a while and having that time with her own family. After encouragement, she finally was able to squeeze a little "no, I won't come to see you this weekend," and was shocked to find out that her mother was happy to spend that time with her friends. It turned out the mother felt guilty about telling her daughter to skip a few weekends because she was afraid to hurt their special bond! Imagine if Anna had set boundaries long ago, she would have been happy with no resentment!

Another significant boundary that ACOAs are afraid to enforce is accepting physical touch or sex when they don't want to or not calling out someone who mistreats them. I find this boundary especially hard for women to implement. Naturally, in our society, women are looked at as "weaker creatures" compared to men, especially in the work environment. Only recently were many courageous enough to speak up about the sexual harassment they encountered. Cecille worked in an office where most of her coworkers respected workplace etiquettes and behaved professionally, except her immediate supervisor. He would come to Cecille's office and touch her back or grope her buttocks without asking permission. Since he was her supervisor and Cecille was afraid to be fired, and on top of that being ACOA, she never said anything, just put up with the harassment. I encouraged her to push the aggressor back and was very happy to hear that Cecille used her Judo Black Belt skills to good use. When the supervisor touched her inappropriately again, she grabbed his arm, twisted behind his back to cause pain, and whispered into his ear: "Don't you ever touch me again, or it will be more painful next time." Of course, there was no next time.

Other boundaries of yours that might be violated come from people-pleasing or just wishing for peace at your own expense. Such as adopting another person's beliefs or ideas about complicated or straightforward things so you would be accepted, even if they are against your integrity and values. You might allow other people to say things to you or in front of you that makes you feel uncomfortable, like inappropriate jokes in the work environment, someone deceiving other people, lying to others, or taking advantage of others. You might feel bad about it, but you might not have enough courage to speak up out of fear of authority or fear of becoming unlikable.

In the workplace environment, you might be afraid to speak up in the meeting when you have some great idea that would benefit your team or you are afraid to say no to new projects. Instead of concentrating on your own time, energy, and projects, you might be allowing yourself to be interrupted or distracted to accommodate another person's needs and wants.

You might be giving away too much of your time and energy in a relationship, which can be romantic or a friendship, just to be seen as beneficial—or not defining and communicating your emotional and physical needs in your relationship out of fear of being rejected.

I hope that the examples above helped you see your boundaries and where you are not keeping them. I read on Instagram once: "Each time you set a good boundary, an energy vampire loses a fang" @ mindfulboundaries

Few Things to Know about Boundaries

Before we set healthy boundaries, let's talk about something significant: how to honor yourself. Since many of your needs, and your whole self were not honored, you grew up with the feeling of unworthiness and learned to dishonor and abandon yourself and your feelings. It might take time and effort, but it is necessary. So how do you honor yourself?

First, start with acknowledging that you, and only you, are responsible for yourself. It is enough of the blame game and it is time to mature. With that, your need to prioritize your needs. You, feeling happy and healthy, should be your priority. And I can hear you say, "Is that selfish?" What do you say when you hear "put your mask on first and then help others" on the plane? It makes sense to put a mask on your face first to breathe, and then you will be able to help those with you. Same works with self-care. You can't give yourself to others when you are empty.

Second, ask for help from your family, friends, strangers, angels, higher power, whatever works for you. But you have to ask for help because, as you know, it is tough to do it all by yourself. We were created as a group. We belong and depend on a group, so we can and should ask for help. You are not alone, even if it feels like you are.

Third, let go of the guilt for what you did or didn't do in the past. Let go even of the things you think you did but didn't. All that responsibility goes back to your childhood; let that go, and don't feel guilty about sins you didn't commit. Finally, let go of the guilt of being you, wanting more, and doing more.

Fourth, communicate clearly with the people around you that you live with or work with. And above all, communicate with yourself genuinely, don't lie to yourself no matter how painful the issue is. And at the same time, take credit where it is due and give yourself praise. Talk to yourself as a good friend would talk to you.

Fifth, always honor the "no," no matter what circumstances, and stay to your truth. If you are afraid to look rude when someone asks for your help and can't help them, just tell them, "I care about you deeply, but I can't help you with this." See, it doesn't sound rude. If someone invites you to go where you don't want to go, just say, "Sorry, I have other plans." That's it!

Sixth, listen to your body regularly, don't wait until you get sick. Don't be a martyr and punish yourself by punishing your body. Instead, make sure you treat your body as something special, get enough high-quality food and water, and exercise. Make sure you take care of your mental health as well, meditate, pray, and do whatever works for you to ground yourself. Your body is part of you, and you are responsible for it.

Seventh, let go of what doesn't belong to you. That includes other people's opinions, let them have them, but it doesn't have to be your opinion about something. Just because someone thinks differently from you doesn't mean it is wrong, just different. Stay with your truth. If you don't know what your truth is, find out! Don't let other people's opinions of what you do influence you, no matter how big your fear of abandonment is. When you start setting boundaries, you will see that it is possible to keep both people and your boundaries. And those who can't honor you should not be around you anyway.

Eight, stop seeking the approval of people who don't deserve you. Being an ACOA, it is hard to have high self-esteem, and there is a need to see approval from others, get validation, bounce your ideas off, or just ask for the opinion of others. You can, but you have to make sure that the people you are talking to are experts in the opinion they can give and have your best interests at heart. It is not a good idea to ask for approval and validation from those who hurt you, although it feels natural to do that.

Ninth, focus on progress, not perfection. It is very hard not to be a perfectionist, and I have been one since we worked very hard during our childhood to be perfect and loved. But you are an adult now, and you know that you are lovable, so there is no need for perfection. And remember, there is no perfection in nature. I think perfection is a matter of opinion, and it is just an agreement that something is good as it is. So, it is up to you to decide if something is good enough. Honor your choice as long you move in the direction you want to be.

Process to Set Boundaries

Now we are ready to set boundaries. Are you ready? There are a few tips that you should keep in mind while setting boundaries. Start with permitting yourself to set boundaries, say no, and speak out. Many get stuck in the childhood mode and are still waiting for permission to say no to something. If you can't permit yourself, I am permitting you. Yes, you can say "no." After you are ready to set a boundary, you have to be honest with yourself. That is what you want and what you don't want. What are your needs? Don't be afraid of yourself. Find out what your needs are.

It might be daunting at first to set boundaries with those who need them, so start with your best friends who can understand and support you. Start with something small that will not influence your life that much if you won't be able to do it. Then move to the other people who need to hear it, as those who hurt you.

As you start telling no to others, you will notice that it will get easier and easier with time. What surprised me the most was that others were okay with that when I started saying no. That gave me more confidence in realizing that other people can change their plans or ask someone else for help or companionship.

There will be times when you feel that your boundaries don't work no matter what you do. Don't take it personally if your boundaries don't work. Just let them be. Some people won't get your boundaries, or even worst, start criticizing your boundaries. You can expect that out of narcissists especially. Don't try to change others. It never works. That is the time to remove yourself from the situation. If someone is pushing you to do something you don't want, just leave the room, the building, or hang up the phone. In a situation where you see your boundaries are not being honored, leave the situation without fighting over it or trying to justify to the other person why you need those boundaries.

There might be instances when you constantly need to keep boundaries with some people, and they will try to test it and push against you. The key is to see it and enforce the boundary without feeling guilty or "giving a break." Don't be afraid to speak up and let others honor you.

Exercises

Here are a few exercises that can give you a jump start to feel comfortable with setting boundaries. And like any exercise, it works when you work it.

Exercise #1. If you are one of those people who are afraid of the word "no," I recommend you stand in front of the mirror and say out loud, "No." At first, you will be ashamed of yourself, you can be afraid to look at the mirror altogether, and it's okay. When you finally manage to look at yourself in the mirror, say loud and clear, "No." Repeat to the point that you are not afraid to say it.

Exercise #2. Go to the mall and walk around where they have salespeople standing around and pushing you to buy or try out their product. Usually, it starts with something simple like, "Can I ask you a question?" Or they just hand you things, and naturally, we grab things, even if we don't want to. Your job is to not pay attention and pass by. Or have enough courage to answer "no" to them. Make it a game, go around the mall and collect ten "nos." If you do not feel comfortable going alone, bring a friend and make a game. The friend will keep you accountable and give you advice on how to respond to the next sales attack. I recommend you come up with a reward that you will give yourself after collecting all ten "nos'" because you deserve it!

Exercise #3. Call the person you know who will want you to do a favor for them, like come over, take care of their kid, watch TV with them, something that you don't want to do. Keep a conversation until they ask you to do it. Then, gather the courage and tell them "no," because you are busy doing something else.

Exercise #4. Think about the situation in your life where you feel obligated to do something that you don't feel like doing anymore. Maybe a coworker keeps asking you to pick up their slack or a supervisor who gives you too much to do. It can be a sister who constantly drops her kids at your house. Write a friendly "no" note to that person who asks you to do too much. Don't include an explanation of why you can't do it. Instead, get to the point, sweet and straightforward. Something like, "I care about you deeply, but I can't help you with that, sorry." If the matter is more serious, reply, "I would love to help, but that sounds very challenging, and it seems like this issue should be handled by a professional." Or "I would love to help, but unfortunately slapped with work myself." Keep that note handy, so when you get a request asking you do to what you can't do, just copy and paste the answer. And do it quick, so you don't change your mind. If they come back with why you can't do it, just don't reply and don't negotiate.

Exercise #5. Write your activities during the day. Do you spend time on actions that are not necessary? Maybe you are talking to people randomly or going to meetings that take up your time. Keep a log of your activities for a few weeks and decide what meetings are essential and what are not. Maybe instead of a meeting, you can do a short phone call? Maybe you can just write an email or message someone? That will save you time and energy. If you are afraid to propose such a thing to the other person, don't be. You might be surprised that they agree on such time-saving techniques because we all need more time.

Exercise #6. Having a healthy connection with people in our lives is very important to our mental health. But it can get overwhelming to hang out with many people and say yes to every meeting we are invited to. Observe your connections, write a list of people you hang out with most of the time, and observe your routine for a few weeks. Then decide what connections are important to you. Decide what connections are worth cultivating further and what connections could be discontinued or done more sporadically instead of spending lots of time on them. The same goes the other way. Evaluate what meaningful connections you don't have time to meet with, especially those who uplift and support you. Make plans for quality time to focus on one-on-one connection, weekly date nights, or unique girls' night out.

Exercise #7. Make a list of people you constantly meet that you don't want to meet that often. Then, next time you plan to meet, take a more extended break in between. If you have a meeting set up already that you don't want to go to, send them a short message apologizing that you won't be able to meet them and postpone the meeting to a day that you feel comfortable.

Exercise #8. As we all know, we have needs that need to be met. Sadly, like ACOA, we get into sacrifice mode and neglect ourselves. That can be fixed by setting boundaries with ourselves and others. Evaluate your daily routine that comes to sleep, eating healthy food, having sex, playing, having off-work hours at night or on weekends, and other physical and mental needs. What routines would you like to be? Make an action plan, set boundaries, make time for yourself, and stick to it!

Your Superpower

Because you have difficulty setting and keeping boundaries with others, you are very agreeable and approachable. Your coworkers and friends love you for your dedication and loyalty.

CHAPTER 11

Anxiety and Hypervigilance

I don't think it is possible to live on this planet and never experience stress or anxiety. Occasionally I come across a person telling me they've never experienced any stress whatsoever. Then I ask them if they ever wear a sweater when they are cold. Anything out of the ordinary, something your mind or body isn't used to, causes stress. It may be physical or emotional stress. Stress and anxiety cause inflammation in the body and lead to different illnesses, primarily heart disease. In order to be healthy, one needs to manage stress and anxiety levels.

Anxiety is just a feeling that you are in danger. It is a protective mechanism that lets you know when to pay attention in order to save yourself. Sometimes, there is a real danger, and you should take appropriate action. Any stressful situation can be handled by fight, flight, or freeze. If you grew up with childhood trauma, you usually freeze.

How Anxiety Serves Us
You might understand what I am talking about. When you are a child, you know you cannot leave the house no matter how bad it gets. So,

you definitely cannot flee. Where would you go? Those are your parents, that is your house, and you have to be here. You also understand that you cannot fight with your parents. First, you are way too small physically, and even as you become a teenager and maybe bigger and stronger than your parents, you probably will not have enough guts to fight back. The only way to handle anxiety-inducing situations is to hide in your room or freeze, and mentally disassociate yourself from the situation.

Something I read the other day changed my perspective on stress as a coping mechanism. Turn out, from an early age, whenever we feel unsafe, our survival instinct kicks in. We become stressed and anxious about what's happening around us. Our brain tells us we must fight, flee, or freeze. Here's the catch. Whenever we survive a stressful situation, our brain remembers that anxiety. It remembers that being anxious helped us survive. It remembers that we fought, we fled, or we froze. So, the next time something stressful happens in our surroundings, it tells us to do precisely the same thing. Anxiety creates more anxiety. It is a tool to survive. When something stressful happened to you but you survived, it is remembered as a great tool and coping mechanism.

Stress and anxiety, like any other PTSD, may be triggered by multiple factors in everyday life. Someone can talk with a louder voice. Someone can do a physical act. Even music on the radio can make someone remember their childhood trauma. Abandonment triggers anxiety in a lot of ACOAs. Abandonment is mainly associated with fear of being rejected.

A long time ago, when humans lived in the wilderness, they depended on a group of people, on their tribe, to survive. The relationships with other people and families were significant. Being abandoned or excluded from the group likely meant death. And that's how humanity advanced. It is normal for a mother to feel anxious when she doesn't see her baby. It is normal for a child to feel anxious when he cannot find his mother. If there is no anxiety, the babies may die.

How can anxiety triggers show up in everyday life? Let's consider the example of a man who has felt abandoned in the past. He goes to a party and he talks with three people. He has amazing conversations with two people. The third person he talked to had to leave to help somebody else and cut the conversation short. The man who has abandonment issues totally forgets about the other two people he had fun with and only remembers the one who left mid-conversation. Has that ever happened to you? It has definitely happened to me. You may dwell on the worst part of the experience and feel unworthy and rejected. What you need to do is to broaden your view, think rationally, and remember what happened at that party as a whole. Not all people reject you. Also, even if someone walks away from you at a party, they may have their own trauma and their rejection was not about you.

Another way to approach this, especially for those with social anxiety, is to set goals where you feel good about things that you can realistically do. The goal is to always care for your own feelings, not about others' feelings and their reactions. If you set a goal, for example, to go to a party and talk to three people, even if one of them walks away, your goal is still achieved because you talked with three people. You have to pay attention to the positive and whether you achieved your goal. Your goal is not to control other people. You have to direct your goals from outward to inward.

In addition, since you grew up in an environment where you constantly felt stressed, that state of mind became a habit. You had to deal with uncertainty every single day, and you had to be on alert constantly. You didn't know what the next moment would be like. You had to make sure you would not let yourself relax. You still carry that from one day to the next, even though you're no longer in danger. I remember my childhood as very stressful. It would be easier to count the days when I was not stressed, not on alert, not hypervigilant. Even when my father would not drink, and that was not often, I could not turn off my hypervigilance. I carried that into adulthood until stress made me physically ill.

Here is another thing that I read about stress that makes sense to me. Since you grew up in an environment where stressing out about your surroundings was normal, you got addicted. I know, it sounds absurd. When stressed, chemicals such as adrenaline, cortisol, and norepinephrine are released into your bloodstream. That is when our nervous system goes into a flight response. And that feels like going and going with no end in sight, which resembles your never-ending stress in your environment while growing up. You see, for you to survive, like any other trauma, your body releases dopamine. That is a feel-good chemical. So, in the long run, we're going after dopamine, and we encourage ourselves to repeat the stressful behavior that leads to more dopamine. Some people thrive in this stressful situation. That's a workaholic, a person with a very high-pressure job, who is always in conflict, or who is stuck in highly toxic relationships.

If you think you are not addicted to stress, ask yourself simple questions. Are you stuck or have chronic patterns of high-level conflicts and relationships? Do you have difficulty sitting still and doing nothing? Do you feel guilty when you can't do anything? Do you suffer from a lack of boundaries? Do you overload yourself and others? You see, when you're not stressing, everything else feels uncomfortable. This subconscious, automatic process makes us wired and tired simultaneously. So when we don't stress, we feel empty and bored. It makes us put ourselves in situations of more stress because our high threshold for stress makes us feel like ourselves again.

You may also feel like your life needs to be stressful because you didn't experience life any other way. Your parents, caregivers, and the household authorities were always stressed out. It is tough to live around an addict and not be stressed. Especially if the addict is the person that you love and cherish. And you don't want to suffer. You don't want them to suffer. But there is just a constant battle between the survivors and the addict, the battle to make them change. For children who grew up in that stressful environment, it feels normal. It may be that you are constantly stressing yourself out. Because your siblings or your parent who were not alcoholics were constantly stressing out, that's what you learned. Because there was no normal day. You don't know what normal is.

In my childhood, I remember that any situation would be blown out of proportion, even when it did not need to be. Everything was a big deal. A simple conversation about the weather could be seen as something very negative and harmful. Or at least, it could be talked about with an aggressive tone of voice. We might be having a simple conversation, not even arguing about anything or even joking about things, which people outside the situation would perceive as fighting. That was my normal tone of voice. That was my normal way of speaking. I spoke that way to blend in with my family. As you know, children learn from their parents and mimic them to be accepted into the family unit.

Even if you are now an adult and do not do anything addictive, like drinking, doing drugs, shopping, gambling, or sex addiction, if you are putting yourself into stressful situations to get a fix, you are still an addict. Like any other addiction, it is very unhealthy and will cause physical and mental harm.

Hypervigilance Is a Tool to Survive

As if that was not enough, let's acknowledge something else. Since you grew up to be very sensitive to your environment and be able to read other people's moods to save yourself, you may misinterpret signs that are happening around you as an adult. For example, you may see a message from someone as threatening when they were joking or didn't mean to hurt you at all.

This reminds me of an image I saw online. There was a drawing of a girl wearing a cape and a big "A" on her chest. On top of the image, it said Anxiety Girl: "Able to jump to the worst conclusion in a single bound." Yep, that's me, alright.

So here is a great way to deal with overreaction. Peter Fonagy, Ph.D., developed this technique called "mentalization." This technique works for people who have difficulty with emotional regulation. We start by acknowledging that, to help us survive, we will always try to figure out what others are thinking. Usually, we'll jump to conclusions that are different than what the person was actually thinking. A person who grew up in a stable environment may experience a negative situation with another person and think that person was having a bad day and that there is nothing to worry about. But ACOA will default to thinking the situation has something to do with them. The key is to recognize those patterns by observing the behavior, writing it down, and then working with those patterns. So next time, when a person ends a conversation with you, notice what you're thinking about that person, why you think that happened, and how the situation makes you feel. Ask yourself if you are falling into your default pattern where you think someone doesn't want you and is rejecting you. When you realize that you have those patterns and can catch them immediately, you can change your thinking.

If you have not managed your stress and anxiety, it may become something bigger and more challenging to let go of. Because a child is exposed to constant stress and anxiety, it grows into hypervigilance over time. ACOAs constantly feel state of increased alertness. That basically means that one is extremely sensitive to their own surroundings. It's constantly reassuring themselves that the people around them will not cause them harm. The physical symptoms are very similar to the ones of anxiety: a fast heart rate, shallow breathing, and sweating. Behavioral symptoms include jumpy reflexes and fast, knee-jerk reactions to the environment. ACOA may tend to overreact to a situation that doesn't look threatening. For example, maybe someone will raise their voice in a conversation to make a point or make a joke, and an ACOA may perceive it as violent and cause them anxiety.

There are also emotions and symptoms that come with hypervigilance. A person can feel constant severe anxiety. They may fear seeing other people and being around them. They can even feel panic while being in a crowd. ACOA might fear judgment from others while judging others extremely harshly because that's what they are used to. A person can look at everything as black and white and go from one extreme to another in the blink of an eye. One moment they could be very calm and even withdrawn, and the next moment they can experience outbursts of emotion. They may also experience paranoia.

Worrying every day, unexpecting the worst, can be exhausting. It is very similar to just being pessimistic. Hypervigilance takes a toll on the body and mental state.

Triggers can cause hypervigilance: feeling abandoned or trapped, hearing loud noises, especially those that are emotionally charged, such as arguments, yelling, anticipating pain or judgment, feeling judged or unwelcome, feeling emotional distress, or physical pain. It also can be triggered by memories of past traumatic events.

And the best solution is to avoid pain and fear by not getting yourself in situations where you would experience it. Let's say you are afraid of crowds and feel uncomfortable going to a party. You tell everybody that you're not going anywhere from now on, just not going to leave the house altogether. But you have to go somewhere eventually and meet other people, such as the work environment. And then what? How are you going to protect yourself from harm? Will you buy a weapon? Isolating yourself from other people may give you peace and a feeling of safety, but it eventually does more damage. Humans are herd animals, and we do need other people. So instead of just not hanging out with other people altogether, you have to find ways to be open to others, to interact, and feel safe.

Exercises

There are, of course, other ways that you can try to approach handling anxiety. You can try different therapies such as exposure therapy, cognitive behavioral therapy, or even eye movement desensitization and reprogramming. I believe you should seek medication only in extreme cases. Here are a few tools that can help you deal with anxiety and hypervigilance. Try out a few of them and see what helps you the most. Exercises described below should be used repeatedly until they become a habit that you naturally gravitate toward when you feel threatened.

Exercise #1: Anytime you feel threatened and your heart rate rises, you should recognize that something triggered you. The first step is to stop. Pause before reacting because you might be overreacting. Things may not be as they seem, so if you overreact, you may put yourself in harm's way or place yourself in an embarrassing situation. Then search for objective evidence in the situation. Things may not be as bad as you think they are. Remind yourself that there is a lot of childhood trauma and intense emotions and fears that come from your past and that you are just projecting it onto the present moment. Imagine that your friend is in a similar situation. What you would tell your friend to do?

Exercise #2: Create a ritual that helps you when you get anxious. Start with positive affirmations that you can repeat to yourself that can be reassuring, such as "I am calm, confident, and collected." You may use other affirmations that include the words "I am." They should not have a negative tone, such as, "I am not scared." Instead of that, say, "I am brave." You may also pick an inspiring quote that brings you peace. In addition to that, you should physically touch and soothe your body. Research shows that physical touch helps the mind to relax.

You should breathe deeply. There are plenty of breathing exercises that you can try out to find the one that fits you the best. Next time, when something triggers you, you will stop, and start repeating affirmations in your mind, not allowing any fearful thoughts to come through, all while breathing deeply and stroking your hand or massaging your neck. Do this for at least five to ten minutes, or until you feel calmer.

Exercise #3: If you tend to get anxious about bad things happening to you, then take time to sit down and write down all of those things that you think can harm you. And then find a solution for them. Prepare yourself ahead of time in case that happens. For example, let's say you think you will lose your job. Brainstorm and write down all the solutions and how you would approach this. You could update your resume now and start sending it to other places. You could find a friend to hire you until you find a job. You could tap into your savings to pay your rent. Maybe you could ask your parents to let you live with them. You may have a friend who will lend you a couch. Maybe now is the time to start a business you have always dreamed about. Prepare yourself for the worst-case scenario. If it happens, though hopefully it never will, you will already have mentally prepared for it. You will have already planned what to do so that you will stress less. So when the next time your boss invites you into his office, it will be easier to handle your anxiety because you already know that the worst could be and are prepared. If you get fired today, you already have a plan to implement and survive. Then tackle other topics you're most anxious about, including relationships and goals.

Exercise #4: When you catch yourself stressing after something triggered you, ask yourself how it is serving you. We all do things that we believe help us, no matter how painful. Let's say someone is late to see you. You may get anxious and afraid that something happened to them. Ask yourself what caused this fear. Maybe it is your fear of abandonment. Then ask yourself if this belief that you will be abandoned is helpful in this situation. Is this fear helping you? Does it make you happy? Does it serve anyone else? If your answers have been "no" to all those questions, then it's time to let them go. Take a deep breath, stop overreacting, and find out what genuinely happened so that you can take reasonable action.

Your Superpower

Because you are used to stressful situations and may thrive in a high-alert environment, you are very good at managing extreme situations. So if something happens around you, you act when others may freeze. That way, you can help others when they cannot help themselves. You may be an excellent person to go to ask for help and advice during a stressful situation.

CHAPTER 12

Eager to Please

Overall, people pleasing is common in humankind since we are born so weak and have to be taken care of until we can find food and shelter on our own. The problem arises when we grow up but still believe that we need to please others in order to survive. We will do anything to ensure we are not excluded from the group so we survive. We can like the same foods as our friends, we might participate in the same activities with coworkers, we might share the same belief with our family members, even if we don't like them or disagree with them. It is such an ingrained behavior that it is hard to get rid of it. Many keep behaving like hurt toddlers, looking for approval and validation, until they die. And some parents act like their children never grow up and try to run their lives as if they were not 55 years old but five.

People pleasing is very common, no matter what kind of family one comes from. One child in the same family might be learning a different approach compared to his sibling, who grew up with the same set of parents. We all take people pleasing differently. It is so common that we are not ashamed of it. That is just something that we do. I read a joke online that someone posted on their Twitter account, "I am done with people pleasing. I hope you are OK with that!"

People-Pleaser or Manipulator?

Many can "grow out" of people-pleasing tendencies by realizing that now they are adults who can take care of themselves. In the case of ACOA, this realization is much more complicated. For us to survive as children, we had to work very hard. There was no peaceful day and there was no dull day. There was no reliable routine needed to assure a growing child. We learned that we need to be entertaining, happy, of service, to never complain or show our feelings. There was never a day about us or our happiness. Not even our birthday party, because that was opportunity for someone to get drunk, turn violent, and hurt us. We knew that we needed to be friendly and please others so that they would take pity on us and see us. It sounds cruel, but many children of alcoholics felt like beggars growing up.

We learned early that when you are "a good girl" or "a good boy," you get what you want. In ACOA's case, what you want is any care, safety, or just leaving us untouched. We learned that your goals would be supported if you are "a good person" and are liked. That would work in the immediate family and outside of it. Because we were so dependent on people outside the family to take care of us, if not physically, but at least emotionally, we would keep those people close to us. That meant giving them what they wanted and doing anything for them.

I always tended to tell others what they wanted to hear and not the truth. I would do what they asked me, even if I didn't like doing it. I learned early that the concepts of being liked and getting what I want are linked. If other kids liked me, they would invite me to come over, they would invite me to play, even for dinner. When I grew older, I realized that alliances were also made by belonging to a group that liked me. Of course, I had to prove my loyalty to them, but it was worth it because I was accepted into that group, as opposed to my own family where I did not feel safe. I believe that is one of the reasons why people join cults and political groups, no matter how negative or violent they are. If a person is not feeling safe and supported and doesn't get his physiological or emotional needs met at home, he will go to find a group where they get those needs met.

Now, with reflection, I understand it was a way to manipulate others to survive. I would please others so they would do what I wanted. To me, it's bargaining and exchange. If I gave something to you, I expected something in return. I would give affection to get affection. I would do something nice to another person to be treated nicely. It took me years to work on it, and now I can say that I give my energy and attention to other people because I want to, it makes me happy, and I don't expect anything in return. That change happened because I understood that my survival doesn't depend on whether others like me.

I had a friend whose mother was an alcoholic. Most of the time, she was left with her grandmother. Her mother had her own demons to fight off, and spent very little time with my friend. Her mother would come home only when she felt so bad from drinking that she would just lie in bed until she could stand up and leave again. Those were the only days when my friend would have her chance "to be with her mother." And, of course, that was not quality mother-daughter time. It was more like the daughter acting as a maid. My friend would clean the cigarette buds and vomit from the floor, bring food, try to feed her, and listen to nonsense and yelling. She would do anything to please her mother in hopes of being seen. For the longest time, she hoped this care would teach her mother how to care for someone else. She hoped that one day her mother would see how meaningful their relationship was.

Sadly, it never changed. My friend left the house as soon as she was done with high school. One day she just had enough. She closed the door and never came back. I heard her mother died of suicide, and my friend told me, "I did the best I could and was there for her when she was never there for me. To be called a mother, one needs to take care of their child and not just bring one into this world. I never had a mother."

You might have had a childhood that taught you to please others and you don't see any other way. Or you might be in a place that understands that others don't impact your life as you do your own, and I salute you. But there is hope if you are still on the edge of knowing that people-pleasing is wrong but you're not sure how to do it. Unlearning the people-pleasing habit can take time, but it is worth it.

It can be very stressful when you believe your survival depends on other people. You might feel very hopeless because you can't control those other people, and you feel angry, alone, and burnt out, since no matter what you do, nothing changes. It is because you are waiting on others to grant you what you want. You want them to change because you believe there is no other way. But there is!

You Can Take Care of Yourself

We have to separate this concept to get out of this pattern. Think for a moment about something you want to have and ask yourself if you need to be loved and liked by others to get it. Is it a prerequisite for getting those things? Of course, when you were a child and you wanted to eat, your caretakers had better like you or you would starve. But things have changed. You are an adult now. So, do you need to be liked if you want a new job? You sure need to be a good employee, but plenty of people are hated in their workplace and still hold the job and are paid well. Being liked, loved, and approved of and getting what you want in life are separate things. I am sure you know people who "don't deserve" what they have but still get what they want.

You might be thinking, "OK, if I go for what I want, then I will look like someone who doesn't care about others." You might think that you look selfish or like an unloving person. But, you see, the practice of love is the practice of taking another person as a part of yourself. It has nothing to do with getting what you want.

Realize that you do have a choice no matter what decision you make. This one can be hard to understand, primarily when you used to be accused of just being born into this world. You might feel guilty about anything that is happening around you. But ultimately, you are not a child anymore, and you should understand that not all things in this world revolve around you, so you cannot influence everything around you, for better or worse. Since you are not a child anymore, you don't depend on other people and you can take care of yourself. So, you do have a choice to decline an offer, to tell them to go and do their own things, to tell them that no, you won't be doing this anymore. Your happiness and getting what you want don't depend on you being liked.

Stopping people pleasing doesn't mean that from now on, you won't want to have anything in common with other people. You will be lonely, pushy, and stubborn and get what you want no matter what by telling others to leave you alone. You still can be an essential part of a group of people, participate in it, be of help, and not be a people pleaser. There is a difference between when you can be of assistance, be there for someone, and when they are just taking advantage of you.

First, start with observing the other person. Collect the simple facts. What are you seeing about that person and hearing? That is not the same as what you think you are seeing. Pay extra attention to what they say and how you understand that. You might tend to misunderstand the person and project your trauma onto them. So, it is essential to be clear that you received the information as it was presented. If you are unsure, ask them, "What I hear is that you are telling me that..."

Second, you should identify if the other person is expressing their need or request. There is a difference between those two. Next to essential physiological needs universal to humans to survive, there is also the necessity to be safe, protected, and loved. I would try my best to help others fulfill their physiological needs.

Requests are different than needs, and they are not life-threatening. The other person should be open to saying "no" to their requests, and they should honor your choice without guilting or shaming you. That might not be easy with anyone you think you should please.

You should also be able to take "no" from the other person and understand that it simply means that your request didn't meet their desires. Same as someone's request might not meet what you want. But it doesn't mean there should be a standstill if one party doesn't agree. In a perfect scenario, both people can get their wants met, and it is possible to work on ways to meet in the middle.

As people-pleasers, we should remember that we are not responsible for other people's feelings. We also understand that it is OK if someone doesn't like our decision. We don't have to rebel against their decision and should honor their feelings. It is enough to hear other people's feelings and let them express themselves without losing our center and control. You can help someone more when you are centered and grounded. We can give them empathy, but we don't have to fix everything they are going through or give them what they want if it doesn't align with us. Respecting what they feel and hearing them out doesn't mean we need to do what they ask us to do.

Exercises

Here are a few exercises that you can use to make a habit of pleasing other people manageable.

Exercises #1. Let's see how big of a people pleaser you are. Try to remember when you said "yes" to people when you actually wanted to say "no." Make a list of times and find a pattern when you did something for other people to please them. It can be something big such as going to a school that your parents wanted you to, to something small such as trying a new restaurant with a friend when you didn't feel like it. Write those instances down and look for patterns. Do you tend to please particular people but not others? Maybe you believe that you must please your caregivers, your family members, and anyone who is involved in your immediate life. Or you might think that anyone at your work can boss you around. Or do you think that you must do everything for friendships no matter what, even if you are not honest? After you identify those patterns, then stop doing them. Be honest with yourself and others. Start with small steps if that sounds like a hard thing to do from the get-go.

Exercise #2. Question yourself before deciding to please or agree with another person. If someone asks you to do something for them, ask yourself how that impacts your life and what difference it will make. Are you being manipulated? Ask yourself if you are being fair to yourself and others by doing what is asked of you. For example, do you think it's fair if you have been asked to meet someone at their place and it is a long way to go? You might think it is acceptable to drive that far, even if it is the third time you are doing this, but why are you doing it? How do you think it is serving you? If you have a great time, you get something in return instead of going elsewhere. But if you are going there because you don't want to offend that other person, so they don't leave you, then it's people pleasing. If you find it unfair to you or the others, don't do it.

Exercise #3. Pull your people pleasing away in small steps. It can be difficult for you to start saying "no," not agreeing, or doing something you love without asking other people's permission. If you are not feeling comfortable, take some small steps to make you comfortable. If you hang out with someone for half a day but don't feel like it, start with the shorter time limit, more like an hour, and set your alarm to go off, leave the place with "I've got to go to do something else." You also can agree to see someone every second time they ask, tell them, "I can't see you this week, but what about the next?" Then you won't feel guilty about not seeing them right away. If you identify some individuals that you have difficulty keeping satisfied, withdraw from them by not responding to their calls, being busy with something else, or limiting the time you are with them. Better yet, if you know that the person always demands the same thing from you, have the answer ready ahead of time. That way, you will be prepared and won't feel so guilty. Take time to prepare those answers, have them handy.

Exercise #4. Dare to set your priorities. First, you need to under-stand what your priorities are. You have things to do in this world since you are an adult and probably responsible for your family, job, and well-being. What are your priorities? If one of the priorities is to keep other people happy, that is not a priority. Your need is to please yourself first. Yes, I said it. If you believe that is selfish, where did you get that idea from? Have you been told this by the same people that told you to please them? Did they tell you that being selfish is bad, but somehow pleasing them and them being selfish is OK? So, rethink this right now, and set your priorities. Make a list of your priorities and implement them every day. Don't feel guilty about those that include influencing only you, such as good nutrition, sleep, mental health, and other priorities that must be met. You might have been neglecting yourself for years, so it might feel awkward to make a list, but you should. And remember, if you don't take care of yourself, you can't take care of others. By setting your needs right, you are pleasing others because you will be able to please them. You can't pour out of the empty pitch. You have to fill yourself in to be able to give to others. Create your to-do list that includes your priorities, and ensure you are done with them by the end of the day.

Exercise #5. Don't apologize if it is not your fault. Are you one of those who apologize to others even if it wasn't your fault? As an example, someone else bumped into you, but you are the one who is apologizing? Or you voiced your priority to someone, and after they didn't agree to grant that, you apologized for your need? Think back and try to recognize those times when you expressed regret for no reason, better yet, when someone else was at fault. You might have always believed everything is your fault, so you should apologize and "be nice." You might also see that the adults in your life were not apologizing for what they did, and you took it as a norm. So, when others don't acknowledge their fault, you are OK with that. Logically, not everything is your fault, and you know that. So, stop acting like it is. Take time to make a list of when you acknowledged your fault, then next to it, write whose fault it was. Do you see the pattern? Change the habit of feeling like everything is your fault and start seeing the situation for what it is. At the end of each day, write what happened in your diary and whether you apologized for something. It might be hard to catch yourself initially, but later, you will see that your inner voice will tell you to stop. In a situation when you feel inclined to say something to the other person, ask yourself if you should or if you do it out of habit.

Exercise #6. Give yourself praise for every time you would have pleased another person, but you stopped yourself from doing it. Keep a list of times you stood up for yourself, declined an offer, said "no," did something for yourself that you used not to do. It is also important to record how the other person reacted when you stood up for yourself and what they said to you. You might be pleasantly surprised when the other person is OK with your choice, and nobody got their feelings hurt. You might also run into a narcissist that will not agree with you, but you have to understand that it is their problem, not yours. It might feel weird but feel the feeling and do it anyway. Then reward yourself, acknowledge that and celebrate it. Count your victories, build that list with time, and read it when you feel like you need encouragement to do something when you must stand up for yourself and say what you mean no matter what.

Exercise #7. Ask yourself, "If I know that it doesn't matter if others like me, I still can get what I want, what would I go get?" This can involve anything in your life, from taking care of yourself to achieving your goals to changing schools, jobs, and relationships. You are worthy, and nobody needs to permit you to do it. Make a list of things in your life that you are not happy with and ask yourself if someone is keeping you away from them. Then change it. Ask others for help to make changes in your life and learn new things about yourself and others to make that change.

Your Superpower

Because you want to make sure that people around you are happy, you are willing to help others, and you make others comfortable in any situation, you are there for others and are trusted. People come to you with their problems and know that you will come up with some solution and console them. You are mostly a person that others like being around.

CHAPTER 13

Being an Empath

We are all empaths, just on a different level. An empath is someone who has the ability to relate to what others are feeling and experiencing on a deep level. Not all people are empaths.

A joke comes to mind. A man consoles his friend: "Yesterday. I got into another argument with my wife. And she told me that I didn't have any empathy for her. Honestly, I have no idea why she would feel that way!"

Why You Became an Empath

How do you know if you are an empath? Let's say you are having a peaceful day at work. And suddenly, you realize that your feelings and emotions have changed. You thought you were doing pretty well, and suddenly you feel sad, depressed, and maybe even angry, and you don't know why. You used to having those high and low emotional waves appearing out of nowhere. If you happened to be reminiscing, or talked with a friend that knew you from 20 years ago, or saw a picture somewhere that reminded you of the past, and that brought your negative feelings, that came from you. Some things can trigger us to remember our childhood pains. And those need to be addressed. But let's say you were going about your day, not necessarily thinking negatively. And then, after talking with someone or seeing something on TV, you suddenly feel all fired up. Maybe you agree with another person who was angry about the way things are, maybe you're feeling sad for them. If another person was involved in determining how you feel, you are just an empath who brought others' feelings onto yourself.

Since early childhood, ACOA empaths see and feel how other family members suffer and want to help them. For example, an empath wants to help the alcoholic father or mother. They may feel the caregiver's pain and would love to change that, so the parent or caregiver will stop drinking. An empath child may also see other family members suffering from the pain that an addict causes. There may be a family dynamic where one person hurts the other, and the child sees the painful situation and wants to change things. Many children who grow up in dysfunctional families feel responsible for their families. It is absurd to think that way because children do not influence their parents. But being a child in such a family and being an empath can be very hard, especially when the child realizes that she is helpless in changing others and the situation itself. That could be very stressful and injure a child's belief in his abilities. And that can carry on into adulthood, continuously having no boundaries.

There are a few theories on why empaths become empaths. First, it is observed that babies are already born with their temperament, and some are more sensitive than others. For example, some babies respond more to sounds, movement, touch, light, and smells. So, those babies are already better at reading these surroundings than others from the day they are born. Then there is a theory that empaths become that way later in life, affected by their surroundings, especially childhood trauma.

An ACOA becomes an empath due to fear for his survival. When a child lives in an unstable environment where he is unsure what the next hour of his life will look like, he learns how to adjust. As a child, he understands that survival depends on how adults feel. If an alcoholic father walks in drunk and is not in a pleasant mood, the ACOA child knows it is better not to show his face and hides in his room. Or it could be the opposite: if the child sees that the parent is not feeling well, he jokes around to make the parent feel better. So, empathy was learned out of the need for survival.

That's what happened to me. When my father returned home, I could tell right away how drunk he was and what kind of mood he was in. There were some moods where I knew I'd better not show my face. There were some moods where I knew he would demand my presence, so I would laugh at his jokes and show him attention. I intended to please him, so my ability to read his mind was crucial. I was very good at reading my mother's mood as well. Even if both of them were watching TV, and there was just silence between them, I could walk into a room and decide if it was safe for me to stay there. There were plenty of instances when I felt I should leave the room and do something else instead of staying with them. And as soon as I would leave the room, they would get into an argument. Thinking back, there was a constant silent dance of me knowing where to be at a particular time, how to behave, and what to say. My survival depended on how they felt about themselves and me. So, my skills, reading their minds, and feeling what they felt were critical.

The Positives of Being an Empath

Either way, no matter how one becomes an empath, being one has its benefits. Empaths have excellent social skills; people like to be around them. Because an empath mirrors the other person's energy, feelings, and mood, the other person feels understood and accepted. They feel as if they met someone like them. Empaths are also excellent listeners. They are great at counseling and coaching. Others feel so at ease around empaths that they don't mind opening themselves up to anything raw and painful inside themselves and telling the empath their life story and even their secrets. Others are willing to talk about their problems and seek advice from empaths.

If you are sensitive, you may also be a natural healer because you know when someone is in pain, you know what to give them, what they need. You may feel like you know things without even explaining how you know that. You have great intuition, and you can tell when people are lying to you or about to deceive you. Although many times even if you feel that the other person is lying to you, you may not say anything about it or take any action to change it because of your wish to please others. You might be afraid to tell others that they are lying to you out of survival instinct.

If you are an empath, you might be very creative as well. Because you can read into others and understand feelings, you can have multiple different experiences daily and write about them. You can create literature, music, or any visual art and express that emotion to see for everyone else. You may not differentiate where those emotions are coming from, but they can be expressed beautifully. Because you are experiencing things more in-depth than other people, you are open to adventures, experiencing new cultures, talking with others, and discovering their life stories. You love to travel, try new foods, and do something different to enjoy it.

In addition, you may be sensitive to crowds, bright lights, and loud music, and you may not like movies about war and seeing other people suffering. You may not enjoy horror movies because that is just way too stressful for you. I remember once my friend was in the hospital to remove her appendicitis. She was telling me in detail what the doctor did. As I was listening intently to her, I realized that I was about to pass out. I don't know how, but it felt like I had a procedure on my body. Up till now, I cannot bear to see blood. If I cut my finger with a knife, someone else must attend to it because I faint.

The Negatives of Being an Empath

Now let's talk about the downside of being an empath. It can get very stressful because you can get very easily overwhelmed. Because you're constantly reading other people's energies around you, you lose your true sense of self. You are like a chameleon in that you become someone else as soon as someone comes to talk to you. You can change in a second from being one person to other. That is very energy-draining.

In addition, since people feel very comfortable around you, they may bring their problems onto you. Others may come to just vent and talk about the things that happened in their lives, bringing negative energy to you. And since you are an empath, you take all this in to understand them. And the next thing you know, you are burnt out and stressed. I read somewhere that it says that an empath has 100 problems, but 99 of them are not theirs.

Furthermore, you may get caught up in other people's priorities, and you will try to accommodate them. You also tend to do as they wish; they are in pain and need your help. Because of ACOA trauma, saying 'no' to others can be very hard.

So, this pressure, stress, and burnout cannot last forever. You'll get exhausted, and at some point, you will try to find a solution. You will want to free yourself from this pressure. When something happens around us, we tend to blame others or circumstances that cause us to feel that way. But blaming others is dangerous because blaming someone for your low energy means you lose your seniority; you are no longer able to respond, and you might consider yourself a victim. The truth is that you are responsible for your energy. It is your energy, like a tuning fork, that resonates with others. Therefore, you need to acknowledge your seniority and have boundaries to preserve it.

Let's say you are at a party and have a few drinks, and then your boundaries become weak. Since you are an empath, you are like this tuning fork that picks up the energy from another person and matches it. Let's say they like you and they feel passionate about you. Since you are an empath, you match that energy, believing that this is what you feel. Then you go home with that person and realize in the morning that that's not even a person you like. You can't blame the other person because you did not enforce your boundaries. Similarly, you cannot be angry at the person who comes to your office and disrupts your day and spits negative energy, if you pick up the energy and you are angry too. It's not about them that they came to your office today. It is about your inability to keep your boundaries up and your seniority.

How do you know when your boundaries are weak? Well, are you easily affected by other people's moods? Can someone bring you down? Do you feel overwhelmed when you have a lot of people to talk to during the day? Do you need to improve your priorities because you spend your time preoccupied with other people's priorities? Are you a people pleaser? Do you have never-ending drama at work, home, or in relationships? Are you bored with your own life? Do you feel depressed because you are not living the dream that you wanted? It is because you are getting all that energy from others and operating from that energy. Not from your own.

You have to know your boundaries with yourself and others, and you need to understand that you're the only person responsible for how you feel. You are the one who chooses to feel something or not. So, in the same way, you can let go of others' problems and other people's feelings. You can protect yourself from being influenced by people. Empaths realize how easily we give our power to others because we are used to that. Being an ACOA, we've been told since we were small that we are worthless, that we don't know what we're doing, and that whatever we feel is not valid. So, we need to listen to other people and their opinions, and that's how we choose to survive. But it is not so now. You're an adult now, can choose your seniority, and should take care of yourself.

There are at least three ways how you give away your power to others. First, you blame others for something that happened and say, "It's their fault!" You are the one who chooses how to react to something, so when you say that it is their fault, you feel helpless.

The second way you give away your power in your seniority is when you feel submissive to other people's opinions. You can tell yourself, "They know better than me." But, again, you learned this from your parents or caregivers. They told you that you don't know what you're doing. Maybe in the professional field, in the workplace, there is a coworker who knows more than you. So that statement is correct. But in any situation involving emotions, you know what is best for you. You can identify your emotions and feelings and decide what to do with them. Other people can't know better what you need to feel

And the third way how you give your seniority away is by needing more confidence in your own abilities. Again, that comes from your childhood when you've been constantly told that you are incompetent in whatever you do. You still believe that. So when you hear yourself saying, "I can't do it," that is your wounded child speaking. That is when you need to tell your wounded self that you are safe, you are an adult now, you can take care of yourself, and you are capable of so many things, and you are competent and can do whatever you are doing right now. And if you don't know what to do, you can ask somebody else for help.

As an empath, you should understand a few things about how to protect yourself. And one of the things is to have strong boundaries towards yourself and others. Others might not like it, but you have to do it yourself. When you have firm boundaries, you know who you are and know what is yours and what is not yours. You can easily release other people's energy without getting tangled up. You can choose what story you live in because you choose your own priorities, and you can live the life of your dreams. Because you are doing what makes you happy, you can make your own rules. There is a separate chapter in this book that talks more about boundaries.

You also must understand that you must take care of yourself first. You cannot help others if you are broken. So many clients come to me and ask me for stress management techniques. And when I tell them what they need to do, or I ask them what they can do, they respond that they don't have time for themselves because they have so many things to take care of. So I ask them who would care for them when they get sick from stress.

In addition, being an empath, you need to realize that sometimes you cannot help everyone that you want to help. You cannot save everyone, no matter how hard you try. What helped me the most was understanding that each of us comes to this life to experience different things. Some may be positive, and some of them may negative and be painful. To change the situation, it has to include both people You can help them, but they also need to help themselves. I like this saying: "You can take the horse to the river, but you cannot make him drink." If they choose to suffer, you must honor their choice and let them do that. You cannot make them better.

Exercises

The bottom line: no matter how one becomes an empath, it is essential to keep self-care as a priority. Learning to feel safe enough to embrace your sensitivity and set healthy boundaries is essential. Here are a exercises that can help manage stress while being an empath.

Exercise #1. When you interact with others, whether your spouse, family members, friends, coworkers, or even strangers on the subway, pay attention to how you feel. First, determine how you felt before they arrived at the scene. And then see what emotions you have now while they present. Pay attention. Do you follow their lead? Do you do what they tell you to do, even without speaking? Please write down in your diary when you take on somebody else's mood. For example, you may have been having a pleasant and peaceful day at work. Suddenly, your coworker came in to vent to you about their workload, another coworker, or their personal life. You want to be helpful, so you pay attention to what your coworker is telling you and empathize with them. If they were sad, suddenly you become sad with them. If they are angry, you suddenly feel angry with them. This exercise aims to highlight how fast you take on other people's energy, so you can place boundaries and protect yourself from that in the future.

Exercise #2. Make a list of people with whom you interact daily. Next to each name, try to remember how you feel when you're with them. Did you notice a difference between how you felt before seeing them and after? Is there a person that constantly makes you feel negative? Or is there a person who always makes you feel inspired? This reflection aims to identify particular people in your environment that influence you a lot. It's OK to keep people around that inspire you and encourage positive emotions. But what is it that you do with the others who bring negativity? When you identify those people, you must apply boundaries to protect yourself from negativity or remove yourself from the situation and those negative people in your life altogether.

Exercise #3. Create a list of affirmations you should repeat to yourself when triggered. When someone comes to you and tells you about their lives, you may be drawn to solve their issue for them. They don't even need your solution. They need you to listen. You can tell yourself an affirmation: "I don't have to fix everything for everyone." And let go of the need to give a piece of advice or even take action for them. Take action only if they ask for your opinion or your help.

Exercise #4. After acknowledging that you have taken on another person's energy even though that person has already left the room, make an intention to let go of that feeling. Tell yourself, "It is not mine, and I am commanding it to leave." And then let it go. Don't be afraid of it, do not keep it, ask it to leave you.

Your Superpower

Because you are an empath, you are a natural healer. Because of your empathetic openness, you feel what others feel and know what they want and need, so you can be outstanding in expressing through art, cooking, teaching others, coaching others. You draw other people towards you and make them feel better.

CHAPTER 14

Feeling Not Good Enough

Not feeling good enough is a widespread feeling among many. No matter what family one grew up in, there was always a situation in their life where one felt less than others. And it all happens when we do something wrong or different from other people's expectations. We also make mistakes, and we can see unwanted consequences. And then, over time, when we add one mistake onto another, onto another, we form the feeling that we're not capable of performing well at all.

There should always be a balance between positive and negative affirmations from others, especially when a child is growing up. In a balanced family, parents recognize that their child is incapable of performing well in some situations because they don't have experience or wisdom. Supportive parents will show the right way to do it, teach them how to fix their mistakes, and empower a child not to give up and to try again until they succeed. In a healthy family, a child's mistakes are not taken as a sign that a child is not good enough, it is taken as a sign that the child needs to practice more to succeed.

Never Good Enough

In a family influenced by an addict, there is no stability, balance, or support for a child to form healthy expectations of themselves and their capabilities. If you grew up in a similar situation, there was no way that you were good enough. You were constantly criticized. You believed that your family would be better off without you because you were the cause of their trouble. You may have been criticized for things that made no sense. As a child, whatever you did needed to be better. No matter how hard you tried, it would help if you had tried harder. If you got an A in school, you should have gotten an A+. Since there is no way for you to meet the standards of perfection that you have internalized from childhood, you are always falling short of the mark you have set for yourself, even while being an adult. And that is very stressful.

It's like that cartoon that I saw the other day. Superman was asked to come to see his boss at the office. The boss tells Superman, "Well, you did a super job! But I was expecting a super-duper job!" That is how most ACOAs feel in dealing with their dysfunctional parents.

When someone asks you how you are, how do you answer? Do you tell them everything is excellent and that your day is going well, even though you're dying inside? Do you tend to people please and continuously give and give without expecting anything back? This may be because you need to feel you need to do better. And there were plenty of instances in your childhood that groomed you to feel that way.

You also might have been told that you must act like everything is fine in the family and no outsiders need to know what's happening inside. So obviously, you just continued appearing to be a happy and perfect child to the outside world. But, because your feelings were also negated, and you were not allowed to express and feel, you even hid negative feelings from yourself. You were not allowing yourself to be an imperfect child because you were afraid of rejection. And since you never accepted the way you are, by default, you decided you needed to do better, and no matter what you do, you will never will.

Some dysfunctional families intentionally create jealousy and sibling competition. For example, an addict may have "the favorite child" that he pays the most attention. And that child may be seen as worthy and an example to others. So the other siblings try to be and look like "the favorite child" to achieve approval and validation from the addict. In the process, those children pretending to be someone else deny and lose their identity.

You may always be compared to your siblings, cousins, or neighbors. Maybe your parents constantly say that other kids are much better than you. Maybe they try to make something out of you that you are not. Maybe the family had high expectations of you following your father's or mother's footsteps, and you were not up for it. And then, by default, you assume you need to be better at something. That was accompanied by the family's disapproval of whoever you are and what you're doing now. They were disappointed that you were not validating their feelings and expectations. So you decided that you are not worthy since you cannot please them.

Lack of Attention

In addition, in the family with an addict, there was much pain and suffering carried by the rest of the family members. Your mom, dad, or other caregiver was consumed with keeping the balance and cleaning up after the addict's messes. Maybe there was not enough time to pay attention to you. But overall, no matter their reasons, you felt like you didn't get enough parental love. When your parents and caregivers dismiss your needs and don't give you enough compliments, support, affirmations, and validation, you fail to develop a healthy self-esteem. You assume your parents don't love you when you don't meet their needs. You must be doing something wrong, then.

As a child, I did not get attention when I did something right. Mostly I got attention when I did something wrong. The most painful experiences I remember were when my father returned home drunk and decided that he would teach me something. Most of the time, he would decide to teach me how to cook. I would feel like a complete failure. He would not have the patience to show me tricks with a knife that he knew would help me to quarter a chicken before I put it in a pot. Instead, he would be annoyed and yell at me angrily for not already knowing everything. And it didn't matter whether I was shaking or crying, he would continue yelling at me that I was stupid and didn't know how to do anything. But when he was sober, he paid no attention whatsoever to any achievements of mine. He never came to see me in a play, and he never came to a concert when I was playing the piano. I did not get positive affirmation from him; however, that was my expectation because I never got any. So I continued as if nothing happened because lack of validation was typical.

In addition, being a child and seeing your parents being unhappy, mainly seeing an addict in the family, you felt that you were responsible for their happiness. Yes, I know, it's a ridiculous thought. But from a child's perspective, it all made sense. You might try to be better, funnier, more entertaining, and much better than your sibling, but you didn't see any results in your parents' happiness. Hence, you concluded that you are not good enough to change things. This also could influence your adult life. When you have already concluded that you're not good enough and helpless, you don't even try to change things in your adult life and relationships.

More than that, when you realized that you could not change your parents' feelings, you started punishing yourself for not being good enough. And you would not acknowledge anything you did right and worth celebrating. If you believe you are self-loathing, ask yourself how well you accept compliments. I still need to work on accepting compliments for a job well done and for my appearance. When someone compliments me, the first thing that comes to my mind is, "What do they want from me?" Many times I would disagree with the compliment and say that it's not a big deal, that I shouldn't be complimented at all. I was doing all this because I felt unworthy.

Do you automatically disregard compliments? When something goes right, an ACOA dismisses it with, "It just happened." Or, "It was easy." Do you do the same? You may call this humility, but it perpetuates your negative self-image. It does not allow you to give yourself credit for what you do well so that you can begin to feel better about yourself. Because something is easy for you does not mean it is unimportant. Try to be aware of the things that you do well. Do not dismiss them. Use them to build on to become a whole person.

If something goes wrong, an ACOA tends to take full responsibility for it. Are you also harsh on yourself? Ask yourself what you gain by judging yourself. I don't remember you picking out those things that make you extraordinary. What is your need to belittle yourself? The answer is simple. Misery is familiar, and you have learned how to deal with distress. You may find comfort in your poor self-image.

The Stressors of Overachiever

Another way an ACOA copes with not feeling good enough is to choose one of two paths. The first path is to stop trying to be good enough altogether. Those ACOAs stop taking care of themselves, their work, their appearance, and any other task given to them. It may seem from an aside that they were doing things on purpose to make other people angry. I remember a few teenagers in our neighborhood who grew up in alcoholic families. They were the worst students. They were skipping school on purpose, they would always get in trouble with the police, and they were cautious of all neighbors and teachers, including us kids. We always expected the worst of them. Sadly, they gave up on themselves, and the rest of the community also gave up on them.

The second path to manage this uncomfortable situation is by trying to compensate by being an overachiever who can gain praise and attention from outside the home. An ACOA might become a straight A student in school because teachers love good students. One of my friends whose parents were alcoholics was one of the best students in class. In addition, she was a great gymnast and represented our school in competitions. Gymnastics was one of her passions, and she gave everything to it. We were very proud of her as friends. Sadly, her medals and prizes never were noticed by her alcoholic parents. She may have even gotten a college scholarship, but her parents decided that she needed to be better to attend one since they did not have any education.

Because of being overachievers, ACOAs want to be leaders and be noticed among peers. They may have a great sense of humor, be great storytellers, and be "the life of the party" no matter where they go. Since the outside environment is something that the child can control, he spends the most time and effort to please other people outside of the family. The child learns to separate those two environments as a reprieve from the stressors at home.

I have been searching for personal validation and worth as a human being from outside my family for a long time. I leaned towards perfectionism at some point. Since I did not know what normal looked like, I developed unrealistic and unattainable expectations in the work environment and relationships. I chose to be a perfect child who should always be productive and achieve many goals. I wanted to be the best at school not only to receive positive and validating feedback that gave me some temporary sense of personal worth from my teachers but also to please my parents by having good grades.

It may seem from the outside that it served me well, being an overachiever, but my parents were not impressed with my good grades and my achievements. After all, they didn't know how to appreciate me. Since I lived in two different worlds and received a very different support system, I still felt emotional and social isolation. Constantly pushing myself to be better, I imposed additional stressors upon myself.

I grew up with the same feelings of being an impostor no matter what I did. If I continued being successful in a chosen field, I might start being afraid of the worst, that someone would find out I'm not good at something, that I am not an expert. Impostor syndrome is experienced by many, even those who are very knowledgeable in their field and are experts. Since I never received validation for what I did and never felt good enough no matter how much I achieved, I feel like an impostor to this day.

You can change your life when you decide that you cannot take this pain anymore, and you have to allow yourself to feel sovereign in your life and your decisions. You have to make the decision that you want to be free. This may be difficult to achieve because you need help with authority as an ACOA. You learn to be afraid and obey authority no matter what because your survival depends on that. You grew up believing that everything outside of you is an authority, and anything that comes from inside of you is not. More than that, anything that comes from inside of you is flawed and wrong.

Exercises

It is time to put an end to that. Below are a few exercises that you can use to silence your inner critic and start appreciating and giving yourself credit for things that you have accomplished. It may be that you will not feel like using some of the exercises due to feeling humble, but you need to carry it through to heal.

Exercise #1. Silence your inner critic by giving proof of things that you do well. When your inner critic throws a negative statement toward you, question it. First, question yourself about where that critique is coming from. Does it sound like your father or your mother? Or your big brother, teacher, or other authority figure? Were they criticizing something that they were an expert on? Or was that just their opinion about something? Then ask yourself, is that critique even true? Just because someone believes you did something wrong doesn't mean it's true. Maybe you didn't even do anything wrong at all. For example, let's see, your inner critic tells you that you don't know how to cook, but others enjoy your food. Ask yourself where that belief is coming from. Maybe your mother criticized something you cooked when you were a teenager. Your cooking skills are improving, so you should silence that inner critic.

Exercise #2. Practice self-praise. Self-esteem comes from what we think, feel, and believe about ourselves. Practicing self-praise can fast-forward your progress regarding your self-esteem and make you radiate confidence. When you say kind words to yourself, your mind doesn't know or care where they came from; it just takes them in. However, praising yourself is even more potent than praise from others because every word you say to yourself forms a blueprint, and your body reacts to match the commands you give to your mind. Write down ten different ways to praise yourself, and take the time to dig deep into all the things that make you unique and special. Examples: "I am funny/I am a great listener/I am great at solving problems." Read that list to yourself every morning.

Exercise #3. If you are not feeling good enough in the workplace, ask yourself if you are as good as others. If the answer is no, that's a good time for you to reach out for more education. For example, you may talk to your supervisor or ask for recommendations from your coworkers. Pursuing knowledge and skills will add to your value. And then, over time, you can look at yourself and give yourself credit for your growth. If you don't have time during your day to learn something new because you are overwhelmed with work and family responsibilities, record your activities during the day in as much detail as possible. Next to it, indicate how long it took you to do it. Also, include conversations with other people. After you have observed yourself and your activities for a week or two, look at the patterns of where your time is going. See where you are spending time that can be enhanced by learning. For example, if you spend 45 minutes driving to work in a car every day, you may listen to an audiobook that helps you increase your knowledge in your workplace. Or you spend three hours every day watching your favorite shows when you could instead watch two hours and then dedicate one hour to reading a book or watching online training.

Exercise #4. Surround yourself with positive people. Since we are already conditioned to think badly about ourselves, our environment must support us and not reinforce our negative beliefs. Make a list of people that you hang out with the most. Next to their names, indicate whether they are positive or negative people. Do they give you too much criticism, never agree with you, and constantly tell you that you need to do better? You need to hang out less with that person. Do you work in an environment full of negative thinking and critical people? Hang out with them less, interact less, and tell them you don't have time to talk to them because you need to work. Do you have enough friends that can support you? Now is the time to look for new friendships.

Exercise #5. Collect praise from your coworkers, supervisors, clients, and anyone who commented positively about things you did. For example, let's say your supervisor sent you an e-mail thanking you for your hard work. You can put that e-mail in a special folder where you can look at it later. Also, keep that yearly review by a supervisor or your coworkers praise for your work for later. If you get a message from a friend thanking you for your help, complimenting you on how good our friend you are, save it somewhere. Later, when you need the inspiration to achieve something, start something new, believe in your capabilities, be worthy of receiving good things in your life, and be happy, read those messages to yourself.

Tool #6: I recommend listening to and doing everyday meditation by Marissa Pier, "I am Enough." I am not an affiliate of any of the products or services, but it changed my life, so I wish it would also change yours. You are welcome to Google her name or the name of the meditation, and you can access plenty of free content from her.

Your Superpower

Because you feel like you need to be better, you always try to put your best foot forward. You constantly try to improve yourself by learning more about yourself, your surroundings, and your occupation. As a result, you are productive, achieving your goals, and moving forward by building new ones.

CHAPTER 15

Difficulty Having Fun

Most of the time, when we see childhood depicted in the movies, we see a group of kids running around, hiding, participating in something, or taking an adventurous path. Most of the time, they laugh, giggle, and enjoy themselves. When we see an adult's successful, happy life, we see someone walking down the beach into the sunset, jumping out of an airplane with a parachute, dancing, talking loudly, and laughing with a group of friends. If you rolled your eyes just now, you are not alone. Not everyone imagines having fun that way. Having fun is believed to be something of a luxury for many.

I found this joke online that one out of five people suffers from loneliness. "If you take a look and you don't see four people around you, they are all out having fun without you." Having fun is very different from one person to the next. And having fun should not necessarily involve a group of people. There are plenty of fun activities that involve only yourself. I think of "fun" as an activity that makes your heart sing. You might be happy reading a book, walking alone on the beach, and sipping a cup of tea. Having fun can be defined in many ways. It doesn't need to include jumping off the plane or vacationing in faraway places. Fun is very personal. It's like taste: we all have different preferences.

You Have to Earn Fun

Having fun and relaxing is essential to having a less stressed and more energetic, productive, happy, and long life. However, not everyone can have fun, and some people have difficulty having fun even if they are from "normal" families. There is even a medical term for not being able to have fun: anhedonia. It can be caused by eating disorders, a history of abuse or neglect, recent trauma, heightened stress, major illness, etc. Most people experience it at some point in their lives, and for many, it comes and goes in waves. For some people, it can last a few hours or days. However, the brain does heal, and damaged dopamine receptors may regenerate within 6 to 12 months. That sounds promising, but not for ACOAs. How was your childhood fun? You probably didn't hear your parents laughing and joking and fooling around. Life was a very serious, angry business. The tone around the house put a damper on your fun. The spontaneous child within was squashed. How often were you really able to let yourself go?

If a person understands what it is to have fun, feels enjoyment by doing something, and then occasionally, for some reason, doesn't feel like doing it anymore, that is fixable. The difference is that there are reasons that ACOAs cannot relax and enjoy themselves. What can be done for a person who grew up without knowing what fun is? How can you understand something outside your experience? Do you allow yourself to have fun? If not, there are some reasons why you are not able to.

You might have grown up in an environment where working hard was the only way to earn fun, at a price. If you have low self-worth, you have difficulty having fun. How is that related to being unable to relax and let your hair down? By not letting yourself relax until you feel you are worthy. If your caregivers didn't acknowledge you, give credit and celebrate your achievements, you might take this invalidation as a sign that you are just unworthy. You might even be a workaholic right now who thinks that only when you achieve something can you reward yourself. Sadly, the more you work, the more you need to achieve. So that finish line keeps running in front of you, and you can't reach satisfaction. Due to your low self-esteem from being ACOA, you can't even give yourself credit for things you have achieved and you sincerely believe that you don't deserve a reward.

You just can't relax. You might think that relaxing is only for lazy people. If you grew up in an environment where your caregivers had multiple jobs, you believe you should work overtime, not complain, and have no fun. You might be honoring your caregivers that way without realizing it. You feel guilt when you're not doing anything at all. You might believe that you don't deserve to lie down on the beach and watch the waves crashing to the shore. And when you do take a vacation, you feel guilty about enjoying it or showing others that you are having a good time. That was me on my last vacation to the beach. I was the only person that had a laptop while sunbathing. I got some comments from strangers about that.

Another reason you may have difficulty having fun is that when you were a child, your home was supposed to be your playground, but where were you supposed to feel safe? Since your immediate environment was unsafe, there was not much fun to begin with, living in an alcoholic addict's house. I would only feel the most relaxed when I was alone, by myself, at the house. When my dad was home, he would be sleeping most of the time, and my mother would tell me to keep it quiet to ensure my father would not wake up. Let's face it: we are all in danger if he wakes up while drunk. And if my father was not drunk or asleep, we still couldn't make any noise because he probably had a headache from a hangover. So, most of the time, I would hang out with my neighbors and outside with other kids. I knew I could shout and run and jump outside but doing all that fun stuff inside my house was non-negotiable.

Having Fun is a Serious Business

You also may come from a family with few siblings where your care-givers were not necessarily taking care of you. You might be the one who parented your siblings. This is very common if you're the oldest child and feel the duty to take care of your other siblings. This pattern is typical in "normal" families when the oldest kid takes care of the rest. But the difference is that if you grow up in a family with an addict under the same roof, you may have felt constant pressure to keep your siblings in line and safe. You probably had no time to be a kid, relax, do something silly, and have fun with other siblings, neighbors, or friends. You knew that the situation could change quickly to something violent, so you were always on alert and expecting the worst. You might not even enjoy sleepovers at your friend's house, fretting what is happening back at home while you are here "having fun." You might even feel guilty about having that time for yourself.

One of my friends whose parents were alcoholics had to take care of her other three siblings. Often family celebrations and holidays were the most terrifying to her. Multiple times, she had to watch family members getting into violent fights, and she had to take care of and make sure that other children were safe. She was the one who started hiding the bottles of alcohol to make sure that her parents would not drink too much. She would be the one who would make sure that her siblings would go to bed with full bellies. She was the one that would clean up the broken glass after the fight. Although she was the only mature adult in that house, she was just a teenager. How could she even have time to discover what fun was? She felt responsible for every waking hour of her and her siblings' lives. Having fun and relaxing was not something she understood naturally, and it took her years into her adult life until she learned from others that relaxing is OK and should be done to keep yourself healthy and sane.

As a kid, I saw many celebrations and parties where adults had fun. And you guessed it, every party would involve alcohol. There would be plenty of food, lots of great stories, and dancing until someone would drink too much or fall asleep. That would be the best outcome, but sometimes someone would become violent and there would be fights, things breaking, and women crying. ACOA grew up knowing that it is all fun and games until someone gets hurt. They learned from the experience of watching the adults have fun. Dreading growing up and having to deal with those drunk consequences. When I think about it, those "fun activities" were learned from a generation before them. That was fun, so how could caregivers have other fun if that is all they saw growing up? Getting drunk was the only way to relax and forget the pain and everyday suffering. I bet not many grandparents were taking a stroll after dinner or playing ball with their kids in the backyard. Back in the day, work was the only activity from sunrise to sunset. Only rich people could have time to do nothing or do something they loved. Having fun is still a luxury in many countries and families.

ACOA children grew up afraid of their birthdays or other holidays due to drinking and fighting. And it doesn't matter if it is Christmas and it should be a sacred time with the family. There would always be some story about someone getting hurt. My best friend's family would get together with their aunts and uncles for Christmas. Her mother came from a large family that argued about the inheritance her late father left them. The evening would start nice, with Christmas gifts exchange, wishes for a better year, laughs, a delicious meal, and then someone would get physically hurt, rushed to emergency to sew up the wound inflicted by the hatchet. Those holiday get-togethers would end in the middle of the night, and sunrise would leave embarrassment and early departures home.

March 8th was a big day in the Soviet Union. Even into the Independent Lithuania days, this International Women's Day would continue. There would be plenty of flowers for sale on the streets. There would be the spirit of celebration, smiles, giggles, gifts, and, yes, parties. Lithuanian Sheriffs would stop women on the roads and give them flowers. Yes, true story! My dad also would remember his woman at home and bring flowers for my mom. By the time he would come back home, we always knew that he would be drunk. My mother would go home knowing for sure what to expect. I remember her saying every year to my dad: "I don't need your flowers. The best gift you can give me is to come back home sober!"

I also heard stories about families that would disapprove of any fun due to losing their child. I had a classmate, let's call her Paulina, who lost her twin brother to leukemia at a young age. Her mother took her son's illness very hard and was in emotional and physical pain for years. Finally, exhausted, Paulina's mother started using painkillers to soothe her pain and insomnia while dealing with her son's illness. Unfortunately, after losing her son, she drowned her sorrow in alcohol.

In addition to all other alcoholic problems at home, Paulina also experienced the guilt of staying alive. Since her brother was a twin, they shared the same birthday. Every year Paulina's mother would remind her that her brother would have been that old this day as well. She would go on for hours about how sad she was and how her son would never be alive and happy and have an everyday life. Paulina's birthday parties were unfortunate. The first time I went to her birthday, I was amazed that the overall mood was more of a funeral than a party. Paulina's mother would be extra drunk that day, embarrass my classmate, make her cry, and make everyone at the party uncomfortable. How would Paulina grow up celebrating her birthday after an experience like that? She felt guilty about being alive and felt that she didn't deserve anything that made her life joyful. She was one of the saddest kids in my class.

So, think about it, do you have enough fun in your life? Or do you get uncomfortable when somebody around you starts having fun? Why do you think that's happening? Remember what your childhood looked like and how much fun you and your siblings were allowed to have. What about your parents, your caregivers, especially those that were crippled by addiction? Did they know how to have fun? Did fun always involve substances? What do you do now in everyday life as an adult that makes you happy or helps you to relax? Do you struggle with finding something fun to do? Since you're not a child anymore, you can change this right now. Now, choose to change something in your daily life to bring you more relaxation, joy, and happiness.

Exercises

Below you will find some exercises that you can use to help you on the path to more fun. And as with any tool, remember, the key to success is taking action!

Exercise #1. Keep a daily diary of things you do that make you happy. I bet you already have things in your life that make you laugh and you enjoy doing. It doesn't have to be something complicated; it can be small things in life that make your heart sing. Maybe you like a cup of coffee and a great conversation with your coworkers in the morning. Maybe you look forward to the end of the day when you finally stretch your legs on the sofa, pour a glass of wine, and watch your favorite show undisturbed. I bet there are things in your life that you do without paying attention that are fun for you, so start writing them down. Take a piece of paper and write down all the fun things you do every day. Create a list of "things that I enjoy doing," and when you feel a low vibe, do something from that list. Now, if you don't even have one thing that makes you happy during the day, it is time to find what it is! Proceed with the other exercises below.

Exercise #2. Watch funny movies, TV shows, or just plain stand-up comedy. If you don't have time to watch a whole movie, it's OK, and you can go on YouTube and watch something very funny for five minutes to get your mood up. I heard that the most searched item on YouTube is funny cat videos. When working on myself, I would take 5 to 10 minutes every day to stop whatever I was doing, and this would be especially true when I was getting mentally tired. I would go to YouTube and watch some funny animal videos. It would always put me in a good mood and take me out of any irritability, tiredness, or negativity. Invest time every day in watching something funny and uplifting. If you frown at searching funny animal videos on YouTube, why don't you just look for other inspirational outlets? Videos or an inspirational book that gets your spirits up will also work. It doesn't have to be funny animal videos. Anything that gets you out and over low negative thinking or burnout will work. When you find something that works for you, add it to the general "things that I enjoy doing" list, keep it a habit, do it every day, and always turn to that outlet of laughter when you feel negative or need a pickup.

Exercise #3. Be open to spontaneity. If someone invites you somewhere, be open to it and go! Not all fun things happen when you plan them. Let others invite you somewhere and enjoy it! Those invitations to spur-of-the-moment getaways, last-minute movie invites, parties, museum visits, or just hanging out with a friend can be very beneficial. If you just said, "Nobody ever invites me anywhere," I dare you to make a list of the invitations you get every day. It can be small invitations to do something like going for lunch, trying out a new dish, or someone inviting you to help them with something. If you still don't have others inviting you anywhere, or you are just not in the right work environment or around people that much, then be the catalyst to try something new. Be the one who invites your friends to come over, go to the park, check out that new exhibit, or watch a movie. Create a schedule of fun stuff to do with your friends. If you have no ideas, call a friend and ask what they would like to do, then do it!

Exercise #4. Seek new things to try. It doesn't have to be something that you have to pay for. Look for a chance to do something new, even if that is just changing your route back home. Boredom is not fun, but it can be changed quickly by just trying. Check out clubs in your community or your work. If there is a book club, activity club, or dance group, join. You will be surprised how much your fun levels will increase by doing something new and meeting new people, which can lead to more fun and adventure. If you are in an environment lacking group activities, make a new club yourself. In the work environment, ask around who would like to participate in something new. Maybe you will discover some coworkers have similar hobbies and would love to share that love with others. Make an effort to create new groups, and that way, you will help yourself have fun and others! Make a list of your interests or what you would love to do, search in your community to see if a club already exists, and check out the Meetup app where people have started lots of groups. If there are none, create a new one! If you don't feel like creating something that lasts more than one day, search for activities happening in your town this week. Just google it, plan to go there by yourself or a friend, and go!

Exercise #5. Make your environment more fun. We spend a lot of time at work, so make your environment inviting, relaxing, and enjoyable. Decorate it with things you like, and put up photos of your family, friends, pets, and times when you had fun. Place a picture of a place you want to visit or a goal you want to achieve. I always feel better when I have something to look forward to. Rearrange your work environment, if possible, change up the décor where you live, and move furniture around. If you spend most of the time at home, paint the walls, rearrange the furniture, buy a new rug, lamp, or plant.

Exercise #6. Revisit things that you liked to do when you were a kid. Did you like to look at plants and insects? Did you like to play video games? Maybe stitching made your day? Did you collect images of antique cars? Participated in a book club? Revisit those interests, and maybe they still make you feel good. You are not a child anymore but an adult can also do those things. Expand on your hobbies. If you like collecting images of old cars, you could now visit museums where you can find them in person, read more about them, and join a club of people who also love those cars! Did you like to ride a bicycle when you were a child? Maybe you can sign up for a riding club and tackle a long and complicated route with a new group of people. Now is your time to do all the silly things you might not have been allowed to do when you were growing up because there was no money or time, and the family situation didn't allow that to happen. If you have kids, do activities with them instead of standing nearby and watching them have fun. When you do that with them, not only do you have more fun, but the bond between them and you will grow. Make a list of new things you can try. Are you choosing to sit and be grumpy, sad, and angry with the rest of your world because you have no fun, or are you doing something about it?

Exercise #7. Reward yourself by doing something fun. I hope you know by now the things you enjoy doing, those that make your heart sing. As long it doesn't include hurting yourself and others, anything can work. You might like things to do by yourself or with a group, they might be free, or you might have to pay for them. You might like doing nothing, just sitting outside yourself, stretching your legs, and watching people pass by. You should have a list by now. If you don't, please go back to exercise #1 and figure out what that is. If you work a lot and give other people a lot of your energy and time, it is time to reward yourself for hard work by giving yourself time. If you finish a project at work, reward yourself by doing something fun. Better yet, come up with the reward to do something fun before you start working on something. That will help you be more motivated while you are working. Reward yourself if you did an excellent job at home by handling something. Be sure to do it, and don't put this for later when you have time. Make time for yourself. You are worthy and deserve it, no matter what belief you formed from childhood.

Your Superpower

Because you are a "serious" type, others look at you as someone who is mature and "means business." Others might look up to you for mature solutions and expect you to be "the voice of reason" in many situations. You might also look like someone who is always responsible and won't let others down.

CHAPTER 16

Difficulty Trusting

We humans are herd animals and belong in a group. Whether we want it or not, we depend on others. Unless you live by yourself in the middle of the woods, you depend on someone putting food on your table. And living in a community, you need to trust that other people will do their part for you to be safe. Mutual trust is the most important thing for any healthy relationship, friendship, or give-and-take relationship. That is how we differentiate between enemies and friends; we trust friends won't hurt us. The moment they hurt us, they become enemies. Trusting in someone means believing in them and expecting them to be honest and reliable. Obviously, we need to be trustworthy to others as well.

Trusting family members and intimate partners determines our survival. No relationship can stand the test of time without trust. We have to feel safe around someone to open up to see others and let others see us. Without trusting others, we can't show up as who we truly are without being guarded, and we can't depend on others to watch our back. Trust brings safety, security, reassurance, comfort, and affection. To relax, perform our day-to-day tasks, and be healthy and happy, we need to trust in other people and ourselves. We can pick romantic partners and can have control of our surroundings when we are adults, but we can't pick our family members and who we grow up with. Sadly, many of us pick romantic partners based on what kind of family members we have because that is safe, familiar, and feels "normal."

It is tough to find someone who has never experienced betrayal. Many struggle with trust issues because others have broken trust, especially those close to them. We all encounter relationships where we expect someone to be there for us, but they aren't. Then we move on from relationships like that and grow a wall around our hearts to protect us in the future. If the person who broke our trust is a family member, we are still related to them for forever, and it is hard to sever the ties. Often, that hurt stays there and keeps reminding us of what has been done to us.

When I looked for a joke online to include in this chapter, I found: "I don't trust stairs. They are always up to something." Or "Oatmeal raisin cookies that look like chocolate chip cookies are the main reason I have trust issues." It is funny, but as soon I read it, I thought, "I wish my trust issues came from cookies." Being an ACOA, my trust issues were being built over the years any time someone lied to me, as small as, "I will come home on time tomorrow," to big lies such as, "I will be there for you."

The Constant Disappointment

My parents, the people teaching me what trust was, were repeatedly breaking that trust. The most significant influencer of my trust issues was my father's alcoholism. Everything in our lives was influenced by it, whether we wanted it or not.

I remember my mother telling me a story that when I was a toddler, she asked my father to pick me up from preschool. I bet you already know how that ended. Yes, he got drunk and forgot to pick me up. Imagine a toddler waiting, the last kid left behind, forgotten, abandoned.

I can't even imagine the terror and grief my little heart felt that day. I was probably asking myself why I was not good enough to be taken care of. What did I do wrong to be left alone? I didn't know it had nothing to do with me, and it was my drunk father who broke his promise.

Trust issues are widespread and especially impact children that grew up in dysfunctional families. They have difficulty trusting other people from the get-go and expect to disbelieve what others say. They might be suspicious of what others promise and may question other people's intentions without evidence that they are lying. I learned early on that adults are not always reliable and trustworthy. Since there is a profound denial of alcoholism in society, I have often been told that nothing is wrong. I learned not to even trust my own eyes and heart. Whatever I was seeing must not be accurate. Whatever I was feeling was not valid. I have often been told that abuse and terror I experienced weren't so bad and others have it worse. I am not sure what "others" my mother was referring to. And just because someone else had it worse didn't make my pain and suffering less.

Other times I remember being with my father on the bus after he picked me up drunk from preschool and fell asleep. I still remember being terrified as we passed the bus stop where we were supposed to get off the bus and kept heading somewhere I didn't recognize. Finally, I woke him up, and we got home eventually. But the image of unseen places and my helplessness to change the situation was terrifying. He had not broken any promises that day, but the overall faith that the parent should take care of the child and watch for the child's best interest was broken.

I learned early that just because my father was with me didn't mean I would be safe, protected, and taken care of. More often, it was the opposite. He was either drunk or angry because he was not drunk, which created a complicated and stressful situation for me. I didn't particularly appreciate spending time with my father. I was terrified. In short, my needs were not met. Those who supposed to be there for me, give me love, support, and nourishment for the body and soul, were not there. As a result, I wouldn't trust my parents with my well-being. I lost trust in my father for not being a provider and protector of our family. And I lost trust in my mother for not being there for me and being unable to protect me.

In addition, I would break my trust in myself when I would give them another chance to prove themselves. I would forgive and love again. Over and over, I would hurt myself by being trusting, loving, and naïve, believing they won't do this to me next time. But it kept happening over and over until today, and there was not much I could do. It is hard to push those you love away, especially if they are your family members. You might be pleading with them to change, helping them as much as possible; but don't see results. It can be heartbreaking giving them another chance and hoping "this time it will work." In situations like that, the best you can do is to take care of yourself and your family and keep yourself sane, strong, and healthy. It is not your fight. You did the best you could. Stop doubting yourself and keep faith in yourself, because the success of them quitting their addiction has nothing to do with you or your abilities. You can forgive and forget but be cautious about what is coming your way.

If you grew up in a dysfunctional environment, you might also be suspicious of other people's intentions. You might feel like others are trying to deceive you somehow, even if their words and actions tell you otherwise. You don't trust someone to be there for you. If they make a promise, it might sound too good to be true. You might be a more "I believe it when I see it" type of person. And even if someone kept a promise, it might seem suspicious to you, and you might think, "well, what do they want from me that they are so nice to me?" You might have learned this from your addicted caregiver. You might have been in the situation when they coerced you into doing something you knew was terrible by giving you praise.

One of my friends, let's call her Louise, had an alcoholic mother who constantly needed money to buy booze. Her alcoholism was so bad that anything they owned that wasn't broken had already been taken to the pawn shop to get money to buy alcohol. There was not much to sell at that point. Like her other two sisters, Louise was taken care of by her grandmother, who didn't have much money. To get money, the sisters were constantly coerced into stealing from other kids. Small things around the house would be gone as soon Louise showed up. One day I asked my friend why she was stealing. And she answered me with, "if I bring more things to my mother to pawn, she would tell me that I am her favorite daughter and she loves me the most." It is sad to think of such a negative influence on a child by her mother, but the addiction would take over, and there was not much we could do.

How Trust Issues Can Break Relationships

People with trust issues have difficulty building healthy relationships with others because it takes a while until they allow others into their hearts. Used to being lied to, many even sabotage a good relationship from the beginning. Trust issues don't allow the person to allow time for a relationship to unfold and see where it takes them. Used to disappointments from the past, those with trust issues assume it will end badly anyway, so what's the point of giving it time and trusting the other person? At the same time, by guarding the heart against betrayal and disappointment, ACOAs often do something hurtful to make the other person leave the relationship first. And then say, "Aha, I knew it wouldn't last. All of them betray me."

It might be hard to focus on the good aspects of relationships, of good characteristics of the person. Focusing on the negative and being "prepared" for the worst is safer. Lack of forgiveness is also common in relationships. Little things can be blown out of proportion, remembered forever, and used over and over in self-defense. It is hard to "forgive and forget" anyone who hurt us. Sadly, by experiencing all this, we wall ourselves in, not letting anyone get in. As a result, we might feel isolated, lonely, and misunderstood. We think we are protecting ourselves, but we are also hurting ourselves in the long run.

Lack of trust influences many of our relationships and might cause stress not just to ourselves but to others involved. In romantic relationships, we might encounter trust-related infidelity, be unwilling to commit to someone, or even have difficulty apologizing when trust is broken. Due to our trust issues, other people might think they are not worthy of love, understanding, and care. Others need reassurance and validation from us as well. If we want trust from others, we also need to be there for others.

Lack of trust negatively touches friendships by not allowing you to rely on your friends for help, not trusting that they will deliver when promised or will not be there to watch your back. You might be reluctant to make new friends and open up to others about your true feelings, past, and issues you are facing because you are afraid they will laugh at you or undermine your feelings, just as adults did in your childhood. Instead, you should invest in other people, open up to them, be there for your friends, and grow mutual trust.

Your workplace relationships can be impacted due to a lack of trust. You might think that other coworkers are conspiring against you, or you might not trust that they can deliver on time with the quality you want. You might decline someone proposing to help you with a project. You would rather put in overtime than take their help. You might have difficulty delegating your work to someone as well. For example, I would agree to take on way too much work and would prefer to do it all myself so I would know it was done. If I was asked if I needed help, I would decline and respond with, "I am fine." But soon, it would backfire since I would make errors and need to redo things. I would also be exhausted, and my trust in my abilities would start declining. I had to stop and pace myself, ask for help, and trust that others would do a good job.

Children who can't trust their parents respond with an intense need to control things themselves. It might be a good thing, but it also can be a bad thing. So I wrote the whole chapter in this book on how to deal with control issues.

Ask yourself whether you have trust issues. Does it affect your relationships? We all have some, and the intensity depends on how we learn to handle that. Not trusting yourself or others might be very stressful and impact your life, health, and happiness. However, it is never too late to address the issue and make adjustments, no matter how hard it is to do it. It takes willingness.

Exercises

It might be that you won't entirely get rid of trust issues and will always have to live with them, but it is possible to make rational changes that will help improve relationships. It can be small or big steps to change as long you believe they need to be done. Below are a few suggestions on how you can approach this.

Exercise #1. Ask your close friends if you have trust issues. I don't recommend asking your family members, especially those who inflicted your childhood trauma, because their answer is unreliable. Close friends will be able to answer you honestly. Just tell them that you are working on your childhood trauma and that you wonder if they think you have trust issues. Listen to what they have to say and also ask for details. You might be surprised by what you hear. You might hear that you have very high walls around you and it takes an effort to get to know you. You might hear that you trust people too much because you want to please them and belong to a group. Since childhood trauma distorted your belief and trust in yourself, friends' opinions are precious. Ask a few friends, acquaintances, partners, and even coworkers. Make a list, look for patterns, and adjust accordingly for the future.

Exercise #2. Learn to trust yourself by keeping your promises to yourself. You have been abandoned by those who were supposed to keep their promises, but they didn't. You learned to break promises to yourself as well. Now is the time to keep them no matter what. Start with small promises that you can keep. Don't tell yourself that you will buy a gift when you finish this project and then never buy it. Don't tell yourself that you will be able to work out five times a week when you know that you won't be able to. Agree with yourself to start three days a week and then see how that goes. When you keep promises to yourself, you keep your boundaries and respect yourself more. You gain more confidence in yourself, which makes a difference in your life. Keep a log of promises to yourself that you kept. When feeling doubtful about your abilities, read the list.

Exercise #3. Face the truth no matter what it is. Don't close your eyes on something and say, nothing is wrong when someone is abusing you, mistreating you, putting you down, or hurting you. You have been accustomed to that and it might be "normal" to you. But it is not. If it is hurting you, it shouldn't be there. It is a chance for you to be on your side and stop abandoning yourself. When you call things the way they are, you have a chance to change them. If you keep lying to yourself that nothing is wrong, there is nothing to improve. Even if something feels "off," that is a sign that change needs to happen. Don't try to squeeze yourself into something. It would help if you didn't keep the peace. If it feels off, it is off. Instead, take a piece of paper and brainstorm what things in your life feel off. It would be best to change those things, no matter how uncomfortable they make you feel. Come up with a plan and take action.

Exercise #4. Tell the truth to other people no matter how you feel. If you are happy, tell them you are happy. If you disagree with something, say so. If they are hurting you, you tell them that. Have the courage to voice that out. Call it what it is and stand up for yourself. Tell your genuine opinion about something when asked instead of telling what they want to hear. Some might not like it, but they sure will respect and trust you more. On the other hand, tell others that you appreciate them, love them, adore them. Tell others when they inspire you make you a better person. We all need encouragement and validation. Don't be afraid to be sincere and genuine. Write a daily list of the truths you voiced to others, be proud of it, and celebrate it!

Exercise #5. Build trust in your relationships slowly but surely. Don't jump into trusting someone too fast, but don't take forever to trust someone. When meeting new people, keep a diary of things about them and what actions and words you have encountered from them. If you have difficulty trusting others, this diary will show you if that person is worth the trust or not. Time will tell, and it is easier to lean towards trust when you have written proof that they are trustworthy. The opposite goes for people who break your trust. Be careful not to overreact on the small stuff and be kind and forgiving of things. But be careful to know your deal breakers and leave a relationship when they break your boundaries. Some people are worth forgiving and trusting again, and some don't.

Exercise #6. Don't be afraid to talk about your trust issues, especially when entering a relationship. There is no need to go into details of your wounded childhood, but letting the other person know that you are super conscious and will take time to trust someone, is the right way to do it. Tell them more if they want to know more, but only if you feel comfortable. You might find others who struggle with similar issues so that you can support each other. When you open up to others, you also might see that you are not alone with this issue and that others will understand. Communicating about that with your partner might help them to go the extra mile with reassurance when needed. They will be more understanding if you would react in a particular way or get triggered in situations. If you open up about your fears and are met with ridicule, that is the wrong person to be around, and you should keep your distance from them. Find those people who can and are willing to support you.

Exercise #7. Let others help you in day-to-day activities, let go of control, and trust they can help you. It is understandable if you feel uneasy letting that control go. You learned to rely on yourself for years. You might even be convinced that others don't do their job and you are always left to do everything for them. This has to change now. It is time to let that control go and allow others to step in. Learn to allow other people in your life to take care of things. Delegate tasks at work to others and assign chores to your family members. Trust that they will do it. Keep a diary, if you like, of who is supposed to do what and when. Keep those records handy when you don't trust someone, then read back to reassure yourself that they delivered before, and they can deliver again. If you have a feeling one day that you can't trust anyone, that is a good list to look at it again to remind yourself that there are people in your world who can help you and are trustworthy.

Your Superpower

Taking time to trust someone can protect you and those you love. It might take time for you to trust a new relationship that will assure that relationship that you are in is worth keeping it. Taking time to trust new opportunities will give you a more settled way to approach them and can save you losses in the future. Not rushing into something from the beginning but taking a second look will reveal how things are instead of how you wish them to be. But, of course, be careful not to go over the top and take too long to trust a person or take that opportunity, or you could lose it.

CHAPTER 17

Blind to Red Flags

It is a human basic need to belong to others and to be loved and appreciated. We long to belong to the group and be accepted the way we are. At the same time, we should understand that others are different than us. We are not perfect, so we cannot expect the other person in a relationship to be perfect. Based on this logic, we should accept others the way they are, even if they display some behavior that obviously will not work for us.

We all have different preferences, needs, and values. That's how it should be. We should attract and have relationships with others who will benefit us, help us grow, and bring joy. The difficulty arises when we are not able to recognize the people in our environment who would fit with our preferences and help us fulfill our needs. And in some cases, another person's needs and behavior can even hurt us. Unfortunately, people do not walk around with labels on their foreheads that say, "I'm a narcissist, and I will hurt you."

It is safe to state that many of us, no matter our backgrounds, overlook warnings in relationships, aka red flags. Some red flags are more significant than others. One red flag maybe a deal breaker for one person, while another person would not count that behavior as a red flag at all.

A joke comes to mind: "I think I was a bull in my previous life because I am attracted to red flags." Here is another one that makes me giggle: "When you look at red flags through rose-colored glasses, all flags look like, well, just flags."

A child who grew up in a more balanced environment, who was allowed to understand his values, was allowed to understand himself and express himself, will be able to identify what life partner they want. More than that, they may have been given great examples from the parents and caregivers about warning signs in relationships. They may have seen the examples and clarifications about relationships between siblings and other people around them. Their parents may have explained the warning signs and taught them how to identify them in any relationship and decide whether or not they should stick around. They may have been taught to recognize warning signs by looking at or talking to someone. "Listen to your gut feeling" came from a loving parent who taught their child to trust himself by listening to himself.

When Listening to Your Gut is Not an Option

When it comes to ACOA and identifying warning signs, it is a very different story. Someone who grew up in a dysfunctional family, in a traumatizing environment, can have a lot of things in their adult life in order. They may be financially stable, have a career, have plenty of friends, have a place in society, and it may look like they have their relationships in order too. But for ACOA figuring out relationships, it's tough. When this traumatized adult falls in love and tries to create a meaningful intimate relationship, the old childhood survival mechanisms rush right in. Many times, in any sort of situation, an ACOA needs to have a clear mind and use common sense, but because of childhood traumas, they tend to disregard those red flags. "Listening to your gut" doesn't exist in adult life. They grew up in a dysfunctional family. First, they were taught to do the opposite. Anytime the child tried to identify a feeling and express himself, he was told that it isn't so and laughed at. Often, a child could see something and feel something worrisome, but was told to ignore the feeling and proceed anyway.

Since I was a little child, I knew I was an empath, so I had a good intuition about many things. When I felt anxious about something, I knew it would end badly. And when I was at peace, I knew I would be safe. Sometimes my father would come back drunk after work, and I would feel that the rest of the evening would not go well. My gut told me I needed to go to another room and hide. My gut told me I needed to leave him alone because it was unsafe for me. But then my guilt would kick in, and I would feel like I needed to be there with him in the same room. The part of me just telling me that it's OK, that's my dad, he cannot hurt me, and I need to do whatever he tells me to. It was my job, my purpose, to be there. Even if I didn't want it to, even if I felt it was not safe for me. Especially when he started breaking things. And I would stay there with him against my self-preservation. Because, in a way, it was keeping me safe as long as I was with him, pleasing him. Because of this twisted self-preservation, I thought I should not listen to my gut feeling. And even if I felt that I shouldn't do something or should not be somewhere, I still should do it because my gut feeling was wrong.

We learn how to deal with other people and build a foundation for relationships based on what we learn from our parents or caregivers. The communication, dynamic, and feeling of those connections carry on to our adult life. We know what we learned. Sadly, it didn't help us who are ACOAs, but it hurt us.

How often have you been heartbroken from a relationship where you thought you could trust the person? How many times have you been in a relationship where you thought they would love and respect you but later on realized that they are a different person? How often have you been in a relationship with someone who is a liar, mistreats you, humiliates you, and is not emotionally available? Have you felt emptiness, grief, sadness, and loss after an unsuccessful relationship?

And then you look back and realize that those red flags about that person were correct from the beginning of the relationship, but you ignored them. It happened because that traumatized part of you changed your perception of that person. And you should not beat yourself up over this, and you should give that part of yourself a big hug and understanding.

Just thinking about myself, I will get into many relationships without seeing any red flags. Only after I've been hurt, looking back, would I see that they disrespected me right from the beginning. They were telling me to my face that they didn't like me. They were laughing at me. In some situations, I got myself in trouble because I not only ignored the red flags, but I turned them into positive attention. I was disillusioned and hurt myself in the end.

When Red Flag Detector is Broken

Another reason you may not see red flags in front of you? You learn from early childhood not to see them because you were denying what was happening to you, especially something that made you feel bad. Ignoring something right in front of you when you were a kid is exactly what saved you. Your red flag detector broke itself so you would not realize what's happening to you and be crushed. It is excruciating to realize that those people who are supposed to love you and care for you are hurting you. And they may not feel like they're hurting on purpose, but their words and actions do that anyway. They are immature and insecure toddlers who have never been heard before. They didn't know what they were doing, but you wouldn't understand that. It was too much to face, so you chose to deny pain.

Something else happens once we have a broken red flag detector. Since we all need love, we start looking for it, even if it is not there. So, when you get involved in relationships with other people, you might tend not to see red flags if they seem like love instead. You may romanticize connections right from the beginning when there is no basis for it. We are humans, and we need to be loved and appreciated. There is nothing wrong with feeling that you want to have another person in your life who loves you and sees you. It gets very complicated when you grow up in an environment where you are not given love attention and do not feel safe. You may tend to confuse the signs of affection and signs of abuse. Since you were a child, you may have been starved for attention. So negative attention, even when you are hurt by it, is still attention. You might rather have negative and abusive attention than no attention.

So, what are the red flags in a relationship? When someone is standoffish, would you be hesitant to decide about your relationship? Or ghost them when they do not give you the attention you need, not reciprocate? When you feel things are going a certain way, and you are investing so much in getting that much back in return, that is not how a healthy relationship should be. And since you grew up with childhood trauma, you may be thinking that if you try to be better, if you just work more on yourself, maybe you will be more helpful to them, maybe you will try to change them, maybe they will love you. It may have worked when you were a child, but it does not work when you're an adult. So, when someone doesn't give you appreciation or respect right from the beginning, those are red flags that you should pay attention to.

If someone makes you feel scared about your relationship, future, and safety and keeps you guessing how things are between you two, those are red flags that show that they are incapable of giving you what you need. You must listen to your gut feelings and understand how they make you feel. We have to be able to relax around someone and be ourselves. This relaxing and being yourself could be very foreign to you if you grew up in an environment where you could not relax. And where you were not permitted to feel yourself and be yourself. Since you grew up in a dysfunctional environment where you feel you have to please others or they will abandon you, you feel the same about relationships.

Someone who wants to be with you and likes you will make sure to let you know, and they will call you and message you regularly. Do they like you or not? They don't want you to leave, and they want you to be happy. So they take actions that they believe will comfort you and make you feel at peace. They will show up for you, have dinner with you, and have plans for the future for you.

Avoid Limerence

You also must be very careful when communicating with others, such as making new friends, coworkers, and neighbors, to read too much into their behavior. You may be starving for love and attention. Did you start to see things where they don't exist? It is sweet to escape into the illusion that a person feels the same things towards you. If you like someone and you are in an environment where you constantly see them, for example, a workplace, church, or a classroom, you could think that you are on the same page. And it might be that you used to be mistreated, so when somebody smiles at you or when somebody helps you with something and is just being nice to you, you start to fantasize that they have deeper feelings for you, more than friendship.

If you have never been in a situation like that, I am sure you have a few friends you heard fantasizing about a friend, a coworker, or a classmate, that they have feelings for. And I'm sure you have seen plenty of movies with the same scenario, where a character is deeply in love with somebody else and believes that mutual feelings are involved, only to find out later that the other person is getting married to somebody else. I am guilty of that as well. Been there, done that. It feels sweet while it is happening to have hope that someone is interested in you. But it is excruciating to realize in the end that all was just an illusion.

But what if the other person, like a coworker or a friend, actually has loving feelings toward you? Then it would help if you saw how they act, not what they say. When you get into a relationship, ask yourself lots of questions and answer them with a clear mind and common sense. How do they react when you have a special day like your birthday? Are you the one who's making them do things for you? Are you doing this all for yourself? Oh, they did something, and you don't need to do anything at all? They surprise and make you feel special by making sweet things for you and organizing everything? The person who likes you will not have a problem telling you that they love you and want to be with you, they will be open to or meet your friends and your family, they will want to be included in your life, and they will let you know.

Ask yourself how you feel about that person. Do you find yourself stepping up? Do you feel better about yourself? Do you feel at ease? Or do you feel like you are being dragged down? Are you trying to fit in, lowering yourself to their level? The most important sign is that they can and will be with you no matter what.

If you are with the right person, ensure that your abandonment issues will not make the best of you. Even though you should not be with someone who doesn't want to be with you every day, you still need to give the other person space so they can come to you. You can set a time frame for when you expect them to come to you, but until then, you should allow them space and let the person breathe. Six months or a year, it's very reasonable to wait and see what happens. Take the pressure off the relationship. Stop asking where this is going. Stop asking if another person is interested in you and if they care.

Exercises

It may be challenging to start to trust yourself and your gut feeling when you evaluate other people in your life. Use your common sense to achieve balance with others. Here are a few exercises that can help you trust yourself more, see red flags at the beginning of relationships, and cultivate healthier relationships.

Exercise #1. Create a list of red flags in the relationship. Try remembering your previous relationships and the red flags you noticed in those other people's behavior. Keep that list as your reference for current and future relationships. Include as many examples as possible for easier identification in the future. In addition, talk with your friends, read articles, and watch videos about red flags in relationships. Learn about toxic relationships and toxic behaviors so that you can identify them yourself. Add them to the list. Use this list to help yourself to identify red flags. Then next to each red flag, give a grade. Is it a big flag that would be a total deal-breaker for you? Or is it a small flag that you can live with if you would change an attitude towards it or if the person would change? Then agree with yourself about how many red flags you will allow the person to display before you disconnect from them.

Exercise #2. Have a friend you can talk to about your relationships. Pick a person who could be very close to you but also will care about your well-being. Do not pick someone selfish, who is jealous of you, who is immature, who cannot see other red flags. That should be a person who one day listens to you. They should point out the red flags that you do not see. And when you start this practice, do not get upset with the other person when they point something out. You may also feel angry at yourself that you do not see what they can see. Be gentle and forgive yourself. With time, you will be able to identify more red flags.

Exercise #3. Keep a diary where you track your relationship's health. It could be a romantic, just friendship or work-related relationship. Record as many details as possible, and write down what they said and did. Don't expect other people to behave as you want them to behave. Do not expect that other people will behave the way you behave. And people when they display who they are. They will do it the way they do. You can't, and you should not change them. And it's your right to accept them as they are or let them go. And then read yourself the red flag list and compare that to what happened. Is that person displayed red flags? How big were they? Can you live with that? Or should you let them go?

Exercise #4. Take time to remember how your relationship was with your parents or caregivers regarding your validation. Were your caregivers teaching you not to pay attention to red flags? Did they make comments to you to be nice to other people and let others take your power away? Were you told to obey your siblings, neighbors, and other people because you had to? That is when you discover your parents created rules of behavior that you operate by. If you've been constantly told to disregard red flags and let other people behave poorly toward you, and you had to be OK with that, you took that experience with you into your adult life. Take time to look closely at the relationships you have right now in your life and ask yourself if any of them have the same patterns you learned from your childhood. For example, let's say your mother told you that you should ignore the insults that your drunk father said to you. You learned that no matter how painful someone's remarks are, you will somehow justify that they didn't mean it, and now when you are an adult, you let other people insult you and you draw no boundaries.

Exercise #5. Listen to your gut no matter your situation. It could be that you feel you should not buy something. You may have the inspiration to go somewhere. You may have a feeling not to trust someone. Or not to take that job offered to you even if the pay is excellent. If you don't trust yourself, start paying attention to what your intuition tells you. Write down every day what insights you get, and then follow them. Record what happened when you listened to your gut and when you did not. Build trust in yourself over time. Prove to yourself that you can trust your inner voice.

Your Superpower

Because you do not pay attention to the red flags as much as others do, you tend to see other people in a more positive light. Since you look for positive attention, you give others the benefit of the doubt in any situation. Since many other people act in self-preservation and from fear from their childhood traumas, you're giving them another chance that can be very positive for your mutual relationship.

CHAPTER 18

Grief

Grief is a feeling known by us all. Simply put, grief is an intense emotional experience that is caused by the loss of something. We commonly use this word in the context of death, when someone we knew, loved, and appreciated dies. But the loss, as we know it, comes in different forms, and grief can be associated with the loss of a relationship, significant material assets, a job, faith, or a pet. In grief, we might feel like things are too difficult to bear and we won't make it out.

There are symptoms associated with the grieving period. They may resemble physical symptoms that can look like depression, including difficulty sleeping, fatigue, loss of energy, loss of appetite, even physical pains, and a suppressed immune system. Grieving also may bring episodes of crying, weeping, and intense physical agitation. There are also cognitive and emotional symptoms. For example, grieving people have feelings of disbelief concerning the loss and can distance themselves from reality. In addition, they can display any negative emotions such as depression, guilt, anger, despair, hopelessness, anxiety, and feelings of isolation.

Grieving Something You Never Had

You may wonder why I am talking about grief in this book. There is something unique to the ACOAs when it comes to grief. When you think about your childhood, you may experience the grief of a childhood that you never had. And you may think to yourself that you wasted all this time, and now it's too late. You may wonder what your life would be like if only you had an amazing childhood like others. Thinking that way might bring you feelings of abandonment, pain, helplessness and hopelessness, depression, longing, loss, and heartbreak. You may feel that things will never improve because of that lost childhood, and you might feel damaged forever. And we might feel like no one can understand and help us.

In any situation in life where you experienced the loss of something, may that be a close person to you, your favorite book, a pet, or, in this particular instance, your childhood that you never had, you may feel like grieving. Proper grieving is when you give yourself enough time to feel the emotions, cry, be sad, and allow yourself to be.

Traditionally, women have said, out of their own experience, that a good cry makes them feel better. And plenty of women feel that they are strong enough, will not give in, and it is not allowable for them to get through all the emotions and be sad and cry. But, in addition, in our society, a man is trained to be strong and is told, "Boys don't cry." For men, in particular, it is hard to go through all the stages of grief because they do not allow themselves to grieve. Hence, they suffer much longer.

It reminds me of a joke. A widow tells her friend: "My grief counselor died last night. He was so good, I don't even care!"

Stages of Grief

This inability to express emotions while grieving can be explained by someone experiencing fear to express the grief. They may be afraid of the reaction that comes with it like they're afraid to be swallowed by it. They are afraid of what people say about their behavior. They are afraid to go deeper into their feelings, afraid they would never return.

They have feelings like if they start crying, they might never stop. It's been said that if we did not stop and resent the feeling of grief, it would run its course in 20 minutes.

If we resist the grief, it will go on and on. Suppressing grief is like another emotion, and it can run for years, causing havoc in our relationships, physical body, actions, and everything else and so our life. We should not be afraid of that feeling. Letting go of the resistance of this feeling allows us to move through the grief faster.

In this process it is common to be angry at some point. At society, your family, or the things that happen to you. It's normal. When we lose something, we experience anger because our brain is protesting against something that is perceived as frustrating or unjust. And if you think about your childhood, you may also feel angry because you might perceive not having a perfect childhood as unfair and frustratingly uncontrollable. Anger provides a way of expressing powerlessness. And you may feel frustrated or bitter towards your parents or caregivers when you think about your past.

All ACOAs feel they want to love their parent, but they have so much pain and unresolved issues. They feel guilty about not being able to forgive them, the guilt that they don't want to love them. They are mad at their parents because they know they have been in pain. An ACOA doesn't know what to do with it. They are stuck. They must move through their feelings and scream, kick, and yell to get it all out. It is imperative to recognize that anger, and it's necessary to express the more profound stress of grief. The grief for the lack of support, love, and appreciation for their parent is the result of shame that causes the ACOA to believe that they are defective as a human beings and unworthy of love.

There is also anger directed towards yourself for not being there for yourself. You may ask yourself why you trusted others to care for you. Obviously, a baby cannot take care of itself, and it needs caregivers to stay alive. You did your best to survive. If you look at things from a different point of view and you would take responsibility for your life fully, the life that you see as a chosen path by you, you may feel a huge disappointment in yourself. You may ask yourself why you would allow yourself to be hurt. You may experience the collapse of your belief system about yourself and your surroundings. And because you feel disappointed in yourself that you couldn't protect yourself, you may punish yourself for not being there for yourself. That may be one of the reasons why you would have difficulty letting go of your grief. You may take this pain as punishment.

If you decide at some point point that this pain is unbearable and you want to let go of grief, it's good to know what stage you're in.

There are five stages of grief. So, let's say that you feel very sad about the childhood that you did not have compared to others. And you understand that this is too late for you to have that, and you will never experience it. So, in the first stage, it may be that you will be in denial of it because you're not able to process the loss. And many ACOAs are in that stage. They believe that their childhoods were just great, and they don't feel any resentment towards the family members, and they talk about their healthy and happy childhoods, although everyone around them knows they've been abused.

Also, someone could argue that you cannot feel the loss of something you never had. So if you never had a happy childhood, you cannot grieve not having it. But if you understand that you have childhood trauma and are reading this book, you understand that something was not given to you that should have been. And the idea that you never got it could be devastating. It also can evoke feelings of unworthiness and hopelessness.

I remember once being in a yoga class where the teacher asked us to do an exercise related to healing trauma. We were supposed to stand in a circle, and we would recall a happy childhood memory where we felt loved and appreciated. And it dawned on me that I didn't have any memories. The old story about a grandmother sitting me on her lap and giving me freshly baked cookies didn't exist in my life. We were not in contact with my dad's side of the family, and my grandmother on my mother's side was mean. And since my dad was an alcoholic, and my days were full of stress and unknown, I was blocking any positive and happy memories. So when my turn came, I said I don't have happy memories. And others were looking at me like I was lying. And I was pretty sure, at that moment, that there were plenty of happy memories that I experienced during my childhood. But I couldn't remember any of them and was blocking them.

I got to listen to other people's memories. And that was one of the first times I realized that I wished I had a happy childhood as they did. An overwhelming wave of sadness came over me. That was when I reached the second stage of my grief. That is when the individual realizes they did have an abusive childhood and were unhappy with it. The childhood they thought they wanted to have, was never provided to them. And they feel like it was big injustice caused to them. Because every child should have a wonderful childhood and be loved, appreciated, and supported, that is the stage when an ACOA may feel angry, frustrated, and bitter at the caregivers. I have been myself in that stage for many years. ACOA can feel worse in this stage, feel guilty about themselves, feel bad about their childhood, and feel like they are betraying their family.

The third stage can lead to depression when ACOA resigns to their fate while still existing in a state of conflict with their loss. An individual might try to reverse the loss of perfect childhood by making it into a sacrifice. Turning to religion might become appealing, and all painful childhood activity might be turned into a spiritual experience where an individual believes he might be rewarded for that later, becoming a martyr. The mind tries to justify and explain what happened. Sadly, in this stage, grief is still intense, and grieving ACOAs may increasingly ruminate over the lost happy childhood, the experienced feelings of guilt and depression to the point where they won't let those emotions go. Especially if an individual felt like a victim and was used to getting attention when weak, they can hold on to the grief for a long time because it serves them.

The fourth stage of grief is when depression and despair are extreme since individuals might continuously think about how all this pain would have been avoided. This can lead to more suffering because

ACOA realizes nothing else can be done. The realization that it is too late, and none of the thinking or feeling a victim will change the past. This may be a very dark place to be. But it has a silver lining. When there is nothing to change, and grief becomes an inevitable state of mind, the individual accepts the situation as it is. It would be acceptance. The resistance to letting go is over.

The fifth stage is the acceptance that the individual did not have a happy childhood and lets go of their loss. They understand that feeling in pain and depression will lead them nowhere. The pain becomes too painful. They stop blaming the caregivers and parents for that lost childhood and then reach a state of peace with that. I reached this stage when I realized that no matter how painful my childhood was, my parents, especially my alcoholic father, never wanted to hurt my mother or me. I understood that my father also came from a broken home and did not know how to deal with his emotions or soothe his pain. He did the best that he could to numb his suffering with alcohol. This type of practice went from generation to generation. When I understood that my father once was a hurting toddler who did not know how to behave or regulate his emotions, I could forgive him with compassion. And by forgiving him, I forgive myself, and my grieving was over.

Within all of us, there are a child and an adult. When the feeling of grief arises, ask yourself what part of yourself is the source of this feeling. The child may be scared of losing something. The adult can understand that it is inevitable to lose something, and he can let it go. It is important to understand that you're not a child anymore. You can be in control, and you should control your life, feelings, and actions. You can choose right now to let that go. Allow yourself to grieve, let go of that feeling, and have a fantastic relationship with your parents and family. And then think about your extended family, your friends, and the great love and support you can receive for the rest of your life if you accept it.

If you feel you cannot just grieve and allow it to pass through you, ask yourself how that is serving you. Why are you afraid to let go of your grief? Maybe because that is the only connection that you have to the pain that you suffer through? Are you trying to justify somehow what happened to you? Those questions take time to hear and answer them. But dig deep inside yourself, and see how that is serving you. Why are you choosing to hold on to your grief? Does that make you feel special? Is that honoring your parents? Does holding on to that grief somehow make you validated? It is painful to hold on to that grief, no matter the reasons. It does not serve you. So, it's time to let that go. The way to go through grief is to leave the right out. Have a good cry, and be done with that. Taking care of grief will bring up anger and blame toward others. No matter what happens, you cannot change that, and you must accept it. After you feel like you've already blamed enough and been angry, sit with the grief and let it happen.

It is also imperative to recognize that future events will cause us grief. How can you soften grief that will arrive sometime in the future? By accepting the inevitable. Nothing lasts forever in this life, so let's accept it. The basis of all mourning and grief is attachment. Look at your life and identify the areas of attachment. Ask yourself what internal needs they satisfy. Do you have things or relationships that bring you emotional fulfillment? We may have an attachment to those. So naturally, when those have gone, you feel grief. Ask yourself, "how can I balance my life so I can decrease the extent and the degree of attachment?" The greater the attachment, the greater the overall fear of loss. We should ask ourselves why we feel so incomplete and empty that we need to reach for solutions in the form of attachments outside of ourselves. We should start looking at our areas of immaturity. Do we need to examine where we get love instead of giving it? The more attachments we have, the more vulnerable without the grief. When we have to acknowledge and let go of all negative feelings, we graduate from the smallness to the recognition of our greatness. Our inner joy should come from the pleasure of giving. Then we have nothing to lose, and we are fearless.

Exercises

Here are a few exercises that can help you to get better at grieving. You may use these exercises to grieve your loss of a happy childhood or anything you will lose over your lifetime. For example, you may use this approach when dealing with infidelity, loss of a job, or any other disappointment or failed expectation about someone or something.

Exercise #1. To let go of your grief and associated emotions, allow yourself to feel all the emotions that you will go through. You may take about 30 minutes, or even more if needed, to write a letter to your parents or caregivers, especially to the addict in the family. Write a letter about how angry you are at them, and express all your feelings about not having a happy childhood. That is the letter to let your emotions out and not to be sent to the actual person. You're welcome to discard the letter to let your pain go. If you don't want to write anything, you can imagine that that person is standing before you, and then you just let everything out. Tell them how disappointed you are, how angry you are, how hopeless you feel, and how you feel robbed of the perfect childhood that you rightfully had to have. If you feel that you didn't get this out in one day and in one sitting, then you can schedule an appointment with yourself where you will let go of more of your grief. And allow all the emotions to flow, even those frightening to you, like rage or extreme weeping. Stand by your side and honor your feelings.

Exercise #2. Another great way to let go of your grief and heal your trapped emotions is to create art. You can start painting with watercolors or draw something with pencils. Try singing and just letting your voice out, or listen to some song you already know and sing along to hear your voice. You may also express your grief and negative and blocked emotions through dance and body movement. The key in those artistic outlets is to allow yourself to feel what you feel and express your grief. Any emotion that we put the label on helps us to heal and release it.

Exercise #3. If you can, it is advisable to have a conversation with your parents or caregivers, especially with the person that is an addict. You may never get an apology from that person, but at least you can vocalize your pain and tell them how you feel. You should not expect anything to change because the person deep into addiction is in pain and cannot deal with his emotions. The conversation should be as closure and to improve your relationship. You're welcome to try your best, but never blame yourself or them if it does not happen as you hoped. Some situations are just tough to deal with and are impossible to heal.

Exercise #4. Have a conversation with your parents about your childhood. Focus on the positive things. If you like, write them down. Try to look through the old pictures and remember fun summer vacations and parties. Try to recuperate any memories that were favorable. I am sure that there were some experiences in your childhood that were joyful. And if you can't remember any happy memories with your parents or caregivers, did you have experiences that warmed your heart with your neighbors, friends, and classmates? Try to find some ray of light in this dark past. You will reevaluate that your childhood was not only painful experiences but also some positive ones.

Your Superpower

*Because you have experienced grief and under-
stand what it is to lose, you can support other
people in their grief. You may help other people
in distress and be a great support system for
them when they are unsure how to deal with
something they lost.*

CHAPTER 19

Can't Stand Criticism

We live in such an opinionated society that it is tough to live without being criticized by someone. It is trendy to judge and be compared to others. That includes everything, the way you look, the way you move, what you eat, what you do, how you behave with others, how you dress, how you sleep, and how you breathe. If you watch the news or social media, you probably find out that someone will always criticize somebody else. Feeling righteous is very popular these days. So you will find someone, always, who will not agree with you. It is very hard to please everyone. It's impossible.

It reminds me of a joke about a man interviewing for a job. When asked what his most significant strength is, he proudly answers: "I am just incapable of understanding criticism." The interviewer raises his eyebrows and replies with, "Well, that looks more like a weakness to me." The man smiles, nods and enthusiastically replies, "Aw, thank you, sir!"

I think not all criticisms are the same. It's good to hear constructive criticism to improve yourself. There is no progress if we never compare ourselves to others. The only way to move forward is to measure how far you have come and how far others have come. Those who grow up in relatively normal families have a healthy understanding of themselves and the environment. They may have strong opinions on who they are and will not be easily manipulated or hurt by others' criticism.

In families without an addict, a child would be allowed to be himself and he would be allowed to express his feelings and emotions. He would be validated, and he would even be asked to express his opinions about things. Since it is impossible to live in this world without hearing criticism and facing other people's opinions about oneself, children from a more emotionally stable family would be better at handling criticism. Criticism in the everyday environment may be a perfect learning tool. But in a family with an addict, criticism was used as a weapon. At least, that is how the ACOA took it.

The Birth of Harsh Self-Criticism

Children can disagree with adults in an emotionally mature family, hold their beliefs, emotions, and thoughts, and be appreciated for who they are. But that is not how it works in a family dealing with an addict. Because children who grew up with an alcoholic felt emotionally unsupported, they cannot take criticism very well. As children, ACOAs did not receive enough attention, unconditional love, and security from their alcoholic father, mother, or caregiver. Those authority figures did not satisfy the child's needs for validation and approval, so naturally, when the child didn't get that, they assumed it was their fault. As a result, they take criticism as very harsh, harmful, and threatening. There was no balance of good and evil, of compliments and criticism. Mostly it was just criticism, not feeling good enough, no matter what they did. At some point, the child concludes that they must not be worthy of receiving love and attention at all.

In addition to justifying why others are critical of them, they make situations worse by being very critical of themselves, no matter how well they do something. They frequently beat themselves up for being less than their parents expected them to be. Even if the result of their actions is better than others expect, ACOAs might see it as not enough. They might become so harsh and unreasonably self-deprecating that they believe their parents were drunk because they, the child, displayed unacceptable behavior. That is just ridiculous to think that way. A child does not influence why the parent or caregiver is an addict.

I had a classmate, let's call him Tim. His parents were both alcoholics. He was always studying very hard for everything. He would be terrified to go home when he got a less-than-perfect grade. I don't know what happened in his house when Tim received a perfect grade, but he somehow associated his grades and performance with being accepted. So it is no surprise that later, once I caught up with him as an adult, Tim had become a workaholic. He was telling me that he didn't understand why his wife left him. He gave his all to his work, being perfect, winning rewards, bringing more business to the company, and but he still was not good enough for his wife. In his mind, to be accepted, he had to work hard, he had to produce something, and he had to prove his worth.

In my case, I did not receive that much criticism from my alcoholic father because he did not even care about me. Or he would drink away from home, wake up hungover, and watch TV all day without talking to me. He gave me no attention, not negative, not positive.

Avoiding Conflict

ACOAs may not have gotten enough positive attention, validation, love, and affection, but they were getting plenty of neglect and conflict in the family. It might start from an addict being just in a bad mood and seeing a child doing something in front of them, and that would set off a conflict. Many times conflict can start with criticism. An alcoholic father accidentally trips on Legos on the floor and yells at his son for being so disorganized. An alcoholic mother could be very critical of her daughter and disapprove of her dress or any other way she looks. It may be just a comment that the addict said without thinking much. But the child took it as harsh criticism, and those words went directly into the heart. And early on, a child also learns that arguing with an addict or trying to prove a point and explain why they behaved one way or another never worked, and it just induces conflict and more yelling. Because of fear of conflict, an ACOA may have learned to avoid conflict altogether.

Do you remember using any conflict avoidance techniques while you were growing up? For example, did you withdraw to your room after being criticized? Did you leave this space physically or mentally? How did you protect yourself? You may have used different strategies to avoid conflict to feel safe and run things smoothly, to keep the calm in the family. This strategy may seem very effective and the proper way to react to the situation to avoid anxiety and stress.

Conflict avoidance is a good strategy while the child is growing up in a dysfunctional family. But does not serve the adult trying to live a responsible, mature life. Avoiding conflict becomes a routine, the only way the child knows how to function in a highly stressful environment. This type of reinforcement and belief that this kind of approach works in any situation, whether it is a work environment or a personal relationship, does not work from the adult point of view in the long run. Nevertheless, that is the usual way an ACOA acts during a conflict. It can change only by creating new coping strategies.

I have seen this happening in my own life as an adult and my friends' lives as well. One of my friends, let's call her Doreen, told me that she will not visit her alcoholic mother anymore because she is tired of listening to how inadequate she is. Doreen had been dealing with childhood trauma for a very long time and decided at some point that she wanted to be separated from her mother because she did not feel like she was good enough. Whenever she sees her mother, the first thing that comes out of her mother's mouth is criticism: "Why did you put this dress on? This is not your color." Or if Doreen has lunch with her mother, her mother will ask, "Why are you ordering this? You're obese as you are." So my friend, instead of confronting her mother about the criticism, chose to avoid her mother altogether. And at the same time, she felt guilty for not being able to see her mother. I advised her to let that go because there was no hope that her mother would realize how much she was hurting her daughter. Doreen needed to change her point of view about her mother, which was very hard for her. After realizing that her mother also grew up being criticized by her mother, Doreen had empathy for her. Only then was she able to revisit her.

Avoiding conflict altogether also doesn't work in confronting an issue. ACOAs never ask for a raise because they're afraid of being seen as ungrateful. They might never confront an abusive relationship and act like everything is fine because they don't want to induce conflict. They may allow others to walk all over them because they don't want to be hurt. Because of fear of conflict, rejection, and abandonment, the ACOA may need to learn how to negotiate successfully at work for a better position or pay, for better personal development, and for being supported and respected. Because ACOA is afraid to create a conflict, it may be coerced into doing something illegal, improper, or even hurtful towards itself or others. It is imperative to learn how to face criticism and be able to give criticism to others. Those skills can be learned and helped to manage everyday stress in the work environment and personal relationships.

Using Conflict as a Way To Get Attention

On the other spectrum of this issue, criticism can be taken as a way of life. Since fights and disagreements were everyday experiences in dysfunctional families, ACOA learned that this conflict, being critical of others, is the norm. They learned to use disagreements and conflicts as a regular part of their lives. An ACOA needs to learn how to communicate appropriately. There is a possibility that learned conflicts are seen as an opportunity to receive attention. And since ACOA is starved for attention, support and affection, causing conflict and being criticized is the only way to get attention from others.

The child who grew up in an environment where they saw that conflicts were everyday communication between family members will grow up into adults who will use such communication with others. They may seem like they are always looking for conflict, like they are constantly criticizing others about how they look or act. The truth is, behind that, a lonely individual is looking for attention. So instead of having an open line of communication with the other person and asking them for support and attention, they do something to invoke conflict. That inevitably poisons any relationship. And ultimately, they may end up losing people in their lives, the people they care for. And just because they cannot express their emotions and ask for help, they were not taught how to communicate emotions and ask for help. ACOA may not see the harm in their interactions because this type of communication was used by their families while they were growing up. ACOA may have learned great ways how to cope with difficult situations and deal with conflict based on previous experiences but may have yet to learn how to act in healthy interpersonal relationships.

Try to evaluate the environment you grew up in and what that has to do with criticism. Can you calmly take constructive criticism towards who you are and what you do? Or do you take it personally? Do you criticize others to invoke conflict, to get attention from them? You can change that. You can change your point of view about the people who criticize you, and you may start listening to critiques about your work from a constructive point of view. You may still change your behavior towards others in your relationships without conflict. Here are a few exercises you should use to identify how critical you are of yourself and how you can handle conflict. As for any habits, it takes time to identify your patterns and create new habits.

Exercises

Here are a few exercises that can help you with criticizing yourself and others.

Exercise #1. When you hear someone criticizing you, try not to jump to the conclusion that whatever they are saying is true. Many things said by other people have nothing to do with you but with their insecurities. Always take other people's opinions with a grain of salt. When you hear someone criticizing you, ask yourself, "Is this person qualified to criticize me? Is this person the expert in what they are pointing out to me? Can this person be trusted?" Judging their remarks to ensure they are truthful and worthy of attention is imperative. Someone can harshly critique your work because they feel insecure, not because your work is worthless. And if you need help with authoritative figures, it may be hard not to listen to them. You need to understand that this fear of criticism comes from your childhood when you believed others could harm you. Now you are an adult and you can defend yourself.

Exercise #2. Remember the remarks about your looks, performance, and actions told to you by your addicted parent or caregiver when you were a child. Write down those remarks on the left piece of paper. Then, on the right side of the paper, investigate how you look at yourself from your adult point of view. For example, did your alcoholic father tell you that you are not a good singer, but your music teacher asked you to join the choir because you have a divine voice? Or your alcoholic mother told you that you are fat, but other girls in the neighborhood were striving to look like you? This exercise must prove to you that your authorities are not necessarily correct. The harsh words often come from the pain; it is time to forgive them and forget their remarks for your own good. If you can't forgive them, then clarify to yourself that their critique was wrong.

Exercise #3. It is a good idea to ask the experts about your work and get constructive criticism. Decide on the area that you want to improve in your life. Let's say it's your career. Do you have a supervisor that can give you constructive criticism? Do you have a coworker who's an expert? You should go and talk to them. Ask them for a review of your work, how you can improve, and how you can advance in your workplace. Just make sure you ask someone who is an expert and capable of giving you good advice. Then listen to what they say, and take action to improve yourself. You can also ask a few of your trusted best friends to give you some ideas on how you can improve your skills or your personal development. You will be surprised how differently you view yourself from how others do. Collect as many opinions as possible, and then decide whether you need to act on them.

Exercise #4. Catch yourself criticizing yourself during the day. In what instances do you criticize yourself? It can be as small as thinking to yourself, "Oh, I could have done so much better explaining what I meant at that meeting." Do you criticize yourself for still losing five pounds, even if you exercise five times a week? Do you want to be happier when you pay for the food you share with your friends? Ask yourself, "Would I say this to my friend?" Probably not. If your friend said they had doubts about how well they expressed them-selves at a meeting, you would say, "You did great. Others didn't say anything at all!" If your friend complained about those last five pounds on their body, you would remind them how great they look and that they lost the other thirty just this year! And if your friend had second thoughts about enjoying a meal with you, you would be offended. So start paying attention to what negative remarks you give yourself. Pay attention and write them down so you can see the pattern and change it.

Exercise #5. Let's look at how you criticize others. If you grew up in an environment where it is normal to criticize others just for the sake of it, you might be inclined to do the same thing to others. Ask yourself whether you criticize others to start an argument to get attention. Start observing yourself daily and list all the times it happens while you speak with your friends, while you interact with your coworkers, and when you talk to service people at a restaurant. Start a list of the times you criticize someone for how they look, what they say, what they thought, or what they did. It does not matter what kind of criticism you give. Ask yourself if it was worth it. The goal is to see a pattern that you display towards others. Are there particular people that you criticize the most? Is there a particular pet peeve that you cannot stand? But above all, you need to ask yourself if your critique was worthy of giving or was just something to prove that you are in control and above somebody else. When you have enough items on the list and you can identify your patterns, it will help you avoid making these comments in the future. Learn to critique someone only when they ask for it, give it as advice, give it as something to inspire someone to change, as constructive criticism. Avoid hurting other people's feelings just to argue.

Exercise #6. Ask your significant others, friends, and coworkers with whom you spend a lot of time to point out when you start criticizing yourself. If you write down your habits, you may identify some particular things about yourself that you don't like. Next, evaluate if criticizing yourself will bring positive change in you. If you think it will, then you should take action to change things. And if you don't, you need to ask yourself why you keep doing it. And if you don't want to change something about yourself, then you stop criticizing yourself about it.

Exercise #7. Think of people that you are in the relationship with. Do you criticize them? Why do you criticize them? Please write down the things about each of them that you criticize, then ask yourself why you want to do that. Is that something you don't like, or is it something your abusive parent didn't like? Is that negative opinion coming from you or your childhood trauma? The opinion you hold about them might not be even yours. Then, decide how badly you want something to change. None of us like to be told what we need to do. It might be challenging for someone to keep listening to you if you always criticize them. If you notice that your critiques of other people don't work, it's time to conclude that they will not change. Then learn how to live with that. If you conclude you cannot live with something you criticize about another person, you should leave that relationship.

Your Superpower

Because you criticize yourself, you strive to achieve more and do it better. You push yourself for better results no matter what you do, are an achiever, and inspire others.

CHAPTER 20

Codependency

Our relationships guarantee our survival as species, and through healthy relationships, we achieve a healthy level of autonomy. Limbic resonance is the idea that we can pick up on others' moods. I read that group physiology and emotional stability resonate among the group. And children depend on their parents to radiate neuro synchrony to regulate their mental capacity for self-directedness to emerge. Parents need to be stable and emotionally healthy to provide safety for their children's mental state. Attachment determines the ultimate nature of a child's mind and guides self-preservation and emotional regulation. Basically, it means we learn how to regulate our emotions from our parents.

Fertile Ground for Anxiety

Due to the lack of a balanced environment, children from a family with an addict didn't get the proper emotional care and felt unsafe. The way that the brain processes trauma makes ACOA hypervigilant of their environment. We might be sensitive and watch for signs from others that we might be disappointed or rejected by others, and we constantly scan our surroundings to detect, treat, and cater to other people's needs and try to predict the next moves to keep us safe. That is how codependency is born.

It causes constant stress and keeps us stuck in chronic anxiety. Cortisol, a hormone released when we are stressed, shuts down the hippocampus, which is the part of the brain that helps us accurately to perceive and read other people and the environment. It helps supply context and helps us understand how we should act towards a threat. When it is not functioning correctly, we tend to disconnect from our true selves, feel lost, and anxiety takes over. And to feel safe, we need to control the outcome. Chronic and unregulated stress can lead to physical sickness.

We tend to misread other people's facial expressions or vocal tones and can misinterpret someone completely. When the other person is making us anxious, we need to control them. Maybe that other person has insecurities and comes with their own traumas that are difficult to manage. Then we get into situations where we get into arguments or misunderstandings only later to find out that, honestly, nothing happened that we should have been upset about.

When we feel threatened, we feel like we need to control their mood in the mistaken perception that if we can get them to change, we will feel less stressed. And it does not come from a feeling of wanting to control them or being superior. It is not like we think we know better and they should listen to us. It comes from self-preservation. When I was living with my parents, I wanted them to be happy no matter what. I made sure to be funny enough to raise their mood, and I wanted to do things that satisfied them. If my parents were in a bad mood, I would start a conversation with an emotional charge and make them direct their anger towards that subject, like politics or the weather, or someone they knew. That would help them just to be upset at something and let that energy go.

I would participate in those conversations and see how the mood changed. They were angry, but not at me. I was safe. When their mood changed for the better, my mood would change for the better as well.

Only then would I feel that the worst was over and I'd dodged the bullet. My strategy was similar to wanting to control the situation or people-please, but there are differences. People pleasing is a way of manipulating others and preventing a situation from going not the way an ACOA wants. Controlling the situation and others' behaviors can be bullying. Codependency is an ACOA's feeling the other person is a part of their unit and can't be safe unless the other person feels good. All of those actions seek the same outcome, to be safe.

Codependency in Relationships

Being codependent and trying to influence the household situation during childhood is one thing. It gets trickier in intimate relationships when one person is codependent on another person's mood. ACOA can feel the need to cheer or manipulate their spouses' moods when they are upset. When we see someone upset, we feel our livelihood depends on it, and we try to change it.

We project our needs onto others because we are not taught how to identify our feelings. Codependency is not postponing one's need; it is the projection of personal needs that we don't recognize within ourselves onto another person. It becomes more apparent when we feel stressed.

The joke comes to mind: "A codependent person is someone who puts a sweater on someone else believing that it will make themselves warm." Because the codependent person is not allowed to identify, validate and take care of their own feelings, they project their feelings onto others and then try to take care of them. It is easier to take care of others' feelings than their own. It is also easier to care for other people's needs than their own. Because we were not allowed to, we don't know how to do it. Because of this, ACOA tend to tune in so much to others that they lose their identity. They lose themselves in others' feelings.

Codependency is extra complicated for daughters of alcoholics. By default, women can tune in to other people's feelings to nurture and help a baby survive. That works well in a family not touched by alcoholism. However, women who grew up with alcoholics in the household report a higher need for control, overreaction to change, feeling responsible for more than they can handle, difficulty with intimacy, and judging themselves too harshly.

Similarities Between the Narcissist and an Addict

Codependency reaches three generations. It starts with a child growing up in a dysfunctional family and being taught how to codepend on adults. The second stage is when an ACOA is grown and forms codependent relationships with other adults. And the third stage is when a codependent ACOA becomes a parent themselves and influences the lives of their children.

ACOA parents carry this codependency on to their children by being overprotective, expecting too much out of them, worrying too much, and not allowing the child to express themselves. It is a good thing to be able to pick up the moods of others, but it is not healthy to project your feelings onto others. Then the mother projects her aspirations onto the child and sees it not as a separate person with its individuality but as an extension of herself. When the child is not getting the opportunity to become the person they want to be and has to act as their parents want them to, they grow up constantly searching for someone to validate them and accept them as they are. Sadly, that search might never bring results because healing trauma truly depends on healing the codependency and finding and loving yourself.

Growing up in an environment where everything is about narcissistic parents, the addict's needs, the child has no space to grow up as an individual. Since their environment is in constant flux and child is stressing about how to please the adults, being fearful of becoming a problem when they express their needs, they learn to stay quiet and well-behaved.

Due to one parent or caregiver being an alcoholic and not functioning fully as a provider, the other parent might be working double time to fulfill the duties of both parents. Ultimately, the child is left without being taken care of as it should be. There are plenty of families where siblings take care of each other. Then there is no room for their child's needs, and the child learns codependency. Since narcissistic parents become the center of the child's universe, it learns to please every parent's needs first before attempting to meet their own needs. Many times, ACOA will glorify the addict parent, try to meet their every wish, and learn not to ask or respond to their own needs. They know it is not a good idea to ask for their needs to be met so they avoid acknowledging their own needs. Many ACOAS don't expect their needs to be met by others. They learn to give and give, but never to receive.

Living with an addict might look like living with a narcissist. ACOA might learn that behavior of demanding their needs be met by The narcissist feels like the other person is an extension of themselves. They expect others to meet their needs, and the different opinions of others or any individual scares them.

Addiction creates a similar environment for others around them as narcissists in that they preoccupy other people with their needs and desires. It is similar because no matter how much you try or how good you are, it is never enough, and you will always come second and be neglected. It is tough when one parent is an alcoholic and another is sober but a narcissist. Those children have adults to take care of first, neglecting themselves, believing that is what life is, always serving and pleasing others without meeting their own needs. That is what happened in my case. I am also an only child, so I had no support or possibility of being consoled. I had, and still have, a challenging time meeting my own needs. I remember working overtime every week to meet my coworkers' needs and wanted to please them so much that I sacrificed my time, energy, and sanity to the point that I couldn't take it anymore.

Addicts and narcissists are immature. As a result, narcissists get do not develop past being a self-centered child where all they care about is themselves.

In that way, a narcissist's needs are similar to the addict's immaturity. Addicts prioritize their own needs above everything else. Both types end up in lavish fantasies and manipulate others by assuring their low self-esteem. The unions of narcissists and addicts are widespread.

Sadly, both types are lonely inside, need to feel accepted, and feel like strangers in their own skin and in relationships. Close ones who love an addict or a narcissist can feel rage and loneliness over time due to not being loved back.

Since narcissists see others as an extension of themselves without individuality, wants, and needs, it is tough on their children. A narcissist looks at others and asks themselves, "What can they do for me?" Children require attunement from mature adults to learn how to live their life. Children learn from their parents how to perceive this world, and when they are not permitted to be themselves, it is a shocking, disappointing, and very lonely experience. The ACOA becomes the parent that narcissists never had. They demand to be admired, seen, cared for, and loved. It just happens that they are seeking this from their children, that the children should be the ones who show care and admiration.

For ACOA not to feel lonely, they cater to addicts and narcissists and try to flatter and take care of every whim and please their parents no matter what. Since the addict and the narcissist don't care how others feel, they soak up all the energy and attention the child gives them. Due to the need for survival, children feel as if their life depends on their parents, so they give themselves away without leaving anything to themselves, as comes from energy to time. More than that, ACOA doesn't even know they should care for their own needs instead of their parents. Nothing is more critical to a child than being seen by their parent, no matter who they are. I am sure you have seen children doing something and shouting, "mom, mom, look at me, look what I can do!" When a child doesn't get the needed attention from the parents, he feels neglected and lonely.

It is tough on the child to choose between pleasing a narcissist by rejecting yourself and your own needs or pushing them away and being discarded as useless. Sadly, narcissists can seem helpless and manipulate the child into pleasing them. If the child disobeys, they ignore the child, degrade them, and even guilt their children into submitting to their whims. Narcissists don't allow the child to grow up and become their individual self. They discourage that because it is convenient to keep the child feeling helpless. It is a harrowing and demoralizing experience. An ACOA understands that the parent doesn't see them for who they are and they know that they can't be ever loved. Since the narcissist would take disobedience as a personal threat and punish the child, there is no way out of this situation until the child grows up and leaves the house. Sadly, this tough codependency is not left behind. ACOA find other people to recreate the same relationship as with their addict or narcissistic parent.

If you are still unsure if you have codependency traits, then answer a few questions. Do you need to check in with the other person and get their permission and validation for whatever you do? When the other person hurts you, do you feel sorry for the other person, even though they were the ones who hurt you? Would you do anything for the other person if they ask you to do it, even though you think it's wrong? Would you agree that the other person's opinion about everything is correct? Do you always put the other person first, no matter how depleted you are physically and emotionally? Do you feel like walking on eggshells to avoid conflict with the other person? Are you afraid to tell them no?

Exercises

The good news is not all is lost. Starting to work on your codependency now, and being persistent with it, will bring results. Here are a few things you can do to help yourself identify your codependency and use different exercises to help yourself to let go of it.

Exercise #1. Take time to remember and write down how you acted when your parents or caregivers were in a bad mood, sad, upset, or angry. Did you try to console them? Did you try to make them laugh? Or did you keep trying to do something different, like talking them into quitting drinking? Do you remember something that you did that worked to appease them? Pay attention to what emotions your memories bring. Identify as many details as possible and look for the patterns.

Exercise #2. Remember how you usually act when your significant other is sad, upset, angry, or any other negative emotion. This also applies to the people in your life that you care about, such as friends, and workers, neighbors. Do you feel personally responsible for their happiness and well-being? Do you honor their emotions and let them just be? Or do you try to change how they feel to keep the balance and peace? How does that make you feel when they decide to do something very different than you expected or want them to do? If you cannot remember past experiences, start writing down new ones as they come up, so you can return and see the patterns. Then, take a very close look and your behavior towards them. Ask yourself if the current situation with them brings up your memory of the past and how you acted while you were in your parents' household. Do you see similarities in how you act toward others? Do you react the same way in your adult life with the people you care about as you act with your parents and caregivers?

Exercise #3. When you identify the same patterns that you are apply-ing in your adult life borrowed from your childhood, now is the time to change that. Pick a few situations that keep on repeating. Then list a few actions you can do next time this situation arises. If you need help with what to do in a particular situation, ask your friends and people who care about you, and understand your situation for advice. Try out different actions to change your pattern. Especially when dealing with other people in a codependent relationship, it could be tough to change your patterns and take action, but do not give up and stick to it to make the change.

Exercise #4. Find your true self by asking yourself what you like to do by yourself. It is time to realize that you are an adult now and can take care of yourself in your own needs. Take small steps, no matter small, toward the separation in the relationship.

Exercise #5. Find new friends and increase your friendship circle. If you don't feel like going to groups where you don't know people, like a church, art group, or any other hobby, then start making friends in an environment where you already feel comfortable. If you are at work and you know that you like to converse with coworkers, ask them out and do activities outside the office. It is okay if your coworkers do not want to engage with you outside the office walls. Do not be harsh on yourself when someone declines your offer. Don't take it personally. We all have our daily lives, and only some look for new friends. Try to be in a place where you can meet new people and start friendships.

Exercise #6. Identify the person in your environment where you feel there is a dependency. Then monitor during the day how often you think about them, how often you want to please them, how often you want to call them, write them, and get in touch with them. Trying to make it less of an action every day. Focus your attention on yourself. If you find it difficult not to text someone and seek validation from them, ask a friend who cares about you to be your accountability partner.

They can help you change your patterns by messaging or calling them instead of the person you feel codependency with. Initially, it may look terrifying to you, but with time, you will see that you are safe even if you do not check in with that person every single day or constantly message or talk to them.

Your Superpower

Because you care about how other people feel and cater to their needs to make them feel better, you may have a lot of friends come on if you allow that. Others like being around you because you see that you invest in relationships.

CHAPTER 21

Difficulty Finding the Right Mate

Let's face it, we are herd animals and need others. We need to keep our relationship with others for better or worse. Relationships are one of the main areas that most people struggle with. Even individuals who grew up in seemingly balanced and loving families may still struggle with relationships. Relating can be stressful; even relationship gurus have stressful days with their partners. Relationships are like dancing with a partner. Some days, the dance flows, and one leads while the other follows. And there are days when both partners step on each other's toes. It is essential to understand that having a flawless dance every day is tough. However, we should realize that stepping on toes is not necessarily a deadly experience. Others help us to see a part of us that we didn't know before. We need others in our lives to grow.

Unfortunately, in our society, we expect others to behave like us out of fear. If someone behaves differently than us, then we are afraid of it and we will fight it. Even if a friend disagrees with the group's opinion and takes a different action, they can be seen as an enemy. For example, I started implementing healthy life choices in my daily life and I say no to certain foods and activities while visiting my friends. I was surprised to see how many of them felt offended by my choices. All this was happening due to fear of different choices. It took time for them to realize that I would not change my food choices to keep them comfortable. I explained that just because I made different food choices than them, it does not invalidate their choice; they can eat whatever they want, and I am not stopping them from doing whatever they want. Obviously, their fear came from the "if you are not with me, you are against me" mentality. This can be seen in any relationship.

Everyone Has Different Needs

The world would be much better if we allowed ourselves to do what we want and others to do what they want. Let's take it further. Do you remember the saying, treat others as you want to be treated? The saying is flawed. Treat others as they want to be treated. We all are different. That is the beauty of living on this planet. Then why not celebrate our differences? Relationships would be so much easier if we would give others what they need instead of giving them what we need. We should understand that being different doesn't mean it is wrong, and it is just different.

I remember a joke I read once. It goes something like this: "they say when you meet the right person, you know immediately. When you meet the wrong person, it takes about a year and a half to figure it out." That made me laugh. If we love someone, we want to give them everything we like. We will do anything to please them, improve their lives, and love them back. We may believe that we know that person so well that we can decide what is better for them. But that's not true. That person knows what is better for them. And if someone came from a dysfunctional family and has childhood trauma, they're afraid even to look at themselves, let alone to tell you what they want. Because they, themselves, are not sure what they want. Anything that you do, you are guessing that your decision will be correct and will make them happy. In addition, if they need to know what you want, but you don't even know what you want, there is no way to find out if you are compatible in the first place.

So let's say that you want them to be happy, and you want to fulfill their needs. That means you will put your own needs aside. Let's say your significant other loves being at home and does not like traveling or being alone without you. Conversely, you love traveling and have a job that fulfills you but keeps you away from home most of the time. Obviously, this is a very extreme example. A lot of differences happen on a more subtle level. With this example, they will not be happy with you being away from home, and you will not be happy if they tell you to stay home. If you don't know that person well, or they don't even know themselves, you may marry them and expect them to be happy for who you are and what you give them.

The problem arises when two people are very different and have different needs. My mother told me long ago that she admired my father for being the life of the party. She remembered him as a funny guy who could make anyone laugh, full of amazing stories, a great dancer, and made everyone feel at ease. But then, when they got married, she expected him to stay home, be happy with married life, settle down, and pay attention only to her. She was not a person to go out much and she expected him to do the same. As a teenager, I had already figured out something was wrong with the picture. My mom was expecting my dad to be a different person, but he had different needs.

Obviously, this type of relationship can only last for a while because the one person will feel like the other person is not giving their best and will feel neglected. And in return, the other person will feel overwhelmed by the first person constantly being in their environment. You may ask why two different people choose to be in a relationship and live under the same roof. It is because both of them have very different attachment needs that were developed during childhood. Childhood is when we define what it means to love someone and belong to someone, what it means to feel safe, and who we can trust. Family patterns from childhood impact our choices of partners, how we reach for love, and meet our needs.

Pain Equals Love

Since ACOA grew up in a dysfunctional family, they might believe pain equals love, and painful relationships might feel normal. Suppose they saw parents or caregivers constantly arguing, abusing each other emotionally or even physically, seeing them invalidating each other, and gaslighting. In that case, they might not have a good and healthy relationship model to begin with. Many stay in relationships out of fear or for survival. Many experienced traumas in their childhood and don't even know what normal is.

If you don't feel loved in a relationship, it means that you are not compatible. For relationships to work, both people must feel they're getting what they want. They need to be loved, accepted, and seen for who they are. And that's true even for relationships that aren't romantic. Any partnership or friendship needs this type of intimacy, where both individuals should feel comfortable being who they are and expressing themselves to the other person.

To be loved, first, you need to start with yourself. Do you need to ask yourself what love means to you? Are you seeking pain because pain equals love? Are you courageous enough to look deep inside yourself and be honest about your needs? If you grew up in an environment where the only attention you were given was punishment, emotional or even physical abuse, you might take any attention even if it hurts. Or you may even want to be constantly rejected. I know it may sound absurd. But after long contemplations, I realized that I was attracting relationships into my life that allowed me not to commit fully to them and keep me at a distance. Investing myself entirely was very scary. I was attracted to emotionally unavailable, narcissistic men who made me feel rejected. Since I thought that was normal, I subconsciously sought them out. Once I took time to find my true self, be honest with myself, discover my needs, and heal my childhood trauma, my relationships tremendously improved. I was able to accept myself and others as they are.

The only way to have healthy relationships and to understand other people is to take time to get to know them better on a deeper level. This means listening to them when they talk without interrupting them, pushing your opinions onto them, or giving unsolicited advice. This means you have to observe their behavior without judgment and see their preferences, what they like and don't like. Even if they like different things than you, you need to ask questions about their thoughts and feelings and encourage them to talk freely, without judgment, and with compassion and forgiveness. Try to understand them and see things from their point of view without feeling threatened. Remember? Different doesn't mean it's wrong, just different.

Then you ask yourself whether you are ready for this. Can you invest in another person to know them better? Or is that something that scares you? Or do you feel like if you help them discover who they are, they will leave you alone because you don't worry about love? Then ask yourself what kind of attachment style you have. What causes your fear? You may have difficulty answering those questions because you were taught not to trust your feelings about something, your feelings were invalidated, and your needs were discarded. You may have grown up in an environment where you thought that you and anything associated with you were unimportant. Since a young age, an ACOA has been taught to sacrifice for the family's good, not to be selfish, and to be subordinate to the adults. They need help identifying and honoring their needs. Martyrdom and serving others became a mantra for the ACOA, which is difficult to break. There are many religions that support and reward victimhood. Do you need to ask yourself why you're doing something? Are you doing this for yourself or for someone else's well-being? Of course, there is nothing wrong with doing something for others as long as you honor and love yourself first.

Relationship dynamics that an ACOA learns are influenced by a few factors. First, we already established that an environment that houses an addict is not the best environment for a growing and developing child. To grow into a happy and well-functioning individual, a child needs to have stability, balance, support, and safety from the immediate environment. The most painful part is that the child does not have a support system from their parents. There needs to be clarity about where the child can go when stressed. If the parents should protect the child, but they cannot do that, where should the child go? It is trapped

Since the addict causes havoc in the family, the child must find that haven somewhere else. It can be a family member that lives with the family, like an uncle, aunt, or grandparent, that gives emotional support to the growing child. Research has shown that children who had another adult as a role model, who gave them love, support, and safety, were in much better shape than those who didn't. And to be honest, I did not have that save haven at my house. I was even ashamed to talk about what was happening inside my family, was ashamed to complain to anyone about what was going on and how we were treated.

In addition, the child must have support outside the family. Was there a place where a child even momentarily could feel out of harm's way and feel supported, soothed, and was modeled a different behavior? Was there a neighbor, friend, grandparent, or teacher the child could confide to? It is also essential to know how long the ACOA spent with the addict in the family. Was it their entire childhood, or only a few years? The trauma tends to be cumulative over a significant period. Less time, less trauma. How old was the child when the parent or caregiver became an addict? If those traumas occurred before the child turned seven, they could be imprinted for the rest of their life. Only through inner work can healing occur and release the damage caused by the trauma.

Attachment Styles

Due to those factors, the child creates a unique image and expectation for relationships. A few different attachment styles influence how we relate to others. Knowing those types will help us understand others better, understand where they are coming from, their needs, and how to make the relationship successful.

An anxious attachment style describes an individual who may be more likely to have concerns about their partner's behavior and doubts about their partner's commitment and loyalty. Those are the jealous types. Due to low self-esteem, the fear of abandonment from childhood, and the belief that they are unworthy of love, they need constant reassurance from their partner that they are loved and appreciated. If they don't get attention, support, appreciation, and constant reassurance that they are needed, they will feel abandoned and unhappy in the relationship.

Avoidant attachment style indicates that the person is more independent and likes being by themselves. They rely on themselves and usually do not accept or hear other people's opinions. Self-reliance learned in childhood makes them uncomfortable depending on and relying on others in adulthood. They may even view themselves negatively, with a loss of judgment, and feel unworthy of love and support. They may even get triggered by an anxious attachment style partner who constantly needs closeness. Avoidant partners will feel claustrophobic in the relationship and need to withdraw to create emotional and physical distance to meet their needs.

The disorganized attachment style may be characterized by lack of consistent behavior and relationships and may confuse their partner. One day they may be needy, demanding attention, and the next day they may be dismissive and distant. As a result, those individuals experience chaotic relationships filled with instability and unpredictability. In addition, they and other attachment styles view themselves negatively and as unworthy of love due to childhood trauma.

The secure attachment style is the most balanced and healthy style that feels confident in who they are. They have a healthy balance between being in close relationships and needing independence. They feel comfortable depending on others, uncomfortable accepting help from others. They have a healthy point of view about themselves, they have done the work, and know their worth. The secure attachment style knows they are loved, appreciated, and worthy of love. Hence, they can help other attachment styles understand themselves better and heal.

Exercises

Here are a few exercises below that will help you learn more about you and your partner's attachment style and how it can lead to a happy, fulfilling relationship. Better yet, have your partner do the same tests as you and have a conversation about each other's needs.

Exercise #1. Be truthful to yourself, your feelings, thoughts, likes, dislikes, and needs. Indeed, ask yourself what it is that you want. Do you have a belief about what you need because someone told you that? Did you come up with the list of needs yourself, or did you listen to someone who told you they knew what was better for you? And be honest with yourself, do not be afraid to tell yourself what you are. Write in your diary every day and then look back and find patterns. Observe those patterns. Did they ever change? This exercise is not here to judge yourself. You need to be forgiving and patient with yourself, and you are just observing your patterns. Being honest with yourself is an excellent start for a change in healing.

Exercise #2. Identify what type of attachment style you have. There are plenty of tests you can do for free online that will tell you your type, give you an extended description of that type of personality, and even give advice on what to do about it. You may also have a mix of different attachment styles, and that's okey. That is just a tool to learn more about yourself, so it can guide you and help you in your healing process.

Exercise #3. Think about your parents and caregivers you grew up with, including your family members and friends. When you get more familiar with attachment styles, write a list of people in your life and, next to their names, try to identify what kind of attachment types they have. Is there an attachment style that is very common in your family?

It would not be a surprise because that means that you learned that from the adults. If you have a family member or close friend with a different personality type, ask yourself how it is that serving you to be in that kind of relationship. Some attachment styles go very well together and look like a happy relationship from outside. Become an investigator and pay attention to how people behave, identify their attachment styles, and see how those types work together. Then ask yourself how you fit in with other people, what serves you, and what doesn't. It may be time to move on if you are in a relationship with someone incompatible, and your attachment styles don't work well together.

Exercise #4. Think about your current relationships. How do you feel about those people? Did you ever try to change them? Did you think to yourself that your life would be so much better and you would be much happier if other people would change the way you want them to change? What did you do so far to make them change? How much success did you have? And then, think about yourself and evaluate your change through the years. How did you act 20 or 10 years ago? Do you act the same? Why did your behavior change?

Your Superpower

Because you learned from early childhood to disregard your own needs and put up with turbulent relationships, you have more patience with the difficulties that arise in relationships. As a result, you may have more patience towards your partner and try harder to preserve the relationship, for better or worse.

CHAPTER 22

Need Immediate Gratification

It is a natural human desire to want things that make us happy and get them immediately. The most desirable things we want are food, sleep, entertainment, and recreation. And some things must be acquired on time, for example, food or sleep. During pre-modern times, decisions that had to do with survival needed to be made quickly. Today, humans don't have predators, and we no longer need to act that fast. So, we focused our attention beyond survival. Instant gratification means giving in to the temptation to receive things immediately, even though waiting to receive those things will be more rewarding. It is all about avoiding pain and seeking pleasure.

Here are a few examples of instant gratification, in case you think you are really good at managing temptations, and you just shook your head at the idea that we do things that hurt us. Have you ever indulged in a high-sugar and high-fat treat, like a donut or chocolate? Even if you know it would be better for you to snack on a carrot? Have you ever skipped a workout and gone out with your friends for a few drinks, even though you know you should not drink empty calories and you know that skipping a workout will not achieve your fitness goals? Have you ever hit the snooze button as soon as you heard your alarm go off, even though you promised you would wake up early and meditate? Have you ever bought anything with a credit card even though you knew you could not afford it? The list can go on.

And let's admit it, we live in an instant gratification world. Starting with the VIP passes, membership specials, watching movies without commercial breaks, clicking a button, and immediately receiving a result. It is hard not to want to receive pleasure right away.

I remember seeing a cartoon showing runners lined up for a start. Above them was a sign: "Instant gratification, zero-mile run." Next to the lined-up participants, a man was standing and yelling: "OK, runners, get ready. Go!... OK, now come fetch your T-shirts." The cartoon made me laugh, but to tell you the truth, I often feel like one of those runners. And I have no patience for slow walkers or slow drivers. I expect immediate results. If I am calling someone, I expect them to answer. If I send a message to someone, I expect them to send me a message back. If I get an idea to do something, I need to do it right then. And waiting to receive something when I want it right away is very stressful. I'm sure you have seen a coworker banging their mouse on the table because the Internet was not running fast enough. Yep, that was me.

The Marshmallow Test

I would have failed a marshmallow test when I was a child. If you have yet to hear of this test, it was initially performed in the 1950s by Walter Mischel. The task consisted of a straightforward situation involving a child who was brought into a room and just sat uninterrupted for a long time. Then, they were presented with a marshmallow or some other sweet or desirable treat. The researcher told the child that he had to leave the room and they should not eat the marshmallow while he was gone. He explained that he would be back with two marshmallows if the child did not eat the original one. If the child could not wait and ate the marshmallow, they would not be receiving a second one.

After the study was completed, researchers followed up with those children. They concluded that their ability to postpone gratification was linked to higher cognitive ability and coping with stress and frustration in adolescence. In addition, they concluded that postponing instant gratification would lead to success in adulthood.

In 2013, a newly published study added to the idea of delayed gratification due to a child's level of self-control. This time, the child was primed to believe that his environment was either reliable or not reliable. Before doing the marshmallow test, a child was asked to do an art project. Children in the "unreliable" group were presented with unreliable conditions: the child was given a set of used crayons and told that if they waited, the researcher would bring them a bigger and newer set. Then, the researcher left the room and came back empty-handed after 2 1/2 minutes. The researcher then repeated the same sequence of events with a set of stickers. After finishing his art project, the child was given the marshmallow test. It was found that those in the unreliable conditions waited only about 3 minutes on average to eat the marshmallow, while the other group in the reliable conditions managed to wait much longer, an average of 12 minutes. Researchers concluded that children's ability to delay gratification was not solely based on self-control. Instead, their environment impacted children's decisions. This shows that a child's decisions are based on his experience.

I think ACOAs would fail that test every time. There were plenty of reasons for ACOAs to become impatient. Having an addict in the house created a hostile environment for a child to be responsible and take care of himself, siblings, or even the addict. There was no happy, joyful, and playful childhood to enjoy due to the constant need to survive. If not on the physical level, then on the emotional. Sometimes it may seem from outside that the childhood of an ACOA is as happy and normal as any other child. It wasn't so.

The Need for Speed

Things were always changing quickly in a family with an addict, so the child had to make swift decisions and only later evaluate whether those decisions were the right ones. It felt like a predator in the house, and an attack could happen anytime. There were plenty of circumstances where I had to act fast once my dad returned home drunk. Sometimes there was no time to contemplate or foresee the best action. Sometimes things would turn for the worse very quickly, and I would need to flee the room.

Since I grew up in a constantly changing environment, I got used to changing to adapt. I remember getting bored quickly in a monotonous situation. I remember feeling uncomfortable in the workplace and bored if I was always doing the same thing. Staying in the same job for a few years made me feel like I was trapped. I always felt like I had to move, go places, and do things all the time. Being constantly alert and on edge became my "regular," which became the normalcy I was craving.

That constant feeling of movement and change is stressful. Due to my need for instant gratification, I would react to situations with little thought. I would interpret a lot of things as threatening. I got myself into trouble multiple times by overreacting to things. Since I would expect things to be worse than they are, I tended to see things from an opposing point of view, then feel offended and need an immediate response. You can imagine the embarrassment when I would respond to someone from a place of hurt and then realize that the person didn't even mean to hurt me. Many times I would incorrectly read into a tone of voice or a word and immediately overreact. I needed to apologize afterward. Over time, I learned to read emails and messages twice, ensuring that I understood them and did not project my fears onto what they said. After embarrassing myself, I saw that this impulsivity led me to misread the environment, and I would feel self-loathing for what I had done.

It's pretty easy to understand why you want everything immediately. Putting things off gives you so much trouble because when you were growing up, if you did not get what you asked for at that moment, that was the end of it. If you said, "I want this now," and your parents said, "You can't do it now, but you can do it by the end of the week," or "We can talk about it later," you knew that was the end of it. You knew that promises for the future were broken. That was one consistent thing in your life. That was the reality of your life. If you didn't do it immediately, it simply would not happen. This makes it very difficult for you to plan for the future. For you to say, "This is what I am going to do two years from now, and this is how I am going to do it," it's a struggle.

I remember many times that things were promised to me and not fulfilled. Some days, my dad would tell me that he would play with me and we would do something together. Those were the days when he was not drunk. Very quickly, I learned that if he told me that we would ride our bicycles later, on the weekend, this might not happen. I learned pretty quickly that if he was drunk and we did not do something together right away, it might not ever happen. I was taught to seek instant gratification, otherwise my needs were unmet.

I may have patience for other people's behaviors, which comes from my tendency to please others and my fear of them leaving me. Still, when it comes to the instant gratification of achieving something in my control, I'm good at it. I am loved in the workplace because I seek instant gratification in achieving work goals. When someone asks me to do something, I want to execute the action and receive the results immediately. Employers loved me. Although it feels gratifying to me to produce fast results, I got overwhelmed because I have difficulty setting boundaries with people and saying no. As a result, I used to burn out quickly and get stressed in the workplace.

This need for speed and gratification also comes in other areas of my life, including starting new programs to improve my mind, behavior, or body. I'm always eager to try out new programs, only to run out of patience if I don't see immediate results and I eventually drop them without finishing. I lose interest if something doesn't work in a few weeks. This is because so many things need time to show up. I have a few books I start reading but never finish because they didn't give me the feeling of interest right from the get-go. I also am OK with stopping a movie and picking something else if the first 15 minutes didn't interest me. I need to have the patience to wait until things get going. Sometimes, all I do is start something new but never finish. My brain does not like unfinished business, and my constant need for gratification keeps me stressed. And when it comes to having things, if I get the idea that I want ice cream, I will buy it now. If I want to buy a book, I need to drive to the bookstore and buy it now. I almost got into trouble signing off on a deal that would have cost me double to produce and being ripped off by someone just because I wanted instant gratification.

Impatient with Yourself and Others

You might also want what you want when you want it because a part of you feels, even though it is probably no longer valid, that if you don't get it now, if you don't go after it now, if you don't grab on now, it will never happen. The sense of "this is my last chance" is always with you. Those were the situations when you felt like the child in the previously mentioned test that keeps on waiting for crayons and stickers but receives none. It is being trained not to trust the environment.

You may have had similar situations when you were growing up. In addition, when you were a child, nobody told you that postponing gratification might be beneficial in some circumstances. I, for sure, don't remember those conversations with my parents. You might also need to learn what the consequences are for some of your actions. Certain rules were applied one day, and the others were not. There was no consistency at home, and you didn't form a framework in your mind from learning that behaving impulsively brought unwanted results. You had to figure all that out by yourself. And you did your best.

You even become impatient with yourself when you decide to work on patience and wait to become patient. Patience, therefore, is something that your mind works very hard to acquire. You want it all immediately. This gets you into a lot of trouble because your lack of patience feeds into everything else that gives you difficulty. Mainly it feeds into your impulsivity and your judgment of yourself.

In addition, you tend to be impatient with others you would rather not be impatient with, like with your family members, friends, coworkers, and other people you like to hang out with. Everyone may not act as quickly as you want them to in situations. Many have different processes for how they approach situations or do things. You may lose patience with your kids because they need to move faster to get in the car. You may get upset at your significant other because they are not listening to your demands to do something right away. You may get annoyed by your coworker taking time to accomplish something that takes you only minutes to do.

Seeking instant gratification can hurt relationships as well. Naturally, to have a fulfilling and trustworthy relationship, one needs to have patience, energy, and time for that relationship to develop. We are all on a unique path. Our speed is not necessarily the same as the other person's. It never ends well when someone wants instant gratification by forcing that upon others. It is seen as immature, pushy, and insecure. The lack of patience turns the other person off and can hurt or end what otherwise could have been a great relationship.

In addition, someone with no patience can demand that a relationship elevates to the next level when it is not ready to move there. Similarly, pushing a relationship to be something other than what it is organically causes hurt. It takes time to get to know someone and get to know yourself to create a healthy relationship. All of it can be very difficult for the ACOA, due to having no patience, also due to having abandonment issues and the need to entangle with the other person for security.

Exercises

Here are a few exercises that you can use to help yourself deal with instant gratification urges and learn how to regulate yourself.

Exercise #1. When you find yourself in a situation that needs immediate attention, stop before deciding how to act. Take a piece of paper and write out all solutions that come to your mind. Try to devise solutions as if you were giving them to your friend. Try to take your emotions out of it. Then take a break, reread them, and eliminate them one by one until you arrive at the solution that you feel would work the best for you. For example, let's say you find out that your company is being sold. That may be a very stressful situation. So instead of jumping to conclusions and immediately deciding that this situation will work against you, take time to write out different paths that you can take. Maybe you can start by staying in the company, while asking friends if they know who's hiring. Maybe you can decide to take a break and be between jobs for a while. After you write down all the paths you can think of, ask yourself and evaluate which of the situations will work best for you at that moment. Not all changes lead to negative results. Try to keep a positive attitude and take action by listening to yourself, but not in a hurry.

Exercise #2. If you noticed that a few times when you decided something in a hurry without thinking much about it and it was not the best decision, try asking others for help. Next time you need to address something, call your friend you trust to ask for an opinion. It is better to ask a few friends and hear their opinions. It will give you more time to settle and make a decision with a clear mind. Also, listening to other people's opinions will help you see the problem more clearly, and you can come up with your own solutions. It is okey if you still end up with your initial course of action, but at least you took time to mull it over and proceed without hurry. You may even have a list of good friends with particular expertise. For example, only some friends will have good advice about parenting, cooking, job searching, or where the best areas to live are. Take time to write your friends' names down, and next to them, note what they are good at.

Exercise #3. If you tend to overreact to things, especially when someone is questioning your intelligence, your capacity to perform, or your integrity, try to take time to process before reacting. Let's say you got angry or annoyed by your coworker for not delivering his part on time. Instead of writing him an angry email and pushing the "send" button, write the email, then save it. Read the email the next day and send it out only if you still agree. You will have a clear head the next day and save yourself from embarrassment. Or you can write that person a letter complaining, explaining why you are annoyed and just pouring all of your heart out. Do not send that letter anywhere. That's just a piece of paper. Throw it into the trash without anyone seeing it. Or just write it out in a Word document on your computer and delete the file after you feel better.

Exercise #4. If you are an impulsive shopper, love things that are on sale, and tend to buy things even if you don't need them, make a plan for how you act. You can try out different things that work for you to help restrain yourself from buying. For example, keep all your credit cards at home, so you cannot charge them when out. If you like shopping online, add items to your cart, but wait to buy them. Take your time until the next day to decide whether you still want the items. You might also set yourself an amount of money you allow yourself to spend, and then don't go over the amount of money allocated for that month.

Exercise #5. Before you take actions that you want to take immediately, ask your future self if that is a good idea. Imagine what will happen if you take action. How will they make you feel in the future? I'm sure you had those moments before when you finished the whole bag of chips, and then you felt terrible and thought to yourself, "Oh no, I should not have done this." So next time you want to eat the whole bag of chips, ask yourself how that will make you feel. Even better, try to record those times when you give in to immediate gratification and then feel bad about it. The key in this situation is to catch yourself immediately after you start thinking of taking an action that will work against you. And then, go to your list and prove to yourself that instant gratification maybe not be the best action to take at the moment. On the other hand, if you are talking about an action that delaying would jeopardize your survival, then you should do it.

Exercise #6. One of the ways to protect yourself from letting go of your standards because of the need for instant gratification is to make decisions ahead of time whenever possible. For example, you are on a diet and going out with friends to eat at a restaurant. Why don't you check out the menu before going there, so when it comes to ordering it, you don't even need to check out other items? You already know what you will be ordering. In addition, you can treat yourself by not giving in to instant gratification. So, if you decide what to eat before getting into the restaurant and are good at ordering a salad and a healthy meal, reward yourself by doing something nice for yourself. You can train yourself to be good at staying away from instant gratification just like any other good habit you want to build. And the reward can be anything from having a cup of tea, taking a bubble bath, or saving for your vacation, but there has to be some treat that makes you happy, and it is just for you.

Your Superpower

Because you don't have patience and seek instant gratification in everything that you do, as long as you don't self-sabotage, you are so eager to accomplish your goals you can immediately execute ideas as soon as you have them.

CHAPTER 23

Feeling Lonely

I wasn't surprised when I read that according to the 2020 Cigna Loneliness Index, three in five adults in the US report being lonely. When you think about it, that is a lot of people. Loneliness is an epidemic. Loneliness is the feeling of not being accepted, understood, loved, seen, listened to, and appreciated. Many people feel very lonely and isolated, misunderstood, and rejected while they belong to and live within a large family. Plenty of people go to different social activities, talk to other people, and still feel lonely. There are a lot of people who live with a spouse and children and feel lonely. The person who feels lonely does not necessarily live alone.

Many feel isolated and lonely because they feel they are different from others. That can happen based on past experiences. Naturally, we all are different in some ways and similar in others, but being different can work against you in a group. Ultimately, it depends on the group, how they accept and approve of different individuals. If the group feels secure, appreciates others being different, and sees the value in it, all individuals in the group will be included. But if a group that isn't accepting sees someone being different, then that individual will be excluded. It is challenging to find families that agree 100% all the time. I read somewhere that even in the closest relationships, if there are no arguments, this means someone is lying. We are all different by default. That's the beauty of this life experience. If we were all the same, we would already be extinct.

I remember this cartoon I saw once. It portrayed a room with a sofa where two parts of a circle were sitting together. Both circles had different indentations, but they were very simply outlined, and if you put them together, they would fit right in to create a complete circle. And on the left of the image, half of a circle was standing and looking at them, but his indentations were very different, full of circles, curves, weird lines, and overall, complicated. So those two circles on the right were asking the half circle on the left: "Have you met your soulmate yet?" Obviously, that is a funny cartoon. But it is sad because it looks like it will take a lot of effort to find somebody as complicated as them to be their match.

Loneliness Starts in Childhood

Many get to know the feeling of loneliness in early childhood. It is rare to find a family where the child can express themselves and do whatever they want. For obvious reasons, parenting needs to take place to protect the child. There is always a delicate balance between being protective and being oppressive. And due to our survival instinct, in our childhood, we will obey what other people, the authorities, tell us to do. Due to our survival instinct, we will figure out early in childhood what part of our personality is accepted by the group and what part is rejected. Naturally, we will display the part that is accepted. For example, if you notice then when you do something silly, people laugh, are happy around you, and want to be around you, you will display this part of you more. If you see that other people don't like when you feel sad, you will try to hide your sadness. Over time, that part of you that is sad is not being integrated into your full character, is not being embraced or nourished. And since you are this wide range of emotions, you start to neglect that part of yourself that feels sad. That is where you feel unhappy and feel split to pieces. And since you understand that a part of you is being rejected, that means not all of you is welcomed and loved. That must mean there is something very wrong with you.

Indeed, we humans are creatures who survive by belonging to a group. Our success is in our numbers. The most significant and painful punishment of all is to be placed in solitary confinement. But what if you felt like you were placed in solitary confinement without walls? That's how ACOA feel.

If you are ACOA, feeling different and lonely is acute. You could live in a big family, constantly surrounded by people, and still feel lonely. And feel guilty about complaining that you feel lonely. One of the reasons we feel alone and lonely is that we are very different people from those around us. After all, they don't understand us. Especially in childhood, being different is a bad thing that threatens your survival.

As an ACOA, I often felt very different from others. I felt lonely and isolated. Having feelings of being excluded from the group. Since I have no siblings, I felt more isolated. Of course, I had neighbors I could go to, play with, and then come back home anytime I wanted. But I was still only one child. I had nobody to console me or talk to about my feelings, and I just had to pretend everything was okey. It never occurred to me that I could talk about my loneliness to somebody else because the feeling of loneliness was just another "normal" feeling, the same as being unloved, hurt, and unappreciated.

In addition, my family thought that you should not tell anyone what's happening inside the family. I was amazed when I discovered a book explaining ACOAs. That was the first time I realized that other people like me grew up with a childhood trauma caused by addiction. I used to assume that everyone else felt normal and felt part of a group, and they were happy the way they were, and the way things worked for them. I assumed that everyone felt accepted, comfortable, and at ease. Of course, as a child, I didn't realize that other kids were also dealing with their issues in the family. I felt that way into my adulthood.

Did you feel as if you were different? Did you feel as if you belonged to a group? Because you were not accepted into a group, or at least you thought that way, you felt something was wrong with you, like you were broken somehow. You thought if your parent did not accept you, there must be something very wrong with you. And you already assumed that others would not understand you anyway, even if you told them what was happening. So you were standing in your own way of actually reaching out for help.

I had a client, let's call her Patricia. She came to me for a stress management consultation. Meditation, relaxation, or other self-love techniques work pretty well on managing stress, but in many cases, it can work only as a bandage. And if the wound is not treated, you can change bandages as often as you want but you won't heal the wound. Patricia told me that she had tried everything: meditation, journaling, exercise, yoga, mindfulness, essential oils. She also read plenty of self-development books that helped her define her goals and vision of how she wants to see herself in the future, power through her resentment and procrastination to achieve those goals, delegate things around the house to her spouse, and be more reasonable with her kids. Yet, she still felt like it was not enough because the results were there, but not life-changing. Patricia felt overwhelmed, burned out, helpless, powerless, and exhausted mentally and physically.

When I asked her, "How do you think it's serving you?" I saw the rage in her eyes. She couldn't understand how I could be so obnoxious by assuming that she enjoyed the suffering. She was doing things for herself, and her family felt like nobody else could do it. Her pain felt justified. To be a victim was a normal honorable thing to do. Obviously, Patricia felt alone in her own family. Because she felt different, she needed to please others, but this type of life was typical. She felt unloved, lonely, and misunderstood even by her spouse and her children.

When we finally got to the wound her alcoholic father inflicted, she realized that she was following her family's standard, that pain equaled love. She based her experience on her childhood. She couldn't change her life back then, so she felt stuck as an adult. She felt as if there was no way out. Because of fear and rejection, Patricia was afraid to connect and talk to her spouse about her feelings and how lonely she felt. She was afraid that her spouse would treat her complaints about being lonely and misunderstood the same way her father treated them, by invalidating her feelings. In a way, her fear of connecting to other people was holding her back from changing her situation and being included in a group. When we start working on her deep childhood trauma, we start healing the wound, and the bandages also start helping.

I was also surprised when I found other people who grew up in a similar environment as me who were also dealing with the same set of issues. Suddenly, I understood that I was not alone in the world, there was nothing wrong with me, and I wasn't so different. I learned that there are groups specifically to help ACOAs. There is a lot of attention on teaching how to deal with addiction, but somehow not as much about the families hurt by addicts, especially children. You don't see an ad on TV saying something like, "If you grew up with an addict, you might have issues; please call our helpline." There is government support in dealing with drugs, alcohol, and addiction in general, but I have not heard of lots of help for the families of those addicts. That shows that as long the families are functioning and not causing other people harm, nobody will pay attention to them. ACOAs need to be supported in getting help for PTSD.

You Are Not Alone

What does an ACOA need to understand? In a way, a person who grew up in that environment is different from someone growing up in a family without addiction. But there are so many other children growing up around alcoholics that, in a way, they are not so unique. Growing up with childhood trauma is not so rare. And no matter how different or weird we feel compared to other people, we actually have more similarities than we can imagine. We all want the same thing: to be loved, supported, validated, acknowledged, and appreciated. Yet, we feel we are different from everyone else because of our experiences.

If this sounds familiar, I hope you understand that this feeling of being isolated and different did not happen only to you. It happened to your other family members as well. For your siblings, even your parents, grandparents, or other family members that used to live with you growing up. That constant pretending that everything is okey was in no way allowing you to open doors to others outside your family group, making you feel more isolated. Because of that, you might have difficulty learning socializing skills and belonging to a group because you feel different. Since you learned that you're not accepted in your own family, you automatically assumed that groups outside of your family would not accept you either. You learned from an early age that acceptance needs to be earned.

I used to believe that I was carrying some curse, that bad things happen to me but not to others. Then this belief developed into some martyrdom to see how much misfortune I could carry and not break. I think it was a survival technique to justify my existence, just as Patricia did. I think it is unfortunate that many ACOAs bring this martyrdom into adulthood while questioning why bad things happen to them. I think it is essential to realize that many other routine and happy-seeming families also have diseases. Many people lose their jobs and get into accidents every day. But no matter what happens to us, we can go on, learn, heal, and adapt.

Feeling lonely can come from the unmet need to be seen. It can be challenging to understand group dynamics when someone is not used to being acknowledged, listened to, or appreciated. When surrounded by others, they feel they are different. They have the idea that everyone is looking at them, everyone noticing them when they are not. When was the last time you saw a stain on a stranger's shirt? I bet you need to think carefully about that. I, personally, don't remember. And if you think that others pay attention to you, remember that everyone only sees and hears themselves. As you hear and feel only yourself, another person also hears and feels only themselves. So, no matter how different you may be, you are safe because nobody is focused on you. Everyone around us has insecurities and fears and tries their best to survive. In addition, we all carry some trauma inside of us. We all have this inner child who needs love, affection, validation, and support. So we all are similar. We all want to be loved for who we are, unique one-of-a-kind individuals. If you feel lonely and different, I encourage you to start talking with others. Do you have the courage to look for help?

Exercises

Here are a few exercises that can be used to help you with feeling lonely, isolated, or different. Of course, not all exercises will feel right for you, but trying out at least a few helps you feel better about yourself and your connection with others.

Exercises #1. If you feel lonely and isolated, list friends you can reach out to. Make a list, and next to their name, describe how they can help you. For example, let's say you have one friend who's very good at listening to what you have to say, so contact that person when you feel like you need to talk it out. Let's say you have another friend who is very good at giving you advice. That is different in that you need contact them when you feel like you have reached a dead end and need to find a solution to a situation that is boring you or making you feel helpless. Then you should have friends who are just good at having fun, going for a hike, playing cards, discovering new things, traveling, visiting galleries and museums, and other outgoing things like dancing or concerts. If you are into arts, make a group of friends who are interested in the same activities as you, and contact them when you feel like you need to do something artsy.

Exercises #2. Watching other friends or people having fun on social media posts can make you feel more isolated and lonelier. If you can, stop looking at their posts. If you still want to be involved in that, acknowledge the reality. I'm sure they're not traveling, being in love, and having the best time of their lives every single day. Remember when you had a good time? If you cannot remember when the last time was you had fun, then invite other people to do stuff with you and create new memories.

Exercises #3. If you feel very different from others, you need to create a circle of friends that you can talk to as ACOA. You may believe that other people will not understand it, so it is essential to find people from the same background as you. Then, attend an ACOA meeting where you can talk freely and be adequately supported.

Exercises #4. You may feel lonely, isolated, or different in your own family. If you have a partner and you feel like they are not giving enough love and support to you, it is time to communicate that. Think back and evaluate whether you have communicated clearly what your needs are. Or do you think they need to read your mind? If your partner cannot support you how you want, you need to seek that support from other groups that can understand you. But do not feel guilty, ashamed, or isolated just because your partner cannot support you. Remember, they also have their traumas and differences; they can be introverted or extroverted, and just not the type of personality that can give you what you need. You have to understand, are they just different, same as you think you are different?

Exercises #5. If you feel isolated or lonely and don't want to contact anyone, go to places filled with people. Go to places like movie theaters, malls, libraries, concerts, and sports events. You can even start a conversation with a stranger and find a new friend!

Exercises #6. Take time to remember childhood and list your beliefs about how isolated and exceptional you thought you were. For example, "I believed I was the only child in the world with alcoholic parents." Or, "I was the only one with three brothers, all of whom were addicted." Try to write down as many of those beliefs as possible and look at them from a different point of view now. Do you seriously think that you are the only one with childhood trauma? You know that is not true. So it is time to let this belief go.

Exercises #7. If you think that bad things happen only to you, and you are so unique, you feel like a martyr, I invite you to take a piece of paper and write things down and compare yourself to people you know. Usually, it is not a good idea to compare yourself to others. But in this instance, it is worth it. Think about your friends, coworkers, neighbors, and people that you heard in the news. What bad things happen to them? Do you have a friend whose mother died from cancer? Do you have a neighbor who lost their job? Do you know someone who got injured because they were in the wrong place and time? Make that list, and then when you have the urge to act like a martyr, blaming the rest of the world that only bad things happen to you, read this list. And realize that everyone faces losses in their life. It doesn't mean that losses that come to your life somehow come because you're special, because you are damaged.

Your Superpower

Because you understand what it feels like to feel lonely and different, you are more friendly and easy to approach by other people who feel different, that might belong to other races, ethnicities, religions, and age groups. You may have more compassion towards others and can be a bridge that helps others to open up, ask for help, and feel included.

CHAPTER 24

Taking on Too Much Responsibility

It is hard to find someone who has never felt guilty about something. We live in a group of people where it is easy to misread someone else's body language or misunderstand what they said. Sometimes you might cause a negative outcome or cause someone to be unhappy, which is definitely a situation that calls for a feeling of guilt. Of course, some people never feel like anything is their fault, no matter if it was their fault.

A joke comes to mind. A doctor tells a man on his yearly checkup: "Sir, you need to lose some weight. It is impacting your blood pressure." The man looks at the doctor and answers: "Can't help it. It runs in the family." The doctor looks him over and adds, "Well, I can guarantee you that nobody runs in your family!"

Taking on the Weight of Blame as Self Preservation

Self-blame usually starts with questioning yourself, "Why did this happen to me?" If you are in a situation that you don't see happening to other people, you automatically decide that it must be you that is the problem. If it weren't for you, this thing wouldn't happen. You might question yourself, did you say something wrong to that person? Or maybe you made the wrong facial expression that another person didn't like? If you decide that maybe your loud laughs turn people away from you or what you are wearing is so displeasing to other people, you can change that. You can act and decide never to wear that thing again, never laugh loudly, and never do things that upset other people.

It is much more complex when the self-blame you feel is characterological self-blame. That is when you hear this voice inside your head that tells you, "This happened because I am so ugly, stupid, naïve. How can I do this? How could I believe this to be true? What was I thinking?" This self-blame is harder to change but possible with positive statements that need to become a habit over time.

Then there is another type of self-blame when you tell yourself, "If only I have done this or that." For example, you might tell yourself that you would not have been hurt if you did not hang out with those people. Or if only you knew that this person was not worth your trust, you would not have given your time and energy to him. All this "what if" needs to stop right the moment you start thinking about it. You need to understand that you did your best. You can't change things in the past, so why keep thinking about it and wasting your energy on it?

All types of self-blame happen because we try to make sense of what happens to us. But, of course, we don't want this to happen to us, so asking why something happened somehow gives us the illusion of control over the situation.

Basically, it all leads to self-preservation. And if you grew up as ACOA, all this self-blame is sometimes exaggerated to the point of self-destruction. There are plenty of rules in the alcoholic household that other families usually don't have. Since there are more rules, there is a higher chance of breaking one and feeling guilty about it. Plenty of mechanisms limit the problems from arising that might interfere with alcoholic parents or caregiver control over the family. Responsibility is a central issue in the family. The reasoning behind the drinking is usually attributed to outside situations or other people and never to the alcoholic itself. ACOA in such an environment can learn a sense of hyper-responsibility where they believe they are responsible for anything that happens to them and their family.

Healthy child development needs a robust and reinforced schedule of day-to-day activities, and there should be patterns that the child will see growing up and can expect to happen to assure safety. That need is never met in a house with an alcoholic because the only sure thing is that there is no predictability of how the day will end. That constant uncertainty causes a child to feel unsafe. Over time, the child develops the capacity to expect the events based on the adults' previous experiences. The inconsistency influences the set of rules. Some days those rules should be followed. Some days they should not. Some days those rules are broken by the adults but still expected to be followed by the child. All this is very confusing to the growing brain. Both negative and positive reinforcers communicate opposites and convey very convoluted messages. The child can't find meaning in these contexts and might conclude that they are in a "no-win" situation no matter what they do.

One of the confusing and heartbreaking situations for me as a child was taking the side of one parent or the other. Obviously, I loved and obeyed them both, but I would get in trouble if I agreed with one of them. No matter whose side I took on the subject, even into my adult years, I was met with "you two." If I agreed with my mother, the father would say, "You two are always against me!" If I agreed with my father on something, I would hear discontent from my mother, "How can you be on his side?" In the situations when I would take sides, the main reason for an argument would be totally overlooked, and I would end up the object of their unsatisfaction and be blamed for taking sides, never pleasing both, and feeling unsafe. Sometimes I would wonder what would happen if I had four parents. Life would be very tricky!

Due to the lack of an adult in the family that should assume the appropriate responsibility for the family's well-being, the child becomes overly responsible for himself and the other siblings. Yet, at the same time, they feel responsible for the alcoholic. An ACOA feels it's worth is determined by how often it is needed and of value to others.

As time passes, this child assumes more and more responsibility for the family members' happiness and well-being. It is done out of self-preservation. As it takes the energy out of the child to take care of things that it shouldn't at the same time, it gives the feeling of control and being seen, important, valuable, and useful. If the child feels needed, that means it will survive. It won't be thrown "out of the cave." But in reality, a child has no control over the events, so it can't be responsible for the adult's alcoholic behavior or actions. There is no way the child can change it. I know from my own experience of trying to change my father and stop him from drinking for years, which never worked. Finally, he stopped drinking when he himself decided to change.

Because there are more and more rules that the child assumes with age, there are more mistakes that they can make, hence more opportunities to be at fault. But it is imperative to mark that all those situations won't happen without the main perpetrator in the family, the alcoholic. Although it never seems as if it is their fault, a family usually pretends that nothing is happening or that others are to blame for it. Since a child becomes overwhelmed with self-blame and hatred towards itself because it can't change things or do things right, it might start thinking of not belonging to the family.

I had a friend whose parents got married because of pregnancy. Both of her parents were alcoholics, and I would see her sad and damaging more often than optimistic and happy. She told me once that when her parents would get drunk, they would blame her for their unhappiness because she was born. Her mother would remind her how much she sacrificed due to her daughter living and how many hopes her mother had to kill to keep this family together. My friend felt guilty for being alive, although we all understood it was not her fault. It might be easy to understand that from the other person's point of view, but my friend tried suicide a few times unsuccessfully. And that would make things worse. Her mother, while drunk, would blame her daughter, "You are such a loser that you could not even commit suicide right!"

Before graduating from high school, my friend got pregnant and left to live with the baby's father. Many laughed, "The apple didn't fall far from the tree." Looking back now, I think it was her ticket out of hell.

Because following the rules is a way of surviving in a dysfunctional family, a tendency to follow the rules leads to being hyper-sensitive to the emotional states of others. Because the ACOA might have learned to be overly responsible for adverse events in the family, although it had no power to influence the situation, it can feel like it is responsible for other people's feelings.

Keeping a Negative Self Image

As the child grows into an adult, they might assume personal responsibility for colleagues' or friends' negative emotional states. The ACOA can replay in their heads over and over the past conversations and interactions with others to understand and identify what they did wrong to cause such an outcome.

In addition, it is important to point out that when ACOAs feel responsible for the happiness and well-being of others, they also feel guilty about many things. The hyper-responsibility doesn't extend to positive events. Understandably, not everything goes wrong in life. There should be things that go right. But here is the sad part: ACOA will never take the credit for things that turn out well. If something goes well, it gets overlooked and downgraded, underestimated. Somehow anything that goes right has to do with something other than yourself, luck, other people, and "easy circumstances."

You might be guilty of this as well. If you are a great cook, you might brush off the compliments on how tasty the dinner is. It was going to happen that way anyway. Or, if it is evident that you are the one who is responsible for a positive outcome, you dismiss it with, "Oh, that was easy." For example, I love decorating, and at some point, I was making money by advising other people on how to put furniture together. I also would make flower arrangements for them. I would have many happy clients who would invite me to come to their house again. Somehow, it is not very helpful because it comes easy for me to put things together. So it was hard for me to accept the compliment on my decorating. Even worse, I would l feel like a fraud by accepting money from my clients. I see how I undervalued myself, but that is what ACOAs grow up with. I think maybe in the way of the experience that no matter how well I will do something, it won't be noticed or be enough. This is not a sense of humility but a distortion of reality.

You might also keep a negative self-image because you are used to it and it feels safe. Accepting praise for being capable means changing the way you see yourself and that you should judge yourself less harshly and be a little more accepting of your own mistakes.

In the alcoholic family environment, the child learns early on that their emotional requests or demands are not met. It is learned that when a child asks for their needs to be met, it can be seen as a negative and bad thing, even punishable. A child's needs are not important at all. Only the adult needs are essential. It is conveyed to a child that his primary purpose is to keep adults happy, which means behaving by their rules. These include never letting down the family, keeping everything functioning, caring for others, and above all, relinquishing façade in front of others.

Sometimes, the child becomes so overwhelmed with all responsibility and dynamics in the family that they do the opposite – relinquish all responsibility. Suddenly those children rely on others for any need or want to be fulfilled. It might happen because they tried to fulfill the expectations of the adults but couldn't and that feeling of not being good enough just made them stop. Or it could be that their self-esteem was shattered, and they won't believe they are capable of doing and succeeding in anything by themselves. That also might happen because the child did not have the example of others who can teach him how to identify, label, and communicate their emotional and physical needs.

Some can't meet their basic needs and need to be hand-held into adulthood. Many start to doubt their abilities and believe their psychological skills and feelings are personal deficiencies. Many become angry because of this failure to develop personal autonomy and have social skills to deal with interpersonal challenges. Sadly, the anger is usually met with punishment and seen by the adults as a rebellion. So, the only way to meet those needs is to rely on and demand others to meet them. This child understands that they need to be good at people-pleasing or they will be abandoned. There is a whole chapter on people pleasing in this book.

So, let's put the blame where it should be. It belongs to the perpetrator, the alcoholic. A small child can't be blamed for his life and for surviving in such an environment. We can agree or disagree with what happened in the past, but one thing is for sure – it wasn't your fault. You can wish things were different; you might ask yourself why they happened to you or how you could have done it differently.

Exercises

But the truth is that you can't change the past, but you can change how you react to it now. It is time to forgive yourself and learn new habits that don't include self-blame. I hope the exercises below will help you to build those habits and live a happier life.

Exercise #1. Take some time to remember your childhood and what things you would get in trouble for. Did you have some habits that your caregivers didn't like? Did you get in trouble for small stuff or big stuff? Were you getting in trouble only with some particular kids around? Try to see those situations with your adult eyes and identify whether it was actually your fault. As an ACOA, you might tend to blame many things on yourself, and in truth, there must be times that you took the blame without being at fault. Identify those instances and give yourself slack. You can even talk to your siblings and ask if they remember those instances when you all got in trouble and whose fault it was. You might discover that a lot of times, when you thought it was you to blame, you were not at fault at all. Write the stories down and see if there is a pattern. Maybe there was a particular person that would get you in trouble, but you were blamed for it? Discover those faults and clear your name by letting go.

Exercise #2. When you get into a situation where you feel guilty about something, investigate it first before assuming the blame. If it is something that you think you did or said to the other person that makes you feel as if you are at fault, take time to look at the situation from the third person point of view. Image your friend is telling you a story of someone else who did that and give them an opinion that that person is guilty or not for what happened. Try to judge your guilt from the least biased point of view. It is a good idea to tell the situation to another person, a friend who is impartial to what happened or can give you an honest opinion. It would help if you heard more opinions on the matter to decide whether you should blame yourself. Be careful not to believe that everything you do is correct and that everyone around you is "doing this to you." It is possible to tend to blame others on the way to healing from childhood trauma. Although many things that happened to you were not your fault, let's just be honest, some things we do are our fault, and we should take responsibility and ownership of it.

Exercise #3. Let's say you got into a situation where you caused another person pain by saying something or doing something, and it turns out it is your fault. You did your best, but that is how it ended. That is where you should be very careful and not drop into all-consuming self-blame and pity for your action. You should take responsibility and ownership of your actions, but you should not go to the extreme that you are a terrible person, don't deserve to be loved, and are worthless. Most worthy people on this planet make mistakes, but they live on by learning from them. So should you, when faced with a situation where it was your fault. Apologize to the other person, take action to improve the situation, learn from it, and grow from it. This should be coming from the place of a mature individual who understands it's their fault and that things can change, not from the child who should throw a tantrum and decide that they don't deserve to be alive because they did such a horrible thing. Make a record of your faults, and next to it, write down how you solved them and how you got things fixed. So when you despair that you can't get anything right or always it is your fault, read this list and see that you can come out of the situation with more knowledge and resilience.

Exercise #4. Catch yourself if you do negative characterological self-blame. You have to battle that with a genuinely positive statement about yourself. Pay attention during the day to your thoughts when a situation arises when you think you did something wrong. Then take time and list your great attributes that are the opposite of what you usually think when self-blaming. Divide a piece of paper into two columns and on the left, write your self-blame statement that you said today. If, let's say, you tend to blame yourself with "I am so naïve, I always allow those things to happen to me, and I never stand my ground!" Think of a time when you stood up for yourself, listened to your gut feeling, and weren't naïve. Then write the positive statement on the right piece of paper, "I do stand up for myself when needed, and I am very good at assessing the situation." So next time when you have thought that you did something because you are naïve and can't stand up for yourself, you give yourself slack that you are doing the best you can right now and remind yourself that there were times that you did stand up for yourself. If you are thinking, "well, I don't have any positive situations that I can remember," then it is time to create those situations!

Exercise #5. In your mind, go to a situation when you were a child and felt like something was your fault. Now, as an adult, investigate whether it was your fault. See that small child and hug them, explain that it wasn't its fault, that they have nothing to do with it, comfort the child, and tell them that you won't leave them. Imagine saying comforting words to yourself at that age. In your mind, hug that child, comfort them, and console it. It might feel silly at first, but it works tremendously with healing your trauma. Take your time with this tool but do it for sure and as often as possible.

Exercise #6. Observe how much responsibility you have in your day-to-day activities and identify how much responsibility you have in your family. If you see that you carry the majority of the responsibility, then it is time to ask for help from others. If you see that the majority of things are being taken care of by others, it is time to contribute more and get the courage to be responsible for things and gain your confidence back. Ask others if you are unsure how much responsibility you take in your family, community, or work environment! Just make sure you ask the individuals who know about proper responsibility and are good role models.

Exercise #7. Acknowledge the things that you should take credit for. Make a list of things that you love to do and are good at doing. If you are unsure where to start, observe yourself doing daily tasks and write them down. At the end of the day, decide whether you enjoyed doing them. If you did, evaluate yourself. Are you good at doing them? If yes, put that on your "good at" list. I recommend asking your family members, supportive friends, and coworkers to tell you what you are good at and put those things on the list. And when someone compliments you, take it, appreciate, honor it, and remember it. You are worth it!

Your Superpower

You are very good at following the rules and ensuring things will work. You are quick to jump into responsibility for what happens and eager to change the situation and help others with that.

CHAPTER 25

Difficulty Forming
Healthy Relationships

Has this ever happened to you? You meet someone and immediately feel this attraction to them that is very difficult to explain, like a magnetic pull toward them. Some call it soul mates. It feels like you know them from a previous life. Such attraction does not equal love. Instead, attraction indicates that you need something in that other person, usually something you're not consciously aware of. For example, they may be fit, confident, or successful no matter what they do, or you may like how they behave with others.

On a subconscious level, we believe we can get everything we want or need when we are around or associated with that person. That's why so many people vote for politicians they barely know anything about, simply based on their character or their image. On a personal level, when we see that person displaying attributes that we would like to have ourselves, we naturally assume that the mutual commitment to keep us around will help us to gain it.

A joke comes to mind. A daughter comes to her father and says:

"Daddy, I read that in some cultures, the man doesn't know his wife until the day of the wedding." And the father answers her: "Well darling, that is true of all cultures."

Learning From the Worst

We want something about another person so desperately that we are willing to stay in toxic relationships just to satisfy that need. So it is essential to understand and be aware that attraction to someone does not equal love. By recognizing what you need or want, you can discover other ways to get it without entering into a relationship or partnership altogether.

There is another reason why an ACOA enters into unhealthy relationships. As a rule, children learn to understand the world from their parents. And since the household of an alcoholic is a very unbalanced, unsupportive, abusive, and scary place, the child who grows up into an adult sees relationships as something to be cautious about. It projects experiences from childhood onto an adult relationship and feels pain all over again.

No matter how hard parents try to create a balance and haven in the family, it is challenging to achieve this in a family with an addict. Most of the time, the non-alcoholic parent is left alone to care for the whole family. This builds tremendous resentment over time, and the single parent becomes numb to the stressors and tries their best to survive. No matter how bad things can get, the non-alcoholic needs to keep the show on the road, continue to carry on with the rest of the family routines, and keep face to the outside world like nothing's happening. It is very stressful, and that stress can be passed on to the children who have nothing to do with the situation.

The issue is that non-alcoholic parents have so little left to themselves after caring for everyone else that they have very little to give to their children. There's not enough energy and time to do it all. In a way, the energy is robbed of both parents. But adding an addict who needs constant care, who ruins any routine, and poses stress and harm to the family, sometimes can be unbearable. Unsurprisingly, the non-alcoholic mother or father can be narcissistic to survive. And then, the child may feel like it has been ambushed from both sides and has nowhere to go.

There are times the alcoholic parent is not always drunk. And when that happens, it can feel joyous, and they can be in a generous mood and have only a few drinks and be relaxed and funny. In those rare moments they can even become a fun-to-be-around kind of parent. If the father is the one who drinks and then becomes funny and suddenly has time for the children, the mother can feel very confused. Because you see, at that moment, the child likes their father because they finally gets attention and approval from him. Those moments are treasured forever as a fun time together, and they are very dear to the ACOA.

The mother in this situation, just like mother did, who always takes care of the children, becomes like a tyrant in the child's eyes. She's the one who's so controlling, overpowering, and continuously pushing the children to do their routines. Sadly, there is a triangle of jealousy because the mother sees that the child prefers their father, even though he has not been there for the child. It invalidates the mother by casting her as the enemy. In my case, my dad didn't care much about what I was doing. He didn't impose any rules on me at all. So if my mom did not allow me to go somewhere, I would go ask my dad instead, and then take his approval and leave. My father seemed to be a more fun person to be around, without any expectations or demands, compared to my very controlling mother.

Because of this imbalanced dynamic in the family, children grow up afraid to be in a group because they believe it is not safe to belong. It caused pain and suffering. Hence ACOA is afraid to belong to other people.

Enmeshment and Disengagement

It can be very stressful to live in a house with so much chaos. There is a constant feeling of fight, flight, or freeze. Children operate in survival mode all the time. And as a rule, the more someone is threatened, the more they stick together. The emotions run high but can't be expressed healthily and moderated. Emotions may explode out of nowhere and cause conflict and fear in the family. Impulsive behavior can be acted out instead of moderated. After a display of blame, anger, rage, and emotional and physical abuse comes rigid control. Withdrawal or behaviors like overspending may not seem so impulsive or outrageous from outside, but they are used as self-soothing mechanisms. And as a non-alcoholic parent runs out of energy and time to create a balanced and safe environment for their children, they become rigid and controlling to keep the family together. Rules and routines become tight to be more easily managed, and the feelings of chaos. There is a lack of middle ground where feelings can be shown, understood, worked on, vocalized, and healed. ACOA learned this behavior and then carried it into adulthood by being unable to regulate their emotions. They can explode one moment or become withdrawn the other. Their partners may be confused about how to deal with ACOA and their mood swings because nobody ever taught the ACOA how to deal with emotions.

To survive, the members of a family impacted by an addict create alliances and triangles. Two people will bond over their feelings and gossip about a third. For example, a non-alcoholic mother might complain about her alcoholic husband to their child. They form a bond because they feel they are on the same team. But a moment later, the same mother could complain to her alcoholic husband about their child, creating a bond between the two. Siblings also can ally together against one or the other parent or against another sibling. The funny thing about this is no matter what the triangle may be, it is still created. Usually, the complains are never addressed to the person being complained about. All this is happening to feel less lonely and feel part of a group, creating a false sense of safety.

There is this constant enmeshment and disengagement, which can be very confusing. Because of a lack of attention and support, the non-alcoholic parent may make a child into a surrogate spouse. They may seek admiration and validation from the child. Suddenly, the ACOA becomes responsible for how their mother or father feels. It is challenging for the child to understand the parent, especially since they do not understand themselves yet. The child may feel shame for not correctly paying attention to the parent. They may feel as if they cause their parent pain. Guilt and the false closeness don't allow the child to grow and take care of their feelings, and they don't have time and energy to understand themselves and grow into a balanced adult. Sadly, ACOA approaches adult relationships expecting their partner to agree with them 100% and always do as they've been told, which leaves very little space for the other partner to express their feelings.

Being different in this environment is not welcomed. Children learn from an early age that being different is very wrong. They start to rebel at some point, tired of the rigidity of their household. They withdraw and ignore whatever is happening in the family. They may break the rules on purpose and try to be individual as much as possible and do everything they can to gain personal space. They may disengage from family conversations, avoiding interactions that can trigger disagreements. From outside, it may look like everything is fine when in reality, the issue is just being ignored.

Things can go the opposite way. Because the alcoholic is not functioning correctly, she cannot care for the family, and the non-alcoholic spouse and other family members must keep up appearances of normalcy. It is common for children to start parenting younger siblings. If the family houses more extended family members, uncles or grandparents can step in to parent the children. There is an imbalance between who does what and how much. Too much work and trying to manage everything becomes tiring, and many will eventually give up. Sadly, dealing with an alcoholic may look like nothing helps, no matter what, and everything leads to chaos. There may be no routine, things that have been planned out don't happen, and a child may be left to parent itself.

Seeing non-alcoholic parents give 110% of themselves through this situation, children learn not to take care of themselves. All they see is that none of the family's needs are being addressed. Nobody takes care of themselves but they control and do everything for others. Martyrdom becomes a virtue. Because of the chaos in the family, everyone tries to control others and fix others' behavior instead of just taking care of their own needs. And because ACOA cannot and were not taught how to connect to themselves, their own feelings, and their own needs, they are not capable of understanding the needs of others. It carries into adulthood by feeling like a victim or a martyr in adult relationships. It may look as if you know best what your partner needs when they are wrong. However, without clear communication between two people, without understanding what each individual feels and needs, those needs will always be unmet. Do you need to learn to honor your feelings and needs so you can understand and honor another person's feelings and needs?

Putting up With Emotional Abuse

Relationships are such a complicated matter that we can cling to others or push them away because of the emotional pain experienced in childhood. Because ACOA did not receive enough validation and support from their parents, they may grow up with low self-esteem and self-worth. Feeling shame, discouragement, and loneliness can contribute to further isolation due to fear of investing time and energy into relationships. After discovering that other people function differently, we may feel that some things are truly wrong with us. And that belief can keep us from understanding others better and wishing to reach out to build healthy relationships.

Feelings of inadequacy and low self-esteem can lead to boasting. This behavior can be taught by an addict who has obviously experienced trauma and doesn't know how to process it. An addict might tell drunk stories about their importance to their friends or workplace environment. Multiple times, I heard my dad brag about himself and how good he was. And most of the time, his conversations revolved only around him and his work, without including anyone else. He would not even be interested to hear how your day was, it was all him or nothing. This fake feeling of superiority above anyone else makes an addict feel like they are in control. It covers feelings of worthlessness.

Every household with an addict experiences violence, emotional or physical. Some may grow up believing their family had no abuse because nobody touched them physically. But emotional trauma is worse than physical. Physical bruises heal, but emotional pain doesn't until it is processed. The abuser injured the other person's self-esteem by invalidating them. Children are much weaker than adults by default, so they grow up to be controlled and subdued by the abuser. Sadly, the child who grew up seeing adults being controlling and emotionally abusive become an abusive adult in their lives and their families. Emotional abuse is seen as something totally normal, something that children should have a taste of to grow up into balanced adults. The victims can create a convoluted way of getting power by subjugating others, being passive-aggressive, becoming entitled. By suffering and falling apart, they get attention and demand to be saved.

Families do not fall apart all at once. They do it bit by bit, in denial, by losing hope. But it may not seem like that from outside because this denial and despair are covered in lies. Denial of what is happening inside and acting like everything is good is a coping mechanism to handle the pain. It is like a frog that is being boiled slowly. Since there is no immediate difference in the water, the frog does not jump out because it gets used to the temperature. This is how the families of alcoholics work. Every day there is more and more pressure on the family to carry on, but it seems from the outside that it is intact and strong. So no wonder that there are plenty of innocent explanations to cover up the addict's behavior. The wife may tell her friends that her husband likes to hang out with the kids while relaxing at home with a drink. A husband might tell his friends she is not feeling well and has stomach flu when, in reality, she's just wrong again. Denial becomes natural, and family members pretend like nothing's happening. Denial is helping them to stay sane. Nobody wants the knowledge that the family is falling apart, becoming a failure. So ACOA learns to lie to themselves and others to justify peace. And when that child grows up, they bring this behavior to their relationships. Still, they may not be able to acknowledge their painful emotions, so they lie to themselves and others. It is no surprise that many ACOAs end up becoming addicts themselves.

Exercises

Below you will find some exercises that you should do, no matter how painful they may seem. Of course, you may read the exercise and, by default, decide that you don't do whatever is asked. But I invite you to take time and contemplate the questions below to uncover deep wounds so that you can address and heal them.

Exercise #1. Think of someone you are in a relationship with right now, which could be a friendship. Then ask yourself what it is that attracts you to that person. What are the needs you expect that person to fulfill for you? What is that you think they're fulfilling for you? And then, brainstorm other ways to fulfill those needs without relying on that other person. Some needs require a particular person to fulfill, while plenty of needs can be fulfilled some other way, with different actions, even by yourself. For example, let's say you are attracted to someone confident who is a go-getter and achieves their goals. Because of the low self-esteem you developed in childhood, you do not believe in yourself, so you associate yourself with the achiever rather than doing it yourself. So the first step is to recognize what characteristic you love in that person, and then start doing things that will make you achieve the same level.

Exercise #2. Next time you argue with your partner, observe how you behave. Do you react to triggers peacefully? Or do you explode with emotion? Do you overdo things and later are sorry for them? Again, it is essential to learn how to self-regulate. Next time you catch yourself emotionally, stop a second, acknowledge that you have an emotion, label that emotion, ask yourself where this is coming from, then evaluate the situation you are that caused you to act out how you did. There might be a situation when it is appropriate to express explosive emotions. But is what you are now reacting to reminding you of past situations? Of course, but it is not a big deal. Practice emotional regulation as often as possible.

Exercise #3. Ask yourself how often you complain about others. It may be that you form triangles in your immediate family groups and with your neighbors and coworkers. Do you catch yourself complaining about somebody else while, in the meantime, you don't have the guts to talk about the issue directly? Do you form those triangles to relate and belong to a group? Take time to reevaluate your connections and your behaviors within the group. If you find those behaviors, now it is time to stop it.

Exercise #4. Observe yourself in conversation when you disagree with a person. What is it you do? Do you talk them into your point of view? Or do you ignore the conversation altogether? Do you agree with them to keep the peace? Then think about the issues that arise in your immediate family. How do you handle issues with your partner? Do you agree with them for the sake of agreeing, even though inside you are disagree? If so, it is time for you to find the courage to voice your concerns, find common ground, take responsibility, and come to better solutions.

Exercise #5. Ask yourself whether you play a victim in any situation or take charge of how you feel. Do you blame others for the way your life turns out? Do you feel like someone owes you something? Do you try to get attention from others by displaying weakness? It is essential to understand that your life is in your hands, and you are not the child anymore that depends on adults. You're an adult that can let go of your traumas and live an empowered and happy life.

Your Superpower

Because you have seen very painful family dynamics, you empathize with other people's suffering. So many can come to ask your opinion about things. You may help them to heal their wounds with understanding and compassion.

About the Author

Lolita Guarin has dealt with stress and tried many stress-release techniques over the years as a busy professional and childhood trauma survivor. After her health deteriorated due to stress, she went on a quest to find a solution that consisted of natural remedies and practices. Managing stress without medication became her priority.

And now, after years of researching stress relief techniques, attending workshops, coaching, and practicing on her own, she found that there is a better and more natural way to battle. And it starts with how we deal with stress in general, which became one of the teaching pillars for managing stress.

Lolita Guarin is a bestselling author, of a book *Crush Stress While You Work: tips and tricks on how to stay energized, organized and happy in your work environment.* She also have been featured in two Amazon #1 Bestsellers *Complete Self-Care 25 Tools for Goddesses* and *Miss-Adventures Guide to Ultimate Empowerment for Women: Harness Your Power and Thrive in Every Area of Your Life.*

Lolita is empowering speaker and has been a guest on multiple shows and podcasts. As well as shared the stage with Mario Lopez, Melissa Gilbert, Toya Wright, and Lynn Richardson. Lolita has organized and facilitated online and in-person workshops for groups, organizations, and individuals to teach stress management.

She is a licensed and certified Stress Management and Life Coach for busy professionals and adult children of addicts. She is also Certified by Sound Waves Heal as a Psychic Reiki Master & Light Language Practitioner, Sound Healing practitioner using Tuning Forks. Helping others in person or remote sessions to release past traumas, stress, and blockages to achieve health and mental balance and move forward. She founded multiple online courses and continues to support those who have suffered childhood trauma due to an addicted parent and others who suffer from burnout, low energy, and stress.

To sign up for one-on-one consultation with Lolita
or get more information about her please go to her website
www.BeAmazingYou.com.

Attend Lolita's course *Life Without Limits*
with Wellness Universe, go to
https://wellnessuniverse.learnitlive.com/Class/
Life-Without-Limits-with-WU-Expert-Lolita-Guarin/22825

To sign up for stress management online courses and
Stress Management for Adult Children of Addicts membership go to
https://lolitaguarinsm.teachable.com/courses

To receive complimentary meditation please go to
https://beamazingyou.lpages.co/free-meditation

https://www.facebook.com/LolitaGuarin

https://www.instagram.com/lolita_guarin

https://www.linkedin.com/in/lolita-guarin-a069a811a/

https://www.facebook.com/groups/513172906499358

https://www.facebook.com/BeAmazingYou

Just scan QR code and it will get you to

www.ingramcontent.com/pod-product-compliance
Lightning Source LLC
Chambersburg PA
CBHW051609120626
46551CB00014B/1735